VISIONS of TEAOGA

Jim Remsen

D1260434

SUNBURY PRESS

Mechanicsburg, Pennsylvania   USA

Published by Sunbury Press, Inc.
50 West Main Street, Suite A
Mechanicsburg, Pennsylvania 17055

www.sunburypress.com

NOTE: This is a work of historical fiction. While historic figures, places and incidents are accurate according to the author's research, the contemporary names, characters, places and incidents are the product of the author's imagination or are used fictitiously, and any resemblance to actual persons, living or dead, business establishments, events or locales is entirely coincidental.

For information about special discounts for bulk purchases, please contact Sunbury Press Orders Dept. at (855) 338-8359 or orders@sunburypress.com.

To request one of our authors for speaking engagements or book signings, please contact Sunbury Press Publicity Dept. at publicity@sunburypress.com.

ISBN: 978-1-62006-451-1 (Trade Paperback)
ISBN: 978-1-62006-452-8 (Mobipocket)
ISBN: 978-1-62006-453-5 (ePub)

FIRST SUNBURY PRESS EDITION: August 2014

Product of the United States of America
0 1 1 2 3 5 8 13 21 34 55

Set in Bookman Old Style
Designed by Lawrence Knorr
Cover by Lawrence Knorr
Edited by Janice Rhayem

Continue the Enlightenment!

Yukwe kulis'ta! – Readers, listen well!

You are about to journey into old Teaoga. Its names and places may be unfamiliar to you, but be assured that they are real. Queen Esther, Eghohowin, Red Jacket, Pickering, Hollenback, Slocum, Hartley, and the Moravian missions all existed. The Pine Creek murders, the 1790 council at Teaoga, the Wyoming Massacre, the War of the Vegetables—all occurred, and all shed light on our nation's tumultuous beginnings. The formal council speeches are largely drawn from Pickering's own written account. Even the Tutelo war pearls that you will read about are a real detail.

The episodes in modern-day Tioga/Athens are another matter. The place names are real—visit today, and you will find the museum, Teaoga Square, the Narrows, Round Top, Towanda—but the modern cast of characters is purely the author's invention. Any resemblance that Maddy and her Rockn crew might have to actual individuals is coincidental.

At the same time, she certainly hopes you could imagine hanging out with her.

Maddy's remarkable visit took place seven short years ago.

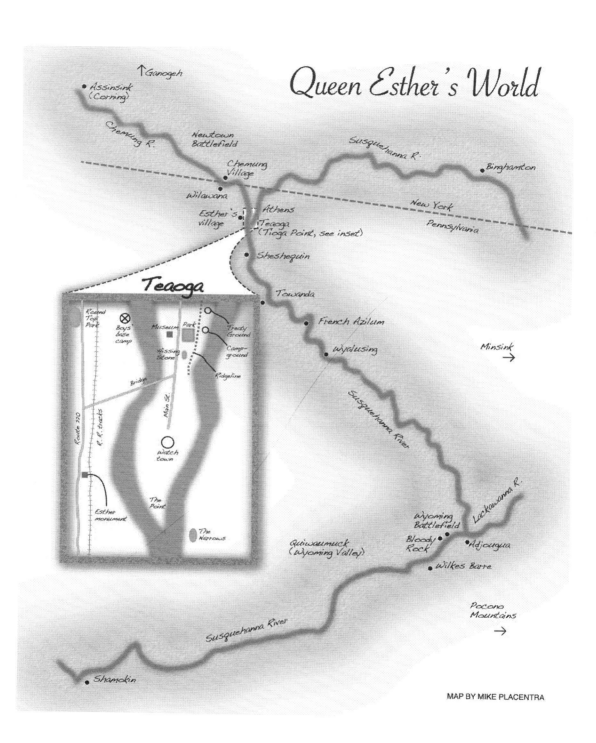

Queen Esther's World

↑ Ganogeh

Assinsink (Corning)

Chemung R.

Newtown Battlefield

Susquehanna R.

Chemung Village

Binghamton

Wilawana

New York

Esther's village

Athens

Pennsylvania

Teaoga (Tioga Point, see inset)

Sheshequin

Towanda

French Azilum

Minsink →

Wyalusing

Susquehanna River

Lackawanna R.

Wyoming Battlefield

Quiwaumuck (Wyoming Valley)

Bloody Rock

Adjouqua

Wilkes Barre

Pocono Mountains →

Susquehanna River

Shamokin

Teaoga

Round Top Park

⊗ Boys' base camp

Museum

Park

Treaty Ground

Camp-ground

Missing Stone

Ridgeline

Bridge

Route 220

R.R. tracks

Main St.

Watch town

Esther monument

The Point

The Narrows

MAP BY MIKE PLACENTRA

Chapter 1

The valley below was bathed in afternoon sunlight, giving it a certain ... *luminance? Luminosity?* Maddy knew one of those was right. From her seat riding shotgun, she smiled as her eyes framed the radiant landscape that sped by.

For miles now, Maddy had been lost in a private game she thought of as Playing Painter. The trees lining the distant riverbank—this was June so they'd want to be a fresh forest green, with dabs of lime for highlights. The wild river gleaming between the tree trunks: definitely one of the silver tones she'd tried in art class. The craggy cliff here to the left, looming just above her dad at the wheel: make it slate gray, charcoal, a patina of fern green.

Hurtling northward along the valley slope, Maddy found the bends and sudden dips of the country road exhilarating, the lacy wildflowers and towering hemlocks postcard-perfect.

But they also whispered *this is so not Texas, girl.*

Any resemblance to home was lost once Maddy had stepped off the airplane from Houston three hours earlier and journeyed into the folds of northern Pennsylvania's Endless Mountains. Her father had picked her up at the airport for this final leg up the winding river valley to his temporary home away from home. It was all brand-new to her—all except her long-lost dad, that is. She loved the zippy red two-door he'd rented, and how he didn't say a word when she propped her feet up on the dash. She'd clicked the AC to full, directed the flow onto her legs, and kept squinting out to see what more vistas awaited in the brilliant light.

Her father, a one-man pep squad, seemed even more pumped than she was to be reunited. "Is that Maiden Madeleine P. Winter I see there?!" he'd exclaim suddenly, gaping over at her in mock astonishment. Every ten minutes or so he'd blurt it, or some equally corny variation, and every time Maddy saluted back, "Present and accounted for, sir." Without her middle school friends, he might be it for company these next two weeks. *But s'okay, if I'm going to head off into the great unknown, there's probably not another grownup I'd rather do it with.*

Unfortunately, as the afternoon stretched on, Maddy felt a headache nagging. She'd been awake since 4:30 that morning. Flying here all by herself was awesome, yet she'd been so pumped she barely slept on the plane. Her eyeballs were in a state of burn from absorbing all the rapid-fire sights. The newness, the total dislocation, were jumbling her high spirits with gut-squirts of anxiety. And why was it so sticky hot this far north, anyway? She needed to wash up in the worst way. Another dip in the rollercoaster road brought a wave of queasies that wouldn't go away. *Not Texas anymore, girl.*

She leaned back, shut her eyes, and tried to think of nothing. Blankness followed, if only briefly.

"Sheshequin, Madd. Yo, how's that for a name?"

Maddy jerked awake. "Wuh. Wha-where?"

1

"We just passed the turnoff to Sheshequin," her father smiled. "Sorry, girl, you were conked out for a few minutes."

Maddy righted herself and peered around. "Sheshequin?" It sounded like another Indian word. Earlier on the drive, he'd had her pronounce the names of other spots as they passed: Tunkhannock, Meshoppen, Wyalusing, Towanda. The big river, she knew that one already: Susquehanna. All were place names left over from the original native inhabitants. And all whispered *not Texas.*

Mr. Winter found an oldies station on the radio and began wah-waahing along to a love ballad. Maddy listened lightly, still too groggy to join in. Once her eyes would stay open and focused, she turned to look outside. They were traveling down on the valley floor now. Not a single cottonwood tree in sight, but those frilly white wildflowers were everywhere. Lots of noisy trucks, too.

Soon something told Maddy to look to the right. Her gaze caught a big slab of rock just ahead. It was sunk in the ground along her side of the road. As they shot past, words flashed by her window: Tea-something. Queen-E-something. *Whoa, that was a monument. To a queen? I love queens!*

"Wait!" she cried. "Stop!"

Her father's eyes widened in surprise, but, with a quick glance in the mirror, he kept moving. "Dang, there's a diesel rig bearing down on us like a locomotive! Let's come back and check it out later, okay. We're almost at the motel. And there's something else I want to show you, too."

THE CAYUGA SUITES WAS an extended-stay place set back from the highway on the edge of town. They toted her luggage up into the carpeted stillness of Suite 210.

Maddy noticed that the two rooms had a pastel vibe, fresh ten years earlier but now a bit road-weary. She also noticed the pillows piled beside the living room sofa. Her dad, she realized, was yielding the bedroom to her. His chivalry earned him a quick hug.

It had been two long months since Maddy had hugged her father or even laid eyes on him, ever since he'd been sent to this woodsy hamlet with the grand name of Athens, Pennsylvania. He was a senior drilling engineer whose energy company wanted him here—for a few more months still—to monitor its often finicky natural-gas drilling rigs. In another two weeks, her mom and little brother would fly up from Houston to join them for a family road trip, but only after she had her own special time with him here.

The cat nap in the car had eased her headache, and Maddy figured a hit of cold water would also help. She chugged a cupful from the kitchenette, then rolled her big suitcase into the bedroom and heaved it onto the polyester bedspread. *I can't believe I'm finally here!* She pulled off her sneaks and eagerly started to check things out. No sooner had her eyes settled on the TV atop the dresser, though, than her father cleared his throat and announced, "Hey, girl, let's have some house rules. One hour of television and one hour of online time per day, max. Call it the Cayuga house rules, okay?"

Maddy felt slapped. Irritation shot through her. *House rules? Here? So stoopid!* She teetered beside the bed and envisioned belly-flopping onto it.

But she didn't collapse. Instead, she squeezed her eyes shut and summoned the promise she recently made to herself: No More Meltdowns. She heard the voice of her best bud Melody, fifty-one days older and ever the lecturer, telling her to "breathe deep and slow, queenie." *Mel's right, I can get my hair in a frizz way too easily. Time to get a grip.*

Mr. Winter, noticing Maddy's frown, lowered the bedroom thermostat three degrees and headed toward the other room. He knew from experience that his middle schooler's moods could turn on a dime, and that it was best to leave her alone once a snit hit.

"When you're ready we'll go grab dinner," he said evenly. "And I've gotta show you my surprise. You can unpack later."

The metal door clicked shut behind him. Colder air was already filling the room. Maddy sat on the bed, closed her eyes lightly, and took stock.

It came back to her how stoked she'd been when the school year finally ended, plus how her folks considered her mature enough to fly up alone on her summer getaway. Also, her father had arranged for her to be a junior counselor-in-training at some kind of history day camp here for both weeks, which sounded outstanding. *So what to make of this TV clampdown? You'd usually rather read or draw anyways, girl. Remember, you were even thinking of shutting off your phone up here, going all retro! The online thing? You'll figure it out. Just breathe deep, take it slow, and figure it out.*

Maddy stretched her arms upward and shook them to release the willies. That helped. It also reminded her that her armpits were putrid from the marathon day. She rose, slid sideways in the hip-hop glide step she'd been working on with Melody, and headed to the bathroom.

THERE WASN'T AN ENCHILADA in sight at Herman's, a crowded calorie palace just down the road. That was fine, though, because Mr. Winter had become a regular, so the waitress, a friendly bleach blonde with the name tag Bev, gave Maddy extra fries and free refills on her root beer. She also complimented her on her glittery green fingernails. Maddy mumbled her thanks.

As Bev bustled away from the booth, he leaned in. "Why so quiet? I hope she didn't think you were rude."

Maddy felt herself blush. She'd been trying not to spiral back into the queasies—but all around her now, in close quarters in this not-Texas world, sat strangers, strangers, and only strangers. "People talk funny here, Dad, and I don't want them to think I talk different, too," she said. "They'll think I'm a cowgirl or something."

"I guess I felt that way at first, but I've enjoyed how most people are friendly and interested in where we're from. It's the small-town way. You'll see."

Maddy begged her innards to believe it, and to please stop tumbling like a dryer gone wacko. If Mel were here, they'd recite their Dracula line together, "I tink I must go mad, I tink I *vill* go mad!" She took another deep breath and looked around.

Herman's was a family-style establishment that seemed to draw half of Athens. Maddy noticed how its rowdy neon bar was barely three steps from the family tables where kids fussed in high chairs and grandmas inched around in walkers. She played with her straw as she slowly surveyed the surroundings. *Be cool. This isn't so different from home. I recognize that honky-tonk song that's playing! These folks are friendly. Believe it. Hey, that girl over there looks kinda like me. This thing is doable.*

She also decided to practice saying the Indian place names again: *Tun-KAN-uck. Muh-SHOP-en. Why-a-LOO-sing.* Her father had to help her get *Sha-SHE-kwin* right. "Aren't they pretty-sounding?" he said. She agreed the words rolled off her tongue.

Over ice cream, her father turned the talk back to his house rules. "Maybe I was too, I don't know, harsh-sounding, Me-Madd," he said. "I know you'll be off to high school before long, and we want to respect your judgment and all."

Maddy, feeling on the upswing, cut him off. "It's okay, Dad, really. Half my suitcase is books and art stuff. It's not like television rules me or anything. You just caught me by surprise."

"Nice," he smiled. "Hey, let's try another deal. I give you a minimum of *daddytude.* You give me a minimum of *maddytude.* What say?"

Tickled by the wordplay—always a family favorite—Maddy extended her finger across the booth for a quick pinkie shake. Her father grasped it tight and looked her square in the face. "I know it's strange to be so far from your buds, Madd. You must be kinda in shock today." He could have launched into a lecture about breaking out of the mold, cutting loose, spreading your wings, but he decided to say simply, "Just try to go with the flow, okay."

Fair enough, Maddy thought. This could be a perfect place to try different things. *Look at him and that sick red car. He even went with the name I gave it: Li'l Red! For an engineer, Dad's a cool guy, not like the other ones he works with. He does have a little pot belly, but he makes up for it with his goatee and that movie star smile. Not a rebel, exactly, but definitely not all solemn, and what was that other word Mom used: dour.*

The problem was, compared to Mister Sunny, Maddy often felt like a skitzy-ditzy, human storm. She had a side of herself she wanted to shake that was moody and spoiled and devilish. It would flare up suddenly with bratty reactions that knocked her off stride and even made her crash. Last year, when it was really bad, she'd named it Mz Snarkley. The other side was Rockn Grl, who was a bundle of fun as long as she didn't get too hyper, which could be exhausting. Maddy shut her eyes and prayed that her Rockn self would rule—or at least that she would go with the flow.

Their check paid, Mr. Winter slapped his wallet shut and flashed that bright smile. "C'mon, let's giddy up. We've got things to see!"

He swept Maddy toward the door, past display cases offering Herman's cornucopia of baked goods, clothing, souvenirs and gee-gaws. As she stopped to ogle the fresh blueberry pies, he balled his fist like an intercom mike and announced, "Attention, attention, is there a Maiden Madeleine P. Winter on the premises? The tour bus is now departing." Maddy drummed his shoulder while he winced in delight, and off they went.

THE AIR HAD COOLED and an evening breeze was kicking up. They opened the windows on Li'l Red and drove toward the center of town. "Ready for a windshield tour?" Mr. Winter asked. Popping a fresh stick of gum, Maddy was Rockn ready.

She and her mom had done a bit of online research about Athens and gotten the basics: population 3,400, one of a cluster of river towns known as "The Valley" on the Pennsylvania-New York border. Has a high school that graduates 190, way smaller than hers, and a middle school named Rowe that she'd have attended if she lived here. Athens's sister town directly to the north, Sayre, used to be a big railroad center that had the second-largest locomotive yards in the world a century ago. Maddy thought that was pretty cool, and had tried to identify where the first-largest was. No luck. Also, she knew Athens was at the confluence of the Susquehanna River and a tributary with the Indian name of Chemung. The juncture itself was called Teaoga by the Indians but then was renamed Tioga Point by the settlers in the olden days. Beyond that, Maddy didn't know too much about the area except that it had mega amounts of natural gas underground and, from the looks of it, lots of big old trees and green mountainsides.

"Wait until you see all the twisty back roads," Mr. Winter said. "Hey, want to try fishing? A fellow I work with, guy named Charlie, has been after me to go bass fishing some weekend. He says he has all the gear."

"Fishing?" Maddy exclaimed. "Dad, the only thing you fish for is those teeny screws to your model trains."

"Har-har. But let's try it. Maybe we can kayak, too. And I'll take you out to see one of our rigs. The well pads in the forests are a sight to see."

He kept the car at 25 mph as they took in the sights. Athens and the other Valley towns were between the two rivers in the bottomland that narrowed to its southern tip at Tioga Point. They were driving south on Main Street, which ran straight down the middle like an arrow shaft for several miles.

As they bounced across some railroad tracks, Maddy's eye caught the sign for Valley Playland and some kids shooting hoops on one of the park's courts. *Maybe I'll check that place out later.* They cruised past a Handi Mini Mart, a candy haven where she watched some boys about her age circling the parking lot on stubby BMX bikes. Just beyond that were three blocks of old connected brick storefronts with display windows like a classic Wild West town.

Midway along the stretch of stores was a shady pavilion called Teaoga Square that had a bandstand and an ice-cream shop in the rear. As they drove past, Maddy noticed packs of lively families working on their cones.

"See that sign? It says they have band concerts there every Wednesday night," she said. When Mr. Winter didn't answer, she began to muse. *This town is like that Herman's place, with one of everything for people. I can handle this. It'll be fun, maybe.*

"The Valley is a proud area," her dad said. "Seems its boom time was almost a century ago now, and it's lost a lot of industry and jobs over the years. They're worried about families moving away. I know people at my company have met with the town fathers to be sure we hire local folks and train them for management and skilled jobs. Let's see how that goes."

The commercial zone gave way to a noticeably fancier stretch of Main Street. Suddenly, Maddy felt like she was entering a Hollywood movie set. Large, elegant, wood-frame homes lined the street. Mature maples and oaks spread their branches gracefully overhead. On the left was a handsome old stone church. The homes were set back on broad lawns and many had immaculate flower gardens wrapping around. The sights—homes of patrician gray or white or steel blue, the canopy of beautiful trees— reminded Maddy of New England towns she'd seen in movies. Her dad slowed Li'l Red to a crawl as they purred along.

"This is the original part of Athens," he said. "I think they call it South Main. Pretty classy, huh? Must be where the big shots live."

He pulled over and parked. "Hop out. This is what I wanted to show you."

They had come to a small park. It was hardly bigger than an empty lot, but it was well-tended with walkways leading to a monument at the center. "That statue over there honors the town's war veterans," Mr. Winter said. "But, voila, here's the good one."

He walked Maddy to a blue iron plaque mounted on a pole next to the sidewalk. It displayed the fancy seal of Pennsylvania above an inscription in large yellow letters.

STEPHEN FOSTER
America's beloved writer
of folk tunes and ballads
attended, 1840-1841, Athens
Academy which stood here.
The Tioga Waltz, Foster's
first music, was composed
at that time.

Mr. Winter turned to Maddy with a goofy grin. She cocked her head in confusion. Looking again at the sign, it came to her. "Stephen Foster. Camptown Races! Omigod. Doo-dah!"

Her dad threw back his head, pumped his arms like a rooster, and sang out, "Daddy Haddy Funny Fun, Doo-dah, Doo-dah!"

Maddy, shoving aside embarrassment, leaned back and answered, "Maddy Haddy Better One, Oh De Doo-dah Day!"

It had been years since they'd sung their nonsense song. She was amazed at how the words came back. It wasn't just that they shared the same stubby build and hair like straw. They also reveled in the same cockeyed humor and zany wordplay, plus a love of singing and, curiously, she realized more and more, of history. How many other people learn about old Stephen Foster when they're four years old, she thought.

When she was little her dad would lift and spin her in merry circles when they sang their doo-dah ditty. Maddy was glad he didn't try it now. They stood side by side, humming the tune, as they read the sign again.

"I saw this when I was visiting the museum to see about your counselor position," Mr. Winter said. "The lady who's going to be your supervisor, Mrs. Tulowitsky, told me Camptown is a real town that Stephen Foster was referring to, and it's actually nearby. That's one of the excursions we'll have to take, okay?"

Maddy had her first look at the Tioga Point Museum, which was directly across Main Street from the park. It was a compact but grand structure, built 100 years ago, with four stone columns gracing the front portico. "What a jewel box of a building," her dad said. "I guess Athens, being named Athens, felt like it had to have its own little acropolis temple." Maddy felt another wave of butterflies—*yikes, this is where I start working on Monday!*—but she took a deep breath, and it passed.

The museum was housed on the second floor, above the town library. Around back was a shaded garden and picnic area that led to the riverbank a few yards away. They wandered to the edge and gazed down at the dark-green current. "That's the Chemung," her father said. "I know from the map that it goes northwest up into New York state. About a mile below here it dumps into the Susquehanna. Hey, maybe we can write a song about the mighty Susqy!"

Maddy was hardly listening. The war monument in the park reminded her of that other monument, the one she'd spotted along the highway into town. They were going so fast at the time that all she'd caught was a line about a Queen Elizabeth or Eleanor, some E name like that. Maddy had a thing about famous queens down through history. That's why Melody called her queenie (or, sometimes, Queen Cwazy), and why Maddy had named her kitty Tiara. *So just who is this new backwoods queen?*

"Dad, remember that monument you promised to go back to? Let's do it, okay."

FIVE MINUTES LATER, THEY were rolling out of Athens over the little bridge across the Chemung and back out to the highway that headed along the river flats. Soon the granite block rose into sight on the opposite side of the road. They parked carefully, waited for the handful of cars and pickups to whiz past, and hustled across the road. With evening fast setting in, they had to get close to the thick bronze plaque to make out the inscription:

TEAOGA
A WATCH TOWN
The south door
Of Iroquois Longhouse
Was Situated on the Point
At the Meeting of the Rivers
200 Rods to the Northeast.
QUEEN ESTHER'S TOWN
Of the Delaware Indians
Was 100 Rods to the East
Along the Chemung River Bank.
Both Towns Were Destroyed by
Colonel Thomas Hartley
And His Troops
September 27, 1778
These Flats for Five Miles
Known as Queen Esther's Flats
Were Grazing Grounds
For Their Herds.

Maddy's mind was swimming. Queen *Esther? What was a watch town? Who was this Hartley?* But first things first: "Dad, what's a rod?"

"It's an old surveying term. A rod is equal to 5.03 meters and 16.5 feet. I can't believe I still remember that. What a dork. I had to learn it in school."

Just like an engineer, Maddy thought.

The ground rumbled and dust whipped up from the swift traffic at their backs. Maddy felt exposed and unsettled as she stood on the roadside looking past the undergrowth to the distant water. Her eyes framed the scene. About fifty yards down was a set of railroad tracks running parallel to the highway. Beyond that seemed to be freshly plowed farmland. The field sloped gradually toward the river's edge, which was maybe three football fields beyond and marked by a line of trees in the dim distance. The only sound was the rush of the wind through the high grasses and the cawing of two crows flapping over the field. No one else was around. The scene struck Maddy as desolate and sad. *Weird, that Tioga had a queen. I know about Queen Elizabeth, Queen Victoria, Queen Anne, Marie Antoinette, but an Indian queen? And she had herds of what, cattle? That doesn't sound like an Indian thing. Some colonel destroyed her town in 1778? That was during the Revolutionary War, I think. I'll have to ask Mrs. Tulowitsky about that...*

As her eyes rested on the tree line and the black waters beyond, a finger of light reached out to her. It was pulsing from a single spot on the distant riverbank. She squinted. The light throbbed brighter, then fainter, then disappeared. *What the el. Fireflies? No way. A campfire?* It gave her goosebumps. She turned to ask her father if he'd seen it, but he was facing the other way, scanning the slopes rising to the west.

Meanwhile, cars were flicking on their headlights as darkness gathered. It was time to head back to their home away from home. Maddy shook off the clammy feeling. She wanted to use her hour on her dad's laptop to chat with Mel and maybe do a little research about this Queen Esther person. Plus, she hadn't even unpacked.

Her father, reading her mind, gestured toward their car. "Time to whirl, girl."

Chapter 2

At her seat under the canopy of bare trees, old Esther pulled the shawl blanket over her head and withdrew like a turtle into a shell. The November chill ached, made worse by the damp wind off the nearby Saosquahanaunk, the great river the white man's tongue called "Susquehanna."

Cold seemed to be Esther's constant companion, yet that was not the real reason she concealed herself.

Two large yengwes—white people—were coming close after leaving the nearby treaty grounds. They must not be allowed to see her. One was Pickering, the gaunt, straight-backed leader who had come to the Teaoga treaty grounds to address the assembled Indian nations. The other was Hollenback, the trader. Hollenback once knew Esther well, but she had been avoiding him for six long years. The two men strode along quickly, deep in conversation.

"Have they passed?" Esther muttered to the other native women seated around the campfire. It pained her to hide like a coward, but she had heard that some hot-blooded young yengwes were out for her scalp.

"Yes, Sister, they just entered Pickering's quarters," Cakoanos replied.

Cakoanos, her dear old friend, lowered herself back to her seat at Esther's left, her customary place, and they resumed their meal. The two had shared experiences over many winters, and their reunion to witness these grand public peace talks at Teaoga had given Esther special pleasure. Cakoanos was one of the uprooted Tutelo Indians who had been part of Esther's mixed Indian village here in better days. Then, twelve summers ago, they had fled from Teaoga together to escape the advancing Colonial army and their torches, in the time they called The Burning. Unlike Esther, Cakoanos had returned here to live with a few other determined Tutelo families, and had stayed to weather the difficult days that had settled upon them since then.

Esther peered back toward the treaty grounds. She had arrived at Teaoga this very day—and her dread had only grown. The six winters since her last visit had left her more bent and haggard, her hair streaked with white. She could only hope Hollenback and the other settlers would look past her now as just another faceless old squaw. As a precaution, she had not brought the large white Christian cross she once displayed around her neck, a gift of the missionaries she had befriended long ago. Wearing it would surely draw attention—nor was she still confident of the yengwe creator's protection.

It had taken a personal appeal from another of Esther's esteemed friends, Sagoyewatha, the Seneca chief known as Red Jacket, to convince her to come here at all. One morning a month earlier, Red Jacket visited Esther's home in Iroquois country, five days north of Teaoga, where she had been living in quiet safety for several years. This was at Ganogeh village, Red Jacket's birthplace.

Arriving with gifts of tobacco and three strings of wampum beads, Red Jacket had stated with appropriate formality, "Mother Esther, I desire you to give ear to me." As they puffed slowly on the kulukuneekun, the traditional mix of tobacco and sumac, to help their thoughts mingle, he explained the importance of the peace talks. It would be the first council that any Iroquois nation would have with the peculiar new yengwe government that called itself the United States. The council fire would be lit at the ancient treaty ground at Teaoga. Red Jacket would hold the high position of Pine Tree chief, the one who would stand and speak for his Buffalo Creek Senecas.

Other chiefs, sachems, and male elders from the various tribal councils were expected, and Red Jacket wanted the wisest matrons to be there as well. He was known for seeking the women's advice first. The Seneca matrons would accompany him to Teaoga, and he wanted Esther along, too. In their prior conversations, she had demonstrated insight into the yengwe mind and wisdom about how native groups might live in harmony through these harsh times. Although Esther was not a Seneca, Red Jacket knew she had once led her mixed village with distinction as a sakima—a female civil leader—and was trusted by the other Indian nations that would be represented at the Teaoga talks.

Esther listened patiently to Red Jacket's appeal. She knew about the peace council already. Travelers had come through Ganogeh with the news. They told about the recent murders of the two Seneca trappers by drunken yengwes, the Seneca demand for ceremonial gifts to the bereaved families, and the request that the great Washington himself meet with them.

Esther knew this was the year whites called 1790—the Moravian Christian missionaries had taught her their time counting system. Furthermore, she knew the yengwe settlers had created their great council of states that seemed to be like the Iroquois Confederacy. The settlers had won their long war to throw off British rule—but because most of the native people had fought alongside the British in this Revolution, the sky remained dark and the hatchets sharp. Esther believed the young United States did not want more bloodshed with the mighty Seneca warriors.

Contented by the tobacco and Red Jacket's sonorous voice, Esther considered his invitation. She was intrigued and honored. His final comment, "Tutelo hunters came to us saying their women at Teaoga desire a special purpose for you," clarified her thoughts.

Taking the wampum strings in hand, Esther gave her reply. She held the strands of sacred shell beads aloft in her open palm, letting them spiritually receive her pledge as was the custom. "Brother, I have heard your words and my heart is stirred. Perhaps the Preserver has brought me to this time for this purpose. My Tutelo friends have endured many dark days. If they need my presence, I cannot refuse. If you need my presence to help keep the treaty fire bright, I cannot refuse. My sixty winters have worn down my body and weakened my eyesight. Let us hope it has not dimmed my vision."

THE JOURNEY SOUTH FROM Ganogeh was more tiring than Esther expected. Her current husband, the sturdy old Onondaga chief, Kanistagea, known to the yengwes as Steel Trap, was away with his men on the seasonal hunting party to the west. Her grown children had left long ago to make their own families, three of them with the Moravian Christians far to the west in Ohio country. She knew she must depend on younger companions from other native families to smooth her trail to Teaoga.

Overland they trekked for three chilly days. As they wound along ancient footpaths, they came upon the remains of Seneca villages and orchards put to the torch by General Washington's soldiers years earlier and now inhabited by a few stray Indian families. During the terrible Revolution, many of the Seneca villagers had fled west to Niagara and perhaps on into British Canada. Esther prayed for the ones cut down by the measles or other wasting sicknesses in crowded Niagara. Shequaga, the thundering waterfall where it is said Red Jacket practiced his speeches, soon emerged into view. She was comforted to see it towering majestically over the desolate site.

Finally, they arrived at the Chemung River for the final leg by bark canoe and dugout. As they set out on the rapid waters, Esther felt she was entering a dream world. Memories rushed forward with the current. There was the old Forbidden Path, wending along the riverbank on its route westward into the Seneca homeland. She pictured the stern guards posted along the trail previously, in better days, when yengwes knew they faced certain death should they set foot on it.

Soon the canoes passed the remains of Assinisink village, where Esther and her first husband had presided many winters ago until yengwes attacked. Those had been some of her best years, when the people had been strong and confident, her children vibrant. There were the shallows where her young sons had bathed year-round, breaking the ice in winter, as part of their daily hardening ritual. The rocky outcroppings, the eddies, the slopes beyond, all called to her. Assinisink had become the place, on many quiet days, where Esther's heart still traveled. But as they floated onward, she forced the memories away. She knew the ache in the center of her chest must be stilled if she was to remain strong and useful.

More and more canoes joined from other bands and villages. People greeted one another with shouts and song. They began seeing white farmsteads, the settlers and their cattle lifting their heads to watch them pass. Grim looks were exchanged. A few of the long rock piles the yengwes called boundary walls ran down to the shore, hulking symbols of the new order.

The travelers grew silent as they slipped past the hilly Newtown battlefield. Here, during the Revolution, brave warriors had been killed or maimed in a desperate attempt to stop the white army's advance up from Teaoga into the Iroquois heartland. The soldiers later bragged of their Newtown victory—and she knew some had even boasted that she, the hated "Queen Esther," had been found among the dead.

Esther's pulse quickened again when people pointed out the rugged cliffs of Wilawana rising before them. On its slope was the forested glen where she had once led her villagers to safety, just ahead of Hartley's marauding army. Those painful times still haunted her sleep.

Soon, nearing Teaoga, the canoes came upon a pocket of Indian huts that hugged the riverbank. Esther knew this was the isolated Tutelo settlement, but she did not recognize the two young women who raised their right hands in greeting as the flotilla cruised past. One wore a cradleboard on her back, her baby's glossy hair peeking out of the top. The sight cheered Esther, then brought a stab of worry. How often she had prayed for her old Tutelo villagers—

Teaoga's last remaining natives, hemmed in now by yengwe settlers. Were they safe? Were they healthy? Had they forgotten the old ways, the generous spirit and beautiful manner of speech she so admired? Soon she would know.

They paddled past more and more yengwe fields and rail fences, drawing ever closer to their landing point at Teaoga. She detected the smells of yengwe animal herds and their waste souring the air.

Soon, on the western shoreline, Esther noticed one of the watering spots used by her old village, at a break in the trees where the riverbank dipped low. How many times she and the other women had crouched there to fill their jugs and pots! A footpath had snaked from that point inland to the site of her doomed village. The path could still be seen, but yengwes had cleared the ruins to make way for more pastureland for their hundreds of horned cattle. Esther felt her eyes mist. She yearned to see the promontory where her home had stood, the wood-frame home, which the whites called Queen Esther's Castle. In times past, Esther could spot a single robin clearly on a distant mountain, but now sights beyond a hatchet toss were cloudy. Perhaps that was best. She knew what she would see: the settler Snell had claimed her high ground as his own and built his cabin there.

As the procession passed the settlers' new wharves and approached the landing, curious yengwes lined the Teaoga bank to stare. The Indians now numbered nearly 100, four or five per vessel. What a sight we must be to them, thought Esther. Native leaders sat high in their long boats, displaying their finery of beaded headbands, feathers, and long bright ribbons. Silver brooches, bells, and ear and nose rings shone in the winter light. Many of the men were tattooed, the women with vermilion dye lining their brows.

Esther, however, crouched low in the middle of her canoe. Hollenback and the others must not recognize her. She had carefully returned a few times in the early years after The Burning to see friends and visit graves. But ever since 1784 when the treaty was pushed through that surrendered all remaining Indian land in Pennsylvania territory—yengwes laughingly called it the Last Purchase—Esther had known to stay away. The Iroquois, the Delawares, the Shawnees all rejected this Fort Stanwix treaty, but to the land-hungry settlers, Pennsylvania was not Indian country anymore.

Also, travelers from the south, from other settler communities, brought gossip that some sons of the captive soldiers bludgeoned that horrible night of battle twelve summers ago were now young men themselves and seeking vengeance against her. So she huddled low in the boat, enduring this final passage into Teaoga as if it were a gantlet menacing her with piercing eyes.

The canoes continued in silence. Esther, glancing sideways, noticed settler parents drawing their children close to their sides. They need not fear, she thought, we are in the hunting time so most of our young men are away in the forests far to the north. This will be a council fire without the "burnt knives," the restless young warriors who attend councils to linger, give opinion, and often fall into the rum and make trouble. No, she thought, you yengwes are seeing the elders, our wise old men and women, and young mothers, and our children not yet of age. May your eyes recognize and respect that, Esther prayed.

At last the procession reached the famous Carrying Path, the trail for portaging canoes across the narrow neck of Teaoga between the two rivers. As their vessels were beached and hauled into rows along the shoreline, the passengers stepped out. Esther stayed back near the water's edge, in a sideways crouch, peering at the mixed crowd waiting before them. A woman stepped toward her, perhaps thirty winters old, with a familiar oval face and eyes that shone in friendship. It was Cakoanos.

"Sachoo-ca-cho," she said. "How are you, my friend?"

"Sachoo," Esther replied. They touched cheeks lightly and studied each other with quick smiles. Aware of Esther's peril and sensing that she was tired and uneasy, Cakoanos whispered, "We are honored you have come, Sister. We are here to care for you. Rest assured that few others know you are among us."

At Cakoanos's direction, they pulled their woolen trade blankets over their heads and, with faces lowered, slipped through the crowd. To their left, Esther knew, was Hollenback's trading post and water well. The pair moved off in the direction of the long-abandoned Cayuga watch town. Within moments they were skirting the trampled field where the wooden fort of Washington's occupying army had once stood from river to river. Seeing the site pained Esther's heart. It contained ancestral tribal burial grounds. Now, white soldiers' bones lay there as well.

Shortly they arrived at the sprawling campground area. It was already occupied by more than 100 other Indians who had arrived on foot or by canoe over the last several days. Just to the north, on a plateau beside the Susquehanna, was the open treaty ground.

"We have made a shelter for you not far from the ridgeline but out of view of the yengwes," said Cakoanos. "My shelter is next to yours. It is fine earth, with a fire circle and among our women."

She walked Esther to her low-slung shelter. Like a small wigwam, it consisted of branches tied into a dome frame and covered with blankets and reed mats. Crouching low to enter, Esther uttered a prayer of gratitude for safe arrival, then placed her plates and her pouches of cornmeal, herbs, and medicines at the far end. Cakoanos had brought her an extra bearskin for sleeping. Esther recognized it from the wound next to the animal's left eye—it was the very fur-skin she had left with Cakoanos after The Burning. She spread it out carefully. The ordeal of this journey had left Esther with an aching head. She would rest before joining the others at the circle.

"SISTER, WE HAVE PREPARED boiled cakes and yengwe beef." Cakoanos stirred her old friend awake. Esther wrapped herself in her white blanket and emerged from the shelter to take her place at the fire circle. Sunset had sharpened the winter chill. Esther was pleased to see meal fires burning throughout the busy campground. Four other women and a girl sat waiting around their circle of logs. Three of the women were Tutelos, the other a Mohawk war widow. All could have been her daughters. None were Shawanoes, proud Shawnees, like Esther. In winters past she would have recognized their various tribes by the dress and quill work, but these days everyone seemed to wear the same trade goods of European cloth and metal jewelry.

After a round of greetings in Delaware, the tongue most commonly known among the natives, the women began to fill their wooden dishes with hot corn cakes and chunks of beef that Pickering's men had made available. At that moment, she spotted Pickering and Hollenback walking near. Esther withdrew into her arched blanket.

Once the danger passed, the women settled back to their supper. They ate readily, ladling the food down with cold river water. Though Esther's tongue found beef tasteless compared with rich deer venison, she ate it gratefully.

Afterwards, as the group relaxed in the warmth of the fire, the Mohawk woman, a saga singer, began to chant. It was in the Mohawk tongue so the others could only hum along. The chant, low and vibrant, seemed to fill the air with peace. As its melody lingered, the Mohawk woman stood to face Esther. Raising her arm, she intoned in Delaware, "Sister Esther, we are honored to have you in our company. In winters past you have cared well for many of our scattered people, as a sakima and a healer. Sister, we have heard often of your deeds. We long to benefit from your wisdom before the breath leaves you and you pass on to the land where the spirits lie. Sister, let us thank the Preserver for bringing us together safely. Your journey has been especially trying. With our gift, let us wipe the dust from your body and the grief from your heart so our thoughts are clear and our time together bears fruit."

Cakoanos motioned to the lone girl seated at the fire to come forward. This was Cakoanos's daughter, Sisketung, a thin girl perhaps twelve winters of age. She presented Esther with a ceremonial bundle of tobacco. The old woman moved into the firelight to spread out the leaves carefully. She noticed it was not the traditional kulukuneekun mix and that it was wrapped in paper, not corn leaves.

"I am honored," Esther said. "It is from where?"

"Hollenback's store," young Sisketung replied quietly.

"Surely it will smoke well," Esther said after a pause. The women brought out their pipes while the leaves were distributed around. Esther retrieved her best effigy pipe, which bore a carved wolf's head on the bowl. It had belonged to her first husband, the now-dead war chief Eghohowin. The wolf was the totem of the Tùkwsit, his Munsee Delaware clan.

Aware of the harshness of straight tobacco, Esther puffed lightly so as not to cough. Others did likewise. Two puffs later, one of the young Tutelo mothers let out a cough, then a hack of smoke, then a loud laugh. Soon they all were guffawing and rocking on their haunches. The sister is young, Esther thought. We will teach her, gently.

Winking at the young woman, she declared, "It smokes well."

The evening wore on and her companions fed more timber into the fire. In the darkness, other groups could be heard talking and singing. Some danced around their fires. Many stories, good and bad, were being shared. Esther knew that most people in the campground would not want to sleep on this precious night. The Teaoga council had let them break their isolation, perhaps look past old tribal grievances, and forget the yengwe stranglehold for the moment.

Cakoanos rose to speak. "N'petalogalgun: I have something to say. Listen well. Sister Esther, my heart sings at your arrival after your long absence. We Tutelos wish to hear about the pure ways, about the ancient traditions that our families are quickly forgetting. Sister, there are so few of us left and the yengwes hem us in. We are like their cattle behind fences. You have seen this happen, but you came alive in a stronger time. Teach us as you were taught. Help us teach our children. Sister, surely you are weary tonight and wish to rest. In the days ahead, please sit and bring us your knowledge."

As the others called out "yo-hah!" in assent, Cakoanos continued. The words came easily, carrying thoughts she was longing to express. "Sister Esther, I have something else to say. My daughter owes everything to you, her very life! I wish the women here to understand your bravery. Twelve summers ago, my family lived in your village here, one of the many scattered people you took in. My body was heavy with child. The time of her birth, Sisketung's birth, had come. As the white army moved in with murder in their eyes, our people were fleeing like birds. You saw to it that I was not abandoned. You ordered that a litter of branches be built to carry me. We all fled into the night until we reached safety in the glen at Wilawana. There the next morning, on a bed of moss, my Sisketung came forth."

She turned to face Esther. "I might have died if not for your healer's hands. You stayed with me until I was well. Most of our others continued north. The soldiers soon passed near, trying to hunt us down. But you stayed for two days to nurse me and protect us."

Esther recalled it all too vividly. The children crying in fear. The treacherous nighttime climb across the rocky slope. Cakoanos moaning in a labor that would not end. The sickly newborn emerging in a gush of blood. The bittersweet tea and juniper bark compresses she administered. The deerskin strips they tied to the baby's wrists so the ghosts would see the tiny girl was tied to earth and leave her alone. Finally, in the predawn darkness, making her own reluctant farewell as she left them to their fate and headed north.

Slowly, Esther rose to Cakoanos's side and looked into her eyes. They touched cheeks and let their tears mix. From the circle, another Mohawk chant began.

Cakoanos cleared her throat and continued. "Sister Esther, my young Sisketung wishes to be of service to you during this time. She holds you special in her heart. Sister, please honor her. She will stay at your side to see that you are in comfort and will be grateful for any words you might share."

Sisketung had already gone to Esther's shelter and waited dutifully in the doorway.

The old woman turned to the circle. "Sisters of Teaoga, you have wiped the dust from my body and the heaviness from my heart. You have much to teach me. We have all endured hardships. Sisters, I am honored by your gifts and your beautiful words. I will answer your questions as my mind permits. Cakoanos speaks true, my body is weary now. Let our sharing begin tomorrow. Now I will let your chants be my night song."

She moved toward her shelter. Sisketung had made the bearskin ready.

Chapter 3

The winter sun was just appearing above Teaoga's eastern slope when Esther stirred awake. She glanced over to where Sisketung's blanket lay. The girl had already left. Morning fires were crackling outside, and Esther became aware of another sound rising in the distance. Her spirit leapt in sweet recognition.

In a clearing south of the tree grove, several dozen natives of various ages stood together in rows. Some elders were droning a chant to signal that their ceremony was about to begin—the beautiful, age-old communal sun ritual. Night, the people's Aunt, and Moon, the Very Old Uncle, were returning to sleep. It was time again to welcome Sun, the Father, and offer thanks for sustaining the people, animals and plants.

The sounds brought forth strong memories. Esther had performed this collective ritual nearly every sunrise during their days upriver at Assinisink, but only occasionally since then. She found a patch of sun outside her hut and let its warmth ease her stiffness while she watched.

The people stood in lines facing southeast. Slowly they lifted their hands in unison and shouted a tumult of sacred greetings to the sun. So many tongues could be heard! Esther recognized Delaware, Seneca, Cayuga, and thought she heard Mohawk. Six times over they chanted the prayer-greetings to the steadily rising sun.

The elders called out with confidence and ease. Others in the group looked to the elders, and many were hesitant at first with their own sixfold chants. Parents stood beside their children, demonstrating and prompting. Among them, Esther observed, were Cakoanos and Sisketung.

Cakoanos was bent close to her daughter, who stood frowning and stiff. They exchanged what seemed like unhappy words.

Soon the chanting slowed to a stop. The worshipers clasped hands in greeting. Although many were strangers to one another, the greetings grew lively and loud. Esther noticed how the elders seemed renewed as they walked about in the mixed congregation. She knew, as they did, that this was a rare opportunity to blend voices in prayer across tribes and to show the old ways to a scattered younger generation.

Following custom, the crowd dispersed for the morning meal at their campfires. By now, Father Sun was spreading his warmth generously into the frosty air. The camp was in good cheer. And Esther saw that young Sisketung was nowhere to be found.

Cakoanos had returned to the fire and was stirring a cauldron of dried eels and hominy. Another woman was preparing salawpawn, fried cornbread, on an iron skillet. Morning chatter was all around.

Esther approached her friend's side. "Sachoo-ca-cho, Sister. Your night dreams were well, I hope." After a moment, she added, "Your daughter departed from me without a word this morning. Is she well?"

Cakoanos sighed. "This council gathering has left her more troubled than I knew. So many of our brethren here, so suddenly, so many tongues. Sister, understand that Sisketung is quiet but very alert. She knows some yengwe settlers have made angry talk about our gathering. We live near them. We hear their words of hate and experience their shameful acts."

They sat as Cakoanos continued. "There is a yengwe girl she has known since they were infants. The girl's family claimed the land where our few wigwams stand. Her mother took pity because we had suckling infants among us, so they let us remain near the river's edge, away from their fields. Over the years, Sisketung has learned some of their tongue. I worry that her innocent mind is drawn to their ways. You saw that she ran off from our sun greeting."

"Perhaps I can speak to her," Esther said. "The old traditions have much to teach."

"Perhaps," Cakoanos replied. "But the yengwe girl—she is called Sarah—talks about us as savages. Sarah is afraid of the Senecas and the Munsee Delawares. It seems this Sarah has heard stories of their punishments and has told them to my daughter." After a pause, she added, "Sisketung has heard dark stories about you, too, Sister. The settlers feed and spread these stories like crops in their fields. I have tried to explain about the fighting, the Burning, all the yengwe lies, the blood our people have shed. Sisketung listens, but her ears seem closed."

The cheerful mood of the morning was flying away. While Esther and Cakoanos were speaking, the other Tutelo women had returned from their huts along the Chemung to spend the day at the camp circle. They sat now with their bowls of hominy, listening.

"Will the black clouds never lift from our people?" Cakoanos asked, eyes troubled. "What is left for us?"

The other women stirred. They had already discussed what to tell Esther, how to explain their worsening struggles. One of the women rose and began pacing. "Sister Esther, the yengwe land treaty brought the settlers in like a thousand noisy birds!" She jabbed the air with her spoon. "Their big men come with surveying chains and poles and cut up the land for themselves like slices of meat! They say it is theirs alone! In your time the yengwes might have sent their Bible-talkers out to work with us, but these new ones simply wish us gone!"

"Yo-hah! Sister, all our fishing spots they take, and our hunting lands," another said disgustedly. "We are like beggars!" Voices shrill, the women took turns telling how they had lowered themselves to make baskets and brooms for the yengwes, and to forage for berries. Their few men rented themselves out for coins to chop woods, clear fields, "do the labor of beasts!" No longer could the men hunt and fish freely—and many, they said, were lost to rum. Taunting was routine, and even assaults. Their sons risked danger swimming in the rivers or entering the forests on vision quests.

"Perhaps we should have left for the Ohio country or Niagara long ago, like the others," one young mother lamented. "Yo-hah, even if the bones of our ancestors cry out at us."

"Sister," said another, "has Cakoanos told you that a group of yengwe boys has been stalking our settlement, throwing stones at our homes, and shouting curses! It is a game for them to see what wickedness they can do until we chase them away. It began after our two men departed for the hunting grounds far to the north. Now, even during this council gathering, two of our women stay behind each day to protect our homes. We have one musket and a handful of powder and balls."

"Still your tongues," Cakoanos called to the agitated women. "A yengwe approaches."

THE FAIR-SKINNED YOUNG MAN strode towards them purposefully. He had just left a neighboring campfire where the people were still buzzing and keeping their eyes on him. Though clad in a wide hat, cravat, and drab broadcoat—simple clothing of the peaceable Quaker people—he bore the fierce demeanor of a warrior. His formal style of speech, distinctive to the high-minded Quakers, jarred further with his hostile tone.

"Dost any of thee speak words of English? Which of thee speaks English best?"

From their circle of bristling anger, the women responded with frowns. Cakoanos stood to face him.

"I am William Slocum," he announced curtly. "I seek my sister, Frances Slocum. She was kidnapped from our home in the Wyoming Valley. Frances was a tender lass of five when she and a wee lad named Kingsley were taken in bedclothes—stolen!—by three of thine Delaware braves and carried north. 'Twas twelve long years past. We understand Frances was spirited through Tioga. 'Tis said she might be found to the east, among thy Mohawk brethren. What dost thou know of this?"

The women sat unmoving.

"Have mercy on the poor lass! Surely thou hast heard something! Verily, what dost thou know?"

Cakoanos understood his odd English words well enough. She shook her head stiffly and muttered in English: "Know nothing."

"Nothing?!"

Slocum glared at them one by one before wheeling and marching off.

Esther and Cakoanos exchanged glances. The girl Slocum had been taken captive just one moon after The Burning. Quiwaumuck, the broad river valley three days south that yengwes call Wyoming, was still being raided by warriors at that time, months after the battle that had changed Esther's life. It was during the yengwe Revolution, that terrible time. Esther had heard that the girl was taken not east as her brother thought, but west where she was adopted by the Maumee tribe. Esther remained quiet. Let others tell the impolite yengwe what they knew.

The memory of Teaoga's captives had never sat easily with Esther. Thoughts were rising within her that demanded voice. The sisters wanted to learn about the old ways and hear her lessons. Perhaps this would be a good moment to set out on their wisdom path together.

Esther had kept her eyes on Slocum as he hurried up the sunny ridge to the north, past native children playing and a few families basking in the thin light. She spotted Sisketung walking there among the younger children.

"Cakoanos, I see your daughter beyond," she said, gesturing to the ridgeline. "Please bring her to us. I have something to say and wish her to join our circle."

Sisketung was led back without a word. "Daughter, I ask you to sit behind me, against my back," Esther said gently. "I will face away from Hollenback's store so you can watch for yengwes coming near. Also, your young body will warm my bones." The girl moved into position as instructed. Esther turned to her with a smile, but Sisketung avoided her eyes.

Once logs were added to the fire and everyone was seated, Esther raised her right hand. "N'petalogalgun: I have something to say. Sisters, listen well. Together we have cleared each other's eyes and ears so our minds are made ready. The great council fire will soon be lit. At the same time, you have called on me here to share the lessons of my years. Sisters, I pray that I may bring those years to life so you may understand all our times, the fat harvests and the starving winters. I will take you back as far as my youth. But first, I must speak of a certain burden that is upon my heart. You saw the yengwe Slocum descend on us like a thunderclap, speaking of one of the greatest wounds between us, one that will not heal."

"The yengwe captives?" Cakoanos uttered. "There were many."

"Yo-hah, Sister," Esther returned. "Let us take that, like one burning log from our fire, and examine it for lessons."

The young women settled in to listen.

"Sisters, did you know that for generations, before the Tutelos and even the Munsees came to Teaoga, war parties brought countless captives through here on their return to their villages in the northland? Others remained here and were held captive for many moons. These early captives were from other tribes. They were taken by the Cayuga and Seneca as we fought among ourselves for control of lands for our beaver trade with the yengwes. Later, when the yengwes pushed and crowded onto our land, caring nothing for their treaty promises, we lifted the hatchet against them. Many yengwe men were cut down, and then their women and children were brought captive into our midst."

"Sisters, I saw the yengwe captives when I was a child," one of the Tutelo women said. "I saw them crying. Some of our people laughed and taunted them, but I kept away. The fear in their eyes frightened me."

"Yo-hah," Esther said. "Our people could be harsh in wartime. In the first great war, many years ago, when we joined forces with the French, hundreds of Delawares and my Shawnees went on raids from here and returned with many yengwe prisoners. I can still hear the excited cries the warriors would make as their canoes drew near to us—one yell for each new captive they were bringing."

Esther found her voice slowing. These were difficult memories.

"Women among us, often our war widows, would beat many of the yengwes. Always the captives were left to find their own food. They lived on berries, roots, fish they caught with their hands, perhaps dog flesh. With our men away fighting, we often did not have enough food for ourselves. Some of the prisoners nearly starved. Others died of illness. I saw this. I saw one, the churchwoman Nitschmann, die from a sad heart. She was Moravian. The Western Delawares had attacked her mission town and scalped her man. She told me her two small sons escaped into the woods. She never saw them again. She lasted six moons here at Teaoga, praying, barely eating or stirring, until the breath left her."

A Tutelo mother broke the silence. "Sister, we know there were gantlets, too."

Esther gazed sightlessly at the fire. "Yo-hah, but not always. Sometimes when fresh captives arrived, our people would form two long lines, the gantlet lines. Even our children would join. The yengwe captives would be forced to run through and be struck hard with clubs and sticks and rocks. If they survived, they were worthy of being adopted. Sisters, know that yengwe children were spared running the gantlet! They were adopted, usually by our families that had lost members to war or disease, and they would be treated well. Older captives were left to die or might be sold as servants.

"Sisters, you know I was born Shawnee. Among the Shawnee are special people called peace women. They are the mothers or kin of the leading chiefs. The peace woman appeals to the war chiefs to spare the innocent. She can protect captives. When warriors would return with fresh captives, the women's war society, the miseekwaaweekwaakee, would rush out to meet them. If they touched a captive first, they could do what they wished with him, even kill him. But if the peace woman touched him first, he was safe.

"I know this," Esther said, "because my aunt was a peace woman. She told me I might become one, too, someday. As I grew older and saw the sufferings of war, I decided to take on the work of a peace woman to honor my people. When I became a sakima and led my village here, I kept that purpose in my heart.

"For a time we had no more captives at Teaoga. Then came the yengwe Revolution. The British from the north sent their fighters to drive away the Patriot yengwes who had begun to settle on these lands. Our warriors joined with the British to protect our lands. The raids brought yengwe prisoners back to Teaoga again. Our fighting was right, Sisters, and keeping captives as ransom was right. But this time I spoke out against cruel treatment. The gantlets returned. There was one yengwe family I knew well, the Stropes. Their children came as captives early in the year of The Burning. I protected their son from the gantlet. Their daughters I protected from harm as well. And there were others.

"But did it matter, Sisters? Did the yengwes notice these efforts at mercy? Were they grateful for the good treatment many of our people gave to the adopted yengwes? Did this change their hearts?

"Listen well. Once we harmed any of their women and children, that was *all* they remembered! Their *own* cruelties they forgave! We buried the hatchet. We took their condolence gifts to settle our own losses. But they continue to keep the stories of war captives like strong tinder for their hatred. You saw the hate in Slocum's eyes. I fear hatred is all they feel now. Perhaps it is a wound that they *wish* to have fester."

Esther rose slowly to her feet. "Sisters, though I pray it were otherwise, that is what I think. I ask you now to reflect on it. My bones are telling me to move into the open sunlight while it remains. Sisketung, please join me."

AFTER A SLOW WALK away from the ridge, the two reached the vast clearing south of the campground. The sun was nearing the western mountain, and only a few other people were in sight. Esther directed Sisketung toward the nearby Susquehanna shoreline.

"Daughter, here were the clay beds the Cayuga had for making their pots during the days of their watch town," Esther explained. "Some of their women came to our village to show us their cording and firing methods. Have you learned these ways?" The girl shook her head no.

Esther pointed to the southwest. "Around that bend was an inlet where they sunk a rock wall to catch the shad that filled these waters. They made nets of willow and lowered them from canoes. The men also used spears and arrows to bring them in. Such strong nets! Such fine harvests of fish! Then came the feasts and songs. Daughter, I can hear the laughter still."

They walked on silently. Sisketung kept her eyes averted.

"Child, what is on your heart?" Esther said finally. "Do not be silent."

They halted. Sisketung faced her.

"I ... you ... My, my mother puts words in my mouth!" The girl's voice tightened. "Last night she, she said I would be of service to you. Yes, I will. And that I owe my life to you. It may be true. But that I hold you special? I, I cannot say that. You are an elder, and I must respect that. Perhaps the spirits will punish me for speaking to you like this. But I, I scream inside!"

Sisketung gulped for breath and shook. A cold dread gripped her. She'd felt it ever since the yengwe boys' recent stone-throwing and terrifying taunts of "Savages! Killers!" She'd kept her fears to herself, as was her nature, but as the Teaoga council date approached, her dreams had grown dark. Now, the notorious Esther was visiting her own dangers upon them all. Peril seemed everywhere.

As Sisketung faced Esther in the ebbing light, tears welled in her eyes. "You call yourself a peace woman!" she exclaimed, lips quivering. "You tell us you tried to show mercy. But I have heard! You, you killed twelve yengwe captives! Butchered twelve yengwe men while they lay defenseless on the ground! How can we honor that? What kind of person are you? What kind of people are we?"

Never had she spoken like this. As the girl breathed back sobs, Esther studied the crows aloft in the distance and considered her reply.

"Daughter, it is wrong to raise your voice to an elder," she began evenly. "Your understanding is clouded. The yengwes try to make a hard story simple. Daughter, those men were soldiers who would have killed our people. We had suffered greatly in battle that day. I had suffered a great personal loss. It may be true that twelve captives were killed, but know that most did not die at my hand.

"Daughter, you do not understand what the yengwes have done. It is true we have shown wrath along with strength. But you must understand *their* unprovoked treachery and wicked deeds."

She took Sisketung by the shoulders. "Daughter, listen to what is said at the fire circle. Hear as I speak more about the events of my life. Listen to the council talks, where you will hear some of our wisest chiefs. I do not seek an apology. I only ask you to listen. And please, stay with me."

Through her tears, Sisketung held Esther's gaze. Her emotions sparked wildly, caught between two world views clashing like great flintstones. As the girl struggled toward a reply, something caught her eye. A runner was approaching from the campground.

ESTHER WAS SUMMONED TO Red Jacket's quarters. The runner said the chief had waited until darkness was closing in to help protect Esther from notice.

Red Jacket was seated at the far side of his expansive shelter. A large circle of women, the Seneca matrons, sat murmuring. The chief signaled to Esther to take her place near him.

Barely thirty winters old, Red Jacket was already known across the land. His well-practiced eloquence had recently given him the formal name Sagoyewatha, "He Keeps Them Awake." He was proud of the name, and of the embroidered greatcoat the British had presented to him for his wartime support.

All eyes were upon him as he rose to speak. Red Jacket seemed taller than his modest height. Carefully, he arranged the silver ornaments, medals, elegant gorgets and royal sovereignty tokens he wore. He smoothed the folds on the blanket draped over his shoulder like a toga. Raising his right arm, he began:

"Mothers, Sisters of the Seneca nation, your presence at Teaoga strengthens our will and firms my voice. Other nations join us at this great council fire. They understand that an injury to one is an injury to all. In that spirit, I have asked a great Shawnee sakima, Esther, once of Teaoga, to join our circle and make her wisdom available to us.

"Sisters, I have news about the council, and your advice I seek. First, let us share a smoke so our minds and spirits mingle." The women brought out their pipes as the kulukuneekun was passed around. Red Jacket sat watching puffs of aroma fill the dimly lit space. At the proper time, he rose, smoothed his blanket, and resumed his measured tones.

"Sisters, I can tell you the great council fire will soon be lit. The yengwe speaker Pickering waits in his tent. Many leaders of our nations are here already. We await Ojageghte, Fish Carrier, the old Cayuga chief. Once he arrives, we will begin in a day, maybe two.

"Sisters, let all who come know why we are here. Five moons past, during the Month When Corn Is in the Milk, three yengwes cut down two of our best men in the Pine Creek territory to the west. Our men were trapping and causing no offense. The three yengwes were taken to their courts, but nothing was done, no punishment came. Three moons ago we called for the leading men of Pennsylvania and of their new big government to come here with condolence gifts for the families. We also told them they must brighten the chain of friendship with the Senecas. They have neglected this friendship too long."

The matrons sat silently. Some bent sideways, eyelids low as if asleep, but Esther knew all were alert, listening deeply. One of them lifted her right arm.

"Brother, your words are true," the woman said. "The two grieving families are here waiting. Brother, the time is good for this council. Tribes far to the west continue their fighting to keep the yengwes out of lands beyond the Ohio. Some of our young warriors have joined them. The murders of the two Senecas cause fresh talk of the warpath. The yengwe settlers at Pine Creek are afraid we will lift the hatchet. Their leaders surely will have an open ear to our words."

"Yo-hah," a few others uttered in agreement. "Yo-hah!"

"The sister speaks true," Red Jacket said. "And listen well: I believe the yengwes' new big government also wants to take the chain of friendship away from New York and Pennsylvania. I believe it wants to be the only voice speaking with the Senecas and all our nations.

"Sisters, we have seen how New York is working to break apart our confederacy. Its leaders desire to put each of our six nations onto separate lands that they will surround. Let us call on Pickering to promise that his new big government will prevent this wickedness and will recognize our full Six Nations council as the true voice of our people!

"Sisters, the time is right to push the big government to stop the land merchants who are everywhere around us. Two of them used their smooth words to trick our Seneca chiefs into putting their marks on paper selling away land. Now they will cut up this ancestral land and sell it to settlers and make us leave it forever!

"Also, messengers have brought word that the yengwe leader Washington tells Pickering to declare that our people should take up their agriculture. With plows and fences and single crops! With men doing the planting like women when they should be hunting and fishing! This is not our way. Our men are not plowhorses in harnesses! I wish to speak against that, too. I will bring these matters to the elders, but first I desire your counsel—and, if my words satisfy you, your consent. You matrons have as much authority in council as the men. In all important business you have equal say."

An extended discussion followed. The matrons agreed with Red Jacket's objection to the New York land sale and his demand that Pickering recognize the Six Nations. Many voiced anger at the idea of putting their men behind plows, though a few said the other native nations might see it as offering them a better future. Esther said nothing, sensing that silence was expected of newcomers.

"Brother," one woman said in conclusion, "the time for supper has come. Let us return to our fires. We will consider your words and hope to deliver our answer before you sit with the elders."

As the meeting broke up, Red Jacket took Esther by the arm to thank her for attending. Esther departed toward the opening. Before her stood Sisketung, waiting in the doorway, where she had been listening. Was that a new look of understanding in the girl's eyes?

Chapter 4

IT WAS 5:35 BY THE TIME Li'l Red bounced over the curb and jerked to a stop beside the museum walkway. Mr. Winter cut the engine and cried out, "I am so sorry! Our staff meetings can be brutally long!"

"No prob!" Mrs. Tulowitsky called as she and Maddy rose from the portico steps where they'd been waiting. "We got your message in plenty of time, Russ. And if you get in a pinch again, just text me, and Maddy can come home with me and my Katie. Right, Maddy? Your daughter is super, by the way. And she's a history missy like me, I'm happy to see! Can't tell you how much I enjoyed talking with her."

"Thanks a big bunch," he said, stooped in apology. "I tried to arrange my days so this late stuff wouldn't happen, but you know ..."

"Hey, you gave me a perfect excuse to make my husband cook tonight!" Mrs. T said with a bright laugh. Being head of both the history museum and its summer camp, Peg Tulowitsky was a friendly fixture around town, known to most as simply Mrs. T. With her big, twinkly manner, she could have been Santa's kid sister.

"Oh," she said, "and why don't you and young missy come over for dinner Wednesday? We can chat and the girls can hang."

Mr. Winter looked at Maddy, who gave a "sure, why not" shrug. They quickly agreed on six o'clock—he'd bring one of those belly-buster pies from Herman's. With a breezy "okay, you betcha then!" and a jingle of her keychain, Mrs. T headed off to her SUV parked in the rear.

Mr. Winter didn't waste a second: "So, my wild child, how was day number one? I am all ears!"

Maddy hopped in. She was tired and sticky. She sort of wanted to take a nap, and sort of wanted to shower, and was getting hungry—but mostly she wanted to talk. She'd talk Melody's ear off if her bud were here.

"Was this really only one day? It was, I don't know where to begin. The campers were cute and—wait, wait, stop the car. I've got to show you something."

They pulled over in the museum driveway. Maddy pointed to a stone slab lying on the ground ten yards away. "That's covering an old Colonial well hole that's way over 200 years old. Mrs. T showed it to us today when we went on a group walk. It was a big deal to dig a real well, and here it still is. Cool, huh? And down there where the road forks is where a huge Revolutionary War fort used to be that went from river to river. Honest! There apparently are bunches of soldiers and even Indians buried there."

Her father cocked his eyes toward the spot, which was maybe two blocks to the south, where some especially fancy houses lined the street. "Really? Kinda gives me goosebumps. It's wild how all these things are mixed right in with the town."

"Yeah. And in the other direction, remember where that stone church was that we drove past the first night? That's real old, too, but guess what? Behind it is where the Indians used to come from all over to hold big treaty talks from, like, time immemorial. They used to do it right outdoors. I guess that makes sense. I just never thought about it. She walked us up there. It's all weedy and overgrown, but she said it used to be a big open treaty ground. Some of it's been washed away in floods and stuff.

"She says she'll take the campers on her walks a lot. She calls them our 'camp outings.' It's part of the history thing. Mrs. T has this way of making everything seem amazing, so even the little kids were paying attention."

"What are the kiddos like?" Mr. Winter asked.

"Wait, wait, look at the Stephen Foster park. Remember the sign said there was a school there that he attended? Mrs. T said the first settlers who came here were really into book-learning. They made sure each town had land set aside for a church and a school, first of all. They came together from Connecticut, like old Puritans, and wanted everyone to be able to read the Bible. The schools—they called them academies—were free, too, which she said was unusual. So lots more of them could read than other settlers in Pennsylvania."

"Yeah," her father broke in, "that was definitely a Protestant thing to train everyone to read the scriptures on our own. The Bible is a big reason literacy spread, Madd. So I get it, that's why there's the academy here. And that must be why this spot has such a New Englandy look."

"The park is even officially called Academy Park," Maddy added. "Also, Mrs. T told the campers that some of them came from those first Connecticut settlers. She knows their families and said it's true, that they should be proud. The kids were looking at each other like they didn't know."

"She sounds like some teacher," Mr. Winter said as he pulled out onto Main Street. "She sure got you thinking. Good old history can do that. History Missy. I like the name! So meanwhile, what are the kids like?"

"Nice. Squirrelly. Loud. Cute," Maddy said with shrugs. "There are seventeen of them, I think six to nine years old. Plus, there's me and Katie, who's Mrs T's daughter, and Trevor, a town kid my age, as the junior CITs. Plus Mrs. T and a college girl named Beth, who's actually a summer intern at the museum. We're inside and outside. We'll be out in the back lawn a lot when the weather's right."

He pressed for details, so Maddy explained that they'd divided the campers into the Senecas, the Cayugas, and the Oneidas—all tribes that were part of the Iroquois Confederacy that was big in that region in the Colonial days. Mrs. T taught them a handy way to remember the Iroquois tribes: COSMO, for Cayuga, Onondaga, Seneca, Mohawk, Oneida. Maddy had already committed it to memory.

The group Maddy ran was called the Senecas. She said they'd be doing a daily mix of table crafts and cooking, Indian sports, and local history stories. That day, the little campers had strung beads, made popcorn on a grill, and begun designing their own Indian painted posts, sort of like totem poles, first on paper and later on actual wooden poles they could take home.

"You should have seen it, Dad! The kids were getting marker and glue all over themselves, shouting like, 'Look-look, Maddy!' And a few were draping themselves on me. I'm still sticky."

"Wish I could be a camper myself," her father said with a big sigh. "Sure beats borehole analysis. And the other CITs, how were they, Madd?"

"Nice. I mean, at first, well, Katie and Trevor greeted me, as soon as I walked in, with a big 'Mucho gusto, amiga!' and some other Spanish, like I was Mexican or something. I just kinda looked at them."

"You didn't say anything?"

"I think I said, 'Uh, hello to you, too.' And I told them I knew that was Spanish, but I take French. They seemed surprised. Trevor said he figured everyone in Texas could speak Spanish nowadays. But they didn't make fun or anything. I sort of made fun of myself, actually. I taught them how to say y'all the right way, nice and drawn out. They thought that was funny. They were asking about cactuses and longhorns. Katie's kind of noisy and in my face, like a puppy dog or something. But mostly they were pretty normal. Katie said she liked my nails. I said I liked her hair. I don't really. It's just so-so. She invited me over to ride bikes. That's big around here, I guess."

"Great!" Mr. Winter said. "You knew they'd be nice to you, right?"

Maddy turned away with a gulp. *What a stupid question! Dad is so out of it sometimes. Kids will be not nice over nothing. If they're in a nasty mood, or having their cramps, or to impress their crew, or just to give themselves some evil entertainment. New kids always get the treatment. I've been known to mock a few kids in my time, not that it was my finest hour. But Dad doesn't seem to have a nasty bone in his body. Same with Mrs. T. That's one of the mysteries of life, how some people, especially grown-ups, keep their snarklies in a cage.*

She said nothing, letting her father hold onto his innocence.

"So what did you and Mrs. T do while you waited for me?" he asked.

Maddy closed her eyes and felt the car rumble along. "That was actually pretty intense," she said as her mind drifted back to their drive down to Tioga Point.

"COME ON, MADDY, THAT was the last of them," Mrs. T had said. Two cars were pulling away from the museum, driven by chatty moms car-pooling seven of the campers back to their homes. "It's 4:05. Sounds like your dad won't be here for an hour or so. I want to show you the Point. We have time."

They'd driven slowly down South Main, past the bridge turnoff and due south for another half-mile or so. The houses thinned out, and the street became unpaved and bumpy. At the dead end was a turnaround area. Mrs. T parked the SUV as Maddy looked out at the dramatic change ahead. The tall oaks came to a stop at the turnaround, giving way to a wide, vast field of tilled soil baking in the direct sun. The field was roughly triangular and sloped away from them as it narrowed gradually to a distant point. It looked to Maddy like a giant slice of crumbly brown pie.

"So, my dear," Mrs. T said, "you were asking me about Queen Esther before. It was a little nutty when the kids were running around, but I can talk now. I'm really glad you asked. If you like history, and I know you do, you've come to the right place. Let me do a little show-and-tell, okay?"

The day's heat had built up, so they had the place to themselves. Mrs. T left the engine on and the AC running as they got out to look around. They walked onto a grassy bluff beside the parking area, into the sun, and stood side by side. A warm breeze off the field riffled their clothes.

Maddy let her painterly eyes ramble. Along both far sides were the two ever-present rivers, glistening silver through the trees that bent over the riverbank like thirsty cattle. The low green mountainsides rose beyond like protective levees to the left and right. It brought to mind a favorite image her Sunday school teacher had recited to the class from one of the Psalms about how the mountains "melt like wax before the Lord." If you melted the big, jagged Rockies halfway down, she thought, this is how they'd look, comforting and eternal.

Billowy cumulus clouds, her favorite, floated peacefully above the hazy southern horizon. Maddy raised her face to the breeze with a smile.

"Behold Tioga Point!" Mrs. T declared, sweeping her right arm in an arc.

"The two rivers join at the actual point south of us down there. Think of that point as two o'clock on the dial, okay. Now look at the top of the mountainside over there at twelve o'clock. That's what locals call 'The Narrows.' There's a tight squeeze where the trail rises through a pass over the top. It follows an old Indian trail. The settlers used to haul their wagons over The Narrows somehow. Nowadays, a few bald eagles nest in the trees beneath it and dive for fish at the Point."

Bald eagles, here?! Maddy gaped at the thought of the famous, hunky birds flying out of a picture book into the wind. She'd always wanted to see one in the wild.

"Now, look down. We are standing on the site of the Cayuga Indian village, right on this high ground. The Cayugas used to be like security guards, stopping outsiders from continuing north into Iroquois country, up in New York State. I'm talking about the 1600s and 1700s. The mighty Iroquois Confederacy dominated most of those Indian lands, and they wanted to be the only ones to deal with the Colonial governments. Guess what historians call that Iroquois territory?"

Maddy stared, clueless.

"Iroquoia," Mrs. T said. "Like it was its own distinct nation and place. They're right. It was."

"So this was the Iroquois watch town?" Maddy said.

"Right! You probably read that on the monument out on the highway, right? The Iroquois Confederacy, the Six Nations, saw itself as being in a big longhouse. The Senecas guarded Iroquoia's western door. The Mohawks had the eastern door. This was the southern door, guarded by the Cayugas. We call the spot Tioga now, but they called it Teaoga: Te-a-O-ga. Drawn out into four syllables."

Mrs. T kept squinting across the field. Her voice slowed. "So much happened here. I feel close to it somehow, especially when I'm here at the Point. Do I ever! I feel honestly privileged to live around here, Maddy. History is my thing, almost as much as being a mom. I tell you, I come down here a lot.... I'll look around and take it in, then close my eyes and let it settle in more.... It's almost magical, you know what I mean?" She had a misty, distant look in her eyes. "Oh my, here I go."

Snide thoughts jumped into Maddy's head. Mz Snarkley projected a picture of Maddy's friends in the school lunchroom chortling that a middle-aged mom would get all teary over a field of dirt. Maddy mentally shouted back. *Go away!*

This IS an amazing place. I know how Mrs. T feels! Maddy took a deep breath to regain her focus. *I really do know how she feels.* She recalled times when she, too, felt overcome. Times, with books she loved, when she would stop reading and close her eyes to let the images open up like flowers. It would be intense but in an exquisite way. Or when she would be listening to a sermon in church and shut her eyes, and Jesus would be right there, comforting an old lady or riding by on his gentle donkey. *I know what you mean, Mrs. T, I really do!*

The realization went through Maddy's mind in a flash while she stood surveying the hazy distance.

Just as suddenly, Maddy spotted a dark shape out above the far treetops. Her heart pounded. "An-an-an eagle!" she spluttered. "There's uh, a big bald eagle!!"

Mrs. T turned her eyes to the solitary creature riding the warm updrafts. "Nice. But probably a crow. Wait, no, it's a turkey vulture. Balds aren't usually out much at this time of day. If you're lucky, you'll see them in the early morning."

Maddy frowned in disappointment—but then had a quick, welcome image of the vulture snagging Mz Snarkley, who jabbered angrily as she floated off in the bird's talons.

The bird sighting put Mrs. T back in teaching mode. It was becoming clear to Maddy that her new boss wasn't only fun-loving but was way sharp, too. All day she'd noticed how Mrs. T would effortlessly move out of her hearty mom self and begin reciting amazing amounts of information like a professor— pulling words out of the air as though she had an invisible teleprompter. She'd gesture, change voices and pacing, go silent, sigh over a thought, maybe crack a quick joke. She'd stop at intervals and scan the campers' faces, maybe ask a question to be sure they were following—all to help them *inhabit* the story. Sometimes last year, Mr. Ramage managed to cast a spell like that in world cultures class, but Mrs. T was able to do it with little kids, too. Maddy found it hypnotic.

Mrs. T was in the mode again.

"Back in Indian times, Maddy, this area would have been just *filled* with eagles and hawks. And with flocks of grouse and pigeons and turkey and other birds like you wouldn't believe. I imagine it as an Eden. There were elk, and foxes, wolves, wildcats, otter, beaver, bears, coyote, rabbits, big herds of white-tailed deer, you name it. The Indians would go out hunting in the late fall, usually in teams, on long trips into the woods. The rivers were full of sturgeon and haddock, pike, turtles, eel, and huge runs of shad, millions of shad in the spring, that they'd catch in traps and nets. Then they'd dance and feast and give thanks for the bounty. Right here, I'm sure. It's just amazing to imagine.

"Picture it, Maddy. We're seeing a cleared-out field now. But originally, this land was covered with deep forests that went on and on for days. And the tree trunks were massive! The settlers called them—get this—'big butts.' I've been reading about this. They said a squirrel could jump from treetop to treetop for a week without touching land!" She was sweeping her arm from horizon to horizon. "Can't you just see it? I sure can. That was what they call the forest primeval. It's said the branches of the big butts were so thick that they shut out the light, that it was always so dark on the ground that some settlers went nuts, like they were stuck in a damp dungeon."

Maddy pictured Hansel and Gretel in the deep, dark woods with a cackling witch. She blinked herself back to settlers and Indians.

"The Europeans were nervous in the woods. But guess what," Mrs. T grinned, "so were the Indians! We think of the Indians as blissing out in the forests, right? Not exactly. They had kind of a mixed view. The forest provided animals for their food, and their boys went there on vision quests to seek personal guardian spirits. But here's the thing, Maddy, they also believed the woods were filled with sorcerers, stone giants, witches, mysterious forces that would try to bewitch you and lead you astray. It was the realm of wood dwarves. So the Indians would hustle their way through, leave shelters with supplies for each other, and make tree carvings with news and trail directions so people wouldn't get lost. There was one stretch of the Towanda Path south of here that was so loaded with tree paintings it was known as the Painted Line.

"I love this: when travelers emerged from long journeys, other Indians would greet them with what they called Edge of the Woods ceremonies. These were done right away at the clearing to remove any spells the lurking spirits might have put on them! They'd pace around and chant things like"—she lowered her voice—"'I wipe the dust from your eyes and pull the thorns from your feet to free you from uneasiness so we may speak in good cheer.' The settler diplomats even tried it during their treaties with the Indians, saying they wanted to clear everyone's eyes and ears and hearts to open the way for good negotiations.

"Imagine doing that today?" she said, giving Maddy a long look. "Actually, I wouldn't mind having someone clear the truck exhaust from my nostrils sometimes."

Maddy looked wondrously toward the distant treeline, imagining big butts and forest elves. She was getting a bit overwhelmed, not to mention prickly with sweat.

"Yeah, the woods were alive for them, full of forces and omens," Mrs. T continued. "A bird landing close might be a sign of good fortune. But sudden, say, shadows or patterns of maybe clouds or rocks might be seen as bad omens, as warnings of danger."

Just then, near the treeline at three o'clock, two figures trotted along. Maddy saw spears in their hands. Her pulse quickened. *Braves!!* She pointed, speechless.

Mrs. T spotted them, too. "Whaddya know, I think that's Sam Jenkins and his son. Yeah. They're chasing woodchucks away. I've seen 'em do that with their poles before. Sam owns this farm. It's all potatoes now. I'd go say hi, but he really doesn't like visitors. He used to let people look for arrowheads and things along the shoreline, but ever since some knucklehead kids started using it for booze parties, he put up the no-trespassing signs. Too bad, but such is life, I guess."

Maddy squeezed her eyes shut. *Not braves?* Noticing that she looked flushed and woozy, Mrs. T directed her back into the car. "I'm clobbering you with a lot of stuff, aren't I?" she chuckled. "Oh well, we should head back, anyway."

She turned up the AC full-blast and directed the cold flow at Maddy. They sat for a minute in silence. Maddy took some long breaths. "Thanks," she said. "Hooo, that feels good."

Mrs. T appraised her out of the corner of her eye. "You looked almost frightened back there, my dear. Tell me, did you think you were seeing things?" Maddy returned a sheepish look. Mrs. T decided to open up more.

"You *know*," she said, voice rising, "sometimes when I'm here alone I swear I hear things. Chanting in the wind. *Songs*. One time, I was looking down toward their old clay pits there, and I closed my eyes, and right away, I *swear* I saw squaws at their drying racks full of fish. It was vivid. Felt like I could even smell it. Say, we're quite a pair, aren't we?"

Backing the car around, she continued, "We haven't even talked about Queen Esther yet. Watch out, my dear, I could talk about her all day. Can I give you a little bit for starters?"

Maddy had meant to research the queen the other evening but got sidetracked. So she gave a faint smile and leaned her head back.

"Esther's kind of a passion of mine, you might say," Mrs T began. "She's maybe the most fascinating person Tioga has ever seen. What a time she lived through! You've got to understand that in her time, the 1700s, this corner of the world was often a hot war zone. There was bloody fighting and plundering back and forth. French against English! English against settlers! Indians against English! Indians against settlers! Sometimes Indian against Indian! You know what a vortex is?"

"Like the eye of a storm?"

"That's the idea. This area was a vortex, because it was on the very border between those groups, and important rivers and trails came right through here."

As the SUV bounced along, she explained that during Queen Esther's lifetime, all sides coveted The Valley. Many smaller Indian groups were being shoved around by the whites and even other tribal groups. Essentially vagabonds, these remnant Indian bands were thrown together and had to coexist, learn each other's dialects, and put aside mistrust.

"We talk about multiculturalism today—this was multiculturalism to the max! So Esther led one of those mixed groups in a little village right over there"—she jerked her thumb to the left—"on the far bank of the Chemung. It was very unusual to have a woman lead an Indian village. The whites were the ones who called her queen. They even referred to her house, which looked kind of like a big settler cabin, as a castle!

"The problem is our Esther is kind of a murky figure—stuck in the shadows of history, you might say. Lots of people think she was part-white, French on her mother's side, with the famous name of Montour. But I've read that Moravian journals of the time list her mother as full-blooded Shawnee, and I tend to go with that even though it wrecks the Montour theory.

"In any case, I think of Esther as part Earth mother and part my crazy Aunt Sally who was unpredictable. There's one account of Esther as being stocky and big-boned, but another that said she was slim and elegant. They say she was friendly with the settler neighbors and kind to white captives. But then there's the dark side. You know what infamous means?"

"Like famous in a bad way, right?"

"Yupper. And that's definitely Esther," Mrs. T said as they walked to the portico steps. They'd just arrived back at the museum. Maddy was feeling cooped up, so Mrs. T suggested they sit in the shade while waiting for her father.

"Our queen lived in infamy toward the end of her life, Maddy. It's a nasty story that the settlers told far and wide back then. Basically, during the Revolutionary War there was a big battle downriver, near where the city of Wilkes-Barre is today. She was down there with the Indians and apparently went ballistic. They say she took a big war club and—oops, we'll have to continue this later. Here's your dad now."

"SO THAT'S WHAT SHE told me," Maddy said, resting her head against the side window. Braves with spears still loped across her mind's eye.

Mr. Winter stared out the windshield from their space in the motel lot. He put Li'l Red in park but kept the engine running and the AC blasting.

"Your Esther sounds a bit psycho, no?"

When Maddy didn't reply, he continued, "I think I'll study her up online. Maybe look into the Connecticut academy thing, too. Our quiet little town is getting curiouser and curiouser. Right, history missy?"

Maddy was in her own world, dog-tired and thoughts spinning. *Not braves? I could have sworn I saw what I saw. My eyes were open. I was tingling ... amazed more than scared, really. Like with that weird light down by the river the other night. So Mrs. T sensed something was going on with me! That's a relief to have a confidante. Stupid snark thoughts. Does everybody have them? Maybe I was born with my nerve endings too close to the surface or something. Little Mz Snarkley probably wants me to flop around now, get an attitude, act all sweaty hot and woe-is-me. Nah, no phony fits, if you please. This is too interesting. Bald eagles? Stone giants? Chants in the wind? A forest queen who helped her white captives, but later snapped out? Definitely not the kind of trip I had in mind. I imagined lots of Mister Softee and river rafting, Monopoly games, summer stuff. But this is fine, more than fine. I'm Rockn ready for adventure.*

"Hey, dad, bet I can down a bigger Softee sundae than you."

"You're on!"

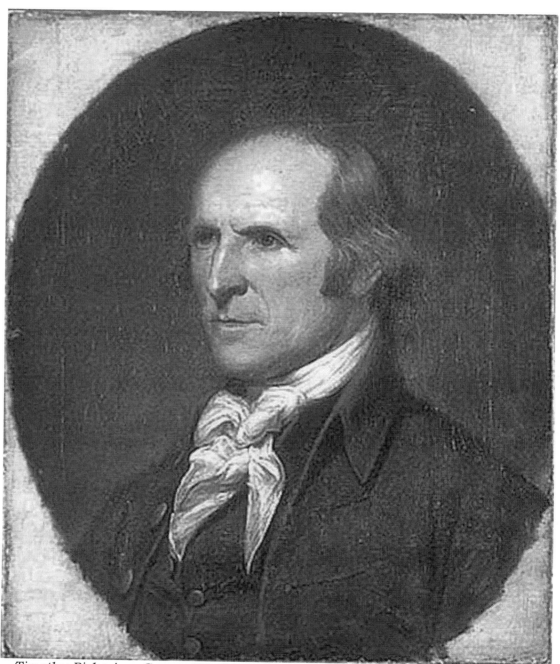

Timothy Pickering, George Washington's emissary to the 1790 Teaoga council.

RED JACKET.
SENECA WAR CHIEF.

Published by Campbell and Reprint

Red Jacket, the acclaimed Seneca chief who jousted with Timothy Pickering.

"Queen Esther Inciting the Indians to Attack Wyoming," a 1902 painting by Howard Pyle. Seated to Esther's left are the Mohawk leader Joseph Brant and British Col. John Butler.

MASSACRE OF WYOMING.

A popular 19th-century engraving of the Wyoming Valley Massacre of July 1778, in which British rangers and Indian allies routed undermanned Colonial settlers along the Susquehanna River near present-day Wilkes-Barre, Pa.

"General Sullivan at Tioga Point," a 1941 mural by Allan D. Jones Jr. installed at the Athens Post Office. (Image taken by Jimmy S. Emerson, DVM. Used with permission.)

The capture of young Frances Slocum as depicted in a 1869 newspaper illustration.

A wigwam of the sort used in the 1790 Teaoga campground.

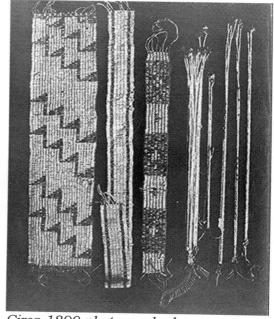

Circa 1890 photograph shows traditional wampum bead belts and strings. The beads are carved from quahog seashells.

A 1872 engraving shows Frances Slocum in old age, when she was known as Mocanaqua and refused to return to her white family. A Pennsylvania state park bears her name today.

These are the two historical markers that Maddy and her father visit on the first day of her visit, in Chapter 1.

Tioga Point (taken from The Narrows), with Queen Esther's village site at far left and Round Top in the central distance.

The Tioga Point Museum building.

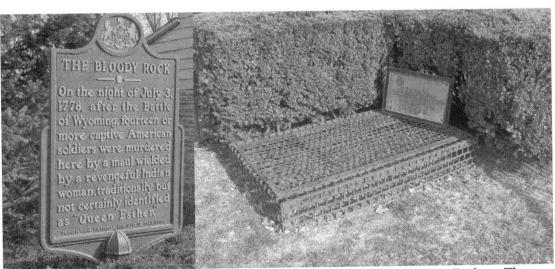

The landmark in Wyoming, Pa., near Wilkes-Barre, that implicates Esther. The grill protects the infamous rock below.

The objectionable monument (left) that Curtis and Tommy called 'the hissing stone.'

Chapter 5

The air bore a different smell here. It was the sour odor of large cattle herds carried across the lowlands on the morning wind. Esther recognized it from seasons past. Her village here had once kept cows, but few enough that their smell never overcame her. She was grateful that her time in upper Iroquois country had cleansed it from her system. The Tutelos spoke of the swarm of recent settlers to Teaoga. With them must have come this stench, lingering even in the months of ice and snow.

She wondered if this was the very odor of the yengwes. Many times she could recall her people being repelled by callous trappers and settlers, not only by the hairy faces, loud voices, and lack of hospitality, but by the harsh smell. Even in peaceful times, they could be as rude as their clamoring cattle and swine. Our people know to bathe and to rub sweet herbs and grasses on our bodies, she thought. Even the bear fat we apply to our skin to stop the biting insects is pleasant next to yengwe sweat.

The irritable thoughts increased Esther's restlessness. She fingered her wampum strings as she sat on the old bearskin inside her shelter—confined by the latest yengwe disturbance outside. Her Tutelo companions had insisted she slip out of sight until the danger passed. Now, beneath the hut's low dome, the dank odors seemed to close in as if a herd was circling outside.

The yengwe disturbance had erupted moments earlier at the dawn sun blessing. Esther had been outside the shelter offering her own invocations. The worshipers in the nearby field began sending up their ritual greetings to the sun when, suddenly, she heard a native voice shouting, "Stop, Brothers! Stop, Sisters!" She could tell it was one of the campground's few Lenape Delaware elders. He had rushed to the front of the crowd. Accompanying him was a yengwe man she did not recognize, dressed in black and holding a book aloft in his right hand. It was the familiar book they called the Bible.

"Repent!" the yengwe man cried out. "Give up your heathen ways lest you be condemned to eternal damnation! Savagery has no place in the kingdom of God!"

Esther understood enough of his tongue to know that this was a Christian preacher. Word of the sun ceremony must have flown to him from the mouths of Indian converts. Over the years, the yengwes had turned some Indians, particularly those in smaller groups or in close contact with their settlements, toward their Bible promises. A few of these converts mingled among the campground population, and one of them must have alerted the yengwe preacher.

The minister kept up his thundering: "Do not let your children be damned to hell! Do not desecrate our land with your pagan rituals!" Alarmed, the natives ceased their ceremony but disregarded his demand to fall to their knees. Esther saw the Tutelos, including young Sisketung, standing stiffly with the others. At that point, a few yengwe men pushed in from the right and tried to force the nearest worshipers to kneel. Some Indian women rushed over to protest. Two native elders hurried to the preacher, took his elbows and brusquely led him off the field. Holding his Bible high, the man shouted back to the crowd as he was forced to the edge of the woods where the trail led back to Hollenback's store and the yengwe settlement beyond. The Indian women were doing the same with the other yengwes, who resisted for a few backward steps, but then stalked off to join the preacher at the trail head.

By then, dozens of Indians had poured over from the campground. From the sounds along the ridgeline, Esther could tell a few settlers had gathered to witness the disturbance as well. The yengwe intruders were withdrawing reluctantly along the trail. She could understand their shouts. They were vowing to return. Esther felt relief that none of the young warriors, the fearsome burnt knives, were present. Violence would have resulted.

SOON CAKOANOS AND SISKETUNG slipped inside the old woman's shelter, the girl holding a bowl of hominy for Esther. "Sister, we are all near, watching out," Cakoanos said. "The Bible preacher and his people are gone. Some yengwe children remain along the far ridge, but they have returned to their idle games. Our elders are telling Pickering more protection is needed. Sister, eat now. We will return to visit."

Alone again in the cramped wigwam, Esther sat in silence and ruminated over her morning meal. She willed the cattle stench out of her nose, letting the oaky scent of the campfires overtake it. At the same time, she willed herself to be calm and to think carefully—disciplines gained from long experience through other hazards.

She wished to be outside in the moving air, with the women, speaking and learning. The night before had already worn her patience thin. She had lain awake too long, watching the moon's pale face through the cracks, hearing the owls and coyotes sing, thinking about Red Jacket's requests, pondering Sisketung's outburst.

Also, recent dark omens beset her mind. On the journey south, she had seen young saplings mysteriously snapped along the river's edge and left to decay. She had spotted more here, on the banks near the Carrying Path—rows of straight and healthy trunks, but fallen before their time and abandoned. She read them as fresh warnings of trouble.

Mostly, Esther thought about what to tell the fire circle. The Tutelos had sought her wisdom and deserved her best teaching. The council fire would soon be lit, interrupting their time together. There would not be time for everything. She prayed to the Preserver for focus and guidance.

The glimmers of understanding that had first come to her in the moonlight grew clearer by day. These women and girls were living in a nightmarish new time, broken from the land in a way she had never been and surrounded by yengwes whose hostility had fully hardened, unlike in her time. The women would need different skills, added endurance, great abilities to change and adapt as they entered a time that seemed ever darker. It grieved Esther to face this bitter truth, but she knew it was as real as the odors assaulting her. Yes, she would draw from her memories of the old ways, but only where it would be of use to her precious listeners. She must not weaken their spirits any more than these settlers were already trying to do. She would explain knowable skills to them. She would carefully answer direct questions. And she would offer thoughts about their way forward. This, with the Preserver's help, would be her teaching path.

Esther relaxed with the assurance that her middle way was the wisest. Uttering a prayer of thanks, she let the pleasant aroma of the campfire and the sumac branches that framed the shelter carry her from her worries.

SOME TIME LATER, AS the thin winter sun was beginning its descent, a figure appeared in the doorway. "Sachoo-ca-cho. Sister, I bring news." It was one of the Seneca head matrons. She saw that Esther had fallen into a daytime slumber. The stout woman sat smiling while Esther gathered herself drowsily and rose to a crouch.

"Sister, the day's events have been difficult," the matron said. "To see you rest peacefully is good. I carry news to add to your peace. Pickering has sent out some of his men to watch for our safety. They will pace the high ground to keep trouble away from our campfires. The men are in place already."

Esther nodded. "Do they carry muskets?"

"They do not. It seems they carry wooden clubs. We can only hope they will help. I approached one of them, and he could not understand my tongue. If more is needed, we can ask our men to stand watch, too."

"It pains me to burden the people," Esther said.

"Sister, these Bible-talkers assault all of us who keep the old ways. Yo-hah, extra care must be taken to protect you, but we are honored to have you with us and to join in your safekeeping. Sister, the matrons wish to gather now to set our voice as Red Jacket requested. It is best you remain under cover here in your shelter. I have come to receive your wise counsel about the Pine Tree chief's requests."

The long night past had given Esther time to arrive at her judgment. "Sister," she began with little pause, "there were three matters Red Jacket brought to us. He wishes to protest the evil workings of the yengwe land grabbers who have been at work in Iroquois country. Sisters, I too have seen how their paper promises drive us from our lands and prevent our return. I agree with full heart that Pickering must be told of their dishonorable ways. We must listen well to see if this yengwe will promise to act.

"Sister," Esther continued with a practiced confidence, "Red Jacket wishes to demand that the yengwes' big government declare the full Six Nations council to be the true voice of the people again. Sister, over my years I have seen both good treatment and bad from Six Nations domination of our scattered bands in the river valley. But the time for those grievances is behind us. Our fates are knitted together now. I believe our strongest voice, our best way forward, rests now with the influence of the Six Nations, as Red Jacket believes.

"Finally, Sister, our counsel was sought on Washington's plan to have our men take up the yengwe plow. Like other matrons, I fear we risk burying our pride and culture with their seed crops. But out of respect to those matrons who believe the plow might hold promise, I counsel that Red Jacket should demand more information from Pickering. Sister, on these matters, this is how my heart speaks. I am honored to be a voice in your council."

The visitor straightened herself. "Sister, your words are clear and your advice sound. I will repeat them to the other matrons when we meet.

"Sister Esther, I have other news. Today a messenger reported that another large group of our people is approaching down the Chemung to join us. They should arrive just before this day's setting sun. Their arrival will draw yengwes over to the river, which will make it safe for you to rejoin your own circle here.

"Sister, very soon the Teaoga council fire will be lit. Let us all be ready."

ONCE TWILIGHT WAS DESCENDING, Esther draped herself in her blanket and emerged carefully to sit near the open fire. The new arrivals had reached the Carrying Path moments earlier. That had attracted the yengwes and many of the natives to the riverside. The crowd would soon head to the other end of the campground for a welcoming ceremony led by the chiefs and elders.

Realizing the value of this sudden, intimate time together, the Tutelo women and girls promptly gathered around their fire and asked Esther to speak. As they leaned in expectantly, Esther studied their open faces.

With a prayer to the Preserver, she began. Taking a loose stick that lay at her feet, she drew two long, roughly parallel lines in the hard earth to indicate the great rivers. "Sisters, here is the Saosquahanaunk. And here, five days east, toward the rising sun, is the Lenapehanna, the river the yengwes call Delaware."

For the next hour, as the sound of the welcoming festivities rose in the distance, Esther told her story. She added trails and towns to her markings in the dirt. She paused often, asked occasional questions, waited before proceeding.

Esther told them how, many winters past in the rocky Minisink country along the Delaware, the Munsees had welcomed her family along with other Shawnees displaced from their homelands far to the south. The Minisink was wild and rich with game then, the harvests abundant. At Pechoquealing village, her parents had taught her and her brothers the ways of quillwork and healing, skinning and trapping. She saw no quillwork on the trade cloth her listeners wore now. Did they know how to work with porcupine quills? Would they wish to learn? Would they want to acquire the healing skills she had been taught? When she asked, a few spoke eagerly of their wish to learn. Hopefully there would be time.

Though Sisketung sat silently, her heart, too, opened to the idea of learning the healing ways. Awakened by the words of Red Jacket and the matrons and sickened by the Bible preacher's insults, she was letting go of her stubborn resistance to the old teachings. Listening to Mother Esther now, she found herself entering the history of her people and seeing events unfold as if she were there. She decided she would strive to commit Esther's recitation to memory—one of the most demanding oral traditions of her people.

While Sisketung listened acutely, Esther told the group about the bitter end to her early years in the Minisink country. A few foolish Munsee men, drunk on rum and yengwe promises, put their marks on land papers, she said. As a result, her people were forced four days west to Shamokin town on the Susquehanna. There she had her first exposure to a mixed refugee community. She recalled the ragtag crowds, the tension, the drinking. Sisketung stared at the ground as the words sunk in. The girl felt aloft on an eagle and witnessing what Esther described: cabins and meager huts teeming with restless Indians speaking a dozen tongues.

Great changes arrived at Shamokin, Esther said, changes that brought argument among the elders: clay pots steadily gave way to iron kettles, deer sinew to linen thread, fish bones to sewing needles, spears to muskets, deerskin to wool and cotton. At Shamokin, Esther tried without success, after days of fasting and waiting, to summon a personal spirit guide. At Shamokin, she also came to womanhood, experienced the period of ritual isolation, put aside her cornhusk doll, and felt new stirrings in her body.

The old woman paused to ask the Tutelos if their few boys still went on spirit quests. The yengwe land surveys had made it too dangerous, they replied, except for one remote area near Wilawana. Did they isolate the girls when they first bled? Only in their own wigwams now. There was no safe place for a ritual isolation hut away from their tiny settlement.

Esther closed her eyes to summon the memories clearly. The Susquehanna lands at the time, forty-five winters past, were under the control of Iroquois overlords from the far north, she said. Iroquois-yengwe land deals forced her people to uproot from Shamokin to Wyoming. From there she soon moved a half-day's journey upriver to an island at the mouth of the river Lackawanna. She had met the handsome Munsee chief Eghohowin and agreed to take him as her husband. There at the Munsees' island base, she began to raise a family while he fished, hunted, counseled with the elders, traveled to other villages, made alliances, and developed the skills of war.

Sisketung let the words of her history fall like seeds and take root in her memory.

Esther's voice thickened with emotion as she recounted the onset of war in the yengwe year 1755. The Indians at Wyoming rose up in pride at the news that warriors to the south, many of them Shawnees, had ambushed and destroyed the redcoat army and killed their foolhardy general, Braddock. French messengers brought a promise that if the Delawares and Shawnees joined them as allies, the French would help reclaim their tribal lands. This offer reached welcome ears, because the previous winter, a Connecticut trader had gotten some sachems drunk and tricked them into signing away tribal rights to the Wyoming Valley.

Did the young Tutelo women know of these dark events? Only vaguely, Cakoanos replied. Sisketung's heart fluttered at the premonition of violence ahead.

Esther pressed on, telling with scorn how the Iroquois sided with the British and arrogantly demanded that the Delawares join them against the French. Most Delawares favored the warpath against the English forces instead. Eghohowin was among the rebellious chiefs calling for war to regain Delaware lands—and Esther said she had felt the same.

"Sisters, understand that here where we sit, right here, was our proud stronghold during that time of war," she said, jabbing a finger at the ground.

ESTHER PAUSED TO DRINK a ladle of water, then cleared her throat to resume. Suddenly, an object whistled through the air past her head. Another skidded across the ground into the campfire.

They were stones, being flung from the darkness.

An instant later, Sisketung, seated behind her, cried out. Esther turned to see the girl clutch the side of her head. A jagged stone had struck near her left ear and thudded to the ground. Sisketung wailed in shock as her hand flew up to cover the wound.

The other women circled tightly around them and scanned the darkness. The stones had come from the direction of the woods, near the ridgeline. The attackers must have crept near to be so accurate, Esther thought. Yengwe patrolmen were nowhere in sight.

Two of the Tutelo women grabbed sticks and walked in a low crouch towards the woods. Seconds later, two boys burst up from behind a log and dashed away into the darkness. They were yengwes with straw-colored hair and white leggings, perhaps Sisketung's age. The girl might even know them, but she was curled on the ground, consumed in fright and pain as her mother bent down and whispered words of comfort.

Esther went to the girl's side. Gently she pried away Sisketung's hand to examine the welt swelling along her hairline.

"Daughter, be strong," she said quietly. "There is little bleeding, and it will stop quickly. Your ear is unharmed."

She turned to Cakoanos. "Sister, we must clean and dress her wound. I have good medicine for that."

The circle dispersed. Esther asked that the attack be reported to the elders. While Cakoanos went to the fire to find a torch to light their work, Esther led the dazed girl into the safety of their shelter. She lay Sisketung on the old bearskin and began gathering herbs from her kunhoksena, the beaded medicine bag stored in the corner.

"Daughter, your head will ache for a day or two. Those were yengwe boys in the dark, attacking us with rocks. Lie on your side so we can treat your swelling."

Cakoanos held a glowing branch, whose embers cast enough light for Esther to prepare her medicines. First she dipped a strip of trade cloth into a pot of cold river water and dabbed it on the girl's wound, gently cleaning out loose dirt and blood. She gave Cakoanos the cold cloth and a handful of grated pokeweed berries, instructing her to wrap the berries in the cloth and squeeze until the juice soaked through. While Cakoanos applied the compress to the bruise to ease the swelling, Esther prepared a poultice of mashed balsam and juniper bark.

Sisketung looked up intently as Esther leaned in to press the poultice to her temple. The girl said nothing, but her tears and fright had given way to a thoughtful expression. She reached up and placed her fingertips on the old women's healing hand.

From the doorway, a man's voice broke in. "Balsam?"

It was Red Jacket. When word of the attack on Sisketung was relayed to him, the chief left the evening's festivities to check on the girl. Though he was no doubt alarmed, Esther could tell by the scent of grog liquor that he was also in good cheer.

"Balsam and juniper, yes," he said, theatrically sniffing like a wolf as he stepped inside. "Sister, it is good to know the girl is in your healing care."

"Sachoo-ca-cho, Brother. We are gladdened by your presence," Esther replied. "This child, Sisketung, and her mother, Cakoanos, are Tutelos, once of my village and now living on the edge of Teaoga. Brother, we were sitting at our fire circle when yengwes attacked us with rocks. We believe it was boys, two or perhaps three of them."

"Does the girl know the attackers?"

Cakoanos conferred with her daughter in low tones, then turned to Red Jacket. "Sachoo-ca-cho, Brother. We are honored that you visit us. My daughter knows the boys of this yengwe settlement. They sometimes taunt us. She says she did not see who attacked us tonight but believes they might have been aiming at both her and Sister Esther."

"Cowards!" Red Jacket bellowed. "Their men raise a crop of cowards who attack women and girls without cause. May they drown in their own yengwe hate! And where were the guards Pickering promised? Our men will keep watch over the campground.

"Sisters, in two days the council fire will be lit. Pray that the talks begin in peace."

Chapter 6

From the Tulowitskys' porch steps, Maddy looked down the rutted driveway toward the makeshift starting line. There sat Katie, poised on her trusty bicycle and raring to go. Maddy, as instructed, barked the countdown from five and yelled, "Go!"

The scuffed purple dirt bike thrust forward. Katie whizzed along the dirt driveway past Maddy, daredevil grin on her face, and gained speed as she bore down on the croquet stakes that marked the finish line. The instant she crossed, Katie punched her flip-flop on the foot brake with practiced skill and leaned back in a triumphant, skidding wheelie. "Woo-hoo, baby! Try that, Maddy!"

Maddy shuffled out into the late-afternoon heat. Wednesday had come, and they were killing time waiting for her father to show up for dinner. Maddy was curious about her boss's house. She thought she should try to connect a little more with Katie, anyways. She hadn't counted on the girl being a speed demon. Oh well, she thought, go with the flow.

Trading places, Katie stood on the steps and counted down to "Go!" Maddy cranked the pedals as fast as she could. The pastel workhorse lurched forward but quickly tilted rightward. She dragged a sneaker on the ground for balance and slowed to a wobbly stop.

"No sweat, go again," Katie called out from the steps.

Maddy got back into position. Don't overdo it this time, she said to herself. Yet that's exactly what she did. After a solid takeoff, she pushed for top speed and twisted her torso awkwardly to the left. The bike leaned left and left, lower and lower.

With a shriek, Maddy skidded sideways across the dirt and gravel as the bike clattered out from under her. She sprawled to a stop in front of Katie, who yelped and tumbled off the steps to help. Maddy, brushing dirt and pebbles from her legs, was aware of a stinging on her left calf and a familiar flush of embarrassment on her cheeks.

"Oooh, ouch!" Katie exclaimed in sympathy. "But you were cranking good!"

Maddy limped to the porch steps and sat to examine the damage. The BMX bike lay crooked beneath a lilac bush, its front wheel spinning, seemingly no worse for wear. Her leg was a different story. The skidding left ugly streaks of dirt from ankle to shorts. The outside of her calf had taken the brunt, producing an angry red and pink abrasion that was beginning to throb. She touched the open wound with a wince.

"That's happened to me, too, girlfriend," Katie said. "Wait, I'll be right back."

Katie smacked the screen door shut, leaving Maddy alone with her sinking thoughts. She leaned forward to pick flecks of dirt from the bruise and examine her exposed pink tissue. *Why do these things always happen to me? Stumble-bum, that's what Dad might say. I almost had it, I think. Not that I care. I'm glad she didn't laugh at me. Not that I'm trying to impress her. We should have had a sketching contest. I would have showed her. Or a pop quiz on the presidents, yeah. She called me girlfriend again. Dunno. Maybe.*

Katie returned with a small tub of first-aid supplies. "Mom has this stuff for us in the pantry. Let's start with the antiseptic." Methodically, she wiped the streaks of dirt off Maddy's leg, dabbed the abrasion clean, and gooped on some extra calamine lotion. Maddy watched silently, frowning but grateful for the expert TLC. She wasn't sure what to make of this girl. *It's nice how she's hearty and open like her mother. It's just that she seems tres jocky and not particularly quick in the deep-thinking department. Too, like, boisterous. We're not really clicking.*

It was hitting Maddy that she didn't have to impress anybody up here, or worry about being in the cool-crowd, or even be friends with anyone at all if she didn't want to. She'd only be here two weeks, and then they'd never see each other again. She welcomed this liberated state of mind. It wasn't snarky exactly. She just liked the feeling of freedom. She didn't have to think about boys, either. Maybe she'd see a cute boy or maybe not, and so what? She didn't want to be one of those girls who had to have a boyfriend to feel good. She could follow her heart's desires here, work on her art, take a break from annoyances, and be her true self. *Girlfriend? I'll think about it.*

Katie seemed oblivious to Maddy's brooding. Her medical mission accomplished, Katie hoisted up her wayward bike, tested its wheels, and gave the handlebars a deft jerk to the right. "Good as new!" she declared. "Ol' Cowgirl has taken some worse licks in her time. So we probably should give your leg a rest. What's next? How about some checkers?"

Maddy nodded gratefully. She hadn't played checkers in years, but it was about her speed right now. For the next few minutes, they sat in the shade, dangling their legs off the edge of the porch, and chugged glasses of icy Kool-Aid. The checkers helped Maddy calm down. They matched each other's captures—occasionally interrupted by Katie's proud displays of burping—until Maddy trapped Katie's last king for two straight victories.

"You girls okay out here?" Mrs. T said, emerging from the side door in a well-worn flowered apron. "Maddy, I hear you got a scrape. Let's look.... Ouch, you'll be feeling that for a day or two. Leave it exposed for a little while so a nice scab can form. We'll cover it with a bandage later."

She pointed to the driveway. "Look, you can see the skid marks where you must have slid. Katie dear, please move Cowgirl off the driveway, okay. Maddy's father will be here any minute. I'm making a big pot of spag with meatballs. Where's Curtis, in his room?"

The girls gathered up the checkers pieces just as, sure enough, Li'l Red pulled into the driveway and around to the steps, pumping out dance music. Mr. Winter turned off the oldies station and climbed out, beaming.

"Hi, Mr. Winter!" Katie yelled, bouncing down the steps. She ran her hand along the car's slinky front fender. Maddy could already tell she was taken with the cool coupe, and probably with her dad's sparkly grin. "How was your day, Mr. Winter? Maddy had a crash on the bike. We were doing stunts. She was going great until she spun out!"

"Aw, Madd," Mr. Winter said tenderly. He bent down to look. "Such a bummer. Hey, I have just the thing!"

He reached into the car's side window and carefully lifted out two Herman's Bakery boxes. One was magic-markered "Choc. Crème," the other "Lem. Meringue."

"Just what the doctor ordered, eh?" he said, holding them out with a flourish. "I'll bet I can smear some meringue right on that bruise, too. Like a nice salve! Sound good?"

Maddy rolled her eyes. "Don't be dopey, mopey."

"Dopey? Why, I've never been so offended. Where are your manners, young lady? I guess this dessert will have to be all mine then."

"Yes, whatever did happen to children's manners these days?" Mrs. T chimed in. She was standing in the front doorway, holding open the screen door. "So glad you're here, Russ. Do come in. Jack, Curtis, come down and meet Maddy's dad!"

The aroma of tomato sauce and fresh basil beckoned from the stovetop. Katie slid her flip-flops on and headed indoors. Maddy rose and shuffled behind, resisting the impulse to limp.

THE TULOWITSKY HOME REMINDED Maddy of her Grammy Winter's eccentric old farmhouse in Indiana. Besides the wrap-around porch and big lilac bushes, this one had creaky floorboards, all sorts of carved wood paneling, quaint wallpaper, ancient brass fixtures, scattered throw rugs, layers and layers of paint, and sticky old windows that you had to bang open and force closed. Katie's family also got by with only window air conditioners and ceiling fans. Maddy took it in dreamily. *Not Texas, girl.*

For dinner, they took seats around an oval oak table in the dining room. An ornate chandelier cast its light onto the center, where the mound of spaghetti was quickly disappearing. The plan for the evening was to have dinner, then walk over to Teaoga Square, four blocks away, for the weekly band concert. The adults were enjoying a bottle of dinner wine, which had them talking gaily. Maddy had noticed that effect before. She worked on her spaghetti and green salad—stopping often to press her palm delicately around her sore spot—while listening to the adult chatter. She noticed that Curtis, Katie's quiet younger brother, seemed to be listening intently at his seat across from her.

The conversation barely touched on the kids in the room, which was fine with Maddy. They did cluck about her injury a little and Mrs. T praised Maddy for her work—especially for her latest idea that the campers make their own Iroquois cornhusk dolls. Maddy had seen directions online for creating the dolls. "Super idea, Maddy," Mrs. T said, smiling at her and her father. They agreed to talk the next day about the project.

Mostly, though, the grown-ups turned their attention to swapping information about their jobs and families, and passing around a bunch of photos. After a few pleasant minutes of that, Maddy's father raised his wine glass toward Mrs. T and said enthusiastically, "Peg, if I may, I've been dying to ask you more about this Queen Esther person. If I have it right, she was an Indian queen, and she ran a village here? And the early settlers thought she was a killer-villain who went off her rocker? Amazing."

Mrs. T took a deep breath and looked around the table. "Ah, Queen Esther. Is that where we want to go? Always happy to oblige."

When no one objected, Mrs. T pulled her chair closer to the table and leaned in. The chandelier cast a dramatic light on her features as though she were a seer presiding at a séance. She turned to Maddy's father.

"Yes about the village, Russ, and yes, apparently, about the killing. That was in the 1770s. But to really understand Queen Esther, you have to go back earlier, to the French and Indian War times."

Mr. Winter cocked an eyebrow in curiosity. Maddy noticed Curtis smiling faintly.

"That was the huge war between England and France that started in Europe and spread over here," she began. "We all learn about it in school, and then seem to forget what it was about. It was known as the Seven Years' War, though it really lasted longer, 1754 until 1763. Over here in the colonies, it was about trade and territory, very big stakes. Both sides recruited the Indians. The Iroquois tribes sided with the Brits, because they thought they could win favors —but most of the other tribes went with the French. That's because the French were already providing them with trade goods and weapons and promised to always respect their land rights."

Mrs. T had slid into her commanding teacher's cadence. "Here's the thing. The Iroquois tribes had been lording it over the Delawares, the Shawnees and other smaller tribes for years, saying those groups couldn't do their own land and trade negotiations, and making them pay tribute gifts to them. The Delawares said they were 'living under the Cayuga armpit.' Groaty, huh? So when the war starts and the British suffer some defeats, there's an absolute outpouring of Delaware pride and belligerence. They go on the warpath on their own to strike hard at the settlers—and just as important, to show the Iroquois they won't be told what to do anymore! It gets ugly. There are brutal raids, and scalping of settlers. Hundreds of Delaware and Shawnee fighters come up here to Tioga, using this spot as their base of operations.

"That's when Esther and her man, a tough Munsee Delaware chief named Eghohowin, come into the picture. We don't know too much about her until then. They pop up in the historical record at Tioga. Their war leader then is Teedyuscung, a bantam-rooster guy who actually declared himself 'King of the Delawares.' He's boastful and warlike at first, especially when he gets into the rum, but then he gets kinda wishy-washy when Pennsylvania declares open war on the Delawares and sets a bounty price on Indian scalps.

"Around this time, tough-guy Eghohowin breaks away to keep on fighting. He takes his Munsees farther up the Chemung, probably with Esther, to regroup at a place called Assinisink. This was around 1756."

"The Munsees, you say?" Mr. Winter asked, squinting.

"Yes, M-u-n-s-e-e. They were one of the Delaware bands, more mountain people than the others. Until they got pushed out of their homeland by the settlers."

Katie, seeing her mother focusing mostly on Mr. Winter, reached an arm toward Maddy and whispered, "Hey, want to play another game of checkers?" Maddy—who'd been trying to figure what a bantam-rooster chief might look like —kept her eyes locked on Mrs T. "Maybe later, okay."

"Aww," Katie said. She gave her father a yearning look. "Checkers?"

"You betcha, Sweets," he replied. They headed off to the living room, where Maddy could see them setting up the game board on the coffee table.

Right here was where Maddy wanted to stay, listening to Mrs. T. She'd been thinking about her the night before, lying in bed after reading about the cornhusk dolls. *What is it I like about Mrs. T? Her enthusiasm. I guess you'd call it passion.* Maddy pictured her lunchroom gang going on all snippy about how they didn't like this girl or that teacher. Maddy wanted to think for a change about whom she did want to be like, in a serious way. *I wonder if any of them know that sometimes, when they're blah-blahhing, I'll pull away like I'm on a helicopter. Like I'm floating above the room, wondering about stuff like why we're here in this Texas cafeteria, where we come from, if girls jabber like this everywhere and always. History helps you figure that out, because you learn about different ways in other times. If nothing else, it's not as boring as fashion and boys. And the Indian stories really are, like, powerful. Mrs. T seems to feel that, too, like we're on the same wavelength.*

Mrs. T unfolded a paper napkin and carefully drew a river map for the others. "Here's Teaoga-slash-Tioga-slash-Athens. And here, about two Indian days upriver"—four inches on the napkin—"is Assinisink. It's across the line in New York, right where Corning, the famous glass town, is located today.

"The Munsees set up quite a stronghold there under Eghohowin and Esther. I've read where Assinisink had thirty or so large cabins, which was a lot for back then. There were a few other Munsee war towns along the Chemung River as well. They doubled-down with their fighting and raiding, and returned with loot and a stream of white captives. There were some ferocious warriors there.

"Once, in 1760, a white peace party made it up to Assinisink and wrote in their diaries how they stayed in Eghohowin's cabin."

"Wait, Peg! I know this!" All eyes turned to Maddy's father as he pulled some printouts from his back pocket. "I read about that very trip online last night and brought it along for you."

He flipped through the papers and found the right one. "So it says one day some of the warriors at Assini-what-Assinisink got loaded on rum and threatened to roast the white visitors alive! The chief— it's Eghohowin himself? Wow!— had to drive his own men out of his house three times, until, finally, the whites scooted into the woods for safety."

"Yupper, that's the story," Mrs. T smiled.

"The white guys stayed in a room with some ferocious brave who had a bed board painted with seventeen human figures representing his seventeen war prisoners, one of them a woman. Other figures were painted with no heads!"

"That wasn't just any brave, Russ," Mrs. T said. "That was Captain Jachkapus, a Munsee war leader who had massacred a Moravian Christian settlement. He must have been one of Eghohowin's henchmen."

"And another Indian's bed showed six war raids and four prisoners, two dead, two alive," Mr. Winter added. "Not sure I'd want to stay there overnight!"

Maddy was agog at her dad's find. The images bloomed in her mind—the plunder, the leering drunks, the scary beds—and she shuddered. Her eyes were drawn to the window as if Indians might be roaming the back yard.

Mrs. T continued: "Awesome, Russ. I consider this Assinisink phase a bit of a Munsee golden age, maybe their final one. They were able to live in the old ways for awhile. The diaries showed they did the daily sun blessing, and had their big dream festivals, where they recited their personal dreams and visions to each other. The Delawares had some religious prophets who were on the move here and there at the time, urging people to reject white ways and white religion. Did you see anything about Old Teacher, Russ?"

"Who?" Mr. Winter said.

"Assinisink had its own shaman, who was called Old Teacher. He had a picture book with images of heaven and hell and rum and a white trader, like an Indian bible. Every morning he would walk around singing to the sun and sort of read out of his book as he preached that the people should keep the native ways. It's said books like these had a kind of magic totem power in the Delaware spiritual worldview."

"But wasn't all this happening right in Iroquois territory?" Maddy broke in. "They were allowing these Munsee Indians to act up, like, right under their noses?"

"Great point," Mrs. T said. "The Munsees were definitely a thorn in the side of the Iroquois. The Munsees were fighting when other tribes, even other Delawares, were gradually laying down the tomahawk. But it seems none of the other tribes wanted to directly take them on. So the Munsees kept fighting, even through some bad harvests and brutal winters of near starvation on the Chemung. It's said that their own women sometimes demanded that the men make peace. Esther might have been one of them. Eghohowin would sometimes release their captives under pressure, but the next raiding party would probably bring in new ones.

"Things flared up for the last time in 1763. The British had finally won the war against the French, but then they broke their promise to remove the string of forts they'd built on the borderlands. That made lots of Indians furious all over again, from the Detroit River to the Delaware, and they went back on the warpath against the British."

"Pontiac's War, right?" Mr. Winter said. "Named for one of the western war chiefs?"

"You betcha. And that did it. The king's Indian commissioner in New York, Sir William Johnson, decided he had to stop these renegade Indians. In the winter of 1764 a strike force attacked on snowshoes—picture that—and destroyed Assinisink and three other Chemung villages. A fifty-dollar bounty was put on Captain Jachkapus's scalp. Bunches of Munsees were captured, and others fled west to the Seneca lands or south toward Teaoga."

Maddy's mind was spinning. *So that's who Pontiac was? And attacking on snowshoes! And yuck, money for scalps!* The story felt personal, as though Maddy were a ferocious brave one moment and a terrified captive the next.

Mrs. T continued: "The next year the Munsees reluctantly made peace with the British, but by then, Eghohowin and Esther were elsewhere. They began a new phase down here"—she made a mark on the napkin an inch below Tioga —"at Sheshequin."

Maddy and her dad exchanged glances: *Sheshequin!*

Abruptly, Katie called from the living room. "C'mon, c'mon, everybody! I can hear the music from the square! Let's get going!"

Mrs. T smacked her palms down on the table. "Yes, let's do it. Class dismissed. Help me clear things up a bit, okay?" Everyone grabbed armfuls of plates and silverware and headed for the kitchen.

"And let's get a bandage on Maddy's leg. It's time to head out for some music and mosquitoes. I guess the Winters's wonderful pie will have to wait for later, right, gang?"

THE STRAINS OF SOUSA MARCH MUSIC grew louder as they trooped toward the square. Katie and her father were already well ahead on the sidewalk. Mrs. T walked alongside Maddy's father, asking him more about his boyhood in Indiana. Maddy, feeling gimpy in the leg, fell behind. Curtis slowed until he was in step with her.

The two walked along silently. He must be about nine, Maddy thought. No sign of a growth spurt yet. After a minute, Curtis cleared his throat. "They're called opaskwi ohtasak, you know."

"What?"

"The cornhusk dolls. Opaskwi ohtasak, at least in the Delaware language."

"Uh, how do you know that?"

"I just know. I made one once. I can show you how. It's still in my room. There are lots of Indian legends about them."

Maddy stared over at the boy, who had that little inward smile on his face. He'd picked up a long stick and was bending it in his hands. *Will wonders never cease. So that's why he was listening to everything. He's caught up in this history, too! Here is he, six inches shorter than me, and he's lecturing me about Indians.*

"Your mom taught you this?"

"Some of it," he said matter-of-factly. "And I read. My friend Tommy also knows a whole lot. He's part Tutelo Indian, you know. He'll be here tonight. My mother said you were into Indians. Talk to Tommy."

Teaoga Square was jumping by the time they arrived. Yellow lights strung across the trees and bandstand illuminated a swirl of toddlers, teenagers, dogs on leashes, little leaguers in uniforms, and doting grandparents. Everywhere were drippy cones and cups of ice cream sold at the dairy stand at the rear. On the stage near the street, a high school troupe performed gamely over the clamor.

Katie ran over to offer Maddy a spoonful from her extra-large cup of Mint Ting-a-Ling. "Party time!" she laughed. Maddy got a small cone of Rocky Road Deluxe and walked around with Katie. She noticed Curtis over near Main Street talking earnestly with another boy, neither of them bothering with the music or ice cream. The other boy had raven-black hair and was no taller than Curtis. Maybe that's Tommy, she thought. She decided to let them come over to her if they wanted.

At that moment, a pack of teenage boys rolled in loudly on stripped-down bikes. Their backwards hats and swagger reminded her of the bully-boys back home.

They headed right for Curtis and his friend and began riding in circles around them. At first, Maddy couldn't hear what they were saying. Then a heckle went up, loud and sickening: "Tommy play your Tom-Tom, Tom-Tom, Tom-Tom." One of them added a mock-Indian war cry. Then came tomahawk-chop motions with their forearms and more derisive laughter. "Tommy play your Tom-Tom, Tom-Tom, Tom-Tom" reverberated off the buildings. The young musicians, befuddled by the disturbance, faltered for a moment.

Curtis and his friend stood their ground and kicked at the bike wheels. Maddy could see the dark-haired boy glaring at the teens. It was a look of contempt. His flashing eyes reached across the square to Maddy like a lighthouse beam. He struck her as fearless.

Finally some fathers stepped in and the teens rolled back to the street with a parting round of "Tom-Tom." The band regained the crowd's attention. Maddy saw that the raven boy had already disappeared.

While finishing her cone, she considered whether she and Katie could have done anything to help. She decided to find Curtis. He stood alone at the edge of the square, scowling.

"Yuck, what was that about?" she asked.

Curtis was breathing hard. "Those idiots! Just because Tommy's Indian! Last month at school he told his class he was Tutelo, see. He said he was proud of it even though they were mistreated real bad in history. It was for some heritage assignment. This got back to one of the kid's big brothers, who's a real jerk! He was the one making the stupid war whoops. We were telling them to get lost. Next time we'll get them! Don't tell my folks about this, okay. I think they were sitting in the back and didn't see much."

Maddy nodded. *What spunky kids. Those bullies were my age at least.*

"Hey," Curtis continued. "I was telling Tommy about you. We're heading down to the river on Saturday morning to look for arrowheads and stuff. Maybe see if you can sleep over with Katie on Friday, and you can join us. Tommy said it's okay with him."

Maddy returned to Katie, who had rejoined their parents on a bench at the rear. "Hey, Katie, how about a sleepover on Friday? My place or yours—but yours is cooler."

"Mom! Mom! Can Maddy sleep over on Friday?" Mrs. T glanced over at Maddy's dad, who gave a shrugging smile.

"Sure, if you like," she answered.

Chapter 7

The sunlight streaming into Katie's bedroom found Maddy floating in light sleep. A creak of the floorboards startled her awake. Peeling an eye open, she saw a figure standing over her, silhouetted against the bright window. It was Curtis. He was so close she could smell his milky breath.

"Just checking," he said in his little clipped voice. "C'mon, breakfast. We meet Tommy at ten."

Once Curtis left the room, Maddy lifted her head to size up the situation. Katie had already made her bed and was gone. A glance at the clock showed nine o'clock. Last time she looked it had been 7:15.

Reaching under the twisted sheet, Maddy pressed the scab on her leg. Not too bad. Maybe she'd remove the bandage today. With a grunt, she swung her feet to the floor and pulled herself upright.

Budgie let out a welcoming squawk from across the room. Katie's beloved green parakeet had been agitating in his cage on and off since dawn, when the first peeps sounded in the treetops outside the window. His shrill rooster blasts had awakened Maddy at first light. She wasn't sure how Katie could stand it. Even Mz Snarkley couldn't make an uglier squawk, she thought.

After a few quiet days, Snarkley had been lurking again. It hadn't helped that the last thing Maddy and Katie did last night, at like 1:00 a.m., was play a game of Clue. Maddy was sure she'd solved the mystery in record time—Colonel Mustard with the wrench in the conservatory! But Katie had jumped in first with her own accusation: Mrs. Peacock with the wrench in the library. And she was right! Maddy had high-fived her dutifully but groaned inside.

That downer had followed a frustrating hour of losing at video games ... which had come after a movie she'd already seen three times ... which had followed another round of BMX riding, very careful and uninspiring this time, in the Tulowitsky driveway. To top it off, Maddy had a hard time falling asleep in the stuffy bedroom. It was no fun listening to Katie's whooshy breathing, tamping down snarky thoughts, and feeling far, far from home.

So her morning mood could have been grumpola. But Maddy reminded herself that here it was Saturday, the day she'd been waiting for since Wednesday. And it was a beautiful, sunny Saturday morning at that, so why let this be a wrong-side-of-the-bed day? Vowing to let Rockn Grl rule, she threw on her outfit, chirp-chirped at Budgie, and headed for the bathroom down the hall.

When Maddy arrived downstairs, Katie was leaning over the kitchen table, chuckling at the comics in the morning paper. "These are sooo dumb," she said. Seeing Maddy, she held up her palm for a ceremonial high-five.

"Well hello, sunbeam," Mrs. T said. "Ready for Mrs. T's Sinful Cinnamon French Toast?" She slid a plateful onto the table for Maddy, along with an assortment of syrups.

Katie found the sports section and scanned the headlines. "Does Daddy know the Mets won again? And look, our Binghamton Mets did, too. Cool beans!" As Katie and her mom chatted about the day ahead, Maddy downed most of the drippy plateful, then had a cup of coffee to help perk up.

Her friend—Maddy decided to think of Katie as a friend in the making—was preparing to head off to softball practice. She played catcher and Mrs. T was some sort of assistant coach. They knew Maddy was going somewhere else with Curtis, but they hadn't asked anything about it and seemed to take it in stride. Was this more of the small-town trust her father had spoken of? Whatever it was, Maddy appreciated it. She tried to imagine her mother being so relaxed about her whereabouts.

Katie bounded out to the car, dressed now in a yellow uniform emblazoned with "Valley Ford Broncos" and toting a floppy equipment bag. She gave Maddy a half-hug in the driveway and turned over Ol' Cowgirl for her use. Before driving off, Mrs. T told Curtis, who was waiting restlessly on his blue bike, to be careful. The plan was to regroup in a few hours to go swimming in the town pool.

MOMENTS LATER, MADDY FOUND herself pedaling down the street behind Curtis. They reached South Main and continued along the shoulder of the road. The sweet breakfast, the wind on her skin, the sunlight sparkling through the high branches, the birdsong, the newness of the surroundings, and the adventure ahead combined to give Maddy a pleasant thrill. *Stay with me, Rockn Girl!* She smiled as she thought of her dad out on his own adventure right then, fishing somewhere downriver with Charlie, and wondered if he had actually caught anything yet. That would make for some family fun. As she pedaled past the museum, she pictured her campers' miniature longhouses drying inside, lovingly constructed the day before out of Popsicle sticks, cardboard, glue, and tempera paint.

Curtis had been plowing forward toward their rendezvous with Tommy, never so much as glancing back. Suddenly, she heard his brakes complain as he pulled to a stop. He'd gone to the other side of the street, about fifty yards beyond Academy Park. As he rolled his bike up onto the far sidewalk, he motioned for her to join him.

Curtis stood staring at a dark shape, an oblong boulder that rose from the ground a step in from the walkway. It appeared to be another old monument bearing words on the front. She'd barely noticed it before. A line of pine trees towered overhead, their bark a similar dull gray-brown, so the monument almost blended in like a tree stump.

Curtis, motionless, kept giving the big stone his best stinkeye.

Maddy approached and let her hand play across the boulder's dank, knobby surface. Attached, at eye level, was an old-fashioned bronze plaque with raised lettering that reminded her of the Queen Esther monument. She began reading.

The plaque was celebrating Fort Sullivan. She knew that was the name of the big Revolutionary War fort that once stood just to the south. The opening sentence mentioned something called the Sullivan Expedition—and not just mentioned it but proclaimed it. The 1779 Sullivan Expedition against the Iroquois, it said, was "THE MARCH THAT DESTROYED SAVAGERY AND OPENED THE KEYSTONE AND EMPIRE STATES TO CIVILIZATION."

Maddy gulped, letting her fingertips linger above the jarring words. Her eyes hopscotched over the rest: "FOUR BRIGADES … RIFLEMEN … 250 SOLDIERS," but kept returning to "DESTROYED SAVAGERY." She looked over at Curtis, who refused to come closer. His hostility, along with the musty air and cemetery atmosphere, were giving her the creeps.

"You understand it, don't ya?" he frowned. "George Washington sent General Sullivan and his troops to burn down whole lots of Iroquois towns from here up into New York. We're Keystone, New York is Empire. We're civilization. You can figure out what the savagery meant. Tommy and I hate this thing. I call it the hissing stone."

Suddenly, Curtis bared his teeth like a Halloween cat, narrowed his eyes into slits, and gurgled a ferocious hiss at the monument. Just as abruptly, he wheeled back onto Main Street and was gone.

"The hissing stone," Maddy said to herself. She remained behind to read the inscription again, to let the message sink in. It bore the date 1902. A group called the Daughters of the American Revolution had put its name at the bottom. *So that's what they thought a century ago. Savagery. Civilization. Yikes, so black and white.*

She wasn't in the mood to get lost in gloomy thoughts, though, and happily steered Cowgirl back into the morning sunshine.

By the time Maddy reached the turnoff for the bridge across the Chemung, she saw that Curtis was already at the other end. He stood astride his bike talking to Tommy, who was perched on the low bridge wall. Both wore tan shorts and faded camo tee shirts to help blend in with the woods. Curtis had instructed Maddy beforehand to wear either brown or green, so she'd thrown on a pair of bright green shorts and a chocolate tee. She didn't have moccasins like they did and had decided to make do with flip-flops instead. That felt vaguely Indian.

"Hi," Tommy greeted her flatly. "I hear you saw the hissing stone." He gave her a searching look, then turned and scanned the river.

Up close, Maddy was struck by Tommy's thoughtful eyes and handsome, angular face. In a few years, she knew, his looks would break girls' hearts. But now he was all business. "Let's go," he said. "We ditch our bikes here."

Tommy pivoted over the wall and onto a dirt lane below. Curtis followed, lifting his BMX sideways and showing Maddy where they stashed their bikes. She rattled Cowgirl into place as the boys watched.

Next thing she knew, Tommy and Curtis were loping across a mucky patch and onward into the brush. She hustled behind, sliding out of a sandal momentarily, and had to trot to catch up. A trail wended through the undergrowth and into a clearing beneath the trees, where the boys were waiting. The ground was boggy, so they sat on a fallen tree trunk and motioned for Maddy to join. Curtis pulled a bottle of bug spray from his backpack. As they lathered their arms and legs, Curtis turned to her. "The Indians used to smear bear fat on their bodies to keep the mosquitoes away. Bet you didn't know that. Wonder what that smelled like."

The thought mingled for a moment with the eucalyptus scent. "Good question," Tommy said matter-of-factly. "Let's do some research. And I'll ask my mom. Also, it was *clarified* bear fat, remember? Let's figure out what that was."

"The ground's too wet here," Curtis said. "We should head up to base camp."

The boys rose as one and strode off on the crude trail. Maddy watched until all she could see were their heads floating above the high grass. She stood to look around. The low bank of the Chemung was perhaps forty yards to her right where the trees ended. She was surrounded by dampness and the thin droning of peepers and insects. Cars and trucks shushed over the bridge behind her, breaking the stillness. If she had her bearings right, they were a bit north of the broad plain known as Esther's Flats. She had a quick image of squaws tilling corn.

The willies shot through her as she realized she'd lost sight of her companions. She took off on as quick a march as her flip-flops would allow, doing her best to step lightly, and to enjoy the moment. Fortunately, the scrape on her leg hardly bothered her anymore. Soon the boys returned to view. They were continuing single file along the crooked path, moving effortlessly. The museum was probably across the river from them now, Maddy figured.

She fell in twenty yards behind, careful to avoid the loose stones and alert to any snakes or other critters that might attack her exposed feet. The boys didn't speak a word and never checked on her. She decided not to be annoyed, figuring that they trusted her to look out for herself. This might be how Indians were with one another, she thought. Besides, the silent treatment added to the adventure.

The trio continued on for five minutes or so as Maddy tuned in to the insect drone and to her own rhythmic breathing. Abruptly, the boys left the trail and headed for a particularly thick grove of trees. Tommy and Curtis got there first. By the time Maddy caught up, the boys had taken off their backpacks and were walking around inspecting the grounds.

"This is your camp?' she asked.

Curtis cast a look in her direction but said to Tommy, "Aw, man, where are our arrows?" Tommy was rooting around in the underbrush. "Here, good. This is where we left them, remember?"

In the clearing beneath the trees, the boys had set up a circle of logs around a small fire pit. The charred rocks showed that it had been put to use before. Maddy also noticed a funny round structure off to the side made of branches and bark. It looked to be in tatters.

"Sit," Tommy said as he took his place on one of the logs.

"This is our camp," Curtis said. "We set it up last fall. Welcome, I guess."

Following Maddy's eyes, he explained, "That's our wigwam over there, or at least our try at a wigwam. The frame is tied together right, but it didn't hold up so well over the winter. Tommy thinks we used the wrong kind of bark, right?"

"Right. Let's look for an old birch tree this time. And the cloth twine was all wrong. We should peel off strips of wood from the underside of the bark. That'll work."

"No duct tape?" Maddy joked. That might get a "har-har" from her father, but the boys reacted with silence. "Sorry," she said. "It's nice you want to do it the real way."

"Yeah," Curtis said. "And we want to come to the real place."

Maddy looked around slowly, acknowledging his meaning.

Tommy, sitting Indian-style, calmly set his dark eyes on the girl. "Curtis says you like Queen Esther. Her village and her flats were down there a little ways, you know," he said, pointing south. "She apparently had some cattle and horses but mostly grew crops, probably corn."

Maddy nodded.

"We'd like to have our camp down there on the flats, too, but my parents think it's too far," Curtis said. "They think they can sorta keep an eye on us here since it's closer to them. Whatever. This was all Indian land. You can still find trails down to their watering holes. And the guy who owns this property is nice. He leaves us alone. I guess he figures we're just kids. Right, Bear Paw?"

"Bear Paw?"

"That's the name I took," Tommy answered.

Pleased she didn't smirk, he continued. "You probably know that Indian kids used to go into the woods to do these, like, vision quests to find their animal spirit guide. Even regular kids seem to know that, but they don't know what it's like. We sat out here a couple of times last year, sitting for hours, hardly eating, just listening. The name Bear Paw came to me. Tell her your name, Curtis."

"He-Who-Seeks," Curtis said with a stare. Uttering the name had changed his bearing. He sat erect like a chief, holding Maddy's gaze.

"I'm not sure my Bear Paw name is right," Tommy said. "We may do a real spirit quest later this summer! There are some deep woods up near Wilawana. We'll tell our parents we want to go fishing there. Hopefully they'll let us camp out."

These two are hard-core, Maddy thought.

The boys had recently been making arrows. Tommy retrieved their stack of lovingly whittled sticks from the corner. A few had slots filled with feathers, plus notches on the other ends to hold the arrowheads. There were also two longer branches, notched at both ends. Bows awaiting their bowstrings, Maddy figured.

Curtis opened his backpack and withdrew a tan pouch that looked like it was made of suede. Bangles and a snakelike design decorated the outside. "My manito xesinutay," he said. "My medicine bag. Indians would put their carved totems and other important stuff inside, you know, and carry it with them all the time." He lifted the front flap and took out a handful of flint triangles—arrowheads.

"We found this little broken one down here," Curtis said. "These three I made myself. These two I bought. And don't tell my mother, but this one is from the museum storage room."

He handed the arrowheads to Maddy, who turned them over one by one and fingered the sharp tips.

"We're always on the lookout for arrowheads over here," Tommy said. "The Delawares called them sanakwesink. The early white farmers would find hundreds of them in these fields. People think it's because the Indians had big battles here, even before the white man came. It's hard to find arrowheads anymore.

"But what I'm really trying to find are southern pearls. That would be the best."

Maddy wasn't sure she heard correctly. "What do you mean, pearls?"

Tommy took out his own medicine bag, which she noticed he'd been wearing on a shoulder strap beneath his shirt. He withdrew a pea-sized gray sphere and rolled it around slowly on his palm.

"My people, the Tutelo, had lots of these back in time," he said. "The Tutelo were from somewhere in the South, like maybe North Carolina. My mother says we were tall and strong. When we conquered other tribes farther to the south, we took piles of their pearls as, like, war prizes. Later, we got pushed north, up here, and we brought the pearls along.

"My mother's only part Tutelo. The tribe is long gone, and the language is gone, too. Her mother gave her six of the old pearls. She gave one to me, and one to my sister. Here, feel it."

Maddy held the orb lightly in her fingers. It made her excited and sad at the same time. *If he's right, this little pearl is eons old. It's all that's left of a lost tribe. I wonder what it's seen. I'm holding it in my hand—it's not in some museum. Wait till I tell Dad and Melody. Imagine finding another one! Let's look!*

"Nice, huh?" Tommy smiled. "The ones we have are gray, but the pure white ones are special. Mom says the Tutelo made them be symbols of, like, greatness, and only chosen people got them. " Tommy quickly placed the pearl back in his pouch. "Let's hunt for stuff along the shoreline later. But hey, want to race? We set up two painted posts, like the Indians had for racing, you know, as part of their festivals."

"Thanks, but I'd better not," she said. "My leg still isn't healed. Plus, I'm only in flip-flops."

The boys dashed off towards the open ground. Maddy spotted a low pole painted with horizontal stripes of red and black. The boys were closing in on it fast, laughing and stumbling.

FEELING RESTLESS AS WELL, Maddy left the copse of trees and headed toward the river. She had to step carefully through the grass and skirt a marshy low spot on her way to an opening in the trees at the shoreline. Approaching the water's edge, she stepped out of her sandals and stood carefully, toes in the cool mud. Enveloped by the lush green foliage, Maddy pictured Renoir composing the scene as a painting. A few fallen leaves floated past, carried along on the current's steady journey southward. Across the way was the Athens shoreline. *Te-a-o-ga*, she said slowly under her breath. *How-dy, Te-a-O-ga.* No eagles or vultures were in sight, but she enjoyed the simple peace as she looked about—until an unwelcome thought ambushed her.

So Indians had a village here once. Big whoop. Everything had to happen somewhere.

Maddy squeezed her eyes shut and willed Snarkley under water. It was surprisingly effortless. More and more she was winning these inner contests. She kept her eyes closed lightly, and opened herself to the sensations of the breeze off the river and the forest sounds. She relaxed into the moment. Thoughts dissolved.

Suddenly, the ground seemed to fall away.

Maddy heard herself gasp. *What the?!*

Panting, eyes still shut, she felt something emerging around her—presences, ancient presences, floating toward her as though from across time. They were Indians, women, of different ages. And maybe a girl. She realized she'd sensed them dimly in the last few days. Now they encircled her, not spooky like ghosts, but palpable. She envisioned them with beautiful beaded clothing and melodious voices, drawing water at this very spot, moving lightly, alert for warning signs, looking right through her.

With their presence came intense insights: *This was their riverbank that I'm standing on. They were absolutely real, as real as me. We were invading them, right here on their sacred ground. Did they sense how it was going to end? How would they feel about me being here? Would they take me captive?*

One thing was certain, she realized: they wouldn't be standing in the muck. Maddy stepped back with a squish. The presences all fixed her with the same hypnotic gaze while they slowly receded and then evaporated. She popped her eyes open. *They're gone, but they're not. Were these their spirits—left here for all time? Holy wow! Wow-wow-wow.*

Dizzy and tingling, Maddy squatted on a dry patch of ground. She closed her eyes again. The warm river breeze and the smells were sublime, but otherwise things had returned to normal. *Was that an apparition? A trance? My runaway imagination?* She was dazed, amazed, and, she realized, wanting more. A current of warmth ran through her body. Somehow the spirits had conveyed a message. They wished to be peaceful. Their purpose was not to capture her but to welcome her, almost as if she were one of them. While that was an unsettling idea, it mostly felt good.

Maddy couldn't say how long it took her to rise and wander back to the shade of base camp. The boys were crouched on their logs, busily tying arrowheads onto the shafts with loops of twine that Curtis had brought along. They'd already strung twine onto the two longer branches to form makeshift bows.

She sat silently, feeling outside herself, and watched the boys working.

"I won one race, he won the other," Curtis reported.

Tommy looked over at her. "You know that post we run to? We made it to be like an Indian painted post, but lots smaller. The Indians said that if you danced around it, it meant you agreed to fight. I read about this. Once a tribe decided to go on the warpath, they held a nighttime war dance all around their painted post. You want to know this stuff, right? The warriors would paint themselves white and red and black. They might have streaks of red on their faces like blood. They'd run up to the post and whack it with sticks or even logs from the fire. And they'd sing about what they were gonna do, how many scalps they'd take, stuff like that. Then, when they returned from the war, they'd dance around it again, like a thanksgiving dance."

"Yeah," Curtis said, smiling as he wrapped and tightened the twine. "I love how they'd paint themselves up. They'd take all day, making colors from berries and soot and dirt. They'd sorta compete in who could have the fanciest face paint, with different spots and shapes and scary designs. They'd also grease their hair with bear fat to make it shiny. That must have looked so cool!"

When Maddy didn't reply, Curtis continued. "And Bear Paw, how about the scalp locks? The warriors would actually invite being scalped, Maddy! They'd shave their hair back to just a circle at the top, like a clump of grass, which could easily be cut off! They said it was manly, to expose your scalp lock to the other side in battle. And if they did well, they'd return with the enemy scalp locks they'd collected, all stuck on a pole!"

No one spoke as they pictured that shocking sight. Tommy went next.

"I like how they'd tie up their war captives with burden straps. Maddy, burden straps were these packstraps they'd put across their foreheads to help carry heavy things on their backs, like animals they'd killed. In their minds, the straps were kind of magical. It showed that they, like, controlled the animal's spirit. They'd also, like, decorate the straps to please its spirit. What's that word —to flatter it. So the braves would bring their captives back tied with burden straps to show they controlled the person's spirit. Amazing, huh?"

Maddy could see it all. The boys might have been trying to match their knowledge in front of her, but she appreciated it. It was exactly what she needed right now, to feel in tune with them, and to take in more facts about this lost world that was reaching out to her. A few of the Indian practices could sound weird and scary—savage, old-timers might say—but she was seeing them as logical responses to their circumstances. She had absorbed that much from her riverside vision.

Still, she said nothing. The boys were noticing her remote silence. Curtis handed her his canteen of water and a granola bar. "It's nice down there by the water," he said. "Find anything good?"

Maddy gave the boys a long look. She decided to tell them. "I saw something down there.... At least I think I did.... I sorta did."

Tommy put down his arrows and moved to her side.

"I was having these stupid negative thoughts," she continued hesitantly, eyes darting from Tommy to Curtis. "Then I closed my eyes and felt better. And then ... I suddenly felt like I wasn't alone.... I swear there were some Indian women there, like spirits, floating along the ground. Native American Indian, honest-to-gosh tribal women. In Indian clothes. Indian faces. Indian pots. Stooping to get water, looking around. They were looking through me. Then, boom, I opened my eyes and it's normal again! Yet, it was real, you guys! I still feel tingly."

"Was it scary?" Curtis asked.

"Not really. More like beautiful, actually! But it's never really happened to me before, so maybe I'll feel scared later."

"IT WAS RIGHT HERE," Maddy said moments later, standing again at the river's edge. She could see her footprints where the water and mud met. The boys looked around alertly.

"We usually go farther down, around the bridge, when we look for arrowheads and stone net-sinkers," Tommy said. "But I like this place. It looks like it could have been an old watering spot, maybe. Let's just sit."

The three crouched around a birch tree a few feet from where Maddy had sat moments earlier. She looked over and noticed Curtis had closed his eyes. He had brought along the museum arrowhead and was spinning it slowly with his fingers like a compass needle. Tommy also had his eyes shut. Maddy decided to try it again, too.

The water lapping against the shore, the wind off the water, the bird sounds, were all lovely. But the Indian women were no longer near. After a placid half-minute or so, Maddy let her eyes open. Tommy was watching the river. Curtis was looking at her glumly.

"Nothing," Curtis said.

"I thought maybe for a minute, but then nothing," reported Tommy.

"But the way you described it, Maddy, was how it felt for me that day, too!" Tommy continued. "I heard it more than saw it. I heard the words 'bear paw' in the air. So I'm sure—well, I believe you. And the spirits were looking through you?"

Before she could answer, Curtis blurted, "It was zero for me! Seeing, hearing, feeling, all nothing. Zippo!"

Curtis jumped to his feet. "I know even some Indians never got spirit guides. And Maddy gets it first time, without even trying! I've been honest, you know, calling myself just He-Who-Seeks. But I want to get my spirit guide! I've tried hard enough."

"Yeah, you have," Tommy said. "But whatever, it's probably not just about trying." Maddy felt bad for Curtis, and sensed that Tommy had had to calm him down before.

"You know," Tommy continued, "it may not even have been a spirit guide that came to Maddy. I know just about anything can be one—insects, trees, not just animals—but I've never heard of *people* being spirit guides. I'll ask my mom about that."

Curtis kept frowning at the water, his face in full pout. Maddy figured if he was anything like her own little brother, it was probably best to let him settle down on his own.

After a moment, Tommy asked, "Want us to try again?" Curtis shook his head no.

"Want to look for arrowheads?" Another no.

"We could do some target practice with the new arrows."

"Let's just get our bags and go!" Curtis grumped, and stormed off toward the grove.

Tommy sighed. "He'll chill later. But hey, look at how high the sun has gotten, Maddy. We need to head back anyways. My stomach's growling."

Chapter 8

Timothy Pickering stood erect at the north end of the open treaty ground, a tall, earnest figure with a chiseled face and hawk-like eyes. Seated at his side on the brisk November afternoon were his yengwe advisors and aides.

Before him, the Teaoga council fire burned new and bright. The delegation of leading chieftains sat across the fire, waiting expectantly. Pickering cast his eyes beyond them to the large semicircle of Indians of various ages and dress, numbering well over one hundred, who had come up from their campground to witness the peace proceedings.

Esther, seated low in the middle of this Indian crowd, studied Pickering's demeanor carefully. Though the man looked statuesque in the slanting sunlight, she thought he also seemed tense.

She saw correctly. Communicating with Indians at all, let alone conducting a peace council, was strange and new to Pickering. Now he found himself presiding at a most delicate negotiation with agitated tribal leaders on behalf of his new government. Everyone—Pickering included—wondered how he would do in his debut. The crowd hung on his ceremonial opening words:

"Brethren, sachems, chiefs, and warriors of the Six Nations," Pickering announced with a dignified bow, "I bid you a hearty welcome to this council fire and thank the Great Spirit who has brought us together in safety, though I sincerely lament the cause of our meeting. I mean the murder of our two brothers of your nation at Pine Creek."

A native translator, a Lenape woman who was part of Pickering's party, paced among the assembly, calling out an official interpretation for the people.

"Do her words properly capture the yengwe's meaning?" whispered Cakoanos. Esther, who had the better command of English, nodded to her friend seated beside her that yes, they did. Once the translation registered with the native crowd, people uttered assents of "yo-hah!"

Pickering proceeded as he had rehearsed, with frequent pauses for translation. He announced that the thirteen yengwe fires had become one great fire, and that General Washington was now the great chief of all thirteen fires. He said he was Washington's voice at this Teaoga council. And he asked the chiefs to excuse his ignorance of their customs, since this was his first council fire.

Esther was touched by the combination of nobility and humility he displayed, finding it rare for a yengwe. She could not have known how diligently Pickering had prepared for this moment, nor how much was at stake for the New England Puritan. The man was in desperate personal straits. After proud military service in the Revolution, Pickering had settled in the Wyoming Valley and become a regional land speculator. But the competing border claims between Connecticut and Pennsylvania had tied up his land, throwing him deeply into debt. To avoid the poorhouse for his wife and seven young sons, Pickering had recently turned to his old commander, George Washington, now the federal president, seeking a position as postmaster general in the young government.

To Pickering's astonishment, Washington instead recruited him to be his personal emissary to the Senecas angered by the Pine Creek murders. Washington knew the Indians were demanding that condolence gifts be presented to the bereaved families, and he reasoned that Pickering, his onetime quartermaster general, could come through, because he was an expert in moving large quantities of supplies into the backcountry.

The president also had explained his broader goals to Pickering. He saw the Teaoga council as a chance to tell the chiefs about an important new law that declared that nearly all Indian affairs were to be conducted centrally by the United States—and no longer by the individual states. He wanted the Pennsylvania official who would be present at Teaoga to explain this change to the chiefs, openly support it, and then step aside for Pickering. Lastly, Washington wanted the Senecas to take up white agricultural ways. Pickering's assignment was to win the day on all of those touchy points.

Pickering accepted the temporary assignment as a step toward the further government work that he desperately needed. The council preparations became more difficult than expected, however. The journey upriver to Tioga was trying, as were the housing conditions next to the chilly river. He'd been waiting here nearly a month for all of the chiefs to arrive. At his instruction, the trader Hollenback had shipped in enough food, rum, and other provisions for two hundred Indians—but rumors had emerged that twice that number might come. Other rumors held that the British at Niagara were urging the Senecas to walk out, and that Red Jacket was going to make trouble for him. On top of all that, Pickering had had to calm the local settlers' anger at having so many Indians arrive into their midst and he had to police the grounds after an Indian girl was pelted with rocks. It took some doing, but he persuaded the local pastor to leave the Indians alone for the duration of the council.

Soon it would be over, he prayed. Even though the esteemed Cayuga chief Fish Carrier still had not arrived, Pickering was glad the Indians agreed to hold this initial session, which followed a feast he'd hosted for the tribal chiefs the prior evening. So it was with weary relief that on this date of November 15, 1790, as recorded in his journal, he made his welcoming remarks.

"Brothers," he continued, voice rising, "you now see my commission, which has been read and interpreted, that I was appointed to wash off the blood of our murdered brothers, and wipe away the tears from the eyes of our friends. And this occasion is to brighten the chain of friendship between you and the United States."

Doing his utmost to follow the elaborate rituals, Pickering handed strings of wampum to Farmer's Brother, the principal Seneca chief, and sat. As the translator called out her interpretation to the assembly, Farmer's Brother consulted with his fellow chiefs, then rose with their reply:

"Brother, we thank the Great Spirit, who has appointed this day in which we sit side by side and look with earnestness on each other. We know you have been long waiting for us and suppose you have often stretched up your neck to see if we were coming. We still must wait for Fish Carrier to arrive. Meanwhile, we accept this wampum belt."

Red Jacket spoke next—and complained that Pickering had blundered by failing to ceremonially "pull the hatchet out of the heads" of the chiefs and bury it. Without that customary oath of coexistence and respect, Red Jacket said, "our eyes are not yet washed that we may see, nor our throats cleared that we may speak."

Pickering immediately rose and uttered those missing words. "Brothers," he concluded, "the United States has no wish but to live with you as brothers in perpetual peace. Brothers, I now wash off the blood of your murdered brothers and the tears from the eyes of their friends."

Pickering lifted a mug and drank to their well-being. He called for his aides to serve a round of grog to the chiefs. As the translation was heard, the natives called out a robust "yo-hah!"

"Huzzah!" added Pickering's assistants. The yengwe had passed an opening test of diplomatic prowess. The tension in the air eased.

Farmer's Brother spoke next:

"Brother, you have now taken us by the hand, and washed our eyes. Our women expect that you will show them equal attention. They are here awaiting your invitation to receive the same tokens of your friendship, which last evening you gave us."

"Sisters, I am very glad to meet you here," Pickering said, and walked about and shook hands with most of the native women. Esther managed to keep her distance and look away.

"I invite you to my quarters, where we may eat and drink together in friendship," he announced. "I take you by the hand as my sisters."

The other women smiled and stirred, but Esther knew she must avoid the special festivities. Too many yengwes would be in attendance. Hollenback would certainly be among them since he provisioned the food. The risk was too great that she would be spotted.

Better that she return to Sisketung. The girl had been resting in their shelter with instructions to keep the healing poultice applied to her wounded temple. Earlier, Esther had spooned a bowl of warm apple pudding from the cauldron Pickering's men placed at the edge of the council assembly. The pudding had gotten cold beneath her blanket but had not spilled. She lifted the blanket to show Cakoanos, who smiled. Beneath her own blanket, Cakoanos held an armful of carrots and apples, also from the yengwe provisions. They chuckled as they headed back to their campfire.

THE FIRE SEEMED TO devour the branches that Esther fed to it. Darkness had come quickly, and the air was growing icy again. She sat contentedly beneath her woolen blanket, young Sisketung beside her on the log biting into an apple.

At Esther's urging, Cakoanos had returned to the upper ground to join the other women for Pickering's feast. Esther assured her that the girl's wound was tender but healing well, and that enough Indians were at nearby campfires to keep the two of them safe outside. Sisketung had not objected, which pleased Esther. She wished to spend time alone with Sisketung and sensed the girl felt the same and had grown more open to learning. Sisketung's only request had been that Esther face away from the ridge again and keep her blanket arched over her head.

As they sat in the chill watching the fire brighten, Esther observed how Sisketung carefully spit the apple seeds into her hand and put them aside to dry. A well-trained child, she thought.

Esther held out an object on her palm. "Daughter, do you know what this is?"

"A quill necklace."

"Yes, a simple three-stranded porcupine quill necklace," she said, handing it to the girl. "But it was strung the traditional way, on deer sinew, and it bears a story. This necklace was made by my mother. Look carefully. It combines Shawnee quillwork with Munsee beading. She gave it to me when I was not much older than you. I carry it always but wear it rarely now. Over time, the sharp quill edges have frayed much of the sinew.

"Daughter, it deserves to have new life. Let us remake it into earrings. Watch."

Esther took the necklace and, leaning into the firelight, carefully untied the elaborate knot holding the three twisted strands together. She handed one strand to Sisketung. "Do as I do, Daughter. Feel along the segments for weak spots. There you may snap the sinew. Cup your hand below to catch the beads and quills that fall loose. You will find more knots along the length of sinew. Untie them, and try to save the sinew. Work slowly."

Sisketung caught on readily. Soon their fingers were moving deliberately, and the companions fell into an easy rhythm. As they worked, Esther told the girl about the day's council talks, about how Pickering's formal manner and diplomatic answers had satisfied the people.

"Mother Esther," Sisketung said, "as I lay in my shelter today, my mind returned to the Bible preacher's words. He is an important man in this settlement. Why does he sow hate? We, too, were worshiping the Great Spirit."

"Daughter, you know that the yengwes have a religion that is worthy of respect but that holds other beliefs like ours as false. Perhaps you have not seen it expressed so violently before. Their harsh Bible preachers have made many of our people choke with anger. Daughter, I have been blessed in my life to experience a better side of the yengwe faith."

The girl looked up. "A better side?"

"Daughter, you have heard me speak of the Moravians. They were yengwes who accepted us as equals and showed us love, showed me love and friendship. I will tell you more about them. But patience, Daughter. Let us wait until later, when the others are with us at the fire, to spare me extra words."

"Yes, they will all wish to hear," Sisketung said, eyes on her work. "We all must learn."

The girl's composure pleased and bemused Esther. This was the one whose eyes had flashed with anger the other evening and was now calm and understanding. Esther fell into a reverie. *Sisketung is like my daughter Tarasuwa—and like me. Observant, sensitive, yet with a current of righteousness underneath that can burst into raw anger. Control that, and she could be a leader.*

Esther looked over at the girl with new eyes. Sisketung lifted her head from her work and smiled. She had just completed her disassembling of the necklace strand and held it out for inspection.

Esther declared the work well-done. Then she went carefully to her shelter to retrieve more items from her pouch: a length of cloth thread, an iron needle, and a sharpened fish bone with a threading hole in one end. She instructed Sisketung to practice threading the hollow quills and the beads using first the old bone, which she said had been her mother's, and then using the yengwe needle. She also was to test the durability of the sinew, and use the cloth thread only if needed.

Esther watched as the girl bent in concentration over her assignment. The sight caused another memory to shoot forth—this time of the yengwe trapper. Images rushed through her mind. Esther had been a mere girl of about Sisketung's age when a trapper had assaulted her. It was during the Shamokin years. She was out along the river, crouched in concentration like Sisketung, pulling sticks from a pile of brush. Her mother had sent her to gather kindling for the evening fire. The trapper must have been nearby—and had learned to approach prey stealthily in his moccasined feet. Suddenly, he was upon her from behind. Esther could vividly recall his flaming red beard, his buckskin, his foul words, the odor of his sweat and his sour breath. As he clutched her waist, she managed to pull her tanning blade from her pouch and plunge it into the back of his hand.

Grabbing his wound, the man flung Esther to the ground and fled cursing into the woods. People were never sure who he was, and he was never seen again. Young Esther learned to keep her eyes up and a blade handy.

Would frail Sisketung be able to defend herself if danger struck? More important, why were these memories returning so clearly now? Esther studied the girl and prayed for understanding.

An answer came quickly. These memories lived in Esther but also in her people. The memories were beckoning to be told. She had not shared the trapper story with the fire circle because she felt it was too personal and had no teaching purpose. It did, she now knew. The events then, and the events of the last days, were teaching that the time had hardly passed for keeping their eyes up and their blades in reach. Even delicate Sisketung must be prepared.

Further, she knew now that she must tell the women about the fates of her four children. It was personal, yes, but it was also the story of her people. And would she be able to share the darkest events of the Wyoming battle? It would test her inner strength, but she knew she must try.

Perhaps Sisketung had brought her this wisdom. Perhaps that is why the girl had said, "We all must learn."

Esther examined the necklace pieces, which lay in careful piles on a piece of cloth between her and the girl. Sisketung had taken all three strands and carefully detached the quills and beads. The next day, Esther said, she would show her how to design earrings and prepare the pieces.

Praising the girl for her diligence, Esther withdrew further into her shawl blanket and turned her ear to the matrons' songs rising clearly now from the direction of Pickering's quarters.

WHILE WORKING ON THE necklace, Sisketung sensed it was best to remain silent. She could tell that her companion was deep in thought. Mother Esther had much more to tell. If half the stories told about her were true, she bore much burden. The girl felt regret at her earlier outburst. Her mind was poised and eager to learn more about her own scattered people.

As her fingers worked, Sisketung pondered whether to tell Mother Esther about her surprise encounter with the yengwe girl Sarah. It had happened right at the entrance of her shelter earlier that day, after Mother Esther and the others had left for the treaty grounds. Sarah was the neighbor with whom Sisketung had had years of uneasy contact, the one who would sometimes come near to loudly show off new foods, new words, strange new beliefs, rumors of yengwe plans, vague warnings of danger. Sisketung would listen out of curiosity, yet say little in return. Though Sarah seemed lonely, Sisketung had grown wary of the straw-haired girl.

Having no age-mates in the Tutelo settlement, Sisketung, in truth, often had her own pangs of loneliness. While solitude had grown to feel normal, she often found herself talking inwardly to the animals of the forest. Ever since she could remember, she would slip away to spend hours studying the ways of the squirrels and the fish, the hawks, and the muskrat. The old kingfisher that patrolled the river was her favorite. She would creep close to watch the regal bird on its branch, admiring its stillness and unerring balance. She tried to read the dark waters as it did and anticipate when it would dive to expertly snag a meal. These creatures seemed to accept the girl's presence as though aware they had lessons to teach about patience, alertness, and survival.

Sometimes on warm afternoons, Sisketung would hear a group of yengwe farm boys fishing upstream. She'd creep near to spy, and was often troubled by their rowdy and impulsive manner. Once she saw them ominously bending and breaking rows of tree saplings along the water's edge. Another time she watched them club a snake to death for amusement. Two of the boys that day were Sarah's brothers, and they had brought Sarah along to watch. Noticing how the girl recoiled at the wanton clubbing, Sisketung wondered if Sarah was perhaps different from the others after all.

So Sarah's surprise appearance in the campground had momentarily lifted Sisketung's spirits. The girl had come stealthily to the shelter, saying she heard Sisketung was injured. The two young stone-throwers had told her where she could be found. Sisketung thanked her for her gift of yengwe biscuits and showed her the head wound and the poultice of herbs.

"Luke and Abner were out to smack that dang Esther," Sarah said. "You just got it 'cause they recognized you. They don't actually know what the old witch looks like. Do you? Do you know where she be?"

Seeing Sarah methodically scan the campground, Sisketung realized the girl was on a spying mission. The visit was a trick. This yengwe was no friend. Jumping to her feet, Sisketung hurled the biscuits back and ordered Sarah to leave. When Sisketung stepped toward her in anger, the girl rushed off, crying shrilly as she went, "I hope they attack again! I'm gonna tell 'em to attack again!" She skittered up over the ridgeline and out of sight.

Instinct told Sisketung not to reveal this to Mother Esther. It would trouble her too much. Instead, the girl would tell her mother about the threat—and would double her own vigilance.

Chapter 9

The day felt blessed from the start. Overnight the winter winds had departed, and Father Sun rose bright and clear in the east. The air was new, with little hint of the cattle herds. At dawn, most of the camp gathered for a joyous sun ceremony. The only ones missing, the women remarked, seemed to be the heavy rum-drinkers of the festive night before. Also, they observed with relief, the Bible-preacher was nowhere in sight.

As the sixfold blessing ceremony ended, a messenger came to announce that extra baskets of carrots and squash were being handed out at the treaty ground. He also brought word that there would be no council proceedings for the day. Fish Carrier, the Cayuga sachem, was expected by nightfall, and Pickering and the chiefs had decided it was best to await his arrival.

Esther said a private prayer of thanks. This news of delay gladdened her. She welcomed the prospect of an uninterrupted day with the Tutelo women. And of more time with Sisketung.

A plan came to mind. Esther gathered three of the women and set out toward the site of the old Cayuga watch town. "Sisters," she told them as they walked, "my visits to the watch town long ago leave a certain cloudy memory. Ka'wia, porcupines, visited there often, walking openly on a trail near the sachem's wigwam." She recalled wondering if the animals—revered but normally reclusive—and the sachem were magically drawn to each other, if the porcupine was perhaps his spirit guide. "This was many winters ago. The trail and any nest might be long gone."

Her intuition drew her near the old spot. She stood watching as the other women scouted through the high, dry grass. After twenty paces, one of them called out in amazement. At her feet was the nearly frozen carcass of an adult ka'wia. Esther made her way there and examined the body, still covered from head to tail with its spiny quills. She saw no wounds from weapon or claw. Perhaps the animal had died of starvation or old age. Nor were there any signs of disease. Fortunately, the winter meant flies and maggots were not active. They wrapped the creature in a thick piece of yengwe wool and carried it back to the others.

At the fire circle, Esther placed the stiff body at the women's feet. She led the group in a solemn prayer of thanks to the animal for offering itself, sprinkling a handful of kulukuneekun into the fire so the smoke would meet its spirit. Then, under Esther's guidance, the women prepared to remove the countless sharp quills that covered much of the porcupine's hide. Some quills were longer than a finger, others only a fingernail. She demonstrated how to grip a quill in the center, away from the barbed tip, and loosen and detach it with a twisting pull. Next they were to clean each one. She showed how to gently wipe the shaft with a folded tree leaf to remove any oil, skin particles, and dirt. Then they were to place the quills into a cauldron of river water that was being warmed on the fire.

71

The soaking would clean out any blood or dirt that might be inside the quill's hollow shaft.

They divided up the task. Several women leaned over the porcupine and went to work gingerly plucking. They handed the quills one by one to the others behind them, who snipped off the sharp points, then wiped the quills clean and placed them into the cauldron. Cakoanos had processed quills once before, but was never certain enough of her skills to teach the others and was glad to learn the old ways directly from Esther.

Sisketung, too, took her place beside the animal and worked placidly. She felt warmed by the thin but steady sun and by the women's easy fellowship. These were gifts from the Preserver, the girl realized.

"Sisters," Cakoanos joked, "I wish I had a bed of sharp quill points to keep my man away when he was feeling devilish!"

"Yo-hah," said another, "and as a fence to keep the cattle at a distance!" The women were slowly shifting along the log to keep themselves positioned in the meager sunlight. When two of them bumped hips, they hooted with laughter at how they were behaving like turtles sunning on a rock. The good cheer moved the Mohawk saga singer to raise a song of friendship. The others hummed along.

Their only concern was that Mother Esther's face be covered. Sisketung noticed how the women would squint periodically toward the ridgeline. Several gestured to Esther to drape her blanket higher on her shoulders. Once their quill-drying task was done, Sisketung thought, she would return to her position as Esther's alert rear guard. Her mother would want that. Cakoanos had agreed that Esther should not be told about Sarah's threat of another attack, but said Esther should be watched over tightly.

Sisketung found herself to be nimble at the quill work. She watched the women's pace and slowed herself so as not to shame any of them. From their eyes and their easy talk, she realized they felt not competitiveness but camaraderie. Their focus, at least for the moment, seemed to be sharing time with Esther, learning from Esther, being with one another.

They have the wisdom to embrace sunny moments that the Preserver brings, she thought. They were agitated by the yengwe boys' ambush and know another attack could occur. But they have decided to settle into this gift of time. Do not let the yengwes bow you down or break your spirit, her mother often told her. Even if you feel broken, she would say, you must behave with confidence. You will see that your own inner spirit will rise with your outer behavior. This is what I am witnessing now, Sisketung thought.

Meanwhile, Cakoanos was watching the other women to see if they were learning the quill-sorting properly. Satisfied, she cleared her throat and turned to face Esther.

"N'petalogalgun. Listen well. Sister Esther, the Preserver has granted us this glad day and our short time together. Let us use it well." That brought a round of assent from the others. She continued: "You have set us on a wise learning path, helping us know the old skills and the times that came before. You set us on that path until the yengwe boys' foolish attack. Sister, you have healed my daughter's wound and helped to clear our eyes and ears and ease our hearts to continue. We are prepared to listen again. Honor us with your wisdom."

72

"Yo-hah!" responded the others. Sisketung moved into place behind Esther. She leaned lightly against the old woman's back and kept her eyes on the ridgeline.

"SISTERS," ESTHER BEGAN, "OUR daughter Sisketung has become my beautiful brave bodyguard. Let us all be strengthened by her example." The others called out their approval. Esther reached back and clasped the girl's welcoming hand.

"Sisters, Sisketung has lately told me of her confusion over the Bible-preacher's angry words. I told her that there are other yengwe Christians who turn with better hearts towards us. These are the Moravians. Sisters, though it was a lifetime ago, I wish to speak to you more about them."

Gathering her thoughts, Esther began carefully. Sisketung leaned against her with acute attention.

"Sisters, when we sat in our circle before, you heard me say that redcoat forces drove our Munsee band from our war town, Assinisink, one cold day twenty-six winters ago. We fled through Teaoga to the broad river flats a half-day south of here. This was the place we call Sheshequin. Eghohowin decided to settle the remaining band there. We had lived through years of war. I had seen enough of revenge and captives and cruelty. Plus, we were weak and hungry. I wished to clear a better path to the yengwes. I believed Eghohowin also was open to that."

Esther drew another rough map in the dirt and proceeded slowly to explain the events of those years, events that were now part of her listeners' own family histories. She told them how the Moravian holy man Zeisberger came through Sheshequin and preached well, drawing natives from both sides of the creek. The Christian Delawares asked that a mission be established there as an outgrowth of a larger Moravian prayer town one day farther downriver at Wyalusing. She explained that Eghohowin agreed, not because his heart was moved, but because he saw practical advantage. From his visits to the Wyalusing mission, Eghohowin had observed the Moravian blacksmiths repairing Indian muskets, straightening their implements, and making new tools in exchange for furs. He saw how the Moravian discipline—industriousness in the field, mutual support, no liquor—sat well with the Indian converts. He had promised Esther he would make their band strong again, and he looked to this experiment as a way to perhaps achieve that.

To clear the path for the Moravians, she explained, Eghohowin went to the Cayuga sachem at Teaoga seeking approval since the Sheshequin village was supposedly on Iroquois land. The Iroquois headman quickly approved. Looking back, Esther said, she believed the Iroquois probably hoped the Moravians would pacify the Delawares, Shawnees, and other troublesome tribes they still considered to be under their thumb.

With Iroquois approval, she continued, Wyalusing Moravian leaders created a mission at Sheshequin early in the yengwe year 1769, in the Month When the First Frog Croaks. In little time, the congregants built a chapel with a shingled roof. They planted orchards, laid fences around the fields, set aside Sunday as a day of rest, taught hymns, and gathered the native children for lessons, she explained.

Sisketung perceived every detail as she floated above Sheshequin on her eagle's back.

"Sisters," Esther said, "the Moravians came and helped a few of us build wood-plank houses for our village nearby. It was the first time we had tried that! They built their own people houses with wood floors and stone fire chimneys in the wall. At first, our people wanted to keep dirt floors for our cooking fires and smoke holes in the roof like we had in longhouses." She smiled at the memory. "I favored the yengwe floors and chimneys. Eghohowin refused them, saying they were an insult to the ancestors!

"Sisters," Esther said, "the Moravians did not place themselves above us. They learned our tongues and our culture. They accepted our gifts and generosity. Their leaders would kiss my cheek. I have never been treated with such love by yengwes! Our family would visit the prayer town often to hear their word of God and to discuss the ways of harmony."

Esther stopped to dwell on the warm memory. Her eyes were drawn to the treetops, which brought a more immediate realization. "Sisters, the light is dimming already. It is best we pause to tend to our work."

She instructed two of the women to return the porcupine carcass, now greatly denuded like an opossum, to its resting place in the dry grass. There they should sprinkle tobacco as an offering to its spirit and sing a final prayer of thanks. Once the pair left the circle with their bundle, Esther reached into the cauldron banked beside the fire and removed a quill. Declaring it well-cleaned, she instructed the others to tip the cauldron and slowly pour out the water, then place the wet quills in a loose pile on a blanket. Sisketung, while disappointed the story had stopped, joined in the activities.

Leaning over the pile, Esther demonstrated the next step: sorting the quills by size and spreading them in rows to dry in the fire's heat. She spread out two more fresh white blankets beside the fire, took out quills of three sizes, flicked off the water, and placed them on a blanket to establish the rows. She began with the larger quills that had come from the porcupine's tail and back. The preferred ones, slender and fine from the sides and neck, must be placed farther away from the fire, she explained. These were the delicate quills most prized in jewelry. Too much sudden heat could cause them to crack.

Just then a runner circulating through the campground came to their circle to report that Fish Carrier's group was near, heading south on the Forbidden Path. Wasting no time, the women leaned into their task. As soon as the two others returned from interring the ka'wia, Esther resumed her saga.

"SISTERS, LISTEN WELL," ESTHER began, "For all my time among them, the Moravians held close to their path of peace. I saw how they would soothe anger among our native groups. They would try to feed and comfort captives who passed through. A few times I saw them protect black-skinned slaves who had escaped from their holders. I was weary of conflict, so their manner warmed me deeply.

"Sisters, their approach was so unlike the other Bible men! The others crowded us toward their water ritual, promising we would be reborn into their God's protection. That they must cleanse our heathen blood. But Sisters, the Moravians had the wisdom to demand nothing. They did believe their word of

God was supreme, and they preached it—but they wanted our belief in it to be sincere and strong. So they expected it to grow slowly. They always left the door open to leave."

"Mother Esther, did you have the Moravian baptism yourself?"

"No, although my heart was drawn. When they gave me a silver cross, I wore it proudly as a totem of harmony, as another sign that I wished to be a peace woman to all people. They were confident I eventually would convert, and told me my Christian name would be Esther. Some people began calling me by that name, which is how it came to be."

Esther prayed that her long telling was plain and clear, because the story took many turns.

"Sisters, the Moravians did win three of my older children's hearts. Did you know that? They had visited and studied often with the missionaries at Wyalusing. By then they were of age. They chose, one by one, to be baptized in the white robes of the convert. My daughter became Amalia and married a Munsee convert named Cornelius. The Wyalusing mission became their new home, where they worked in the orchards and the grist mill. Later, my two oldest sons joined her. They took the names Aaron and Ephraim."

She and Eghohowin would visit the children regularly, she said. Their peaceful, open lives made her content. The chief's mind was not at rest, however. Eghohowin had never embraced the Bible lessons and resented his children's foreign lives. As Esther explained it, he welcomed the Moravians' food and supplies but loathed the effect their presence had on his family. He began quarreling with the missionaries and mocking their faith, sometimes very loudly, during the visits.

"He said the Moravians put a spell on our children," Esther said. "We had bitter talks. I was saddened by the children's departure from our ways, but I understood their decision. The war years, the winters of want, had shaped them deeply. They wished to be sheltered by peace, safe from the hatchet and musket—as did I."

Cakoanos spoke up with an observation of her own. "Sisters, understand that Eghohowin was not alone in his anger. As a child in Sheshequin, I heard from my mother about how other war chiefs and sachems grew to distrust the Moravians as well."

"Yo-hah, Sister," Esther replied. "I heard shamans complaining on a visit to Sheshequin. Delaware and Shawnee headmen would pass through the mission towns and be fed by the Moravians and hear their teachings. The chiefs might praise the converts' hard work and sharing, but they were angered by the rules against taking up weapons, against face-painting, against scalp locks. I remember the shaman Wagomen's words. He said the Moravians were intruders. He said the converts were useless in war and should be expelled from our tribes. Wagomen said that if the Preserver wanted us to live like them, we would have been born among them.

"This became Eghohowin's belief as well. As a war chief, he was always on his guard. Sisters, even when he placed his hatchet on the ground, it was always near. He had seen too much treachery from the squatters, from Pennsylvania, from New York, from the Iroquois, to be truly trusting."

Then, Esther said, the darkening clouds grew even worse when land boundaries changed. Leaning over her map, she showed how a treaty in the yengwe year 1768 fixed the upper Susquehanna River as the very borderline between white lands on the east and Indian lands on the west. Sheshequin was on the west bank—just inside Indian-controlled land—but the Sheshequin Indian village had already established cornfields and grazing pastures just across the river on what was suddenly the white-owned eastern shore. Eghoghowin and other chiefs journeyed to the Pennsylvania officials to win the right to remain on the east bank. The governor granted it, but then, in a two-faced move, opened the same land to surveying. A few white settlers soon moved in, causing friction with both the Indians and the Moravians.

Far worse, Esther explained, her people also learned that their supposed Iroquois overlords had secretly sold the western bank Sheshequin land while the Munsees were still living there. The Iroquois had discovered the high value set on the land by the white surveyors. A trader brought the bitter news to Sheshequin that one Iroquois group had sold the land to Pennsylvania, while another Iroquois group had sold the same land to settlers from Connecticut. Yengwes would soon descend on Sheshequin with land papers, meaning it was only a matter of time before Eghohowin's community must uproot and relocate itself. The dark turn of events kindled the war chief's rage anew.

"Sisters, he was ready to lift the hatchet again," Esther said, feeling her pulse quicken at the memory. "I argued for calm. We quarreled privately and in council. There was general agreement that we were too isolated from other Munsee bands and had too few warriors to succeed in battle at that time."

The group came up with an unusual plan, she said. Other Munsees had recently established a new village three days upriver, called Chemung, and asked Eghohowin to become their chief. Knowing the location would place him out of reach of the yengwes, he accepted the offer and invited other Sheshequin warriors and their families to join what became his new stronghold.

Esther, however, wished to remain closer to her children in the Wyalusing mission. So in the year 1770, Eghohowin's community separated into two. She took those who wished to remain with her—Munsee, Tutelo, Shawnee, Conestoga remnants, mostly women and children, with a few warriors for protection—and moved a short half-day upriver from Sheshequin to the river flats on the western shore across from Teaoga. This became the village yengwes later called Esthertown or, sometimes, Queen Esther's Town.

Though living two days journey from one another, she and her husband were in regular contact as they led their twin villages. The sachem of the Cayuga watch town agreed to let Esther's people have the rich bottomland for their use as a gesture to keep the peace with Eghohowin, whose hostile ways still put the Iroquois on edge. Esther, for her part, agreed to pay a tribute of corn and wampum to the Cayuga sachem and to govern her village in peace.

"Sisters, such a time of uneasiness it was," Esther said. "But no blood was shed. We kept our arrows sheathed. Steadily our new villages sunk their roots and the families grew. My remaining young son and I continued to visit my other children and their own precious children at the Wyalusing mission.

"Conditions were not peaceful to the south. Over several winters' time we saw how yengwe land men were marking and dividing the land in the Wyalusing country. Waves of hostile settlers were arriving, making walls and fences. The Moravians told me how the new yengwes spoke ill of them, saying they held the best land and would not sell it to them, would not trade with them, would not buy their wicked rum. The missionaries were afraid for their community. They also saw how the Connecticut men and the Pennsylvania men in their midst competed violently over land, often the same piece of land, and the Moravians wished not to be entangled."

Esther noticed nods of recognition from several of the women. These events were probably among their own childhood memories.

"Sisters, I was not surprised but my heart was pained when the missionaries decided everyone must depart from their Wyalusing and Sheshequin prayer towns. Western Delaware leaders in the Ohio country had invited them many times to escape danger by moving the people west.

"Preparations were made. Then one hot day in the year 1772, in the Month When Corn Is in the Milk, their journey west began. My remaining young boy and I went down to Sheshequin to see the Moravians depart. Eghohowin joined us but said little that day. Their numbers were great, people of all ages, whites and natives, with many horses and oxen. Some traveled by boat with their furniture, but most set out by land into the thick woods. Sisters, we never saw our Moravians again.... I have heard they finally settled on the Muskingum River ..."

Esther lowered her head and fell silent. Cakoanos, recognizing that her old friend was losing herself in the reliving, rose and invited the others to begin preparing the evening meal.

Sisketung worked quietly alongside the women. The telling left her pensive. She had taken the many events to heart and committed most of Esther's intense narrative to memory. That pleased her. She was also aware that somehow during the long telling she had stopped simply observing the events and had left her body to accompany the younger Esther. Such was the magic of the powerful oral tradition.

A KETTLE OF PEETOOCANOHUK, the smooth broth of milkweed boiled with dumplings, was made ready on the fire while two of the Tutelo women headed to the river to draw fresh water. Others carefully folded the blankets laden with their piles of sorted quills and set them aside to be worked on later in the full light of day. Esther remained quiet at her seat, dully poking the fire with a long stick.

Out of the gathering darkness came the Seneca matron who had visited Esther earlier. She said Fish Carrier's arrival at the Carrying Path was imminent. Esther was invited to join the matrons and elders greeting him. "Sister," the woman said, "we will protect you from yengwe eyes. Your greeting can follow in the safety of Fish Carrier's shelter."

Esther asked the matron to wait while she conferred with Cakoanos. Esther's voice was low but firm. "Sister, the day has left me empty. I ask if you and Sisketung might remain with me here." Cakoanos immediately agreed, and Esther turned back to the matron. "Sister, Fish Carrier is a great chief, and I do not wish to dishonor him. Yet weariness is heavy upon me now. I will ask the other women from my fire circle to attend as my voice and to remain for the evening festivities if they wish. Send my welcome to the chief and to Red Jacket and my prayers that the council fire will now burn bright."

Once the others departed for the Carrying Place, the three companions filled their bowls with broth and ate silently in the warmth of the campfire. Time seemed to slow. Sisketung idly watched Moon, the bright and waxing Old Uncle, begin his evening ascent over the mountainside. Soon Esther remarked quietly, "How different my life would have been had I gone west with them."

Cakoanos understood and appreciated that Esther was sharing her heart. She considered her words carefully.

"Yo-hah, Sister," she said. "Your life has taken many forks. The Preserver has been with you. Pray he was with your children on the Muskingum and is with them still. Pray he stays with us through our troubles. Sister, I believe the Preserver meant you to be our sakima. If you had left for the Ohio, you might have dishonored him. How our village would have suffered."

Esther nodded. She drew a long breath and looked the two in the eye. "Sister and Daughter, your presence is a blessing to me. You remind me to remain strong and trust in the Preserver. Pray he will bring wisdom to our Pine Tree chiefs and will help them speak true to Pickering."

"Yo-hah!" Cakoanos said. "Sister, let us all share a smoke together. It is time for Sisketung to learn."

Esther padded to her shelter to fetch her effigy pipe and a handful of kulukuneekun from her pouch. Cakoanos retrieved two pipes and the tobacco they had purchased at Hollenback's store. They sat close as Esther showed Sisketung how to distinguish sumac mix from pure tobacco. She showed her how to rub them together, fill the bowl properly, and light the mix with an ember from the fire. Once all three pipes were lit, Esther demonstrated how to puff lightly and not let the smoke penetrate deep into her throat.

"It smokes well," Cakoanos said.

"Yo-hah," Esther replied. "Is it well, Daughter?"

Sisketung returned an uncertain look. But she puffed without cough or complaint. The trio continued in silence, resting their eyes and feeling their thoughts mingle. Cakoanos hummed the Mohawk friendship tune.

When Sisketung opened her eyes again, she saw Esther's head bent forward. Soon the woman's mouth drooped open and the old wolf's head pipe slipped from her fingers onto the ground. She and her mother exchanged smiles as Esther began to snore lightly and slump toward the fire.

"Let us move our guest to the bearskin," Cakoanos said, "before she falls into the flames."

Chapter 10

Was that "Thriller" she was hearing? It was indeed. Maddy rolled over and stared upside-down at the clipper ship sailing across the oil painting above her motel bed. Even through the metal door, even with her AC unit pumping out white noise, the dance tune throbbing in from the kitchen was way-loud. The monster hit was one of her dad's anthems from what he called his misspent youth. She was sure he'd turned up the volume and pointed the portable speakers right at her bedroom door as a little wakeup call. *OK, I get the message. At least it's not a parakeet.*

Shuffling into the kitchen, she found her father seated at their little round table, hair mussed, mug of black coffee at his side, bare foot tapping. He was lip-synching to the music as he typed away on his laptop. "Morning, Missy Maddy. Sleep well?"

Maddy walked behind him and gave his back a little hug, then turned down the volume and grabbed a one-pack of corn flakes from the cupboard. Folding herself into the chair beside him, she asked, "So how was your big day yesterday? Seems like it kinda knocked you out."

This was true. She hadn't talked to him since his fishing trip with Charlie—hadn't even seen him awake. When Mrs. T had dropped her off on the way back from the town pool late Saturday afternoon, she found her dad sprawled atop his bedspread, dead to the world from getting up so early. She didn't have the heart to wake him, so she'd nuked a dinner for herself, sent her Grammy Winter an email, and stolen a few extra minutes online. After reading about Esther and Sullivan for awhile, she thought back on her unreal, exhausting day, and drifted to sleep. Not a Rockn Saturday night, but that was fine since she was feeling tapped out.

Now, judging from the music, Mr. Winter was full of morning vim. Maddy decided to roll with his energy.

"Yesterday? A blast!" he bubbled. "I caught ... well, I'll show you." He opened the freezer and pulled out two packages, which he carefully unwrapped. "Exhibit A. You are looking at a pair of fillets from a four-pound brown trout caught by the heroic yours truly. Exhibit B, the succulent fillets from two largemouth bass, also reeled in by Mister Do-Dad, the do-it-all man."

"That's so crazy!" Maddy enthused. While she downed her cereal and a hit of o.j., he recounted how he and Charlie had put into the river at dawn a few miles south of the motel. Outfitted in Charlie's canoe, they drifted here, drifted there, and watched the thin morning fog lift. They saw herons stab the water for fish. They saw kingfishers perched over the water on branches. They waited patiently for action on their own lines.

His eyes grew wide. "My line suddenly got taut. I hooked a humongous trout, and it started pulling us downriver! Charlie panicked on me! A storm came up! He was afraid to reach into the frigid water to pull the beast into the boat! I had to hop out onto a rock and spear it so it wouldn't attack! I didn't know I had it in me! It was heroic, herculean! You would have been so proud!!"

"Not-not-not." She flicked a drop of milk at him. "You are so wack! Charlie probably had to put the worm on the hook for you and everything, right? Just like he's the one who cut up the fish for you and everything, right, mister hero?"

He flashed an impish smile. "Oh, c'mon, fishin's made for fish tales. Did I tell you about the one that got away?"

Maddy shook her head in mock disgust. With an "oh, well" shrug, he turned back to the laptop. "Meanwhile, I have a plan for all this fish, for real," he said. "A few minutes ago I called Mrs. T and invited them to dinner tonight. She said great, but unfortunately only she and Katie can make it since Mr. T is taking Curtis to play pitch-and-putt this afternoon at some golf course up near Corning. Since the weather is looking so nice today, she suggested the four of us meet at the Valley Playland and cook out in the picnic pavilion there."

"Sure, awesome," Maddy replied.

His plan, he said, was to use the fresh fish in a special quasi-American Indian, natural-food meal featuring ingredients with a Three Sisters theme. The staple of the Northeastern Indians' diet was corn, squash, and beans, which they planted together in a cluster they called the Three Sisters. Fish worked too, he figured, since it was one of the Indians' regular treats.

"I've been looking up recipes online, and it's coming together," he said. "I'll coat the bass fillets in cornmeal and fry them. For the beans, I figure let's just look for a classy cold-bean salad. Make it easy. And for the squash, no problemo. Mrs. T said she'll bring a butternut squash pie she saw for sale at Herman's. I didn't know there was such a thing, but it sounds made to order!"

In his quest for natural ingredients, he'd located a listing for an organic food store in Towanda, the county seat fifteen miles downriver. "That'll be a nice destination for a Sunday outing, right? And I'll show you our fishing hole when we pass—listen to this—Sheshequin."

AT THE LITTLE HIPPIE food shop, they bought a bag of stone-ground organic cornmeal ("unprocessed, just like the Indians," Mr. Winter chuckled), a tub of bean salad with sprouts ("think they knew about mung beans and adzuki back then?"), and two broccoli and turmeric tofu pocket sandwiches for the road ("I feel so righteous!"). He placed the tub of salad beside the package of fillets in the cooler sitting on the car's backseat, rechecked the condiments, cutlery, and other supplies, and off they went.

After crossing the Susquehanna just above Towanda, they headed back north on a local road paralleling the river's east bank. For miles they had the drive almost to themselves.

"Rockin'-and-rollin' time!" Mr. Winter grinned, sliding one of his mixes into the CD slot. Out blasted "Girls Just Wanna Have Fun." Maddy winced as he began shimmying in the driver's seat. Please, please don't dance on the gas pedal, she thought. She knew how he was. "Can't you just see Mom bopping to this?" he shouted above the music. "I can, anyways. She had the moves!"

Maddy fell in with his crooning. The peaceful scenery rolling past—farm fields on the river flats to the left, undulating mountainsides rising beside them on the right, trees everywhere—had her eyes playing artist again. She matched the hues outside to the crayon colors of her past: goldenrod, pine green, mountain meadow, burnt sienna, even a little ochre. A few of the passing vistas seemed so perfectly composed that she nearly called out to her father to stop, but she hadn't thought to bring her art supplies or even her camera. She'd have to commit the views to memory.

A few songs farther along, the road rose like a roller-coaster. They had reached a stretch where the river loops over to the very base of a mountain. To allow wagons to pass through, a roadbed had been notched into the mountainside long ago, creating a narrow ledge that curved high above the water.

As they ascended the roadbed, Maddy watched the land drop away dramatically on the left, leaving only a dented metal guardrail between them and the treetops that sloped to the river below. At the crest was a scenic turnoff. They pulled over and walked to the knee-high guardrail.

Mr. Winter two-stepped toward the edge, humming the last dance tune, then stopped cold. "Just look at that!" Before them lay the entire valley with its rim of western mountains swelling up in the distance. The overlook was directly above the juncture of the two rivers—the Teaoga spearpoint.

"Hey, that's Tioga Point right down there!" Maddy exclaimed. She turned herself to face south and did a quick calculation. They were at twelve o'clock on the dial. "We're up at that very place Mrs. T pointed out to me the other day! The Narrows, I think it was called. She said settlers took their wagons up over this pass back in the olden days."

Mr. Winter had been turning around with her to get the full picture. "Lordy, a real mountain pass. These are some tight quarters for hauling loads. Wouldn't catch me trying that."

"She said bald eagles nest in the treetops down there and fish at the Point. This isn't the right time of day, but we might luck out if we look."

Maddy scanned her eyes northward. There was the vast potato field. The parking area where she and Mrs. T had stood. Main Street. Athens. In the hazy distance to the north, Sayre.

"Look how the rivers come together," her father said. "The Susquehanna down there is so much muddier."

Just below them coursed the broad Susquehanna, its color this day a mocha brown. The Chemung River, only half as wide and flowing faster, was emptying its dark-green flow into the Susquehanna. The sight was peculiar, like two mismatched crayon streaks, Maddy thought. Somehow, she knew, the colors would blend by the time the waters reached Towanda.

She turned her eyes to the far bank, beyond the Point. There was Esther's Flats. The very site of the village, the castle, the burning. Just a long, lonesome field from the looks of it up here.

Next Maddy studied the shoreline of the Chemung, section by section. Mr. Winter had fetched his binoculars and was surveying the landscape like a field general. Maddy watched him for a minute, then turned her eyes back to the riverbank. *Maybe I'll tell him about the spirits, but later. My gut is telling me to keep it to myself. I haven't even told Mel, and I tell her everything.*

Mr. Winter walked back to Li'l Red and beckoned to Maddy. "We'd better get a move on. I want to get the charcoal started. We can come back some other time and take pictures, okay?"

MRS. T PULLED INTO the Valley Playland parking lot about a minute behind them. While toting the food and supplies over to the covered pavilion, the foursome chatted about their day and looked around at the well-worn grounds. For a nice Sunday, the park was quieter than Maddy would have thought. All she saw were a few parents watching over their youngsters in the kiddie area and a handful of teens shooting hoops and strutting around on a far court. As her father and Mrs. T conferred about the state of the greasy cooking grill anchored in the ground near their picnic table, she and Katie wandered off toward the play equipment.

"Before I forget," Katie said, "Curty said for you to meet him outside the museum after day camp tomorrow, at like four o'clock. He wants to show you something."

The girls climbed onto a pair of big fiberglass dolphins that swayed on metal springs embedded in the ground. After bucking like robotic cowgirls for a minute, they dismounted and headed down the short slope to a dusty, unused baseball field.

From home plate, the girls set out to round the bases, single file, stepping heel to toe as though creeping along a log. It was a balancing game they both knew. Maddy took the lead, pacing herself and flexing her knees to stay upright.

"My brother's something, isn't he?" Katie said after they slowly rounded first base. "There's a lot—whoa!—going on in his little head. You haven't seen his room—whoa, baby, don't fall!—have you? He has posters of Sitting Bull and Red Jacket, and a real peace pipe, and a spear he made— whoa, oh no!"

She tumbled, laughing, onto the rutted base path. Maddy, already at second, walked back and flopped down beside her. Too dusty, Maddy decided, so they moved to right field and sat in the weedy grass watching the town boys shoot baskets in the distance. Katie began humming softly.

"So who's Red Jacket?" Maddy asked.

"Some Seneca chief who lived near here way back when. He was famous as a speechmaker. Living with my mother and Curty, I learn that kind of stuff." As she sat back, Katie plucked stiff stalks of grass from around her and began weaving them into a braid. Maddy joined in.

"I like Indians and history stuff," Katie continued. "Not as much as my brother, I guess, and not like my mother. But it *is* awesome history. I'm glad Curty and Tommy are showing you things while you're here. They really do know a lot. Did they take you to their camp?"

"Yeah, actually," Maddy replied. *So she knows. And she doesn't seem to be jealous or anything. This girl is too nice. She'd get eaten alive as a goody-goody at my school. I don't think I'll tell her what happened yesterday, but I probably could trust her if I did. Should I declare this sorta-friend to be my friend? Sounds like Curtis didn't tell her about it. He's trustworthy, too, for a little kid. Is it just the Tulowitskys, or the small-town way? Either way, I think I like it.*

Maddy decided to open up a bit. "Curtis showed me the hissing stone, Katie."

"That's what he's calling it? It used to be the *spitting* stone."

"Huh?"

"Yeah, I know, gross. They used to actually spit at it until Tommy's mother found out, like a month ago. Curty told me. Tommy said they had to cut it out or else. She must have gone nutso."

Maddy twirled a stalk in her fingers and wondered silently. Tommy's mother really hadn't blown up at him, the girls would have been interested to know, but she was disappointed. Spitting like that was beneath him, she'd told her son. It was undignified. Like him, she felt the monument's spiritual darkness—which was why she'd been going there early every springtime to burn cedar branches, so the sacred smoke might purify the atmosphere. That was the way of dignity, she'd explained. He was old enough to join her next time, she'd added. Tommy thought of inviting Curtis, but knew it was best to keep the tradition private.

Snapping her stalk in half, Maddy sighed, "Why does the thing have that dumb trash-talk about savagery?"

"Yeah, I know. The good guy-bad guy business is pretty gross," Katie answered. "You should hear my mom go on about it. I think she actually tries to keep people away from the stone."

Maddy envisioned the monument emitting a negative force field. A crazy image followed, out of the blue, making her snicker.

"What?" Katie asked.

"Can't you just picture the other monuments in the park banishing it after, like, holding a solemn council!"

"Hah! Poof! Be gone, bad stone!"

"*Monumentally* bad stone!"

"Moldy boulder!"

Once their laughter faded, Katie resumed her soft humming. She reached over to tie her own grass bracelet around Maddy's wrist. It was too short, so she resumed her braiding operation. Maddy watched and was moved. Her own plait was inept, and even if it was good, she had to admit that the pure gesture of giving it away hadn't occurred to her.

Maddy was seeing Katie with new eyes. The day before, while they lay on their towels at the town pool, Katie had let loose with a long, loud belch from close quarters, and Maddy returned an annoyed look. Katie was upset for a minute, then had said quietly, "Sorry. I know sometimes I get goofy, Maddy.... I, I used to be worse. When I was little I was diagnosed, you know, hyperactive. Kids used to, like, keep their distance or laugh at me. They called me 'Katie-Don't.' Get it? Katydid. Ha-ha. Or I was 'Katie-Can't.'" Maddy could picture kids snickering at Kate's expense, thinking they were so clever.

Katie said her self-control had gotten better, and that she'd found she has a naturally good memory for things, which helped in her schoolwork. Also, she said, she's good at most sports. "So crap, all that's me," she said. "Most times I guess I just want to have fun, and help other people have fun, but sorry if it seems too much."

Maddy, impressed with Katie's honesty, had replied simply, "Yeah, let's have fun, no problem. Be yourself." That was the last they spoke about it, but it left Maddy with an empathetic ache.

Now, sitting on the grass, Katie turned to Maddy with a grin. "You'll love this! One day this spring my brother popped into my room and asked me, 'Have you gotten your period yet?' Imagine, my period! My little brother! I'm like, 'What?!' He's like, 'I know all about menses, Katie.' That's what he called it, menses. And he launches into telling me about the old Delaware Indian menstruation customs. He said he was just reading about them. When a girl got her first period, she'd be taken to an isolation hut and watched over by an old woman of the tribe for like ten days. No one else was permitted to see her or talk to her. They'd bring food and everything to her. I think it was called 'the time of hiding.' Then, when the time was up, they'd put away her girl toys, give her all new clothes, and say she was a woman now. It's actually true. Isn't that wild?

"So my brother asks, 'Why the ten days? Is that how long you bleed?' Yikes. I'm not making fun of Curtis or anything. It's just that he can be so, you know, direct."

Maddy had seen it in him, too. "Disarming," she said.

"Yeah, disarming, you betcha," Katie repeated. "Good word for it, girlfriend."

Katie reached over and tried the bracelet on Maddy's wrist again. This time it fit. She took Maddy's and started expertly adding braids.

"You had a game this morning, right?" Maddy asked. "How did it go?"

"Cool. We won."

"How did you do?"

"Good, thanks. I was the catcher for the whole game. Sorry you weren't there."

From the pavilion they heard Mr. Winter hailing them. He was standing over the grill, waving away the smoke futilely.

"Smoke signals!" Katie laughed as she pulled Maddy up. They trotted up the slope, weaving across each other's paths like a human bracelet.

THE CORNMEAL HAD SEEMED like a good idea, but it was so crumbly that half of it ended up down on the charcoal. Mr. Winter was doubly frustrated that he hadn't brought a grilling basket because some fillet pieces had also fallen loose onto the briquets.

"We're really going native tonight, aren't we?" Mrs T said gamely. Mr. Winter scooped a portion of raggedy fillet onto each paper plate and passed the plates around. "Sorry I didn't bring hot dogs, gang," he grumbled. He took his seat and passed around the bean salad that was pinch-hitting as the main course. Katie gave him a sympathetic look. "This bean salad rocks, Mr. Winter! And your fish is really tasty."

As she picked her way across her plate, Maddy realized she'd hardly said a word to Mrs. T, who was seated directly across from her. "So Mrs. T, Katie says the Broncos won this morning. Did you have a good game as coach?"

"Oh yes, I clapped my hands and cheered a whole lot. Very important job. Did Katie tell you she had the winning hit? She blasted a triple! You should have seen the team jump on her to celebrate!"

Maddy gaped. "No way. You didn't tell me that."

Katie blushed. "Easy pitch."

Mr. Winter reached across and slapped a high-five. Then he turned to Maddy. "Not to change the subject, but let me change the subject. Madd, I was just telling Mrs. T about the city of Muncie. Remember the other night at their house she was telling us about the Munsee Delawares? That got me thinking about Muncie city since it's so near where Mom and I are from in Indiana. Turns out the name is spelled differently, but it refers to the same tribe! Lots of

Munsees settled out there in the 1700s. In fact, Muncie is in *Delaware* County, Indiana! But the Munsees got kicked out of there and ended up in Oklahoma. Such a sad story."

"Sad, yes, and more than a little maddening," Mrs. T said. "By the time of the Revolution, the Delawares had broken into factions, and some of the ones in western Pennsylvania tried to get along with the Colonials. I think you'll find those were the ones who went to Ohio and Indiana in the 1770s to try to set up their own state. Some of the Moravians' Indian prayer towns relocated out there as well. But guess what? After a generation, the Delawares were forced out of Indiana because the government wanted to open that land to white settlement. So they went farther west into Missouri. Then around 1830, guess what, they gave up *that* land and had to move even farther west to Oklahoma. They signed crummy little treaties with the government that kept giving them less land and less payment."

"I never learned any of that in school," Mr. Winter said. "You've got me wanting to do more research."

"Good, please do!" Mrs. T said. "Hey folks, sorry if the story keeps getting out of order. The other night I was telling you about Esther and Eghohowin in the 1760s, and now we're leaping way-forward to the 1820s. If this were a book, it'd be tidier, told straight through from the beginning."

"Better yet, we'd have Esther telling us everything herself!" added Mr. Winter.

"Hah, wouldn't that be wonderful? But I'm afraid there's just lots we'll never know for certain about her," Mrs. T said. "I was telling you my best understanding of Esther in the French and Indian war times, remember? And I said they got routed out of Assinisink and apparently took their band to a spot a few miles downriver from here known as Sheshequin."

Mrs. T eased into her authoritative speaking voice. Maddy sensed the others settling in to experience the story. She felt her own mental helicopter revving up in anticipation.

"During this Sheshesquin period," Mrs. T began, "Esther's band apparently lived side by side with a Moravian missionary settlement."

"Whoa," Maddy's father said with a wave, "before you get too far along, I have to say I'm a bit lost about the Moravians."

Mrs. T smiled back. "Fair enough, Russ. I love the Moravians, but they're so underappreciated. They were a Christian sect from Germany, one of the many persecuted groups that found refuge in William Penn's Pennsylvania. They immigrated here and founded the lovely little city of Bethlehem, Pennsylvania. Hold on, let me get something."

She quickly retrieved an expandable folder from her SUV and flipped it open on the picnic table. "This is my main Esther file. Folks, I have a confession to make. If I've seemed all expert about our Indian history, it's only because I've been immersing myself in it in the last few weeks. I'll tell you why in a sec."

Maddy watched as Mrs. T flipped through her papers. "You and your dad have seemed so interested, Maddy, that I brought this along to be sure I gave you my best information.... Yeah, here's the name: 'Civitas Indiana-Germana.' The Moravians wanted to establish a joint community with the natives that translates as the 'Indian-German Commonwealth.' To do that, their missionaries lived among the Indians as equals, learned their languages, and didn't push mass conversions."

"Sounds kind of radical," Mr. Winter said.

"Definitely radical for the day! And it made them the most successful Indian missionaries in the colonies," Mrs. T said.

"The Moravian record shows that at least one and maybe as many as three of Esther's children converted to Christianity. She also is said to have worn a big cross on a necklace. It doesn't appear that she actually converted, but it just shows how much of a shape-shifter she seemed to be. They all had to be in order to adapt to the constant upheavals and the changing alliances. The Moravian records show that even macho-man Eghohowin got along with the missionaries during the Sheshequin period, at least for awhile.

"But then—guess what, again—the Iroquois overlords secretly sold the Sheshequin land out from under the Munsees, and everyone had to abandon their homes ! Eghohowin must have been infuriated, seeing his people be pawns again in this big game. At that point he seems to have skipped back upriver to lead another Munsee town, probably to get away from the whites and the Iroquois. Some people say he died around that time, in the early 1770s. I doubt that. I think he just slipped out of sight. This is when Esther moved up here to the Flats and became known as Queen Esther."

"At Queen Esther's Town itself, right?" Mr. Winter asked.

"Right-o. Maddy, you were out near Esther's Flats yesterday, right? You know those were the grazing lands and farm fields for Esther's Town? That's another place where I feel there's still magic in the atmosphere to this day, kind of an electric buzz. Maybe it's just me."

Maddy felt herself blushing.

"What was her town like, anyways?" Mr. Winter asked.

"I wish I could say more," Mrs. T replied. "The old maps place it on the Flats. Sometimes it's called Esthertown, sometimes Queen Esther's Town. I just finished reading the accounts left to us by two early settler women. One said Esther's town contained about seventy, quote-unquote, 'rude houses.'"

"Rude?" Maddy asked.

"Yes, as in basic. These might have been simple log cabins since the cabins were spreading into Indian culture then, alongside wigwams, probably because of the Moravians and other friendly whites."

She gestured for them to wait while she read a printout. "Yeah, here, it says seventy rude houses. Wanted to be sure that number was right. My ultimate goal, folks, is to memorize this material. I mean really memorize all the times and places and names and events. It's so I can speak authoritatively—but also because I want to honor the Indian tradition of oral history."

"Like an Indian storyteller!" Mr. Winter exclaimed. "Nice!"

"Exactly," she said. "Their storytellers would listen and memorize legends and histories to pass them on to the next generation. These oral stories were critical to the culture, serving like books and television and more! Storytellers were beloved, and they'd train people from childhood to listen and memorize so they could pass it on."

She handed another printout to Maddy. "Here, dear, read this part out loud for us. It's a settler description of Esther. Say it like you're seeing her."

Maddy found the spot and began reciting: "She was a tall but not very fleshy woman—not as dark as the usual Indian in complexion—had the features of a white woman—cheekbones not high, hair black, but soft and fine like a white woman, not the heavy black hair of the squaw. Her form erect and commanding, her appearance and manners agreeable. She walked straight and had not the bend of the squaw; she had not the Indian mode of turning toes in."

Maddy had slowed her voice to help the words sink in. She pictured the woman walking proudly through her fields, head high, calling out to her villagers. The phrase "an air of authority" came to mind.

"Good job," Mrs. T said. "So it's said that Esther's castle was the largest building, in full view of the Point. One of the accounts says her home—here, I'll read it—'... was long and low, built of hewn logs and planks, neatly done, with a porch over the doorway, and surrounded by a number of other buildings.'

"Interesting, huh? They say she was well-regarded by the Indians and well-known to the whites. That's probably because she traded among the whites and even went on trips downriver to the Wyoming Valley settlements. The settlers were the ones who started calling her queen, by the way. She might have even traveled with Eghohowin to peace talks in Easton and Philadelphia, though the records are sketchy on that."

"But wasn't she brutal to those captured soldiers at Wyoming?" Mr. Winter cut in. "Actually, before you answer, let's break for some of that squash pie, okay? I've been waiting all day for that."

THE DESSERT WITH ITS hazelnut crumble was delicious but a challenge to dish out neatly with their little plastic forks. They laughed their way through the messy operation and gobbled it up as Mrs. T resumed her narrative.

"Yes, Russ, it appears Esther was brutal at Wyoming. That's what makes her so fascinating overall! But I'm talking about before that happened. During the heyday of Queen Esther's Village, she seemed to go out of her way to be peaceable, like she was trying to model the way to coexist. Whereas Eghohowin decided to separate from contact with whites, she wanted to stick it out. One of the accounts said that before the Wyoming troubles, she treated the nearby settlers with—here it is—quote, 'uniform kindness and courtesy.'"

She held up two other sheets of stapled paper. Maddy could see markings written in pen in the margin, probably by Mrs. T.

"There are several stories told about Esther's decency during that period," Mrs. T continued. "Once, it's said, she stepped in to see that two executed British deserters were properly buried. This was early during the Revolutionary War. The two deserters made it as far as the Point, where they were captured by their own troops, court-martialed, and shot dead on the spot. The British officers felt deserters weren't entitled to be buried, so they just left their bodies out on the ground for the animals. Esther had her people bury the two soldiers in Indian fashion, which might have meant curled up on their sides. She gave them that respect."

Maddy's mind hovered above the fresh graves. She wondered if she could ever handle anyone's dead body. This was an Esther story she was sure her memory would keep without even trying.

"Also, Esther apparently made it a custom to visit nearby white homesteads to socialize with the settler families," Mrs. T went on.

Katie, who'd been sitting quietly, seemingly focused on the boys on the distant basketball court, said suddenly, "Mom, didn't you also tell me that Esther once helped two visiting settlers escape from some braves?"

"Yes, good listening, love! Those two courageous fellows had come up from Wyoming to try to win the release of another settler who'd been taken captive. This was in 1777, during the war. They recorded that Esther hosted them at her castle and invited them to spend the night. Hospitality was a big thing with the Indians. Guests were entitled to a double portion of food, which I'm sure she offered. These men said Esther told them she was opposed to war and wished for Indians and whites to live in peace. One of the settlers was a Quaker. Here, let me read. The Quaker said he talked to her about religion and she, quote, 'seemed to have correct views.' That evening, it seems some Indians decided to sit outside the castle and sing loud war songs. The settlers said Esther went outside to talk to them, and returned with a warning that the braves were out to kill them. 'I can do nothing with them,' she said. 'Lie down until I call you.' When it got quiet out, she instructed, the visitors should slip down to the river, take her canoe, and paddle away quietly. And they did. They got away by the skin of their teeth thanks to Esther and her canoe!"

Maddy shot her hand up. "I think Esther and Eghohowin were just trying to stay in their own comfort zones! His way was defensive and, like, military. Hers was peaceful. Both were ways of keeping their dignity. They tried each one, and it worked for awhile. But the deal kept changing on them. Finally, the war way won out. Even Esther snapped eventually."

Mrs. T smiled. "I see it something like that, too. They tried to be survivors in a treacherous time. Change was swirling all around. No one had the Munsees' backs, certainly not the Iroquois. Everything they did was an experiment on the fly."

Mr. Winter spoke next. "Do you think Esther's friendliness to whites was sincere or calculating?"

"Seems this is something we'll never know, Russ," she replied. "But in the end, none of the Indians' efforts worked. It kept being a lose-lose-lose situation for them. Esther saw so much of her people's downward spiral across her long life. It's as though her destiny was to be a tortured soul."

"Just so tragic," Maddy's father said. "I wonder what I would have done. Fight, flee, hide, try to blend in? It reminds me of my mother's expression: You don't know a person until you walk a mile in his moccasins. Hers, in this case."

Maddy wanted to reach over and hug her dad. *Look how his eyes are lit up! He's as into this as anyone!* All along, Mr. Winter had been cocked on the edge of his seat, literally leaning forward to meet the story head-on. It's what made him a good engineer, and she knew it was his overall posture toward life—to meet people and experiences with his receptors fully open. As he'd say to her, "I know me already. I want to know other things." Her mother was more guarded, more straight-ahead, more of a clock-watcher, and she admired that, too, but Maddy knew she wanted to be an expansive person like him.

Mr. Winter's reaction also made Mrs. T smile broadly. "Russ, I'm so glad you're here. I have a proposal I've been wanting to make to your dear daughter." Turning toward Maddy, she continued, "Maddy, you obviously have a head for history. I wonder if you'd be willing to help me with a special project. So listen well, as the Indians would say. Here's the thing. I've been reading all this history, because I want to develop a curriculum about our local history for the middle schoolers in our area. I tried something over the spring with a few classes visiting the museum, but it was haphazard. I need to prepare something that's more engaging, more polished, to present to the principal.

"So will you help me develop it? I don't mean as a focus group that only gives me feedback once it's done. I mean now, working out the pieces from scratch. Beth will be part of the team since her college research focus is the settler groups. Trevor agreed, too, but I need to have another sharp middle schooler to help me concoct lots of ways to hook kids into the material. I want the lessons to be sophisticated, but not too sophisticated, you know what I mean? It's good to have a visitor like you who's learning the history fresh so you can say what strikes you, what's confusing, what makes the biggest impression. Katie says she'll be a sounding board for me after it's done. I know Curtis would like to join the team, but he's too young and would be a bit of a loose cannon."

Maddy's mind tumbled with ideas. While she gathered her reply, Mr. Winter asked, "When would this be?"

"A couple of evenings for an hour or two," Mrs. T replied. "At the museum. We'll order in pizza. Since you'll only be here another week, I figure it's now or never. So what do you think, missy?"

Maddy felt tears welling up again. *Me? Be like a teacher, working with the adults? Helping to honor the Indian spirits ...*

"Well, think about it," Mrs. T said. "You've been so good at the day camp, coming up with clever ideas. How about just joining us just for an evening and see if you like it?"

"Yes, yes!" Maddy rejoiced. Rockn Grl was bursting out of her chest. "I'd love to help!"

"That's the right Maddytude," her father said with a smile. Katie reached over for a fist bump.

Chapter 11

Esther leaned forward, quietly instructing Sisketung to keep her eyes on Pickering. "He is being provoked, but see how his face remains calm." Frequently during the council talks, Pickering had maintained the confident air of a brave, the old woman noticed with grudging admiration. "Observe how he responds."

Sisketung nodded, though she was reluctant to shift her attention. She wanted to keep watching Red Jacket instead. The girl had been faithfully attending the council fire after missing the first day because of her head injury. It had not taken long for Red Jacket's dashing style to put a spell on her: the grand gestures, the words soaring in beauty or cutting in scorn as needed. His oratory, and particularly his open challenges to the yengwe leader, enthralled many in the Indian assembly.

A daily routine had developed at the treaty ground. The mixed crowd of native onlookers would wrap their heavy blankets around themselves and tramp up from their shelters and campfires as soon as the leaders made their first stirrings near the great council fire. This occurred when Father Sun was reaching its peak in the sky. The Tutelo women moved together in a loose formation surrounding old Esther. As the general assembly of observers took its place on the ground, the Tutelos sat cross-legged in the middle of the crowd, in two tight rows. They positioned them several rows behind the matrons and elders, who sat at their honored positions in the front. Esther crouched directly behind Sisketung, her face thus half-hidden, while Cakoanos sat close at Esther's left. This precaution was needed, they felt, because Hollenback was frequently nearby now, overseeing the food distributions.

Often during the council, Esther rested her hand lightly on Sisketung's shoulder and might lean in to provide commentary.

The new day's proceedings had barely begun, and Red Jacket was already raising his arm to lecture the tall yengwe. By native custom, Red Jacket announced, Pickering had a special duty, because he was the person who lit the council fire. He should present extra gifts to the Pine Tree chiefs and to their messengers as well. That demand, once translated, brought waves of assent from the crowd. Further, Red Jacket insisted, wampum belts and not only goods must be presented to the families of the murdered Senecas. This, he said, is how it would have been done during the era of Sir William Johnson, Britain's illustrious Indian superintendent who had kept the chain of friendship bright with the Iroquois.

"At that time, wampum belts were used," Red Jacket said. "When a person was killed, a belt was delivered to one of the relations of the deceased to comfort their minds. We supposed you meant to observe the same custom. You have a small parcel of goods to deliver but no belt. It is the minds of us who are here that the rule of our forefather should now be observed. As you desire to know our rules, we have now told you what they are."

Pickering, rather than being offended, was flattered to be considered a successor to the great William Johnson, who had died fifteen winters earlier but whose diplomatic prowess was legendary. Pickering rose enthusiastically and beckoned to his aides. They rushed off and returned cradling gifts. A sack of sugar and flask of rum were ceremonially laid at the feet of each chief, along with six tin kettles for the messengers.

Pickering acknowledged that he had no more wampum for condolence purposes. He asked Red Jacket to obtain more directly from the Indian assembly, for which he would offer payment. Another murmur rose from the crowd when the request for extra wampum was translated. Esther thought immediately of the wampum strings in her shelter. Sisketung's mind turned to the porcupine quills.

Others in the assembly would surely have fine strings and belts to offer, the girl thought. Many of the older people had kept the traditions and practiced the old skills. Surrounded by dozens of parents, elders and children, mostly Senecas, Sisketung had been admiring their clothing and delicate beadwork. She noticed their proud bearing and gracious manner with one another. More and more it pleased her to be in their close company, and she looked back on how their arrival at Teaoga had agitated her. The yengwe girl Sarah had confused her mind with wicked beliefs about her people. Sisketung was coming to realize that part of her had been ashamed to be an Indian. Her fragile little community, her home, her possessions, her future, had seemed so meager compared with the onslaught of yengwes with their stout wagons and river vessels and roomy log homes. Sarah had teased her about this, while also ridiculing the Indian fathers who were lost to drunkenness and the Indian women who came to their farms in frayed muslin skirts to peddle humble brooms they'd made from river grasses.

Cakoanos had often told her how haughty and foolish Sarah was, and now Sisketung's eyes were opened. Her time at the campground and her wiser understanding of her people's struggles and dignity had vanquished any shame. She could easily strike out in fury at Sarah—but knew that was too risky for herself and her vulnerable settlement. As long as she lived at Teaoga, she must keep Sarah at a distance. She would pray to the Preserver to keep her mind true.

An old Seneca man and woman seated nearby had caught Sisketung's attention. The man often smiled over and even offered her his uneaten pudding. She noticed two fingers were missing from one of his hands. Had he been a warrior? Had he killed yengwes in the heat of battle? Or was he a survivor of one of their atrocities? She felt a flash of pride at her own wound, still visible but healing well. The Seneca woman beside him on a broad blanket mostly kept her eyes down, fingering her silver bracelets. Wrinkled and weathered, the couple looked as Sisketung imagined her mother's beloved parents looked. A wasting disease had taken them quickly, years before Sisketung was born. The girl's thoughts also went to her own father. She had only fleeting memories of him. He had vanished from Teaoga when she was an infant. Often she had heard Cakoanos praying that they be reunited. Sisketung had overheard gossip that her father fell hard into the yengwe rum. His absence left an ache that brought her low spirits on some days, blind anger on others. The thoughts weighed heavily on the girl's brow.

A HAND CLASPED SISKETUNG'S shoulder, bringing her back. "Do you understand what he is saying?" Esther whispered. "Let us see if the interpreter can find the right words. It may be difficult."

Pickering had asked the chiefs, the elders, and the wider assembly for their close attention as he explained how the yengwe government had changed and what this meant for the tribes. Feeling this was his main purpose at Teaoga, Pickering hoped his words were clear. He called them out in as clear and strong a voice as he could muster.

"Brothers, Sachems, Chiefs, and Warriors of the Six Nations, the thirteen states have given great powers to their president or great chief. One of these powers is that of making treaties, with the advice and consent of the Senate or council of old men." Now, Pickering said, this council of old men was making a formal promise to the tribes. Sisketung noticed the chiefs and matrons bowing in postures of deep listening.

"Brothers, in times past, some white men have deceived the Indians, falsely pretending they had authority to lease or purchase their lands. And sometimes they have seized on more land than the Indians meant to sell them," Pickering continued.

"Now, Brothers, to prevent these great evils in the future, the Congress declared that no sale of lands made by any Indians, to any person or persons, or even to any state, shall be valid unless the same be made at some public treaty held under the authority of the United States. For at such public treaty, wise and good men will be appointed by the President to attend to prevent all deception and fraud. These wise and good men will examine every deed before it is signed and sealed, and see that every lease or purchase of the Indians be openly and fairly made."

As Pickering's words registered, scattered cries of "yo-hah!" went up. The talk of fraudulent land sales hit raw nerves. Some of the elders nodded at Pickering's promise, while others seemed to shrug cynically.

Pickering pressed on. The next part of the yengwe law touched on the outrage that brought everyone to Teaoga. It covered the punishment for whites who harm friendly Indians. "Brothers, it is proper that I inform you that if an Indian be murdered or in any manner injured within the jurisdiction of any state," he stated, emphasizing each word, "the murderers or trespassers will be liable to the same punishment as if the person murdered or injured were a white man."

This sent a bolt of excitement through the assembly. Many, including Sisketung, raised their faces and exclaimed "yo-hah!"

The Pine Tree chiefs conferred among themselves. Then, the Seneca leader Honayenus, known also as Farmer's Brother, rose to speak. Facing Pickering across the treaty fire, the old man raised his arm and announced, "Brother, your words land favorably on our ears. You have promised to our Six Nations that your great chief, or men he sends to be his voice such as yourself, will now be the ones to make treaties with our tribes. This is good. Brother, you have promised that your great chief will send wise and good men to stop any more evil doings in the sales of our lands. This is good. Brother, you have promised that your people who harm our people will be punished in the same manner as if they had harmed one of your own. This is good.

"These are great promises that bear hope of brightening the chain of friendship," Farmer's Brother continued. "We hold your glowing words in our minds and know there is much to consider. It is time that the chiefs, sachems, elders, and matrons of the council gather among ourselves to share a smoke and let our thoughts mingle. But first, let us end this council day with a round of grog."

Pickering had his aides distribute tin cups and fresh flasks of rum. Then he rose and faced the entire assembly. "Brothers and Sisters, I am proud to bear these new promises to you. As you depart for your meal fires, pray that the path of peace remains wide. May my people's good will be made plain by the extra shares of beef that we present to you today. Also, Brothers and Sisters, I ask you to provide back to me wampum that might be in your keeping, so we may properly cover the graves of your murdered brothers and console the hearts of their families."

AS THE CROWD DISPERSED, Sisketung and Cakoanos slipped away to Hollenback's food area to receive portions of beef for themselves and Esther. Heading back down the ridge toward their fire circle, Sisketung watched the last rays of sun glinting over the sheltering mountains. Somewhere far beyond those slopes resided the yengwes' curious big government -- whose leaders she doubted the Teaoga settlers had ever seen. Even if this government was to be trusted, how could it keep order among these unruly settlers? She considered asking Esther when the old woman suddenly spoke up.

"The yengwe president promises to send us wise and good men to see that land sales do not stink of deceit. Where were they before?" Esther snapped. "My mind rejects this. The demand for our remaining land grows with every passing moon. Pickering may utter honorable words, but who will the 'wise and good men' he promises us be? Who are they? How can we trust them? They must each meet our chiefs' approval."

"Yo-hah!" Cakoanos said. "How many times the yengwe big men have worked behind our backs in their greed for land. Do not give their Washington the only voice in choosing these men. Sister, you must raise this matter with the matrons when they gather."

"Or with Red Jacket directly. I will do it. Consider it my own promise," Esther said with a bitter chuckle. "Now, let us also talk about Pickering's request for wampum. Can any of the women at our circle provide wampum?"

Cakoanos shook her head. "We have none. Nor do we have any quahog shells to string it fresh. I have not seen any at Teaoga for many winters."

"But we do have the quills," Sisketung said.

"Yo-hah, hundreds of freshly prepared quills," Esther said. "Daughter, our minds are as one. When Red Jacket spoke today, a plan flew to me. Listen well. In our shelter are three perfect strings of wampum presented to me by Red Jacket at Ganogeh. Two of the strands are pure white and one is purple. Daughter, did you know that among the Iroquois, purple or black shells are appropriate for condolence? Let us take the purple string and put it to this solemn purpose."

They had arrived back at the fire circle. While the others stoked the fire and began preparing the chunks of beef and hominy for their meal, Esther took

Sisketung into the shelter. Beckoning the girl to sit on the old bearskin blanket, Esther retrieved the wampum strings from a pouch and placed them in Sisketung's open palm.

"Daughter, we can separate the purple strand. Let us carefully remove its shells and create two shorter purple strands for the two families. Then at each end we shall add graceful loops using our ka'wia quills. Daughter, does that design please you?

Sisketung studied the strands in her hand. "Mother Esther, it will be beautiful. We can make use of the yengwes' cotton thread to string the shells, but only if the original deer sinew does not hold. Mother, I would like to test and treat the old sinew. Will you help me, Mother? Will you help me select the best quills and tie the knots to hold true? My fingers are strong."

Esther stroked the girl's temple. "Yes, Daughter, your fingers are strong. And your thoughts are as pure as white wampum. Begin as the spirit guides you. My eyes grow weary."

Chapter 12

Maddy double-timed it down the museum steps on Monday afternoon, ready to call out an apology to Curtis for being late. After a messy time making cardboard dioramas with her Seneca Set, she'd stayed behind to help Beth wash the countertops and floor the campers had bombed with tempera paint, pine needles, and grass clippings. Mission accomplished, she made a quick stop in the bathroom to clean her sticky parts from the sweaty day, then bounded out of the building into the humid afternoon.

The boy was nowhere in sight. Maddy shouted out his name and circled the building without success. She returned inside to check the wall clock—4:15, fifteen minutes late—then marched her puzzled self down to the front sidewalk. Bingo! Across Main Street, propped up on the granite base of the Revolutionary War monument, was Curtis's familiar blue bike. Beyond it, at the far end of Academy Park, sat Curtis. He was squatting on the grass, cross-legged and, oddly, facing away from her. Maddy walked across the lawn and crouched down.

"Hi, Curtis. Sorry."

"Hey." His frowning eyes were fixed on the distance, staring through the border bushes and high grasses that jutted up only a yard or two in front of them. He remained motionless, hands in his lap, a buddha in a camo top. When the silence went on for a long moment, Maddy felt a snark thought—*well, this is stupid*—but tamped it down. Something was going on. She noticed Curtis rotating his special arrowhead in his fingertips.

"This is the spot," he muttered gravely. "Sit and wait."

Maddy kicked off her flip-flops and took her place beside him. Figuring the moody boy was only going to speak in his own time, she turned her gaze outward and waited. Rising beyond the foot-high grasses in front of them were tree boughs thick with summer leaves. The trees had grown wild up out of a low, swampy trough that was just out of view below them, so the upper branches were actually at her eye level, forming a sort of green wall. On the far side of the long trough, perhaps fifty yards east of where they sat, the ground rose up again to meet the bank of the Susquehanna River. Maddy had walked along this edge of the park before and noticed the peculiar, deserted trough. It ran in a long gouge parallel to the river and seemed to serve as a natural overflow area for when the waters ran high. It was dark and dank and vaguely forbidding down there, a sense reinforced by the poison ivy tangled in the grasses on the incline. Maddy knew she and Curtis were sitting atop a ridgeline overlooking the strange trench of land. It placed them a bit south of the old Indian treaty grounds.

"This is one of the places where some people feel the connection," Curtis said finally. He swiveled on his butt to face her. "Tommy told his mom about your vision, Maddy. She wasn't surprised. She told him other people have had visions, she called them inner sightings, down around the Flats like you did.

And at the Point, she said, and on the Chemung up by Wilawana. And right here, too! She told Tommy she had an old aunt who used to come to this very spot, the way she described it. Apparently when she felt bad, like worried or whatever, the lady would sit out here and connect with the old spirits somehow. The aunt is dead now, but she was sure Tutelos and other Indians had been here, and some left, like, messages and blessings to help their people who came later."

"Messages and blessings?" Maddy felt her scalp bristle. *Messages and blessings, still!*

Curtis let her question linger in the air. "Apparently," he finally said with a shrug. "That's what she called them, messages and blessings. And this lady could tune in to them. She told Tommy's mom it would keep her strong and rez-rezilent."

"Resilient?"

"Yeah."

"How?"

"That's what I'm trying to find out."

Curtis pivoted himself back into position, lowered his eyelids, and fell silent. Maddy watched him for a minute, then looked out into the towering canopy of green. Things were coming clearer. Her mind flashed on messages in a bottle, but she knew the Indians of Teaoga country didn't have a written language—and she knew not to be so literal, anyways. *This isn't about actual written messages. The aunt probably heard it in her heart, like a poetic reassurance or something. I felt that, too, the other day. Indians alive nowadays definitely could use them. For strength, sure. Maybe if we dug up their old water jugs, they'd glow like radioactivity and magic messages would float out of them.* The thought gave her a pleasant feeling. She rubbed her palm across the grass, smiling to herself.

"Aren't you even trying?" Curtis was glowering at her. "Help me out here."

"Sheesh, Curtis, okay, you think I'm a sorcerer or something?"

The boy had already closed his eyes again and was fingering the arrowhead. Maddy decided to concentrate. She shut her eyes lightly, just as she remembered doing at the riverside, and let the sensations come as they would. The grass tickled her bare legs. Cars bounced down the street behind them. One thumped out a hip-hop song, the bass set so low she could feel it. Dampness emanated from the lowlands. Her body was still pumping extra heat, and she felt a bit light-headed and thirsty. There was no birdsong this time, no breeze in the listless air. And, surprisingly, no messages, no magic.

Maddy wasn't sure how long she sat. Her mind had begun to empty out. She felt drowsy when she finally opened her eyes. Curtis was studying her. "I must be cursed," he grumbled. "I don't understand. I don't know how this works."

Maddy felt bad for the boy but also didn't want him to fall into another one of his mega-funks. "I don't know, either," she said. "I guess you just can't force it. Or maybe a person can only do it alone. Y'all got me."

Curtis sighed loudly. "One more time." He brought his long lashes together again.

Maddy did the same. And with a crackle, she perceived campfires. The distinctive smell of burning logs hit her as though it had been injected in her nose. "Whuh!" Her eyes flew open, and she steadied herself with one arm. *I just saw campfires down there ... I think. Why campfires? But there were no Indians this time. Maybe I've got heatstroke. Let me try again.*

Her eyelids fluttered and resisted closing. She saw nothing this time, inner or outer. The smell was gone. Everything was normal again. A dog barking down the street dominated her senses—along with a deep confusion. *Either let me have the inner sightings or don't, whoever you are. I'm not afraid of them. But please don't tease. And please share them with Curtis. He deserves it.*

Maddy plucked at the grass. Curtis looked over. "You alright? You look spacey or something."

"Just dizzy," she replied, "and thirsty." She didn't want to frustrate him with the truth. *I'll sit on my own out here later. If I have another vision, it'll confirm that this really is a sacred spot. It's important to be sure of it first, that it wasn't just my crazy imagination. Then I'll tell Curtis everything and invite him to sit with me out here as much as we can. It's so close by. I'll try my best to send the magic beam his way. I'm not sure how, but I'll try.*

"Maybe you should go back and get some water," Curtis said. "I guess we're done. I've gotta get going, anyways. You're lucky you get to be in that history group later. My mom says I'm too young. That's so dumb. But I'm gonna ride bikes with Tommy. First, I gotta go do another *hissss*. See ya."

He scratched at the air like a cat, then leapt up and headed for his bike.

"Thanks," she called after him. "Let's, like, keep trying this. I'll help you."

GRABBING A DIXIE CUP in the first-floor bathroom, Maddy chugged cold water until she belched. She gave herself a long look in the mirror. The girl staring back appeared normal. Maddy felt pretty normal, too. No deep breathing needed this time. The mini-sighting was disconcerting but hadn't knocked her for a loop the way the first one did. Maybe she was just getting accustomed to their zap.

Soon it would be time to head upstairs for the study group, but she wanted to drop in on Katie first. Her friend had agreed to stay posted in the library to wait for the pizza deliveryman.

Maddy toweled her face with cold water, took a deep breath, and proceeded into the library. "Hey, girl, 'sup?" Katie called out. She was sprawled in an armchair in the reading lounge, flipping through National Geographics.

"Woo-hoo, cattle!" Katie grinned, holding out a pullout photo of two snorting creatures being lassoed. "It's actually pretty interesting. Did you know civilizations advanced on the backs of cattle? That's what it says. Here, look at all these cool horns!"

Maddy shoved in beside her. She had no idea cattle's horns came in so many shapes and sizes and even colors. "My dad would go bananas over this," she laughed.

"Yeah, you Texans. Wahoo!" Katie said, and began lurching in the chair like it was a bucking bronco. Maddy gave her a shove. "Plug ya with my six-shooter if y'all don't stop!"

"Uncle, uncle! You better shove off anyways, sweaty sister. I promised my mom I'd bring up the goodies when it arrives." Katie showed her a twenty and a ten rolled up in her side pocket. "Hey, I have an idea for her for an Indian art project. And Curtis gave me an idea that he wants me to tell you guys about. But go now! Rise and shine! Be brilliant!"

"I'll knock 'em dead!"

"You'll go for broke!"

"No holds barred!"

"Rock 'em sock 'em!"

"*Carpe diem*!"

"What?"

Maddy was glad she could flip on the goofy-girl switch so easily. Laughing at their banter, she skipped and stumbled up the stairs to the main floor of the museum.

"Roger dodger!" Katie shouted from below.

Mrs. T had left the air conditioner on full-blast, which was essential during heat waves. Maddy heard people talking in the side conference room, so she headed that way. Walking through the main exhibit space, she let her fingers glide along the antique display cases. Under the glass was a quirky assortment of specimen rocks, shells, pottery fragments, fossils, insects, and, her favorite, the Indian peace pipes.

The conference room was dominated by a long table that had hosted countless formal meetings and public presentations over the decades. Its high walls were lined with landscape paintings and portraits of historic dignitaries, all starchy-solemn, most of them men. Mrs. T, marker in hand, was standing beside a tall easel that held a fresh pad of flip paper. She signaled Maddy to take a seat. Beth and Trevor were already there. Maddy filled a plastic cup with water from a pitcher on the table and nodded to Trevor. The grown-up surroundings gave her a brief wave of butterflies.

"Okay, team, we are all here, thank you, thank you," Mrs. T began. "I know you're all kinda tired. I don't want to keep you overly long, so let's jump right in. I want to start with a quick overview so things are clear."

Her basic goal, she explained, was to prepare supplemental course material about local history for the area's middle schools. Although students learn a bit about state history, she felt the schools miss opportunities to, as she put it, "turn kids on to how many amazing things in our nation's past happened *wherever* you live." Maddy was moved as Mrs. T said, "Maybe I'm a dreamer, but I think learning this history will not only make you smarter and more curious, but will help you appreciate your own community."

The school principal had asked Mrs. T to present something to him by the end of this summer. She said she wanted to be sure the material is engaging, multi-media, and what she called "pitch-perfect" for middle schoolers.

"Trevor, Maddy, you know how kids your age think and react. If something is stupid or off the point, kids will shut down to it, so I need you to flag that. Beth, you've taken courses on secondary education, plus you know a lot about our settler history, so you're an important voice in this.

"Remember, we're a creative team. Let's have lots of give-and-take and brainstorming! I'm looking for fresh ideas. Any questions before we get started?"

Beth jumped in. "What years in time are we covering?"

"Great question. Let's start with the Indians. I hope we can get up to the settler days and the French asylum community and the Pennsylvania-Connecticut conflicts. But definitely the Native American era will be told, because it was so important and kids usually can relate to Indians. In fact, let's focus on Native American themes for starters tonight."

In a loopy script, Mrs. T wrote the word *decorum* on the easel paper. "I've been thinking a lot about how to explain Indian ways beyond the familiar tomahawks and moccasins," she explained. "A big one for me is decorum. The Indians had a strong code of manners and treated others in their community with a formality that might seem clunky to us but that I find elegant. They also spoke to whites that way, too, according to the records that have come down to us."

She held up a paper from her folder. "Let me give you an example. This is from a peace conference held right here in 1790. A famous Seneca chief named Red Jacket was addressing Timothy Pickering, the U.S. representative. Listen to this: 'Brother, we are happy to see you here, for which we thank the Great Spirit. Brother, you say you are not acquainted with our customs. Brother, we are young, but we will describe the ancient practices of our fathers. The roads we now travel were cleared by them.'

"Get it? Everyone was an esteemed brother, or sister, or grandfather, whether they were related or not. By the way, the Quakers of the time had a similar form of grand speaking, using lots of biblical thee's and thou's and thine's when they addressed people. It was called Quaker Plain Speech and expressed their belief in democratic equality. I suppose the Indians also had a sense of equality before the Great Spirit. They had lots of lyrical turns of phrase and repetition and metaphors. It'd be great to have kids try that in the classroom. I imagine asking for volunteers to come forward ..."

"I've got it!" Maddy blurted. Ideas were popping. "Have two kids go to the front. Ask them to greet each other the way they would normally. So they say, 'Yo, bro, what's jumpin,' or something like that. Then have the teacher chime in with an Indian greeting, like, 'May the sun warm your way always, Daughter.' Does that sound right? The teacher's gotta explain that this is realistic Indian talk and get them to start seeing it as, like, graceful and poetic. Otherwise, the kids will mock it and start coming up with crazy stuff. Get them to understand that the Indians saw one another as, like, noble, or, as my pastor would say, God's children. You could have kids pair off and try it with one another. Have them write down some of their best greetings, and have the teacher add actual ones from Indian history. How's that sound? I think it'd work."

Mrs. T was grinning. "You betcha it would, Maddy! Very interactive! Did you just think of that? You're right that the mindset has to be explained. To do it best, the kids should say their greetings slowly and look into one another's eyes. The formality is foreign to most kids' lives today, so it might be a shock, but I think it'll resonate.

"Also, Maddy, you mentioned God's children. That reminds me of another important topic on my list, which is Indian spirituality." She wrote the word *pantheism* on the big pad. "The Indians believed in their Great Spirit, the Preserver, the One Above All. Yet they also believed the world was filled with lesser spirits. In their world, the woods were the home of wise guiding spirits. They'd go on vision quests to find their personal guide. But the woods were also filled with supernatural sprites and dark forces that would knock you astray. That's pantheism, and you don't really understand the Indian mind unless you appreciate that outlook. It's hard for us to grasp today, though, and I wonder how it's best to teach it so it's meaningful and not just strange."

Beth raised her hand. "Mrs. T, actually, I think it may be best to go light on that since it's religion. Religion can be controversial. Maybe not say much more than the minimum about it, with no special activities."

"Aw, I think it's cool," said Trevor. "Wood sprites isn't religion."

"It is where I'm from," Maddy countered. "I don't have a problem with it, but I can picture lots of the parents and even some of the kids not liking it if we were taught about dark spirits, or even the Great Spirit. If some churches found out, they might complain. It's happened before. Sorry, I've got to agree with Beth."

"It's true that religion can be a hot potato," Mrs. T said. "Let me think about it. And I'll discuss it with the principal. But thanks for the input. I'm certainly not looking to buy trouble."

"PIZZA TIME! RIGHT THIS way for your goopy-droopy slices!"

Katie swept into the room balancing two aromatic takeout boxes in her arms. "Me hungry like cave girl! Grabby-grabby!"

"All right, love, thanks," Mrs. T said, placing the boxes in the center of the table. "Everybody dig in!"

The team set out the food along with cold drinks that Trevor fetched from downstairs. Katie sat beside Maddy and gobbled merrily. Maddy was surprised how hungry she was, and even bargained with Katie to split a third slice.

Afterwards, they sat back and crunched the last chips of ice from their drinks while Mrs. T typed notes into her laptop. Maddy was eager to continue. She wondered if Mrs. T could have possibly known how much she dug vocabulary. For her eleventh birthday, Maddy had actually asked for and gotten an enormous reference dictionary. Her parents' har-har card had said "with love, to our most favoritist word nerd!" Maddy welcomed the dictionary as a brilliant friend spooning out the world of words to her so she could say things just right. Like exactly which sort of anger did one feel at a given moment, *scorn* or *antipathy* or outright *rage*? Which degree of delight? Which shade of skin? What type of humor? Any feeling of dorkiness her love of words—her *lexiophilia* —gave her, eased when Mel had happily started poring over the entries as well. They spent hours flipping through the oversize pages together, enunciating the crisply stated definitions and trying to stump each other with oddball words.

As Maddy waited restlessly, wondering if it was correct to say the pizza smelled cheesy, she noticed that Mrs. T's easel pad had caught Katie's eye. Katie mouthed the words *decorum* and *pantheism*.

"Mom, I know the pantheism thing must be about Indians," she said aloud. "I have another subject word for us: *tattoo*. It's from Curty."

Mrs. T cocked an eyebrow. The others turned to listen.

"Curtis begged me to bring it up," Katie explained. "He's dying to have Indians seem wicked-cool, especially to boys, since he feels like some kids make fun of them. So many people around town have tattoos, like massive body tattoos, and he wants them to know Indians did that, too. He thinks they did it way-better. You know how the braves rubbed dirt and charcoal and stuff into lines and punctures they cut in their skin, and painted their faces and bodies with animal shapes."

"Whoa, hold up," Mrs. T interrupted. "Art projects are one thing, but we don't want kids smearing themselves up in school. I can see that getting out of control real quick. And even the very notion of cutting—let's not go there."

"No duh," Katie said. "That's not what Curty was suggesting. He had a pretty neat approach. He said have people make personal face masks out of papier-mache and decorate them with Indian tattoo designs."

Trevor threw up his hand. "Wait, Katie, here's another way! I'll bet there's a program on our school computers that would let kids design an entire body image and then tattoo and paint it digitally. If there isn't one, I'll work with the tech club to develop it, maybe."

"Right, I can see that working, Trevor," Mrs. T said. "Good thinking! I'll bring it up with the school folks."

"Wait, wait!" Maddy called out. Her online browsing of the past week was coming back to her. "You can do more with that. I have an idea for the guiding-spirit thing. Have the kids work in pairs, like you said they'd do with the greetings. Here you go: Pair up boys with girls. They sit and, like, interview each other about their favorite animal from the Indian woods. Not crazy stuff like zebras and heffalumps. I mean owls, wolves, fish, crickets, like that. The Indians believed each animal had a special power—wisdom, strength, trust, gentleness, right? Have that list be available for the class. Tell the students to think about why they're picking their particular animal, how it fits their personality, feelings it gives them, special memories or experiences, whatever. Have their tattoos represent their animals. Have the boy design the girl's tattoo and the girl do the boy's! Tell them it's got to be respectful, and has to represent what the other person shared about himself or herself. So they could paint the animal on one side of the face, and some symbol of the memory or story on the other, or on the shoulders or neck."

Maddy was talking fast. Mrs. T was wide-eyed. "Maddy, you're giving me goosebumps over here! Where do you get these amazing ideas?"

"Yeah, you rock, sister!" Katie said. "I want to build on that, too. I was only gonna bring up Curty's idea, but I've been thinking about wampum."

"Really?" Mrs. T said. "Okay, go for it."

"I'm still figuring it out," Katie continued. "Imagine, like, an art project where the kids get strips of cloth or heavy paper shaped like a wampum belt. You know, something heavy that doesn't rip. They could mark them up with faint lines like graph paper. Then, say the kids paired off the same way. The assignment was to talk to each other about what their Indian name might be. It's sort of like the animal spirit idea, but they're free to just think about something in their personality that makes them special or that they want to represent. I know a boy who gave himself the Indian name of Bear Paw, which is a power symbol. But it doesn't have to be an Indian name. It could be, like, Bleeding Heart if you're a real sympathetic-type person! Or, like, Song Catcher if you want to be a musician! Get the idea? Let the kids think creatively."

"Good, good!" Mrs. T said. She was madly typing on her laptop.

"Thanks, Mom. And then the kids could fill in their wampum belts with pictures that represent their names! There could be traditional images like bears or trees, or modern ones like footballs! What the hey, let's get real!"

"Here's an extra idea," Beth volunteered. "Have each person select a name for himself or herself. But then have the other person give a name for their partner that's based on *their* impressions of the person. Again, it has to be respectful. So then they decorate each other's belts with a picture for that name. So my belt would have both *my* picture of me and *your* picture of me."

"Let me get this straight," Mrs. T said. "Say kid A wants to be a writer, and so she represents herself with a picture of a quill pen. But kid B pictures kid A as real friendly, so maybe he represents her with, say, a heart or a smile?"

"Exactly," Beth replied. "And if they came up with names, they could add them to the belts, above or below the pictures."

Mrs. T finished typing before speaking. "By the way, team, those pictures are called pictographs, which is something we'd want to explain as part of the lesson. So anyway, wow, there's a lot of rich material here. I may have to combine the tattooing and the wampum into one art project. But it certainly sounds like a winner to me. Let me ask you three young-uns: You're pretty confident it would fly with kids your age?"

"Definitely," Maddy replied. "As long as they're serious. The goofy kids can try to mess up anything, so you have to have a good teacher. But here's what I like. Kids my age can be so nasty with each other. These projects can make them pay attention to each other in a good way. And one-on-one is best because there's not a third person you're trying to impress."

"Maddy's right," Katie added. "The Indian stuff itself is great to know, and if it can also help cut through the mean, gossipy crap that kids put out, that'd be awesome."

Mrs. T looked over at Trevor, who nodded.

"Well, gang, this is a super start," Mrs. T said, looking around the table. "I don't know about you, but my head is about to fall over from all the information. And I'm in bad need of a shower. Let's clean up and call it a wrap, okay?"

Katie was already on her feet, whistling, as she gathered up the used plates and napkins. Maddy grabbed the empty pizza boxes. The brainstorming had put her in a Rockn mood.

"These containers are still rather pungently odiferous, wouldn't you agree, dahling?" she announced through pursed lips.

"Oh, quite, indeed," Katie replied, stiffening into character. She gestured to the portrait of a long-ago town father that hung over her shoulder. "Poor old Uncle Roscoe there. We must evacuate this detritus posthaste or his gout will protuberate in a most ghastly manner!"

The girls laughed their way out of the room, Maddy delighted by Katie's wit and surprising vocabulary. *Am I agog, or just stupefied? She's a real hoot. Why did I sell her short?*

Meanwhile, old Uncle Roscoe cast a frozen stare across the room as Mrs. T flipped off the light.

Chapter 13

Pickering awoke long before first light. The news that a runner from the west had brought to his quarters at nightfall made sleep difficult. He lay on his cot staring into the darkness, wrestling with gloomy thoughts, and considering how to proceed.

According to the exhausted messenger's report, one of the four hooligan settlers who murdered the two Senecas in cold blood at Pine Creek—forcing the crisis that brought him to Teaoga—had been set free by a backwoods court. Why? Because no other settlers would testify against him! Disgusted words came to Pickering's mind—*mortifying, heinous*—as he mulled the realization that more and more settlers consider the murdering of Indians in times of peace to be no crime at all.

In his brief time at the council fire, the colonel had come to admire the Indians' honest if forceful dealings. Red Jacket could be prickly, yet Pickering understood the intention behind the Seneca leader's wariness and bold challenges. Overall, the chiefs' uprightness pleased his Puritan honor and military code. To his great satisfaction, the respect seemed to be mutual. The chiefs had actually given Pickering an Indian name, Brother Conni-sauti, and were using it in their formal council speeches.

Pickering had asked Red Jacket what the name meant. The reply puzzled him: "sunny side of a hill." Red Jacket pointed to the nearby ridgeline and explained. Two days earlier, he said, the chiefs had watched Pickering walking along the ridge, checking on the white and native sentries posted to keep the peace. The sun on that bright day had made his chiseled face and strong frame gleam, the chief said, "You carry Father Sun's strength well, like a warrior, and, on that day, like a sturdy hill." Pickering had glowed in private pleasure. How remarkable, he'd thought, to be compared to a hill! What an extraordinary story to tell his sons.

All the diplomatic goodwill he'd nurtured, however, was endangered by this untimely report of the courtroom acquittal. Pickering's tactical mind knew what to do even before the words came clear. The explosive news must be kept secret for the time being. The upcoming council session was too important, and certainly too delicate, to risk disrupting. This was to be the day of the condolence ceremony for the Seneca mourners. The chiefs and the families would find out about the acquittal soon enough. Better to let the dignity of the moment be preserved.

Besides, Pickering could not afford to have the chiefs accuse him of deceiving them about his government's stated good intentions. In fury, they might storm out of the council, making all his work a failure in President Washington's eyes. The Senecas might even lift their war hatchets again. Both possibilities were horrifying. No, he would instruct his aides to say nothing. If this was deceptive, it was for a greater good. He must salvage the proceedings and depart in peace. Later, in his official report, he would express his outrage at the acquittal and call on President Washington to publicly demand that a measure of justice be attained for the Pine Creek victims.

Satisfied with this decision, Pickering rose and went to his field desk, where he spent the next candlelit hour updating his journal. As was his habit, he also penned a daily letter to his family. Before donning his woolen greatcoat, he studied the inventory of food, supplies, and gifts that Hollenback's assistant had recorded in a semi-literate hand. There were checkmarks next to the items designated to be condolence gifts: "camp ketles/crockry, 2 keggs tobaco, 2 casks pouder, 2 sett o bouls." He pictured himself presenting the gifts to the bereaved Seneca families. The image brought a heavy sigh.

BY THE TIME SHE TOOK HER PLACE at the treaty grounds, Sisketung already felt weary. She had worked well into the cold night, straining her eyes by the campfire to rethread the purple wampum. Under Mother Esther's guidance, the girl had been able to carefully reuse the filaments of old deer sinew. She'd gladly set aside the cotton thread from Hollenback's trading post. Knowing their condolence gift would bear no yengwe elements pleased her Tutelo heart.

Working with artful care, Sisketung had restrung two strands of the cylindrical purple quahog shells on the dampened sinew, then prepared decorative loops of the thinnest and most delicate porcupine quills. Already in her young life, she had discovered a way of taking things apart with her mind, even before touching them with her fingers, and letting them speak their wishes to her. In this way she assisted the individual quills, stringing and restringing them patiently until their shaded colors seemed to match just right. Then she deftly attached each loop to an end of both wampum strands.

Finally, Sisketung held the strings up to the firelight, tested the knots, and imagined her work becoming part of a full wampum belt. The finished strings were perfect to her eyes.

She turned to show Cakoanos and Esther. By then, both women were lost in sleep beneath their gathered blankets.

Mother Esther had told her that other fire circles were also preparing condolence strings for the mourners. Grasping her handiwork carefully, Sisketung made her way in the dark across the sleeping campground to the shelter of the Seneca head matron.

Several women were gathered outside the shelter, near the matron's flickering fire. A white blanket was spread out at their feet. Sisketung noticed other wampum strings arrayed on the cloth. Two women were holding torches and humming contentedly as they examined the pieces, turned them in their palms, and discussed the different designs. They lay the strands back on the blanket in different patterns, deciding on possible configurations. These two were the master weavers, Sisketung realized. Mother Esther had told her that their task would be to spend the next hours joining the campground's gifts together into Pickering's two official condolence belts.

"Sisters," the head matron smiled, "see what our Tutelo daughter has brought. Such fine work! Sisters, see how the girl has used only sinew. And the best quills—neck quills that seem to be freshly prepared. Yes, daughter? Are these precious offerings from the same brother animal that gave himself to your circle? His quills will be a blessed addition to the shells and beads."

Stroking the girl's cheek lightly, she said, "Daughter, you have made Brother Porcupine proud. You have made your people proud. Tell your circle we gladly add your nation's condolence gift to ours."

Sisketung smiled politely. She bent to touch and admire the other strings on the blanket, then withdrew to her shelter. Her heart was full as she slipped beneath the bearskin.

CURRENTS OF EMOTION HAD come to Pickering during previous sessions at the council fire. It might be a tension, or impatience, or perhaps his own lingering worry about his public performance. But the emotion this day was different, he knew, and it did not come from within himself. It was melancholy he sensed. An unmistakable atmosphere of sadness was drifting up from the Indian campground. It had begun not long after daybreak, when he heard mournful noises rising and falling from the distant fire circles. He'd been conducting his breakfast meeting with his assistants—informing them about the murder acquittal, in fact, and instructing them to keep silent about it—when the unusual low keening sounds reached their ears.

Pickering summoned the native interpreter, who explained to the men that they were hearing Seneca funeral songs. In preparation for the condolence ceremony, she said, the Seneca adults had congregated around the two grieving families below. The men gathered on one side of their fire, the women on the other, and sang long dirges to console the mourners. Most of the tribe's elaborate funeral customs had been performed months earlier in the two families' villages, she said. This extra round of songs was being offered to honor and support the grieving parents through the emotion of Pickering's imminent presentation.

The interpreter had another bit of news as well. The Seneca matrons had just provided her with the two special wampum belts that Pickering requested. However, she added, they did not want money in return. When one of his aides had offered payment, the matrons insisted that the money be used to obtain extra beef for the two families. The packages of beef could be added to the official gifts, if Pickering approved. Moved by the women's selfless gesture, he instructed her to convey his whole-hearted approval.

Before departing, the interpreter presented him with a beaded deerskin pouch. In it were the two freshly made wampum belts. Pickering held them up to show his assistants. Each contained the customary fifteen sympathy strings. His eye was caught by the lovely purple loops protruding from the ends of each belt. He ran his finger along the delicate porcupine quills, thinking how his wife would admire the skilled handiwork.

The council session began later than usual, long after the morning frost had disappeared. Though the colonel and his men took their positions beside the fire as normal, the natives were painfully slow to arrive. They seemed to drag themselves up the wide trail from the campground. The interpreter explained that the sachems were delayed, because they were sitting with the families for a final smoke that would mingle with the dead men's spirits in the sky world.

At last, Red Jacket and the other chiefs and sachems took their places across the council fire. The native assembly behind them steadily grew in size. Esther and the Tutelos crouched in their accustomed places. Esther had been quiet throughout the morning's dirge-singing. Sisketung saw that the old woman appeared especially careworn, and even wearier than she.

Everyone knew the council was winding down, so the Pine Tree chiefs began the session with formal speeches that summarized Pickering's pronouncements and their responses. Farmer's Brother told Pickering that the chiefs would accept the written copies of his speeches that the colonel had been presenting to them, even though the custom had been to use wampum belts as an official record of treaties and councils.

Red Jacket saw a chance for another verbal jab. He rose grandly to his feet and faced the assembly. "Our forefathers told us that when a treaty was finished, by preserving the belts used, we would know and could tell our children what had been done." Murmurs of agreement followed. Then Red Jacket held out a wampum belt that he said the yengwe Continental Congress had presented many winters earlier. It bore twelve strings and thirteen spots.

"This belt was once before given to us to brighten the chain of friendship," the chief said, staring at Pickering. "You may think that we lie, but here it is. You can look at it. I gave you this to hang upon the chain where it has been hung once before."

The colonel solemnly took the belt in hand. He locked his eyes on it, feeling the history and hopes imbedded in its pictographs. His meditation helped the proper response emerge.

"Brothers, through this belt and our written words, let us pledge to remember the promises we have made," Pickering declared, looking across the assembly. "Let us take care of them, and turn to them often as remembrances, and repeat the pledges to our children. Brothers, know that I have set my hand and seal to my words. Know that you can present my papers as proof to our governments and to our leading men. Brothers, as long as the sun shines and the rivers run, this will be so."

Sisketung listened with care, not to memorize the speeches but to keep the proceedings clear in her recollection. She joined the others in calling out approval of Pickering's translated promise. Behind her, Esther remained silent. The girl would have expected her to lean in with comments. She turned to check. The old woman was impassively watching an elderly Seneca pair slowly rise to their feet nearby. Sisketung observed as well as the crowd parted to let the aged couple walk forward toward the council fire. The man had his hand on his wife's bent shoulder. It was then that Sisketung noticed he was missing two fingers. This was the friendly old man who had shared his pudding with her. He was one of the two fathers in mourning.

STANDING IN PLACE BEFORE the council fire, Pickering studied the two Seneca couples advancing toward him from the assembly. Earlier, Farmer's Brother had discreetly pointed them out and explained that they would approach the fire and stand for the condolence ceremony. Pickering, the chief said, must understand that his people would put less emphasis on a yengwe court verdict for the white killers than they would on properly covering the victims' graves with condolence gifts. By distributing these gifts to the relatives, the colonel would spiritually wash away the victims' blood and ease the mourners' hearts.

Pickering nodded formally to the two couples, then beckoned to an aide to bring him the pouch containing the two new wampum belts. As he took the deerskin pouch in hand, the colonel passed Red Jacket's friendship belt back to the aide. He turned and gestured to a field table behind them where the friendship belt's twelve strings and thirteen spots could be properly displayed for all to see.

As Pickering faced the Indian assembly again, he had to force down a wave of light-headedness. The somber moment had come. Before him stood the four parents, a chilly breeze riffling their braided hair. The two mothers swayed slightly, their mouths twisted, eyes hollow. The chiefs sat in their customary semicircle, silent and waiting, along with the blanketed crowd behind them.

The colonel scanned them all, then lowered his eyes to the two purple belts that seemed to pulsate in his hands. Images filled his mind, of his own family, of the mocking settlers, of hatchets flashing, of President Washington's hand on his shoulder. He knew what he must say. It must be formal and restrained. Any sentiment must be clothed in dignity. It must avoid Bible talk, to not invite unnecessary controversy. He steeled himself and began.

"Brothers, the business for which this council fire was kindled is now finished," he intoned in a strong voice. "The hatchet has been buried. The chain of friendship is made bright. But before the fire is put out, I must address a few words to the relations of our two murdered brothers. My friends, you are now assembled to receive the last public testimony of respect to the memory of our two brothers whose untimely death we have joined in lamenting."

Pickering paused while the Indian interpreter translated his words. Willing himself to speak slowly, and to face the four parents directly, he resumed.

"Mothers, you have lost two worthy sons from whom you expected support and comfort in your old age. You appear bowed down with sorrow as with years. Your affliction must be very great. I also am a parent, the parent of many sons, the loss of any one of whom would fill me with distress. I therefore can feel for yours."

He stopped again to allow for the translation. Some in the crowd had begun a low moan. The two mothers looked at him without seeing as they continued their slow rocking. Feeling the impact of their bottomless grief, Pickering struggled not to be overcome. He inhaled deeply and summoned the strength of pastors whose eloquent eulogies had inspired him in times past.

"Brothers and Sisters," he intoned, "you have lost two valuable relations, whose assistance was useful, and whose company was pleasing to you, and with whom you expected to pass yet many happy years. With you also I can join in mourning your misfortune.

"Mothers, Brothers, and Sisters, let me endeavor to assuage your grief. You enjoy the satisfaction of remembering the good qualities of your sons and brothers, of reflecting that they were worthy men, and of hearing their names mentioned with honor. Let these considerations afford you some comfort. Death, you know, is the common lot of all mankind, and none can escape its stroke. Some, indeed, live many years till, like well-ripened corn, they wither and bend down their heads. But multitudes fall in infancy and childhood, like the tender shooting corn nipped by untimely frosts. Others again grown up to manhood are then cut off, while full of sap, and flourishing in all the vigor of life. The latter, it seems, was the state of our two deceased brothers. But my friends, they are gone, and we cannot bring them back. When the Great Spirit shall order it, we must follow them: but they cannot return to us. This is the unalterable course of things, and it is our duty patiently to bear our misfortunes."

Pickering raised the condolence belts in his outstretched arms. He walked around the fire and approached the two women. Their husbands stood behind them, hands on their right shoulders.

"Mothers," the colonel said, "to manifest the sorrow of the United States for the loss of your sons, and that you and your families may always have with you the usual tokens of remembrance, I now present to you these belts."

The keening in the assembly grew louder, mixed with chants and a few condolence songs.

Suddenly, Sisketung heard stirrings behind her. She turned to see her own mother reach toward Esther. The old woman had risen abruptly and was moving towards the back of the crowd.

"Mother Esther is sorely troubled," Cakoanos whispered to her companions. "Perhaps the past speaks to her. Daughter, come. Let us accompany her back to her shelter."

They withdrew as their companions wished them well. Sisketung noticed that a few other Senecas were also departing, seemingly stricken with their own personal grief.

At the council fire, Pickering spoke on. Sisketung heard him announce the various condolence gifts, which he said would be distributed the next day. He thanked the matrons for providing the extra beef. And he praised the artisans for the condolence belts. "Most fine," he called them.

Sisketung lingered over his words. The recognition pleased her. "Most fine," she repeated to herself. Pausing for a backward glance, she saw the four mourners shuffle back into the crowd's embrace.

Farther down on the trail, her mother called for her to hurry. Esther was striding far ahead with surprising energy. Sisketung, alarm mounting, rushed to catch up.

"Preserver, bring us strength," she prayed.

Chapter 14

Maddy scooched sideways on the grass to avoid the direct sun blasting through the treetops. It was late afternoon. Academy Park was empty and quiet, just as she'd hoped. A few minutes earlier, she'd slipped out of the museum and took up a solitary position at her spot, seated Indian-style. She was determined to continue her vigil from the day before until it was time to head indoors for the study group. *Please, Indian spirits or whatever you are, make yourself known again, and reveal yourselves to Curtis before his head explodes. Or at least before I return to Texas. Time's growing short, o mysterious whatevers.*

She sat quietly, eyes shut, fighting off self-consciousness. Fortunately, Mz Snarkley was absent. Light thoughts loped across Maddy's mindscape like bunnies. She pictured her campers, and little Lucy's tears about the twig wigwam that Jason had crushed with bratty delight that morning. A bead of sweat slid down her spine beneath her tangerine tee. The dead air was oppressive. Her inner eye saw turkey vultures rising on the heat. She imagined the coolness of the river current. *It must be a gazillion degrees back home.* Her thoughts turned to Houston and her gal-pal Melody. On a sweltering day like today, they'd probably be hanging in her air-conditioned great room. She pictured them making fun of some TV rerun, chugging iced tea, teasing Tiara-Cat, practicing their funky dance moves as the Supersonic M&M Sisters.

I haven't contacted Mel for a few days. Some bud I am. But s'okay, I'm sure she's finding stuff to do. I'll see her soon enough. Wow, only five more days here. I've been in another world.

The free-floating thoughts were interrupted by a fly landing on her forehead. Next it tickled her ear. Eyes still closed, she reached lazily to brush the insect off.

She swatted—and felt her breath taken away.

Her upper body was suddenly rising, pulled forward by a gentle force. In the pink world behind her eyelids, she was aware of being stretched and lifted in a long arc above the tall grass. It was as though she were made of taffy.

From the wooded trough below, an elongated being reached out and grasped her outstretched hands. A young Indian woman—no, a girl, about her age— ephemeral like smoke, floating gracefully, drew Maddy upwards in a swaying dance.

Yielding to the spirit girl's soft smile, Maddy was bathed in contentment. She felt herself floating overhead, filled with warmth, fingers entwined with the spirit. Like the two halves of an undulating rainbow, they stretched together towards the treetops. She perceived campfires down below, and women's chant-song. The spirit girl circled her directly above the high grass, revolving over and over, conveying with her eyes that there along the ridgeline lay a source of abiding strength for her.

Then the spirit lowered Maddy back into her sitting body, withdrew toward the trees, and evaporated.

The aura of peacefulness remained. Unwilling to open her eyes or let go of the sweet sense of motion, Maddy swayed in place, humming dreamily. Flies circled her head. She was aware again of their buzzing and of the sticky heat. But far more than that, she felt bliss and a calm inner strength she was certain the spirit had imparted. She smiled in gratitude. *The spirit girl had a message for me. What was it? Maybe like encouragement? It felt that way. Why did she pick me?*

"Maddy. Maddy dear?"

Mrs. T stood in the grass beside her, calling softly. "Are you okay, dear? You've been wobbling down there like you're about to faint. Here, have some water."

Maddy looked up blankly and licked her dry lips. "Hi. Yeah ... uh ... hi. Thanks." She took the water bottle and drank dutifully. The cold water brought her more into her normal body. She splashed some on her hands and rinsed her face.

"Lucy told me she saw you out here alone," Mrs. T said. "Are you okay?"

Maddy rocked her head from side to side and sighed.

"You saw something, dear? ... Mmm, you *saw* something."

"Oh, Mrs. T. Whew." She couldn't pretend and didn't want to. Her guard was down. She'd have to trust that Mrs. T would understand.

"Yeah, I saw something. Just now. That's why I was out here. I heard that this was a, a magic place."

Mrs. T crouched and waited for her to continue.

"I'm not sure what it was.... Sort of a spirit. Wispy. An Indian girl, floating, lifting me. Mrs. T, it was beautiful. It felt *so* good. She didn't speak, but somehow she told me that, like, all was well. It was sort of like in church, you know, when I'd feel Jesus hugging me. But not exactly. She didn't come from heaven—she came from the ground, right here. I must sound crazy. Maybe the heat has fried my brain."

Mrs. T offered an embrace. "Seems Teaoga's veil parted for you," she whispered into Maddy's ear.

Maddy leaned onto the woman's shoulder and unloosed blubbering sobs. Her relief at being able to open up and be understood was mixed with the contentment that continued to pulse through her. She wiped her eyes and looked over. Mrs. T's eyes were glistening as well.

"Dear girl, you are not alone." She straightened Maddy up, took her fingertips in hand, and looked far into her eyes. "Listen, let me tell you a story. One weekend a few years ago, we had a Seneca woman come down to speak at the museum, all about native crafts and healing. She was outstanding. Afterwards, she slipped outside. I found her walking around the building. Pacing."

Maddy understood.

"She wouldn't say much, Maddy—but she did tell me her people believed there was a sacred spot near the museum. That was her term: a sacred spot. I could tell she wanted to be left alone. Later, I saw her standing out here, chanting and swaying. She was standing at this very back spot."

Maddy knew, even before Mrs. T finished. She could picture the Seneca woman and sense her communication. She imagined the woman steering clear of the hissing stone and its negative force. It was good the boulder was a safe distance from the park and ridgeline.

"After that day, Maddy, I came here, too, sometimes. It's definitely a place of peacefulness. Sometimes I'll meditate and nothing special will happen. Sometimes I'll get a glimmer of something across time. Nothing as amazing as your vision and the *liftoff* you felt. Are you sure you're not Indian?"

She rubbed the girl's green fingernails absently. "The last time it really worked for me was just last spring. I was thinking about the local history teaching, you know, and wanting to add to the curriculum. I sat here and got the same kind of *wordless* message you described, of strength in my plan, and a burst of confidence and, I dunno, clarity that it was the right thing to do. My, this sounds a bit crazy."

Maddy had to snicker. "I'm no one to talk." She slurped more water and considered: *Should I tell her about Curtis's vision quest? That's why I was out here in the first place. No, don't. That would be violating his trust. I wouldn't want anyone telling Dad about me. But I'm glad I've told Mrs. T. She understands. She's been there!*

"Mrs. T, crazy is sorta how this vision stuff makes me feel, too. Like I'm happy and confused and embarrassed all at the same time. Do you think we're just imagining it, that it's maybe wishful thinking?"

"You mean is it there just because we want it to be there? In part, perhaps. But Maddy, some of the visions came to you before you knew anything about anything, right? It sounds like enough people have had similar enough experiences, separately, that it's not just our minds playing tricks on us. To me, the challenge is moving back into normal everyday. Remember in Star Wars —'may the force be with you'? I figure the force is with me, but that it's my own force, just with some extra clarity and strength of purpose from my secret source."

"Extra clarity and strength. Yeah," Maddy smiled. "I'll try it. I want to hold on to the super-pleasant feeling, too."

"Definitely."

"Mrs. T, speaking of secret, please keep this secret. I don't want everyone to know just yet. It would, like, weird them out."

"You betcha, dear. It is totally, totally safe with me. And please don't tell my kids about *my* stuff, either. It's personal information."

Mrs. T hauled herself to her feet. "Meanwhile, let's go blow our noses and set up the conference room. We have more work to do. May the force be with us."

ENTERING THE BUILDING FOYER, they could see Katie inside the nearly-empty library, slouched in a reading chair and leafing through a softball handbook. Katie spotted them right away and called out, "Wuzzup, Wigwam Wonder?!" Maddy returned a wave, but Mrs. T steered her away up the grand staircase to the museum floor, whispering "C'mon, you need a little more time to recover, to *decompress*." Maddy nodded in gratitude.

"One extra pepperoni, one Hawaiian Delite, and one special surprise tonight!" was shouted at them from below. "Gobble-gobble!"

In the upstairs board room, the town fathers posed austerely in their gilt frames while Mrs. T and Maddy began to straighten the chairs. They set out water bottles, aimed the floor fans, and positioned the flip chart on the easel in the corner. Maddy worked in a stupor. *I felt cherishment. I wonder if that's a word. It should be. Now, let's see if I can bring my best clarity tonight.*

Mrs. T was also moving slowly. "Maddy," she said finally, "let me ask you one last thing. Do you think Queen Esther was the spirit? I've never sensed her presence, though I'm always on the lookout."

"I don't think so. Hate to disappoint you, but it was a girl more or less my age. It could have been Esther when she was young … but something tells me no."

"No what?" Beth strode into the room, with Trevor behind.

Maddy turned mutely to Mrs. T. It felt like a spell had been broken.

"We were just talking about Queen Esther. Maddy and I both find her fascinating."

"She surely is," Beth said. She and Trevor took seats, cracked open their bottles, and looked up expectantly.

Mrs. T opened her laptop on the table and rubbed her palms together. Maddy could feel her trying to shift into teacher mode.

"Okay, then, I guess we're ready to resume," Mrs. T began with a nod. "Thanks again for being here, gang. I hope it stays cool enough for us. Katie will join us with goodies in a few.

"First off, I haven't had a chance to review the great ideas you all came up with yesterday. I promise to do that ASAP. But let's just keep pushing ahead. Today I want to try out a different exercise and get your response. Trevor, would you come up here?"

She handed the boy two markers, green and red, and had him stand at the easel.

"The goal of this exercise," she said, "is to explain some big concepts about Indian and settler history. I want the ideas to be fresh and new to the kids. And I've developed a set of identifying terms for the concepts that I hope will grab their curiosity. The terms will be introduced like spelling words, meaning this can double as a history lesson and a vocab exercise. Get it?"

She glanced around. The others returned encouraging looks. Maddy was feeling pretty alert. "Sure, so far so good," Beth replied.

"The trick is to have the concepts be a stretch but not be too sophisticated. Same with the words themselves. So, middle-schoolers, I need your feedback on that. Trevor, I'm going to go through each word. I want you to write them out on the easel. If you feel sure you know how to spell the word, use the green marker. If not, use the red one. Clear enough?

Trevor uncapped the markers and saluted with a grin.

From a list on her laptop, Mrs. T called out the first word: FLUX.

Trevor immediately raised the green marker and wrote in a rather clumsy cursive: *flux*. "Easy!"

"Nice," Mrs. T said. "Know what it means, Trevor?"

"Change, right?"

"Right-o. Maddy, remember I used the word with you when we were down at the Point last week. Flux describes the situation for the Indians in the early and middle times of European contact. It was change, yes, but it was really more like upheaval and chaos.

112

"In biology, you might already know, flux refers to the movement of molecules across a membrane. In human terms, think of the Indian borderlands as their membranes. The borders were broken down by land sales and white trespassing. Foreign molecules—European settlers—began pouring in and kept pouring in. It was a dangerous, unpredictable time, particularly in the 1700s, and some of the borderland in flux was right here along the upper Susquehanna."

She consulted her laptop. "Let's do another term. Try COMMODIFICATION."

Trevor screwed up his face. Maddy could sense the gears turning. He's *flummoxed. Flustered. Flabbergasted.* She was in the moment and grateful for it.

Trevor took the green marker, hesitated, and used the red one instead. After a few practice strokes in the air, he wrote *comodification.*

"Ooo, close," Mrs. T said. "Make that a double-M and you're in business." He made the correction to a smattering of applause.

"Okay, so what is this fancy word, team? You'll find it's one of the most important fluxxy concepts of all, one that changed everything for the Indians."

"It has to do with the Indian trade, right?" Beth asked.

"Yes, the trading with the whites." She turned to the group. "Beforehand, Indians in the east would carefully use what they needed from animals for food, clothing, shelter, weapons, cultural things like rattles, jewelry, and so forth. They might trade some of those goods with other Indians as a kind of barter, but it was small-scale and carefully done. When the Europeans came, they brought a huge demand for these things, especially animal skins and furs. A constant, runaway demand! For clothes and hats back home, more, more! The Europeans turned these animal goods into products for sale on the barrelhead— commodities. And they offered new things in return that the Indians came to covet and even depend on. Things like metal kettles and scissors, blankets, cloth, glass beads, flour, muskets, gunpowder, demon rum. This exchange of goods became known as the Atlantic trade.

"So over a few generations, native animals were almost wiped out in some cases. Most of the Indians steadily bought into this new trade. While some resisted because of how it undermined their culture, many others were willing to turn their old animal friends into wholesale commodities in exchange for the European goods. Tribes began fighting other tribes to control the best breeding grounds and trade routes. These were called the Beaver Wars. Beaver pelts were especially prized. Also, otters and foxes. The animal furs and skins were known as peltry. There's another vocab word for us."

"Commodification is such a dry, technical term," Beth interjected.

"And I like it for just that reason," Mrs T said. "It shows the dry, economic calculation involved to plunder those animals for the sake of fashion. We whites did the same with the woods, where primeval stands of trees were just seen as *lumber* to be harvested. There was another huge aspect to this, too—land. The Indians saw land as collectively shared by their bands and tribes, and in that mindset were agreeing in their treaties simply to share its bounty with the settlers, not to sell it away, for goodness sakes. But to the whites, this land was *property.*"

Mrs. T was up and pacing the floor. "Think about that, gang. Land became one more thing, a commodity, to be divided and resold, with titles and exclusive property rights that boxed out the Indians. Very different, and it set up an inevitable collision course.

"What do you think, middle-schoolers? You look kind of grim."

"It's creepy but important," Trevor said. "I think kids sorta know this already in a vague way, but talking about it like it was just turning natural resources into items at the store, and how it changed Indian life forever … that sticks with me."

Maddy was trying to remember if the spirit girl was wearing animal peltry. The whole business of pelts and skins and guns and rum made her uneasy. "I guess we have to talk about it since it's a part of true history, and it explains a lot," she shrugged. "I don't have any group exercises or extra activities to offer for it, though."

"Well, I do want to keep the term. Let's continue. Trevor, next is BACKCOUNTRY."

"Really? That's easy." In green, he wrote out *back country*.

"Okay, but this is kind of a tricky one since historians usually write it as one word. Any idea what it means?"

Trevor shrugged. "Like, the woods?"

"Yes, in a certain way. Here's why I have it. To the settlers, the backcountry was the remote and faraway part of the colonies. They looked at it as the edge of civilization where you'd only go at your peril. But if you were an Indian, the so-called backcountry was your front porch. It was your sacred stomping grounds! They might have had a similarly uninviting word for the faraway white towns, like 'Smellylands' or something. Those were the perilous places for them!

"The point, folks, is to consider perspective. The settlers recorded the history that we learn, and they told it from their vantage point, only and always. And we enter the story from the *settlers'* particular perspective and use the *settlers'* terminology. This gets at what is called historiography—looking at how history is recorded and filtered, at what the historians' biases and goals might be. I'd like to use the historiography concept in the lesson plan, but I think *backcountry* is a more inviting vocab word to hook kids."

She scanned the group. "So what do you all think?"

"It might be too sophisticated for middle school," Beth said.

"No way!" Trevor nearly yelled. "We all tell stories and gossip from our own, what is it, *standpoint*. My teachers always tell us to listen as if we were the other person. That's what this *histori-whatever* is, right, but in a bigger way! I think when a lot of us were growing up and learned about Indians, we tried to imagine being one. So we already sorta knew what it felt like to flip ourselves around. Now, since we're older, we can handle more of the real truth about Indian and settler times, so it's even more interesting."

"I agree," Maddy added. "I don't know how it is up here, but kids in my classes hate being talked down to. Treat us as smart, or you're in trouble."

"Right!" Trevor smiled.

"We always say 'says who?' about things," Maddy continued. "That's really all this is, in a fancy way. Also, personally, I like knowing that history people try to check for their own bias. I'll bet other kids would appreciate knowing that, too."

"As long as it doesn't make them start doubting everything they read, or use it as an excuse to be turned off to everything," Beth said.

"Well, lots of textbooks these days are pretty careful to present alternative perspectives," Mrs. T said. "We're mostly casting doubt on the old histories and journals from a century or two ago, which were filled with rah-rah propaganda. While we have a lot to be proud of as Americans, our Indian history isn't one of them. It's tough stuff, but I feel very strongly that to be educated people, it's important for our schools to tell the whole story. We see our side as freedom fighters during the Revolution, but we've got to realize the Indians were fighting for their own freedom."

Just then Katie bounced into the room, providing relief from the intense material. The surprise she brought was a package of lemon ice-cones. The crunchy treats disappeared quickly, right after the pizza.

DURING THE FOOD BREAK, Mrs. T decided to go for it. Over the last few days she'd wrestled with whether to add a certain monument down the street to the curricular show-and-tell. It was the large boulder she'd once heard Curty call the hissing stone. She despised it, too, and whenever she drove past it she turned away. She couldn't remove the thing, but she didn't have to acknowledge it either. Its cold language about "savagery" and "civilization" screamed of historiography. Sure, it was right under their noses as a handy teaching focus. But she also considered the monument a hot potato. Not being a native of Athens, she worried that if she raised questions about it, some people might see her as an outsider stomping on local pride. Her gut had been warning her to keep away.

Trevor and Maddy's insistence that students be challenged, however, gave her a surge of confidence.

"Gang, come with me," she announced, and headed for the stairs.

In no time they were standing in front of the boulder. From the sour expressions that Maddy, Beth, and Katie wore, Mrs. T figured they already knew its message. Only Trevor seemed unfamiliar. He bent in to read the inscription, then pulled away in shock.

"Whoa! 'Destroyed savagery'? That's pretty rude! I guess I'd never really paid attention to this thing," he said through pursed lips.

"Rude is right," Mrs. T replied with a bitter chuckle, "and I'm bothered by it, too. Nevertheless, gang, this plaque has a lot to tell us. Remember I was saying earlier how relations between the whites and Indians took a giant turn for the worse after the French and Indian War? The brutal attacks and counterattacks brought on what can only be called race hatred, an ugly, mutual race hatred. They saw one another as evil afflictions. The idea took hold that the natives were all savages who needed to be removed or even eradicated because they were 'a scourge on civilization.'"

"Never mind that the whites had committed plenty of atrocities, too!" Beth complained.

"Very true," Mrs. T said. "But that wasn't part of the story we told ourselves. Even the Founding Fathers thought like this, gang, because right in our own Declaration of Independence is language complaining about 'merciless Indian savages' attacking 'our frontiers.'"

"In the Declaration! No!!" Maddy cried.

"Aw, man!" exclaimed Trevor.

115

"And meanwhile, on the other side, many of the native holy men called for a 'purging' of white ways and prayed that the settlers would return back across 'the stinking waters' of the Atlantic."

"Seriously?" Maddy asked.

"Seriously, the stinking waters," Mrs. T replied. "So this monument is a powerful relic of an old mindset—that it was us against them, and that our white way was destined to win out."

Beth swept her fingers across the inscription. "It's true it doesn't say, like, 'the march that pushed back the Iroquois and made us safer,'" she said. "There's no mincing words. They're not Indians but just 'savages,' and we're not subduing them but need to flat out *destroy* them."

"How about we put up a comment box right here, or even a bulletin board," Trevor said. "You know, ask people to write their own inscriptions, and we could post the good ones right beside the monument!"

"Well, maybe," Mrs. T said, doubt in her voice. "That might take some doing."

"Or maybe this is a chance for a classroom vocab lesson," Maddy interjected. "Have the kids look up *savagery* and *civilization*. I bet they're really loaded words."

Mrs. T nodded hard. "You betcha they are, dear. Savages are defined as brutes, little better than animals. While civilization refers to a *higher*, quote-unquote, form of society."

"Well, the Europeans had developed some major things the natives didn't have, like metals and muskets and glass," Beth said. "Even the wheel."

"True," Mrs. T said. "But I'm not sure our way of governing ourselves was any better. It was the Iroquois Confederacy model that inspired Ben Franklin to propose a union of the colonies. In lots of ways, I think the civilization argument was actually being driven by our desire for Indian land. To the average settlers who'd been squeezed out of land back in Europe, all this Indian land sitting wild was intolerable! They wanted to clear it of trees and rocks and dangerous animals and turn it into farmland for themselves. By so-called improving the land, they'd be able to feed their families and make a living selling crops to market. This was the real march of civilization, gang, and they felt Indians were standing in the way."

"Wait, Mom!" Katie erupted. "I just got an idea. Let's try a class debate about the civilization thing! It gets everyone involved."

"Those always worked well when I was that age," Beth nodded. With a grin, she held up her palm. "Try this idea. Resolved: Indians were wasting the land by not developing it."

Mrs. T slowly repeated the topic, head nodding. "Yes, good! There are strong arguments to be made on either side of that one. So you divide the class and give them a few days to huddle before their big debate, right?"

"Try this," Trevor added. "First you survey the class. Hand out a sheet where they have to check yes or no or not-sure to the question, before you've even taught about it. To get their first reaction. Then, put them on the team that goes *against* what they checked. If they said wasting the land, put them on the not-wasting team. To stretch their minds."

"Cool!" Katie added. "And since some of them will say not sure, why not have them be the judges? So the class has the two teams, and an audience of not-sure kids who get to rule on the arguments."

Mrs. T was beaming. "Some of the kids come from farm families," she said, "so this debate might really grab them."

Maddy had been silent, her mind and eyes wandering. Standing beside the moldy boulder still gave her the creeps, and being back near the ridgeline produced a tingle of longing.

Mrs. T noticed and stepped in.

"You've done it again with the super suggestions, everyone," she said. "Applause to all. Now, I need to pack it in. The shower beckons."

As the group headed back to the museum, she put an arm around Maddy's shoulder. "Thanks for hanging in there and contributing. Let me run you back to your motel. Be sure to take a long shower on me. It's been quite a day."

Chapter 15

Cakoanos had never seen her old friend like this. Moments earlier, Esther had marched directly from the condolence ceremony at the treaty ground, paces ahead of her companions, and disappeared into her shelter without a word. Anger had shattered her composure. In quiet discussion, the other women encouraged Cakoanos to go to Esther while they kept a polite distance at the campfire. Sisketung circled nearby, awaiting instructions.

Slipping inside the shelter, Cakoanos found Esther crouched silently on her bearskin. She had tossed her shawl blanket aside and was glowering at the ground, rolling her head from side to side, brow weighted by the gravity of her thoughts. Her fingers worked a white wampum string. Despite the liquid chill off the river, Cakoanos sensed a heat radiating feverishly from her friend.

Esther scowled up at her. "You've come to be with this old fool?"

Cakoanos sat and handed her a cup of river water. "The women worry. Sister, you are troubled. We wish to soothe you."

Esther drank roughly. Her blood was running too high to feel gratitude. In her mind, she was a cornered ka'wia hurling quills in all directions.

A hard realization had come to her. For twelve winters, Esther had privately longed to hear formal words of condolence extended to her and Eghohowin for the killing of their boy. His wartime death at yengwe hands had been at least as brutal as the Seneca murders, her suffering over it every bit as deep.

But moments earlier, when her spirit flew beside the Seneca mourners and she listened to Pickering mouth lofty condolences on behalf of his government, all she felt was a bolt of contempt. And now she saw herself as a fool, a pitiful old fool, for expecting to gain any solace from mawkish yengwe gestures.

Pickering seemed to be a good man. Esther believed that, and that he spoke from the heart as well as the tongue. His sincerity toward her people made him rare among yengwes. It also made him a fool, however, if he thought he was truly speaking for his people's heart.

"Yo-hah, Sister," Esther replied finally to Cakoanos, "truly I am troubled. The yengwe words of condolence fall upon me like dry ash. How much longer will our people sit with these invaders and be mocked by their empty gestures and false promises? I have had a lifetime of them! I have sat at councils and heard their sunny words. I have heard their solemn promises that our ways and our lands—our hunting lands, our fishing places, the lands where our bones are scattered—would be ours forever. They might say this while it serves their purposes. But eventually, like grasshoppers, their people overrun our sacred lands! Over and over, throughout my long life! Look around us now. Even the ancient Teaoga treaty ground where we sit is land they now claim!"

"Yo-hah," Cakoanos returned. "It is so."

"Why did we forever believe them, Sister? Why did I believe their tricks and their chatter? Why did I resist my own suspicions for so long? Why did I defend

118

them? Did my work as a peace woman only encourage them and serve their sly purposes?"

Cakoanos was pained by her friend's torment. "Sister, you honored yourself and your people by keeping the path bright. You did as the Preserver would want."

Esther cast a withering glare. "I kept the path bright—and blood was thrown upon it!"

Cakoanos was considering a reply when Esther grabbed her blanket and rose to depart. She felt as though the wigwam was closing in on her.

"Come, Sister! Gather the women! We must walk while Father Sun favors us. Sisketung can accompany me and steady my steps."

SISKETUNG HAD TO TROT to keep pace. Esther took a crooked stick from the underbrush and used it to pole herself forward. She led them south from the campground across the large open field that once bordered the longhouses of the Cayuga watch town. Cakoanos and the other women straggled behind.

Indignation drove Esther forward. She disregarded her aching body. She was beyond worry about being spotted, consumed now only by the desire to pass her message on to the other women while her mind was keen and the winter light remained.

As she strode on, the rhythmic swishing of the women's frilled skirts—petticoats made of shiny yengwe muslin—began to assault her ears. The supple, brain-tanned deerskin she would have worn at their age allowed for graceful, silent motion. More important, deerskin was the product of their own hands and culture! Was tanning one more traditional skill lost to the lure of yengwe trade goods?

As she strode on, she was overcome with the words of the Delaware prophet Neolin, whose teachings about two separate creations had inspired Eghohowin. Neolin said the Preserver gave him this message: "As to those who come to trouble your lands—drive them out, make war upon them. I do not love them at all! They know me not and are my enemies and the enemies of your brothers. Send them back to the lands which I created for them, and let them stay there!"

As she strode on, she pictured the hordes of warriors encamped in the heat on this very Teaoga field twelve summers past, preparing for their bold attack on the Wyoming Valley forts. She saw Joseph Brant, the great Mohawk chief, in his war council here with Butler, the fat, pale, irritable British commander. She saw the vast encampment of braves and British rangers, the canoes, the war dances, the boisterous departure downriver.

Suddenly, Esther thrust the pole into a tuft in the frozen ground. They had reached their destination.

"N'petalogalgun," she announced once the others caught up. "Listen well, Sisters of Teaoga, for I have many things to say! My eyes are clear. My heart is strong. Sisters, you have asked for my story and my wisdom. While we gather at this sacred spot, I wish to complete that story."

"Honor us, Mother Esther," Cakoanos responded. The others panted their agreement. Sisketung opened her mind fully and stood ready.

"Sisters, do you know what once rose at our feet?" Esther began, scanning their faces. "It was the painted post! Here where my crook is planted stood the great wooden post the Cayugas placed for their festivals and dances."

"It was red, yes?" Cakoanos recalled. "And carved with many figures of humans and beasts."

Esther nodded. "Yo-hah! And it was last used during the yengwe Revolution. Sisters, we must speak of this Revolution. Some of you may have dim memories from your childhood. Listen well. It was a time when high winds were rising. Hatchets and long knives and muskets were unloosed. Old wounds were open again!

"Sisters, I had tried to run my village in peace, there across the Chemung waters. Families from different tribes had joined our number. Our cornfields were rich. Cattle fattened themselves in the lowlands. Eghohowin's village up the Chemung also prospered. But he and his Munsee warriors kept their hatchets sharpened, ready to protect us all."

Sisketung observed how Esther spoke quicker than previously, as though possessed.

The old woman told her companions how, once Revolution was declared, the two warring yengwe armies, the British and the Colonials, brought bloodshed and destruction across the land and to the river valleys. Frontier settlers who were loyal to the British king were targeted by the Colonial fighters. Many of these Tory loyalists were driven from their homesteads, both up in the New York borderlands and down in the Wyoming Valley. Some fled to Teaoga for refuge, she said. Teaoga became a base of Tory strength and a staging ground for many attacks on isolated Colonial settlements. She also told how deserters from Washington's Colonial Army found safe haven at Teaoga.

Sisketung was trying hard to commit Esther's words to memory. Frequently, her inner eye took her aloft to witness the events. It was a gift of perception that aided her clear remembering.

"Our people had to decide which side to support, the yengwe British or the yengwe Colonials," Esther said. "Many long days and nights were spent in council. The wisest voices said the British were more likely to honor the treaties and keep the swarms of settlers from squatting on our lands."

As a result, she said, most of the Iroquois tribes joined forces with the British, as did the Munsees and other remnant bands. Once this great alliance was set, joint raiding parties of warriors and British rangers swept across the borderlands, destroying farms and homesteads of Colonial settlers, driving the occupants away or taking captives.

"Normal life was gone!" Esther said. "Tory families were pouring into Teaoga for protection. Starving Colonial captives would lurk near our fields, foraging for food. Young warriors would fall into the rum and make sport with our livestock."

One of the Tutelo women spoke up. "I remember the loud gunshots and warrior yells. The captive boys and girls with their hungry faces. I was just a girl myself. Nightmares haunted my sleep."

"Do you remember when our few warriors left us?" Esther asked. "Eghohowin had begun leading war parties again. He wanted our village's warriors to join him upriver for training and to raid. It was a sad parting. I counseled patience, but I could see the fire in our men's eyes. Elesoon was among those to go."

Upon saying the name, Esther fell silent and meditated on her youngest child. Elesoon, her thin son, grown to a restless young man. How he prided himself on his skill in archery and in stalking game! Eghohowin said he would make a fine scout. The boy knew his father had a granite strength, and he wanted to test his own as well. She recalled how she could only smile as Elesoon practiced the warrior yell. He longed for battle.

She composed herself and continued. "Sisters, soon the war thunder grew even louder! Summer's heat had come. The British Butler met with chief Brant at the Teaoga treaty grounds. They decided the time was right to send their fighters out in full force. Brant would go northward into New York territory, while Butler would strike south into the Wyoming Valley!"

Esther told of sitting at the council fire as Butler explained how the Wyoming settlements were supplying men and grain to Washington's army. The settlements were lightly defended by a few undermanned forts. Destroying Wyoming in summer before the crops ripened would stop the Colonial supply line, Butler said, and would open many other Colonial settlements farther to the south and west to attack. Butler knew many of his rangers longed to retaliate for the uprooting of their Tory relatives from Wyoming.

Brant and Butler called for Indian warriors to join the attack on Wyoming. "Eghohowin and our chiefs were eager," Esther said. "Our people felt we should never have been pushed out of Wyoming. I remember one chief rising to recite the old words spoken to the Pennsylvania commissioners many winters ago: 'We will never part with the land at Shamokin and Wyoming! Our bones are scattered there, and on this land there has always been a great council fire!'

"Sisters, what did I say at council? I thought of standing and speaking as a peace woman. But I said nothing. I knew our people were beyond patience. The chief's words about sacred Wyoming moved me, too. So much had been stolen from us. In truth, I shared the flame of anger.

"The call to war went out to the tribes. Many village councils were held. The fever ran high. The people shared smokes and exchanged war belts. Soon, warriors began arriving at Teaoga in great flocks! Eghohowin and Elesoon were among them."

"Yes, I remember it well, the canoes and dugouts crowding the shore near the Carrying Path," Cakoanos said.

Esther told the group how the mixed encampment grew until it stretched from the Carrying Path to beneath the Cayuga watch town. Most who came were Senecas, well-trained at war, she said. They arrived with not only weapons and ammunition, but with their own potions, repair kits, amulets, beaded prisoner ties, and scalping knives. They practiced in the fields, held shooting and athletic contests with the white rangers, gambled and caroused. The raucous scenes thrilled young Elesoon, she said.

Sisketung saw it all in her mind and understood.

"Sisters, the day was set to depart for battle. The warriors leapt with excitement as they made final preparations. They streaked their faces with bloodroot and charcoal. They greased their hair with bear fat. As in the days of Teedyuscung, the noise of war cries filled the Teaoga air! I remember some of the yengwe rangers painting their own faces as well! Such a strange sight they were in their royal green jackets and war faces!

"That last night, the warriors gathered here at this very spot to dance around the great painted post. The shouts rang out! The men ran and struck the post to show their determination. Each called out how he would strike down the enemy! They boasted about how many scalps they would take! The women sang their own war songs and choruses."

Sisketung scanned the field around them, her mind alive with the fearsome images. One of the young Tutelo women spoke up. "Mother Esther, wasn't the white dog ceremony held, the one my own mother remembered?"

"Yo-hah," Esther said. "A dog of pure white was brought to Teaoga for the final war feast. The dog was sacrificed and roasted that night. Each of the warriors ate a piece to draw courage and to ward off danger."

"Sisters, the next morning the river was filled with our canoes and dugouts and the British boats. As we headed southward, the hills rang with our men's shouts! The British were in the front, followed by the warriors. I was among the women who had joined to tend the campfires, make meals, and assist with injuries. My pouches were laden with healing herbs and potions."

As the procession floated past the deserted Moravian mission at Wyalusing, Esther recalled, she noticed many of the cabins were nearly stripped of wood. The Colonial settlers who had been driven away in the recent raids had taken rafters from the empty cabins and lashed them together as rafts for their panicked escape south to Wyoming. "This is what the beautiful Moravian dream had come to!" she said.

Esther laughed dryly. Returning to the moment, she noticed her companions had begun slapping their sides to keep warm. Sisketung, though still fully attentive, stood shivering.

"Sisters, Father Sun is leaving us. This is a sacred spot, but it cannot warm our poor bones," Esther said. "Let us return to the fire circle."

THE FLAMES SENT OUT a welcoming heat as the women sat near beneath their woolen blankets, two of them preparing a kettle of boiled corn cakes and eel. Despite the spreading aromas, Esther felt no hunger. Knowing she must continue her story, she leaned against Sisketung's back and proceeded.

The war party's journey downriver to Wyoming was smooth, she said. Then, on the third evening, runners brought word that the advance party of warriors had descended to the upper end of the Wyoming Valley and encountered an isolated group of farmers, some with muskets. The braves ambushed and killed five of the farmers in their fields, she said, while the others escaped back to Wyoming. Two young Indian sentries were assigned to keep watch over the farmers' bodies in case any Colonial soldiers came out of the forts to try to recover them.

"The next day, our party arrived north of that spot and beached our canoes. I joined in the camp preparations.... As I was preparing the evening meal, Sisters, I saw Eghohowin approaching. I saw him approaching.... His face ..."

Esther's voice slurred. She squeezed her eyes shut and prayed desperately for strength to continue. Her frenzied energy was gone. Sisketung felt as if no one was breathing. Finally, the old woman cleared her throat and spoke, her voice now a husky drone. The others leaned in to hear her over the crackling fire.

"Eghohowin had come up … from the battle … exhausted," Esther rasped. "He looked like an old man…. He leaned onto my shoulder…. Sisters, do you know what it is to … to lose a son before his years?"

Esther looked, one by one, into her listeners' somber faces. All held bowls of food, but no one ate. When her unblinking eyes fell on Sisketung, the girl felt a fresh shiver run through her. "Sisters, Daughter, do you know? … Listen well. Elesoon, *my Elesoon*, was one of the two sentries.

"Yo-hah, my young handsome son was there. The soldiers surprised them at dawn and opened fire. The other boy made it as far as the river. My son, my young handsome son, had no chance. Perhaps he had been dozing. The musket balls tore open my son's proud body. The soldiers ended my son's life. My son, the son of a chief. They scalped my son. They mutilated his body…. This is what Eghohowin had to tell me, as he leaned on my shoulder that day."

Esther stared into the fire, lips now quivering. She reached out as if beseeching the boy. Her voice addressed the flames.

"Eghohowin said he must return to the battlefield … to avenge our son. He said he had just visited Elesoon's body to praise his bravery and promise his young spirit he would find revenge that day. Sisters, my husband showed me his scalping knife, and our son's fresh blood that he had streaked on the handle to guide his avenging hand. My duty, he said, was to prepare our son's precious body and see to the burial."

Esther looked up. "He said it must be done quickly, to protect him from the heat and the animals and the yengwes. Sisters, that is what I did. Eghohowin had warriors carry the two young bodies to us…. I prayed to the Preserver for strength, then I cleansed my son's perfect body. I told him of my anger at his reckless courage, and my pride at his reckless courage. I burned his belongings … dressed his body for his burial … my laughing, proud young boy…. Sisters, do you know what it is to wash blood from a son's torn body? To paint a son's handsome face in burial red? To dress a son's body and fold him into the ground? To cover him with dirt and rocks?"

The Mohawk woman began a low, intermittent moan. Cakoanos came to Esther's side. Esther looked through her friend as she continued.

"Sisters, Father Sun was angry that day. The heat did not spare us. I painted my face the black of mourning and led the long choruses of wailing at the grave…. The other mother, a Seneca woman, prepared her son in the same manner. In the distance was gunfire from the battle. Runners came with word of success, but my ears were closed. I spent much of the day in funeral-song, until my voice left me. I ate nothing. I was made to drink. In time, I collapsed and was led to shade."

ESTHER PAUSED TO EAT absently from her bowl, that it might renew her strength. The others ate as well. The saga singer droned softly. Sisketung sat silently, feeling attached to Esther's heart.

"When night approached," Esther continued hoarsely, "Eghohowin sent for me to join him in the valley. Though I may have slept, I was exhausted. Two warriors led me by the shoulder along a river trail. Sisters, they told me about the day's victory. They told me the Colonials had refused to surrender and be spared. This you may know. The soldiers had foolishly marched out of their forts. Butler set a trap that they walked into. The rangers and warriors quickly killed hundreds of them and took others captive. Our losses were very few.

"Sisters, I wanted to be proud of the victory, but I had no feeling. I was outside my body, like a dream. Once we reached the valley, it was nighttime. I remember the choking wall of smoke from the muskets and the burning fields. Warriors ran about in excitement, inspecting yengwe bodies, collecting weapons, shouting war whoops. Our women also wandered about with torches, shouting, laughing, plundering from the yengwe uniforms. The British rangers had withdrawn.

"I was led to Eghohowin. He was in a field near the river with other warriors. They stood over a circle of captives."

So many times the sight had haunted Esther's memory. Sisketung saw it too, as she had seen it in her mind before, and pictured it now in Esther's telling.

"Sisters, they had tied a group of captive yengwe soldiers ... and ordered them to lie facedown around a rock, like spokes on a yengwe wheel. Some were already wounded from the battle. They wept and prayed. The scene and the smells made me ill. Eghohowin approached me. I sensed his wish. He was a war chief. He took my shoulders and said it was our duty to avenge Elesoon's death. He said he had killed many soldiers that day, and now was my time. Do not hesitate, he said. Be strong...."

Sisketung was shuddering as her spirit hovered above the rock.

"He put his powerful war club into my hand. My knees gave. Be strong, he said! I saw my beautiful son's broken body. I saw the trapper attacking me in my youth. I heard Neolin's angry words ... and I cried out. Next came the crash of the club on a man's head ... and another, on another head." Esther's voice trailed off.

All eyes were downcast. The only sound was the crackling of the campfire and the low keening. Sisketung's mind, however alert, was resisting memorizing. The girl had never experienced anyone unburdening themself so. Such a great blessing, she realized, that it could happen in the security, the acceptance, of the women's circle.

"Sisters," Esther whispered, "my next awareness was awakening the following day at our camp. The other mother sat with me. She said I had collapsed at the rock. She said other women had stepped in and lifted the war club against the remaining captives. Sisters, do you know what it is to hear that sound of death?

"Sisters, that day I removed my skirt and placed it on my son's grave. The skirt bore his blood, and now the blood of two yengwes. I returned to my Elesoon's grave and lay that skirt over his earth. I needed Eghohowin with me, but he was busy at war. I had killed, but I was not a warrior. I had been a peace woman, but could claim the title no more. My last child was gone. I did not know how to go on.

"The other mother knew of my village here and convinced me my people needed me back. Yo-hah, young sisters, I thought of you. Cakoanos, you were with child then, with Sisketung. It was best that I departed that cursed battleground to return to my villagers. I sent word to Eghohowin that he must provide some warriors to us as soon as possible. Then I headed back here to Teaoga, ahead of the rangers and warriors returning with their plunder. Sisters, do you remember me among you then? I was but a ghost. Many days I could not leave my cabin...."

Cakoanos spoke up. "Sister, I was told our warriors promised to spare the yengwe women and children at Wyoming—but vowed to show no mercy to any menfolk who raised arms against them. I was told captive fighters had been killed. You were involved, I was told. I heard no more, and we did not want to press you."

"Yo-hah," said another woman. "Sister, soon word reached us that the yengwes were accusing you of murder at the Bloody Rock, of laughing over the bodies—of being a demon! We knew of your peaceful work with the yengwes, so we held this as wicked talk. We shared in your long mourning for Elesoon, but we left you to tell us what you wished."

Esther managed a thin smile. "Your support was a blessing. Seeing your belly swell with child was a comfort, Cakoanos. Tending to our fields and animals on my good days was a blessing. Preparing for the harvest gave me purpose.

"Sisters, you may remember that when the warriors returned from Wyoming with their plunder, Eghohowin stayed with me for a few days. In my cabin, he opened me to talking about our son. He told me Elesoon had died honorably, and that our revenge was honorable. The yengwes had taken Wyoming from us dishonorably, he said. The fighters had doomed themselves when they refused to surrender. Sisters, was he right? I tortured myself with that question for many moons—but now I am of the same mind.

"Sisters, did you know Eghohowin wanted me to move with him to the safety of Chemung? He told me of the evil talk about me and said I was in danger. I refused to go. My place was here with my village. So I stayed with you, my precious families, and with our few warriors, and prepared for the harvest."

Suddenly a runner arrived at the camp circle. Red Jacket had sent him to inform Esther that the matrons would be gathering at dawn in his shelter. Esther assured the messenger she would attend.

"Sisters, let us rest," she said once the messenger departed into the darkness. "My voice is weary. My heart is as well, though completing my story relieves a burden. I pray that my experience helps to clear your eyes. Helps to explain our difficult past. Helps to show the challenges you still face. Helps to forge your best path ahead. We must speak still of this path. But now, let us take our rest."

Esther walked stiffly toward her shelter. Sisketung followed. She would lie beside the old woman to help keep them both warm.

The powerful revelations of the day were telling the girl what else she must now do during their last hours together at Teaoga.

Chapter 16

The pony-tailed slugger swung from her hips with a grunt. *Ping!* Her aluminum bat sent the softball spinning high into the early evening sky. It was a towering pop-up that curved fast and foul. A little whirring sound could be heard as the ball plummeted toward the third-base bleachers.

Maddy, sitting alone in the front row and lost in thought, never heard the grunt, nor the ping, nor the whir. She was only vaguely aware of the spectators behind her yelling to duck.

An instant later, the softball crash-landed onto the empty aluminum bleacher next to her. That she definitely heard. The explosive metallic boom sent her tumbling sideways in panic.

"Yo, girl, you alright?!" It was Katie, suddenly leaning toward her over the low third-base fence. She'd thrown off her catcher's mask in a mad dash from home plate to try to snag the pop fly. Now she stood four feet away in her yellow jersey, breathing hard, face sweaty. She shot a grin at her cowering friend. "That was close! Head's up next time!"

Katie bounced restlessly, chomping on her bubblegum, while a little boy retrieved the ball for her from foul territory. "Nice try, Katie T!" a man in the stands shouted. "Way to fight for it!" When the youngster dropped the ball proudly into her mitt, Katie gave him a wink, and one to Maddy. Then she turned, chucked the ball to her waiting third baseman, and trotted back to home plate like a big-leaguer.

"Okay, baby!" she called to her pitcher. "Count is two-and-one! Next one's right down broadway!"

For Maddy, the fright gave way to a familiar flush of embarrassment. She straightened herself up from her primal hunch and peered around. The dads seated behind her were intently watching the game again, though two of the moms were giving Maddy looks of concern. Or was it pity? She returned a limp wave of reassurance. Her father and Mrs. T, standing across the field at the first-base fence, seemed to have turned their attention back to the game.

Doofus. It was that gut voice, returning after a lull to zing her. *You can be such a doofus.*

Snarkley's right, Maddy thought. *I deserved to get beaned. How hard is it to pay attention to a softball game, anyways? It isn't like I'm an airheaded little toddler.*

She'd come to the ballgame on a promise to Katie. The Broncos were apparently playing the top team in the league. For dinner, Maddy and her dad had grabbed a pair of Double Cheese Whammies, tall lemonades, and a bag of plump green grapes for dessert, wolfing it all down in Li'l Red as they drove over to watch the action. As usual, her dad gravitated to Mrs. T's spot. The two of them were probably talking about work, family, and a little baseball like pitch counts and player substitutions.

But Maddy's head wasn't in the game. Not even close. Try as she might, she just felt *detached*. She knew what it was. The spirit sightings had scrambled her perceptions. Plus, the rapid pileup of information she was getting about the Indians and the settlers, dirty dealing and massacres, propaganda, lies, hatred —all of it had all thrown her for a mega-loop.

The afterglow of the sightings themselves was actually a pleasure. She found that if she shut her eyes and lifted her arms, she could still get an inkling of the uplift and the Indian girl's serene face. She relished the contentment it gave her. No, it was the settling back in with others that still was the tricky part. She kept wondering why the visions had come to her in the first place. Was she weird? Why hadn't the sightings scared her? Did that make her weirder than weird? Were any folks in the bleachers aware that spirit-people still floated around in their valley?

At that moment, Maddy felt like she was watching everyone from a fort deep inside her head, that her eyeballs were binoculars surveying a distant outside world. It was the same aloof feeling she'd get sometimes in the school lunchroom.

She didn't feel superior to people around her, just mystified. She certainly didn't feel negative toward the folks in Athens. Everyone had been really nice. Everyone except the stupid bully-boys, that is. Generally, the simple friendliness almost brought tears to her eyes. She'd never heard so many people say "you betcha!" before—but she'd take it over "this sucks," which was the common refrain back at her school.

Still, Maddy wondered, do the good folks here know, when they bomb around town, that this land was invaded and ripped away from its original inhabitants? When she and Katie were up at the movie theater in Sayre the night before, she'd started getting powerful feelings like that.

It had been a strange night overall. They'd gotten to the theater early and were sitting cracking corny jokes, waiting for the trailers to begin. Katie noticed a couple of girls sitting a row over and called out to them, "Hey, Lexi! Hi, Em!" The girls barely waved back, then started whispering among themselves. Maddy could see them working their phones, probably sending nasty texts. Katie turned back, smile pasted on her face. "See?" is all she said.

Maddy wondered if she'd be one of those girls back home. She hoped not. But she certainly knew the code of the pack. That brought on the memory of what she'd done last winter to a certain girl in art class.

Fortunately, the movie started—a superhero thing with the standard deafening soundtrack, damsel girlfriend and slapstick villain. They laughed their way through it as best they could. Afterwards, the two other girls shot out the side exit before the credits were even over.

Katie took Maddy to a pizza joint a block away. Then they wandered around Sayre, killing time before calling Mrs. T to come get them. Maddy was struck by the street names—Seneca, Oneida, Mohawk, the full Iroquois lineup. She didn't tell Katie, but it set her to thinking about land squatters and whether the people in those houses truly realized a whole other civilization existed here before them.

Now, as Maddy sat in the bleachers, question gave rise to burning question. Do they know when they cruise around in their boombox-mobiles that this was other people's sacred land first? Do they know when they go off hunting that the Indians used to thank the animals' spirits for surrendering themselves?

The hyper-awareness of things unseen made her feel separate—somehow. It was into that trancelike state that the softball plummeted from the sky.

SETTLING BACK INTO HER seat, Maddy was overcome with more musings. This ballfield once might have been part of an enormous tribal lacrosse field. Or maybe a Cayuga cornfield. She instantly pictured the Three Sisters—corn, beans, squash—growing in symbiotic mounds in the dusty outfield. She imagined herself as an Indian watch-girl on a raised platform shooing away the birds.

Whatever. Stop romanticizing! It was the Snarker again, back with a vengeance. *The Indians were subsistence farmers. Don't you know what that means, dummy? They survived from harvest to harvest. A bad year or two, and they'd be starving.* Maddy frowned. She had to admit she would rather live in a society where there was mass production, and food stores to shop in. With candy bars and ice cream and imported grapes year-round.

But the Indians had a lot of wisdom about the natural world, she countered. They had medicinal herbs from the woods. They made healing potions. We're clueless about those things. *Sure, and some of the stuff worked. But c'mon, girl, wouldn't you rather have antibiotics and anesthesia and ambulances and CAT scans? People back then lost lots of babies and mothers in childbirth. Adults were lucky if they lived past forty. Get real. The Indians believed in goblins and sprites. They didn't have a written language. They hadn't even invented the wheel, for pete's sake! Wouldn't you rather have cars and planes and bikes than dugout canoes and packhorses?*

Maddy contemplated all that. She didn't really mind having her Snarkley self jump in with challenges. It kept her on her toes, kept her smart. The Snarker was like a devil's advocate voicing the hissing stone point of view. So back and forth the inner arguments went. *We have central heating now, too!* But if the Indians had the big populations we had, they might have developed other means to support themselves, she thought. She imagined that was the case, anyways. *Remember, they had goblins! And brutal gantlets.* No fair, she thought. The Indians were dealing with the world in front of them at the time. They had their own value system and their own sense of honor. It's wrong to judge them.

"Hey."

Maddy jumped again. Curtis had slipped onto the seat beside her. He pulled on her arm. "C'mon. Let's go. Tommy's here."

Maddy blinked herself back into the moment. She glanced back toward the scrubby field behind the bleachers. Tommy was sitting on his shiny BMX bike, propping up Curtis's bike with his free hand.

She rose reluctantly and headed across the field. "Hi, Tommy. Nice wheels."

"Hi. So Curtis says you had an inner sighting already at that spot in the park." Tommy studied her face. "You must have some Indian blood in you."

Maddy peered at Curtis and back at Tommy. "Indian blood? I don't think so, but thanks."

"Well, want a Coke or something? My mom gave me ten bucks for cleaning the garage," Tommy announced. "Let's go to the Handi. My treat."

Straddling their bikes, the boys began walking and rolling toward the Handi Mini Mart, which was at the far edge of the field. Maddy looked back. No one seemed to have noticed she'd left the bleachers. She trotted to catch up to the boys, and tried to clear her mind of brooding thoughts.

The Handi was a candy heaven. After ten minutes, the trio emerged with twelve cents left. Maddy was in a renewed frame of mind. She held a cup of orangeade that rattled with ice chips, along with—Rockn yes!—a bag of red licorice lace. Just like old times. When she was a little kid she used to roll up the long, skinny strings into wads and gorge herself, but she didn't see the lace in stores much anymore. Anticipating the wicked pleasure ahead, she hummed a dance tune to herself. Her companions, clasping their own goodies, walked gaily towards their bikes alongside the building.

Just then, three other bikes rolled together onto the store's parking lot. The leader of the pack let out a guffaw. "Well, well, if it isn't the great Tom-Tom! Look who's here, men! It's Mister Tom-Tom himself!"

Maddy froze. She recognized the big lug. It was the loudmouth from the other night at the bandstand.

"So we meet again, Tommy-Tomahawk!" Loudmouth jeered. He rolled up in front of the two boys and dismounted his bike. "Mmm, we love cookies, don't we, men! Me Cookie Monster!" His sidekicks brayed as he reached for the candy bag Tommy was holding.

Tommy yanked the bag back and shot a dagger stare at the bully-boss. It was the same dark-eyed glare of defiance that Maddy had seen—had felt—from Tommy that night at the bandstand. It had pierced her awareness then as if it contained all the wounded pride that Tommy's people still bore. In a flash, it came to her where *else* she had experienced it—another time, another place. It was the same look of hurt, anger, and confusion that dark-eyed Ana Estevez, the girl from art class, had shot back at her in their Houston lunchroom. *Oh, Ana, I'm sorry! What a dope I was!*

As Maddy reeled from the fresh insight, she saw that immediate danger was brewing in front of her eyes. She'd have to sort out the Ana thing later. Her two companions were in need. They had slowly backed up onto a skirt of grass and were barking insults back at the bully-boys. Loudmouth kept menacing them: "What do injuns eat? Tomahawk chops?! Candy corn?! Hand over the bag, little Tommy Tom-Tom!"

Raw anger rose in Maddy. Heart pounding, she bolted in front of Tommy and turned to face the big lug. She held her hands up to stop him. "Peace, you! Just cool it! Peace!" she cried. It felt as if she was channeling someone else's courage and voice. "That's right, peace! I mean it!"

Loudmouth halted for a second and eyed Maddy in amusement. Then he shoved her aside. Maddy lunged for his arm, but he jerked free and kept advancing on Tommy.

Another idea struck. Moving fast, Maddy grabbed Loudmouth's bike off the pavement and frantically hopped on. Before the others could react, she was pedaling away across the parking lot. The bullies shouted in protest. This time her body was straight and steady. She gained speed and zoomed toward the far sidewalk. A patch of loose gravel lay directly ahead. She swerved away just in time, but the move sent her over a scattering of ice chips some lazy customer had dumped beside his car. The wheels skidded. Maddy managed to hop off as the bike flipped across a strip of grass and landed upside-down in a ditch full of weeds and litter.

She hustled toward the ditch, panting and trembling, and considered retrieving the bike. But then she saw. One end of its handlebars had smacked down onto a discarded bag—a clear plastic bag filled with dog poop. The impact had burst the bag open and splattered its nasty, summer-hot contents all over the handlebars. Some of it landed on the seat. The front spokes were coated and dripping.

Maddy jerked her hands back and quickly retreated toward the field. Skipping backwards, she watched as the bullies circled the fallen bike. One of them yelled a stream of curses at her. Loudmouth began to lift up the handlebars, realized the steamy mess, and hurled the bike down with a yowl. Their obscenities grew so crude and stereophonic that store customers began shouting at them to get the heck lost.

Meanwhile, Maddy continued to trot backwards towards the bleachers. The sight in the ditch was gross, but her disgust—and any leftover fear—gave way to exhilaration. *Slimed! He got super-slimed!* And the bully-boys weren't making a move toward her. She turned and strode toward the bleachers. Her hand still held the prized bag of licorice. *Total victory!*

She spotted Tommy and Curtis circling wide across the field toward her. Her maneuver had diverted the bullies' attention, so the boys were able to easily bike away. With a shout of glee, Maddy thrust her arms overhead. *Rockn Rocky!!*

"THAT WAS AWESOME, MADDY!" Curtis exclaimed. "*Totally historic!*" added Tommy.

They were back at Maddy's bleacher seat and laughing like fools. The bullies had tried to swagger near until several fathers stood up on the bleachers like armed guards. "Get outta here, you idiots!" one of the beefier dads bellowed. "I should call your folks and tell them how you pick on younger kids. Shame on you! Beat it!"

Maddy and her friends turned to watch, giggling, as the bullies skulked off. Curtis gave her a double fist bump. Tingling with excitement, Maddy divvied up the licorice, even handing out a few strands to other youngsters in the stands. Between spasms of laughter, she demonstrated how to roll the lace into bite-size wads. Her fingers were still trembling, but the boys were too giddy to care. Tommy decided to tie his lace into multiple knots. "Look, a hangman's noose! Suitable for hanging idiots!" He hooked a thumb into the red noose and made choking sounds.

Curtis jammed two sticky wads into the sides of his mouth. "Look, I'm a *shquirrel!*" he slurped. Then, in one his classic mood flips, he stared at Maddy. "How the heck did you know the poop was there?"

"I had no idea it was there," she replied. "I wouldn't be surprised if they brought the bag themselves and were gonna, like, burn it later in some idiot prank. You know, guys, I was only trying to get them away from you so no one got hurt. The rest of it just happened." Giggles came over her again. "You shoulda seen the look on his face when he picked up his bike! Hah, that was worth it!"

"I sure heard their language! Yow," Curtis said.

"Maddy, what you did was *legendary!*" Tommy exclaimed. "You're so in my hall of fame now. Wait'll I tell my mom what happened."

Maddy paused. "Y'know, I hope I don't make it worse for you later. Those turdheads won't forget this."

"Don't sweat it," Tommy returned. "They're just a lotta talk. Plus, I've been working on my karate moves. Hi-*yuh!*" He leapt off to the side of the bleachers, followed by a prancing Curtis. Maddy chewed happily as she watched their horseplay.

Finally turning her attention back to Katie's game, she noticed the ballplayers lining up along the first-base line for the handshake ceremony. The game was over—and Maddy realized she had no idea what had happened.

Fortunately, her father came over first. "Oh well," he sighed, "they played hard. Did you see Katie throw out that runner at third? Wow, perfect."

"Nice," Maddy said, feeling lame again. Her father apparently hadn't seen the Handi incident. It would even be like him to block out all the ugly cursing.

"Hey, Me-Madd, guess what?" he said. "Mrs. T has invited us to join them Saturday at some mountaintop park for a picnic. She doesn't want us to miss it before we leave. It's apparently beautiful, plus it has history. She called it 'an overlook on history.' Sounds good to me. We'll bring the dessert."

Katie walked over next, toting her dusty equipment bag. She looked wiped out, but under her backwards yellow cap she wore a cockeyed smile. "You played great, Katie T!" Mr. Winter said.

"Thanks, Mr. Winter. They were unstoppable, but we tried. Hey, girlfriend, glad you were here. Hope you enjoyed."

"Sure," Maddy said. "Good game. See you tomorrow."

"And Saturday, I hear!" Katie added.

"Mom, I need a shower bad."

Mrs. T swept by for a quick farewell. She led Katie back to their SUV and called out to Curtis and Tommy that it was time to head home.

"Let's pack it in, too," Mr. Winter said. "I could use a shower myself. Plus a bowl of that Mint Ting-a-Ling that's waiting in the freezer! Sound good, bucko?" He danced a Texas two-step toward the car as he crooned, "Ting-a-ling, ting-a-ling, o baby be my ting-a-ling, ting-a-ling."

Maddy, two-stepping along with him, had gotten another idea. Earlier, when she passed around the licorice, Tommy held a strand in his hand and called it "red wampum." That got her to thinking.

"Dad, let's stop at the Handi over there first. And can you spot me three dollars?"

"Sure, I guess. But why, Miss Ting-a-Ling?"

"I want to buy their last two bags of red licorice lace."

"Licorice lace?"

"Yup, licorice lace."

Chapter 17

Tobacco smoke billowed inside Red Jacket's crowded shelter. Esther and the Seneca matrons puffed contentedly on the kulukuneekun mix, soothed by its familiar aroma and the sight of its smoke dancing through the shafts of bright morning light. Esther had joined the women inside the chief's large wigwam soon after the dawn sun ceremony. As they sat together around the log fire, she was sensing a sweet-sad atmosphere—bittersweet like the kulukuneekun, and like the mood she'd felt at the well-attended dawn ceremony in the field.

The Teaoga campground had stirred early that morning so the people could begin their packing and their farewells. Even the old chiefs turned out en masse for the sunrise ritual, knowing the people's precious time together was near its end. The emotional shouts to the waking sun, and the lengthy communal greetings that followed, lingered in Esther's ears. Bittersweet, like a long life, she thought.

After a time, Red Jacket rose to his feet in the hazy interior. He methodically smoothed his blanket while the matrons quieted. Soon, the only noise was their puffing on the assorted clay and wooden pipes.

"Sisters," the Pine Tree chief began, "listen well. The time has come to make our canoes and packs ready again. With your help, Sisters, the work of our council fire has reached its end. You heard the proper words the yengwe Pickering spoke at the treaty ground yesterday. He performed the closing stake ceremony well. Let us remember the words he declared: 'Brothers, the stake has been stuck in the ground, and it has been pulled out in the presence of you all. We have put into the hole all our troubles, and again stuck in the stake, that they may never rise again.'"

"Brother, may the stake hold firm! May the troubles remain buried!" a head matron called out. "Yo-hah!" the others responded.

"Yo-hah," Red Jacket said. He paused to examine people's expressions. "Sisters, the condolence ceremony stirred deep emotions. Know that I have visited again with our mourning families. Perhaps you have as well. They declare themselves satisfied with Pickering's condolence gifts. Sisters, we must thank our women who made the mourning belts. Their hands were swift and inspired. I saw the two mothers holding the belts close to console themselves."

The matrons puffed quietly as they considered his remarks. Esther kept her silence, wondering if the two mothers had truly found a measure of solace. Perhaps she would visit them herself.

"Sisters," Red Jacket continued, "at this council we have tried to keep the path open to the yengwes. We accept their new big government with its thirteen council fires. Our hearts lift that the chain of friendship appears brightened. Our hearts lift at Pickering's promise that we, each of us as we move among them, will be given the same respect as yengwe settlers. Our hearts lift at his promise that his government will raise up our Iroquois League and resist the wicked efforts to break us apart. We now will report these promises back to our communities and urge our warriors to lay down their hatchets against the big government, here and to the west."

The chief consulted briefly with two head matrons, then with Esther herself, before resuming.

"Sisters, I am about to share a smoke with the other chiefs and elders. Then we chiefs will meet privately with Pickering a final time. Sisters, the yengwe has not pressed us to have our men take up their ways of farming. Perhaps he knew it would stir bad dust and wished to bury it by the wayside. I would like to keep it buried, too, and desire your counsel. Further, Sisters, I wish to press Pickering on a matter that Mother Esther brought to me. His talk that their chief Washington would pick only white men to stand guard over the honesty of land sales troubled Mother Esther. She wishes to have our people join Washington's yengwes to share that duty. I agree, and am willing to press Pickering for that, but I desire your counsel."

The circle of matrons spoke almost as one. It quickly became clear that most shared Esther's opinion. The head matrons assured Red Jacket that he had the women's support.

"Sisters," the Seneca chief concluded, "before Father Sun departs this day, the council fire will be covered and many of us will set off on our journeys of return. Sisters, more gifts and provisions are being distributed at the treaty ground. Gather them for your families. Keep the promises of this Teaoga council in your mouths and share them with your villages.

"Now, Sisters, before we depart, let us toss pinches of kulukuneekun into the fire to give us protection for our journeys."

ESTHER BADE FAREWELL TO the matrons and Red Jacket before emerging from the chief's quarters. Young Sisketung was no longer waiting outside the door. The old woman spotted her seated on a sunny rock at the edge of the treaty ground, bent in concentration. Esther wondered if the remarkably determined girl was doing more beadwork.

As she set out toward Sisketung, a tall figure closed in.

"Mighty Queen Esther, you old crow. So it is you!"

The trader Hollenback had spotted her. Esther, feeling trapped, returned his peevish frown. The two hadn't spoken in six winters, when she last visited his small trading post near the Carrying Path. It was a branch store extending his chain of frontier posts up the Susquehanna from Wyoming—and Esther held him greatly responsible for opening the way for the steady onslaught of yengwes into Teaoga following the Revolution.

"Can't rightly say I'm pleased to see you," Hollenback grumbled. "Even before the council there were rumors you were coming. I didn't believe it. Didn't think you'd risk it! Fact is, we ran into some young fellows downriver who were heading here to get your scalp, queenie! I told them don't bother, you were probably long since dead somewhere. Truth is, I thought I spotted you two days ago—but I kept quiet. Figured I'd best not stir things up. Had too much riding on this council running smooth, if you catch my meaning."

Though Esther didn't understand everything he said, she followed the gist of it. When he placed a hand on her shoulder, she pulled away with a fiery stare.

"Esther, you must have nine lives," Hollenback exclaimed. "But here's a word to the wise, old one: Don't press your luck. I don't know exactly what you did at that Bloody Rock, only that there's plenty of folks call you a butcher, yes sir, and wish you dead in the worst way.

"Now, your Tutelo friends here are honest enough. I don't wish 'em no harm. Don't really wish you harm. I've seen enough of war and scalping, just have. But queenie, you're in danger in these parts. Most people don't want you savages here at all anymore—and they'd make an example of you in a second! So thank your stars you're still in one piece, and move along! I'll give you one more day. If I see you around here past then, I declare I'll let on, you hear?"

Esther hadn't budged. She fixed her eyes on Sisketung, who was facing away, engrossed in her task, oblivious to the showdown. Finally, she turned to the looming yengwe and summoned up her best English.

"Trader, this our land," she muttered. "Your people lie. Push us out. Land now sick. Yo-hah, I go, yes."

She strode off toward Sisketung. Hollenback watched her proud departure, and then left with a snort to check on the final food distribution.

The sight of lovely Sisketung at her work had kept Esther composed. She managed to greet the girl pleasantly. "Daughter, it pleases me that Father Sun has stayed with you. It seems you passed the time well. Let us return to the fire circle. Your mother is preparing cattle meat for my journey. After the meal, I must rest. Then let us walk together."

LATER THAT DAY, IT was Sisketung who led Esther in the direction of the old Cayuga watch town. The girl wished to capture the moment before darkness closed in. She turned and headed into a field of high grass. Esther followed a step behind. Soon they came to a fresh mound of dirt.

"Ah, here lies Brother Ka'wia," Esther said.

"Yo-hah," Sisketung whispered. "Mother Esther, I have something to say. It is this. I feel the porcupine's spirit with me, Mother Esther. Ever since our forest brother revealed himself and entrusted his body to us, I have felt a bond. He seems to guide my fingers when I work with his quills. The Senecas regard his spirit-clan as messengers of faith and trust, and I understand. He has helped me to trust in your wisdom and to trust more in my people. He gives me faith that we have a future even in these dark times. See how I have attached his strongest quills to my pouch as a sign of his guidance."

Esther ran her fingers along the raised quills. "Daughter, your spirit is pure like Brother Ka'wia's. You have learned well. I am honored to hear your heart speak so. Daughter, listen well. Yes, this brother is trusting—but he also bears sharp weapons of protection. Know the need for both in your life, Daughter."

"Mother, his hands guided me to create these." Sisketung drew a pair of delicate loop earrings from her pouch and handed them to Esther. "They bear the quills and beads of your own mother's handiwork. See, I have used her deer sinew. See, the old pieces mingle with the finest quills from our Teaoga spirit-brother."

She reached to place the earrings in Esther's wrinkled earlobes. After she had attached one, Esther took the second away, and hooked it in Sisketung's ear. "A treasure of our time together, Daughter," she smiled.

"Mother Esther, I have this as well." Sisketung opened her palm to show a round, glistening pearl. Esther's eyes shone in recognition of the Tutelo pearl. "Mother, I tried to attach the pearl to the earring, but its hardness would not be pierced. Instead, Mother, I offer it as a simple gift. May it speak my thanks, and may it bring strength in your travels ahead."

"Daughter, my heart is full," Esther replied. "You have shown great care and great insight. N'petalogalgun. As I have watched you these last days, I have seen the qualities of a healer. If we had time, I would teach you the ways of our remedies and potions. Our communities always need healers. Daughter, wherever you go, seek out the healers and learn from them."

Esther reached under her blanket shawl. From beneath her blouse she retrieved her medicine bag, the sacred manito xesinutay, which she carried against her body.

"Begin with these," she said, holding out several bunches of herbs. "Daughter, take these as gifts from me. This is willow bark, and this is milk thistle. Both help keep the mind clear and free of pain. These witch hazel twigs and leaves can be steeped as a poultice for sprains and bruises. You may need them in the months ahead. Your mother knows the preparation, and she can assist you.

"Daughter, add these to your beautiful quill pouch and use them well. You will want to create a medicine pouch of your own. It is time to learn healing and to use its powers for your people."

THAT EVENING WAS ONE Esther and Sisketung would never forget. Moon, the Very Old Uncle, had waxed full, the occasion for a communal bonfire and dancing to offer thanks. Though the tradition was age-old, not all children of the remnant groups had experienced it before.

The night was clear and stars dotted the overhead sky by the time people walked from the campground to the old assembly place where the painted post once stood. The crowd was half the size of that morning's dawn ritual since many families had departed during the day on their homeward journeys. They had left behind campfire logs and the frames of their temporary shelters— material that the remaining people dragged across the open field to feed into the bonfire.

Esther stood with the Tutelos and watched the flames grow and reach toward the moon. She noticed old men holding young children on their hips. The children's curious eyes brought a fleeting image of Elesoon, sending her mind into a private place. She fought off sadness with a prayer to the Preserver and a thought that had girded her before: You must be strong for today.

The old Cayuga chief, Fish Carrier, the principal sachem, stood in the bonfire's glow and lifted his arms toward the moon. His voice rose and fell in a long, chanting tribute to the Very Old Uncle. Periodically, he cast handfuls of kulukuneekun into the fire as offerings. Esther knew many in the assembly did not understand his Cayuga tongue, yet still they were transfixed.

Once his chanting was complete, the sachem prostrated himself on the ground. The matrons followed his example, and then the rest of the assembly lay on the warmed ground. Fish Carrier called out a fervent shout of praise, which the others echoed again and again in a noisy crescendo.

135

The dances followed. Matrons sang traditional Cayuga, Seneca, and Delaware choruses to accompany the men, who danced and slowly spun around the bonfire. It pleased Esther to see Sisketung and other young women and girls readily join the singing and boys attempting the dance steps, some perhaps for their first time. Next came the matrons' stomp dances, with the men providing the singing according to the tradition. Esther shuffled along in the graceful stomping step she had learned as a girl. Soon the Tutelo women joined at her side, including Sisketung.

After a time, Esther's legs tired, and she stepped aside to rest. The men's songs had grown louder and quicker. The abler women kept pace. Images of her daughters swaying in their white baptismal gowns crossed Esther's vision. Preserver, keep me strong, she prayed. Her eyes caught sight of Sisketung. The girl had moved directly behind the best dancers and was attempting their intricate steps. Her feet showed the same nimble skill as her fingers, her arms and hips the same grace. Esther looked at Cakoanos, who had come to stand beside her. The two women shared a few tears of pleasure.

Oh, if only Sisketung could have been born in my time, when we were strong. Preserver, please give this girl a good life. May she have dances, and a good man, and safe circles of fellowship. She is so worthy. And let her be a healer in our time of need. Such was Esther's sadness that she had to turn and leave. She walked slowly into the open field, toward the quiet of the trees, and lifted her face to the Very Old Uncle. Across the years, Esther had never asked anything of his spirit, but now she did. She asked Uncle to shine his protection on Sisketung. She turned to the trees and to the mountains and asked them to protect her. And to the rocks. And to the rivers. And to Brother Ka'wia.

Esther stood listening to the world but was not sure an answer came. She closed her eyes and waited patiently. Then a different sound came. It was the murmur of yengwe voices.

A line of yengwes had formed along the treeline near the trailhead that led back to the store. Esther watched their silhouettes silently. They seemed to be observing the bonfire. She didn't notice any weapons. There were no shouts or vulgar taunts. *Perhaps these yengwes, these ones watching us on this special night, mean no harm. Or perhaps it is merely because they know they are almost rid of us.*

Once the singing stopped, Esther returned to the bonfire. People were milling about, visiting with one another and staying warm. Some tossed more branches onto the embers. Sisketung, breathing deeply, was standing and talking to her mother.

"Daughter, your feet have a gift," Esther said to Sisketung. "Your mother's do as well. The old dances give meaning and always give joy."

"She has asked me to teach her more," Cakoanos said. The three stood watching the festivities. Some of the men sang low. A few young women continued to sway in time. Esther noticed Fish Carrier heading back to the campground.

"Daughter, the dances have wearied my old bones," Esther said to Sisketung, "Please return me to my shelter."

Crossing the wide field, Esther spotted several figures silhouetted along the treeline. She drew Sisketung's elbow close.

"Daughter, I have a last request. Yengwes have been watching us tonight. There, see them near the trailhead. Go there now while I wait. Surely one of them will recognize you. Go with a message. Ask that the girl Sarah join us tomorrow morning at the ridgeline near our fire circle."

Chapter 18

Maddy hadn't sat on a glider loveseat since she didn't know when. The last one she even remembered seeing was the vintage wicker model on Grammy Winter's front porch in Indiana. Now, here were two jumbo metal ones side by side, and high on a mountaintop overlook of all places.

She and Katie hopped onto one, the two parents took the other, and they surveyed the panoramic view of the valley far below. Without a word, Katie leaned back and started giving the old glider a workout. The hinge at her end being in an early stage of rust, it squeaked on the backswing and squealed on the upswing. As her feet pumped harder, Katie felt the rhythm and started to bob her chin. Flashing Maddy a Rockn look, she let loose a high-pitched *ree-eek!* in her throat to accompany the metallic squeak.

Maddy understood she was being invited to add her own techno sounds. She managed to bop her head lightly, but she just couldn't flip on the goofy-girl switch. Not now. There was too much on her mind.

Katie picked up her cue. Gradually, they slowed and quieted. The lazy rhythm was calming, along with the warm breeze that rose up the mountain slope onto the girls' faces. Without a word, they turned their attention to the view expanding before them. The rocker's continuous low squealing became a sort of trance music. Before long, Maddy was lost in contemplation.

Her time in Athens was ticking away fast, a realization that made her buzz inside. She felt caught—perfectly suspended—between a peaceful closeness with everyone, a bittersweet remorse at the rush of time, and a remote disconnectedness. Coming to Tioga had let her step outside her narrow routine and see everything fresh. She felt like she was evaluating herself now with her inner binoculars and hovering helicopter.

From the clarifying distance, insights were coming clear. *I, Madeline Pruitt Winter, have a good heart, or at least want to have one. I love other people who have good hearts. I love people like Katie, who's honest and unguarded and accepting. Even with her issues, she wants to enjoy the moment and doesn't get lost in stupid, paralyzing self-consciousness. I love people like good old Melody, who accepts me but also sets me straight in a gentle way. And like Dad, who's such a teddy bear.*

The insights kept coming. *My best self has the strength to take on bullies and bad behavior. My best self is sick of all the bad-mouthers. I need to keep my distance from the backbiters. I don't want to turn into just another mean teen. I want to be confident, and I want to be smart, confidently smart. I want to learn, and be a teacher. I want to know everything about how the world around me came to be. I want to look with open eyes on everyone around me, especially the ones who aren't like me, and the underappreciated ones.*

Maddy's wishes suddenly struck her as being sort of a prayer. Steepling her hands quickly, she added, *Please, God, let it be so, amen.*

She lifted her face to savor the sun and the breeze and the beautiful view for a long minute, then glanced over. Katie had a faraway look of her own.

TURNING IN HER GLIDER seat, Maddy checked out the scene behind them. Round Top Park, atop a mountain on the western slope of the valley, was filling with families. Its craggy acreage was nearly shaved clean of trees and equipped with picnic pavilions, playground equipment, horseshoe pits, trails, and open fields. It seemed to be a popular place on Saturdays, because they were hardly the only ones here for a midday cookout. Maddy smiled at the hubbub. She saw that her father and Mrs. T had claimed a nearby pavilion and were setting out the lunch fixings.

Emerging from her stupor, Katie followed Maddy's gaze. "How did my mom get over there?" she mumbled.

"We're pretty spacey, aren't we?"

"You know, I was just thinking," Katie said wistfully, "some of my earliest memories are of up here. I actually remember the first time on these gliders that my feet could touch the ground. My mom let me just push it and push it all I wanted while she sat with me. Funny, I used to imagine myself as an eagle flying over Athens! This amazing view up the valley first made me see there was a much bigger world out there."

Maddy pictured her helicopter soaring in tandem with Katie's eagle. "Yeah, it is an awesome view. I think the first time I had that kind of wide-world thought was when I must have been about four, and I heard Mexican dance music on the radio and started paying attention. The funny foreign words, like, blew my mind. My dad told me there were all these millions of people right down there in a neighboring land who spoke a whole different language from us. That really stuck with me."

"You mean they didn't say *y'all?*" Katie joked. Maddy poked her on the shoulder.

"I remember one time up here when I lost a Frisbee," Katie smiled. "A blue one. My dad and I used to toss it around over there in the field. I thought if I threw it real hard out over the overlook it would just magically soar over the valley like a bird. So I whipped it as hard as I could. Hah, it went about thirty feet before dropping into the clearing down there. It just disappeared into the tall grass. I was crushed. I cried and cried!"

"Aww."

"And my folks wouldn't let me climb over the fence to get it back, either. Tragic."

"Kids can be so naïve."

The breeze kicked up, and the girls lifted the bottom of their tees to let it cool their midriffs for a minute. Katie touched a fingertip to Maddy's glitter-green pinkie nail.

"Maddy, it was amazing how the camp kids connected with you. I didn't do so well. I should know how to handle boys better. Shoot, I've had enough practice with Curty. Your Senecas were, like, crawling all over you at the farewell party!"

Yesterday had been Maddy's last day as a counselor. She figured something special might happen, like maybe extra ice cream, no big deal. But her little campers had surprised her with lots of hugs and a handmade gift. Somehow they'd all secretly made an Indian-style handbag that was supposed to resemble the pouches natives would sling over their shoulders. It was made of light-brown felt, folded and cutely stapled along the edge. The flap was carefully cut to look like fringe—Maddy figured that was Beth's handiwork. The kids had pasted on sequins and beads and made animal designs with colored markers.

Even though some of the beads had fallen off the bag, and she had to be careful not to grip the still-sticky spots, the gift left Maddy gleeful. She returned the favor by sketching caricatures of each camper with cartoon heads emerging from Indian clothes. They'd giggled as she wrote quasi-Indian names for each of them, like Lucy Lightning Bug and Jason Geronimo.

"Your drawings were awesome!" Katie said. "Another hidden talent, like teaching. My mom thinks you should be a teacher, you know. I know you know."

Maddy smiled. She'd made a little farewell something for Katie, but figured this wasn't the right time to give it. Katie had a gift for her as well—and also privately decided to wait until later.

THE PICNIC LUNCH CONSISTED of hot dogs, tortilla chips, apple juice, and a token Indian dish: succotash. The food kept Maddy upbeat and in the moment. She and Katie spooned some of the lima bean and corn mix onto their doggies, buried it in ketchup, and decided after two bites that they'd never do that again. "Ptooey!" Maddy spit.

"Now you know why they call it thufferin' thuccotash!" her dad quipped. That earned him a shoulder whack from Maddy.

"You brute," he whimpered, rubbing his arm. "Just for that, you don't get to drive the car home! But actually and seriously, help us start to clean up, okay. We don't have a ton of time. I know Mrs. T has some things to tell us, right?"

Mrs. T straightened herself and gestured to the overlook. "Right, Russ. So, Maddy, do you have your bearings? Do you know what's down there?"

A long-lost frisbee crossed Maddy's mind, but she decided to be serious. "Athens," she replied. "And the valley runs straight through from south to north, right to left."

"Yupper. And do you know what's directly below us, at the foot of the mountainside?"

Maddy shrugged.

"Come on, gang," Mrs. T said. "Let's go back to the gliders. It's easier to get the full picture there."

Only one glider was available. Mrs. T, Mr. Winter, and Katie shared its wide seat. Maddy decided to perch above them on the seat back. It made her feel like a sentry standing guard.

"We are on the western slope looking east across the valley," Mrs. T began, shading her eyes as she peered out at the vista. "You see Athens spread out below us, and Sayre off to the left. Looking northward, beyond Sayre, see how the valley opens wider and wider like the top of a funnel as it goes up into New York State. Now, directly below us, out of view at the base of the mountain, is the muddy Chemung. And over there on the far side of the valley, curving away to the northeast, is the shiny Susquehanna, our great mother river.

"I wanted to bring you up here because it's a good place to show you the last stage of our Indian story. Of Queen Esther's story, too. I've been thinking Round Top would make a good place for a field trip for middle schoolers. And I'd like to give it a test run with you all."

"Please do," nodded Mr. Winter.

"Okay, so first, it's helpful to envision the scene down there in a different way. Think of it as a theater—a vast theater of war!" she said. "That's how generals refer to the broad fronts in their wars. World War Two had its Pacific Theater and its European Theater. The Tioga area was exactly that several times, a theater of international warfare. People need to appreciate that. I've told you about the French and Indian War times. It was certainly a theater of war then. Same with during the early years of the Revolution, when there were countless raids up and down our valley."

A theater! What a great image, Maddy thought. Looking afresh at the panorama, she imagined it as a big board game with toy soldiers and natives charging around its squares. Or as a giant, noisy diorama.

"What I want to tell about is the time after the Battle of Wyoming when our humble little area became a major, major theater of war," Mrs. T said.

"Remember, Queen Esther had her mixed village down there on the flats then. Her man Eghohowin was roosting a few miles farther north of here, up the Chemung. We're talking 1778. Most of the Indians were siding with the British, and that summer they made a joint attack on the Colonial settlements downriver at Wyoming. They laid waste to them, and the settler families fled into the hills. It's when Esther might have committed her atrocities at the Bloody Rock. Afterwards, the Indians came back up here with their captured loot.

"The big win only made them bolder. That summer and fall the braves expanded their raids on more outlying Colonial homesteads. Around what's Williamsport today, they targeted squatters who had recklessly set up homes on tribal land. The settlers fled en masse. It became known in history as the Great Runaway. Isn't that a great name?!"

Maddy pictured settler children running around in circles, shouting and crying. Also, tomahawks and piercing warrior yells. A shiver ran up her spine. She noticed the dad on the other glider shushing his kids so he could listen in.

"General Washington didn't have a lot of troops to protect civilians across all that so-called backcountry," Mrs. T continued. "He decided to send a strike force north to do some damage to the Indian and Tory bases, and to test how far up into Iroquois territory the soldiers could get. He picked a young colonel named Thomas Hartley to lead the expedition.

"That September, Hartley and his force of maybe 200 men made it up to Sheshequin and freed some Colonial captives. They then marched up here to Tioga where they put the torch to Queen Esther's Town, the abandoned Cayuga watch town, and some Tory farmsteads. Burned them down just like that! It's said that Esther and her people escaped in time and fled up to Wilawana, around the bend to our north."

"That's where they hid in the ravine, Esther's Glen, right?" Mr. Winter asked.

"Right-o, Russ," she replied. "By that point, Hartley realized he didn't have enough firepower to attack the Indians' Chemung stronghold, so he withdrew. Some braves were in hot pursuit, and he lost a handful of men before managing to make it back safely to Wyoming. Hartley was hailed as a war hero."

Maddy raised her hand reflexively. "What happened to Esther?"

"It's not clear where Esther went next. We know she was already becoming a hated figure to settlers because of the tales of the Bloody Rock. Wait, there's more. But first I need a cold drink. This talking is drying me out. And Katie dear, please get my sheaf of papers from the car."

THE GIRLS FETCHED COLD drinks from the cooler. Mrs. T drank deep and smacked her lips in satisfaction before resuming her narrative.

"So that was Hartley's 1778 expedition. And it was just step one," she began. "A month later, the other side struck back. A joint force of British and Indian fighters left from here and headed northeast into New York to attack an isolated Colonial settlement called Cherry Valley. It was ruthless. The Indians were furious that the Colonials were spreading lies that their braves had killed innocent women and children at Wyoming. It seems they were angry that some of the Colonial men they'd spared at the Wyoming battle on the promise to stop fighting had double-crossed them by turning around and joining Hartley's troops."

Maddy spoke up. "How about the burning of the villages by Hartley?"

"Yes, I'm sure the Indians wanted to avenge that, too," Mrs. T answered. "Gang, the Cherry Valley attack was ruthless and gory. The braves sacked the town and, in this case, did kill dozens of innocent civilians along with armed soldiers. They committed the worst sort of atrocities on the bodies. Let's just say it was a low point of the war. It became known among the Colonials as the Cherry Valley Massacre, and as you can imagine, they demanded revenge. Washington decided to strike back big time at the, quote-unquote, 'Indian menace.' Hartley's early success in penetrating the Iroquois' southern door here convinced Washington that an attack farther up into Iroquois country could succeed.

"He got the Continental Congress to approve an all-out military expedition to punish what they called—I remember this language—'the insolent and revengeful' Indians. Their first target was to be Eghohowin's war town, Chemung, where Hartley had reported a fort was being built. From there the plan was to keep moving northwestward into the Seneca heartland to burn and plunder—burn the villages, destroy the crops and orchards, kill the livestock, take any and all hostages."

"Dang, a real scorched-earth campaign!" Maddy's dad whistled.

"Exactly. The plans were drawn up that winter and spring of 1779. Meanwhile, the Indian and Tory raiding parties kept up their constant attacks across the Pennsylvania and New York frontier, making General Washington even more determined to hit back hard. He gave the command of the expedition to one of his battle-tested generals, John Sullivan.

"That June, Sullivan set off from the Delaware River with his main force of about three thousand soldiers. They hacked out a passage westward over the Pocono Mountains to the Wyoming Valley. Then they pushed north along the Susquehanna toward Tioga, slowly poling their supplies along on barges. Finally, they got to Esther's Flats in August. Their journals describe the troops marching in military formation right up through Esther's Flats, flags flying and drums beating, to make a showing for any Indian lookouts who might be around."

This, Maddy knew, was the Sullivan Campaign. *The March that Destroyed Savagery et cetera, et cetera.* She envisioned a fife-and-drum corps playing "Yankee Doodle Dandy" as flanks of soldiers swept up the flats towards Curtis and Tommy's hideout while Indian spirits swooped above their watering spot in alarm.

"The Indians and British had pulled back already," Mrs. T went on, "so Sullivan occupied Tioga Point as his base camp. I'm sure in his mind it was the perfect statement, to plant his headquarters right at the old southern door! The soldiers pitched their tents near the ruins of the Cayuga watch town, and Sullivan ordered a stockade fort to be built. It must have been quite a sight—like a Fort Apache with walls of high pointed timbers and blockhouses at each corner. It was located just below the Carrying Path, where it went all the way from river to river."

"The famous Fort Sullivan," Maddy announced.

"Right-o. Sullivan's army got bigger because of—well, listen to this clever move. Part of his strategy was to have another brigade of soldiers in New York join them at Tioga Point by floating down the Susquehanna. This brigade dammed the river up around Cooperstown, then broke the dam and rode the wave south in more than two hundred boats like whitewater rafting! Picture them rushing toward us down the mighty Susquehanna, right over there in the distance."

"A giant amusement park ride!" Mr. Winter exclaimed.

"Well, with mortal danger added," Mrs. T said. "It's said that hundreds of their flat-bottomed boats were moored all around the Point. The unified forces filled the Point with their tents and did their daily drills—probably right where their enemy had drilled just one year earlier!

"Then things got intense. In late August, Sullivan and around four thousand men started their march up into Iroquoia. Near Chemung, ten miles or so from here, a much smaller force of Indians and Brits had dug in to stop them. Suddenly, they were in a head-on battle. They tried to lure the Colonials into an ambush a couple of times, but it didn't work. The Colonials pounded their trenches with cannon fire, and finally overwhelmed them. The great Mohawk leader Joseph Brant led a counterattack, but he also got swamped. What happened became known as the Battle of Newtown, and it essentially crushed the Iroquois resistance.

"Over the next three weeks, Sullivan's troops torched about forty native towns and villages. Just torched them, one after another. The destruction was something the Senecas never fully recovered from. The soldiers told later how impressed they were with the Indians' beautifully tended homes and orchards and fields, but they destroyed them anyway."

Mrs. T consulted the papers in her folder. "It's believed that the soldiers burned and trampled—here it is—'at least 160,000 bushels of corn, along with vegetables and fruit without number.' It became known as, get this, the War of the Vegetables!

"The Seneca villagers fled west toward Niagara. They hoped the British could feed and protect them there. That winter was brutally cold, though, and lots of them apparently froze, got scurvy, or starved."

Frozen. Maddy shivered at the image of Indian children struggling through snowdrifts, only to become frozen to death. It blotted out her earlier mental images of the settler children dashing helter-skelter. She also had a picture of Indian mothers moaning with disease in a cold cabin overlooking Niagara Falls. *That could have been Mom. Or me, for that matter! How could anyone who survived such a disaster ever be the same again?*

"Even Eghohowin apparently ended up at Niagara," Mrs. T said. "He and Esther must have gotten separated. It's said he soon died in a drunken brawl with another Indian."

THE FOURSOME SAT QUIETLY for a minute, gliding with low squeals and processing the information. Maddy kept her eyes on the valley. She imagined painting the distant scene, but all in blacks and grays and lots of reds. She'd call it "Valley of Sorrows."

"War of the Vegetables," Mr. Winter muttered from his seat.

Mrs. T nodded. "And so even though we call Washington the father of our country, the Iroquois have their own name for him. They call him Town Destroyer. Like I was telling you kids the other night, it's all a matter of perspective.

"Meanwhile, Sullivan's men returned in triumph to Tioga, where they held a great celebration. Officers' journals recorded it. Here, listen: 'They fired a salute of thirteen guns from the cannon, built thirteen fires, drank thirteen toasts, and lighted the tables with thirteen candles.' A second party was held where the officers mockingly danced like Indians and shouted war whoops.

"The next day, the army started loading up their boats to return downriver. The rear guard demolished the fort so there was nothing left except the graves of their war dead. And off they all went—although actually, we know that many of the men had hatched plans to return after the war and settle in these parts. Seeing all the rich bottomland from Wyalusing north, and then the rolling hills of Iroquoia, had captured their fancy, you might say. Many of them did return, becoming some of our first permanent settlers."

"Didn't you say the Snells were one? And the Jennings?" Katie asked. Maddy was no longer surprised by Katie's unassuming knowledge.

"Yes, love. Good. Plus the Franklins and the Mathewsons and the Spaldings," Mrs. T added. "The Indian raids actually continued on and off across the region until the war was over. But once they were finally defeated and the land was opened up, those old soldiers made our valley their homes."

Katie kept going. "I think you should tell the students to stand here and imagine, like, peeling off the towns below. You know, just rolling back the whole top layer like some huge bedspread to uncover what was here before. That's what you're making me do, in my mind. And Mom, when they're at the museum, go outside and have them look around. Tell them to picture it being the British and Indian war base one year and then the Colonial war base the very next year. I never knew it was so quick."

Maddy leaned against the glider's left upright and pondered. The valley's sad twists and turns left a catch in her throat. She was considering suggesting that Trevor and his geek friends develop a computer program showing an aerial map with overlays of the various war movements. Her eyes settled on the little bald spot atop her father's head, idly imagining it as a vortex.

Suddenly, another realization popped up like one of his cowlicks.

"Dad, don't you need to take care of the car?"

"Oops, yes indeed!" His plan was to swap out Li'l Red for a bigger four-door sedan that the family would use on their road trip to New York City. With her mom and brother arriving at the airport the next day, this afternoon was his time to make the switch. Meanwhile, Maddy was going to stick with Katie into the evening before going back to pack up.

Plus, she wanted to slip away for a final bike ride around town with Curtis and Tommy. It was a personal mission that had to happen.

"Dad, before you go, let me grab my pouch out of the trunk. It's got stuff I need."

Katie accompanied them to the car. As Mr. Winter revved the engine, Katie rubbed the rear fender and swooned, "Goodbye, my Li'l Red! My sweet, sweet Red!"

The girls blew noisy kisses while Mr. Winter waved a melodramatic farewell.

Chapter 19

Arriving early atop the ridgeline, young Sarah noticed with alarm that sentries were no longer in place. Pickering had ordered them removed after watching Indian groups steadily vacate the Teaoga grounds and head back up the trails and rivers. The settler girl, while curious about Sisketung's mysterious invitation, felt alone and exposed without the guards. She decided to conceal herself behind some bushes where she could observe the activity in the native campground below. She chose a spot that also provided a clear view back to Hollenback's store and the reassuring sight of her older brother, who'd promised to stay on the lookout for any trouble.

Soon Sisketung and Esther approached across the lowland. Esther was making no attempt to conceal her face. Once they reached the bottom of the ridge, Sisketung bounded up the steep footpath to look around. The absence of sentries did not concern her. But where was the settler girl? The yengwe boy she'd approached in the woods the prior evening had promised to deliver her summons to Sarah in person.

Then she caught sight of Sarah's brother standing vigil in the distance. Looking about carefully, she spotted Sarah's familiar checkered calico skirt in a stand of bushes to the left. A beam of morning sunlight caught the skirt's bright-red hue.

"Sarah. Come."

Reluctantly, the straw-haired girl emerged from the undergrowth. A vexed look furrowed her brow.

"Come. Come down," Sisketung beckoned as she descended the path and rejoined Esther, who stood below.

Sarah walked to the edge but halted. Her frown etched deeper.

"Is that your Queen Esther with you?" she demanded, pointing in disdain. "Is that the old killer right there?"

Sisketung glared back. "She proud leader," she responded. "Peace woman. Wise woman. Will bless us. Come."

Sarah didn't budge.

Sensing the stalemate, Esther touched Sisketung's arm. "Daughter," she said calmly, "you have done well to bring the girl to us. It is well she does not leave. This is the moment the Preserver has given to us. Let us continue. Daughter, you can share my meaning with her."

Esther removed a beaded pouch from her shoulder and held it out toward Sisketung, then toward Sarah. She felt it best if Sisketung heard her addressing the yengwe as an equal.

"Daughters, listen well," Esther began. She spoke strictly in the Delaware tongue, yet loudly enough for Sarah to hear her speech. "Our council fire is put out. Our assembly is departing from Teaoga. I, too, will return to the Iroquois homeland. Daughters, I do not expect to see this place again. But the Preserver brought me to this moment for a purpose. I have given my counsel to the

Seneca matrons and to my precious Tutelo friends, including you, proud Sisketung."

Above them, Sarah shifted warily. Sisketung kept her eyes on the yengwe—hoping by sheer force of mind to relay Esther's meaning to her.

"Daughters, these have been dark times," Esther continued. "Our two peoples do not abide together well. Much of the land has been reddened with blood and remains pained and sickened. The times have left me bitter. Daughters, the path ahead may be even darker, even narrower. The omens tell me treachery and danger will hover near you like vultures.

"But Daughters, listen well. The path ahead belongs to you now, to watch over and protect through seasons to come. People with good hearts must step forward to guard the path and keep it open. People with good hearts who will counsel understanding, who will listen, who will show patience and respect. It is a hard way. It is a way that people with closed hearts and selfish ends will try to stop. But listen well: It is the way of the Preserver!"

Reaching into her deerskin pouch, Esther retrieved two wampum strings. They were the two remaining strands she had carried to Teaoga—the sacred white strings of peace. She held them out in her open palm.

"Daughters, I ask you to walk together on the bright path, the path of peace. I pray that you will keep the path smooth and wide. I pray that you, Sisketung, will teach you, Sarah, our sacred ways of the peace women. I pray that you will open your hearts to one another and show the bright path to your people as well. These peace strings will give you strength, and they will be clear signs to others of your good intent."

She placed the two long strands in Sisketung's hand and asked her to present one to Sarah. Sisketung paced back up the footpath and motioned to Sarah to open her hand. She ceremonially placed a pure white strand on the girl's half-clenched palm.

Sarah stared at it without moving. "This is what you call wampum, ain't it. But what's the hag saying to us? What does she want, anyway?"

"Is for you. Means peace, Sarah. Wants peace. You. Me. All." Sisketung raised her face toward the treetops and swept an outstretched arm in a wide arc to encompass Teaoga and beyond. "Peace. You. Me. All."

When she lowered her gaze again, Sarah was gone. The girl had turned and was trotting off toward her brother. At Sisketung's feet lay the coiled wampum string. Sarah had hurled it into the dirt.

In disgust, Sisketung watched the two young yengwes slip into the store. She lifted the wampum from the ground and withdrew down the footpath to Esther's side.

"A child of her people," Esther remarked simply. In truth, Esther had been testing Sarah and was not surprised by her hostile reaction. "Pray that our words will speak to her heart in time."

Sisketung brushed the wampum clean and offered it back to her.

"Daughter, keep both sacred strings," Esther said. "Perhaps on a better day, Sarah will accept hers willingly. If not, another use for it will come to you.

"But Daughter, listen well. Seeing Sarah's anger makes plain what lies ahead. Even a peace woman must be prepared for danger. I have spoken to your mother, and she agrees. Here is another gift for your life's journey."

From her sash Esther withdrew a metal blade with a carved and beaded handle. Sisketung had held skinning knives before, but none so ornate.

"It was Eghohowin's once," Esther said. "Keep it near. It holds great power to protect."

MOMENTS LATER, CAKOANOS RAN her fingers over the handle and its carved wolf totem before handing the knife back to her daughter. "You are young to lift a blade as a weapon, but Mother Esther is right. It is best we all remain ready. Daughter, perhaps you can add a ring of quills to the handle, and a pearl, to make it your own."

"Eghohowin's spirit would delight in that," Esther declared.

"Yo-hah!" added the Tutelo women gathered around them near the fire circle. Their morning meal eaten and the fire now extinguished, they knew the difficult time of departure had come.

"Sisters of Teaoga," Esther raised her arm and began, "my companions await me at the Carrying Path. They have put our canoes back in the water. Soon I will see my home and Steel Trap again, which gladdens my heart. But Sisters, I leave Teaoga in sadness. I have listened to your stories. I have witnessed the marking and fencing off of our land. I have seen and smelled the clamor of the yengwe cattle pens. I have heard the whistles of their boats. I have felt the pain of the Earth and the river. I am seeing the death of our life at Teaoga!"

The others listened silently.

"Sisters, know that you are part of a long river of events. Words return to me today from another council long ago. They were powerful words spoken by my Eghohowin more than thirty winters past. They are words I remember well, because they were spoken true!

"We had traveled to the Forks of the Delaware to complain about a dishonest land sale. Settlers were invading and claiming his wolf clan's lands to the east. Some Munsees had raised the hatchet against it. Eghohowin agreed to end the dispute for eight hundred Spanish dollars—but he had something to say to the New Jersey leader. I listened well. I remember his words exactly. They were these: 'We desire that if we should come into your province to see our old friends, and should have occasion for the bark of a tree to cover a cabin, or a little refreshment, that we should not be denied, but be treated as brethren! And that your people may not look on the wild beasts of the forests or the fish of the waters as their sole property, but that we may be admitted to an equal use of them!'"

Esther began to spit out her words. "That is what Eghohowin said in truth, Sisters! That is what he wished, simply that we 'be treated as brethren.' Hah! Only the Moravians did that with us—and the settlers grew to hate the gentle Moravians just as they hated us. They too were shoved aside! Do you know how the New Jersey headman replied to Eghohowin's plea that the paths through the land be kept open? He said that he, the governor himself, could make no promises about his settlers' actions! He would do nothing for us, would not lift his hand of power. At least he was honest! And Sisters, that land was lost to our use."

The others listened gravely.

"Sisters, now they claim the land beneath your very feet—all of it! Now you are the ones treated like pests of the field. We have witnessed how their Bible men speak of us. We have seen how their children pelt us with rocks, and even now cast aside our wampum of peace! Over my many winters, I have heard more and more hatred rise in their throats. They see blood only on our hatchets, never on theirs. They see their grievances alone and are blind to ours. I have watched the yengwes turn into schwannack, poisonous beings.

"Sisters, I wish to speak of the schwannack. Delaware prophets tell us the schwannack are offspring of the Preserver's devious brother. It is said our strange world results from the work of both brothers. While the Preserver makes health, his brother makes sickness. While the Preserver makes plants to sustain us, his brother makes briars and weeds and poisonous vines. While the Preserver bestows the good, his devious brother adds the bad. Sisters, my life has taught me that the yengwes are schwannack. I do not know why this is so, or why they have fallen on our necks—but I know they are a curse to us.

"Sisters of Teaoga, you have been strong. You have been patient. Still, you have become like shad in the mud, gasping for air. The Preserver has kept you to this day, but the path ahead must take you elsewhere. I counsel that you take it toward the setting sun, to the land of the Ohio. Rejoin your scattered families and people there! Depart soon, before another attack—before another Burning! Sisters, that is what the wisdom of my years and the spirit of the land tells me."

Esther lowered her arm and fell silent. Cakoanos spoke next. "Mother Esther, your counsel falls hard on our ears, but you speak true. We too have spoken among ourselves of departure. Our minds are mixed. We have made our lives here. But yo-hah, the omens are surely bad."

"Yo-hah," Esther replied. "Sisters, continue to speak together. Heed the signs around you. The answer will come."

Esther approached each woman and touched cheeks in a final farewell. Then she signaled for Sisketung to join her. As the two walked toward the Carrying Path, the Mohawk saga singer chanted a song of praise.

Soon Esther had slipped into her waiting canoe and was gone.

THE TUTELO FAMILIES DECIDED they would wait until the snow runoff ended and the lowland trails were passable, probably during the Month When the Deer Turns Red. At that point, they would set off together from Teaoga on the uncertain journey westward.

But the yengwe landholder, Sarah's father, soon stepped forward with other ideas. One cold morning, the ruddy-faced man came to their settlement to declare that he was going to clear land all the way to the riverbank to expand his wheat fields. Their wigwams were in his way. They must leave.

Three bitter days later, the Indian families were gone.

Sarah's father and brothers immediately set to work. By the time the Month When the Deer Turns Red arrived, the yengwes had turned the Tutelos' abandoned wigwams into stacks of firewood and were tilling the new field. Before long, animals were nesting beneath the woodpile of Sisketung's old home. They were a family of healthy, scampering porcupines. Sisketung had dreamed such a thing would happen.

For the Tutelos, meanwhile, the overland trip on the Sheshequin and Shamokin Paths was arduous. Ice still clung to the many creeks and rivulets. The families kept out of sight of yengwes, rationed their meager food, and prayed steadily to the Preserver. By the time the first wheat was being sown over their old Teaoga settlement, the weary travelers had reached the Maumee River far to the west.

In time, they located a village containing a few other Tutelos. Their hosts cleansed the travelers' eyes and ears and spirits, and provided what food they could. Though yengwes were not in the immediate vicinity, they said, danger was never far. Sadly, they knew nothing of Sisketung's long-vanished father.

"Sisters, many of our men slip away and do not return," one of the village matrons said solemnly. "Some are lost to drink. Some throw themselves into battle." Sisketung leaned on her mother's shoulder. She knew these truths already, but the words stung. They would have to strengthen themselves, keep their blades sharp.

As the women shared a smoke, Sisketung studied the flames of the campfire. Her thoughts returned to Esther. She remembered Esther's counsel, to keep her weapon near, yes—but also to be a voice for peace. Sisketung decided to share a story. The women encouraged her to speak.

"Mothers," the girl began, "in the darkness just before we left Teaoga, I emerged from a dream and was drawn outside. Night, our Aunt, guided my steps from the shelter and Moon, the Very Old Uncle, watched over me. I sensed that Mother Esther's spirit was with me as well.

"All was still," Sisketung said. "The animals of the forest kept their distance. The yengwes and their farm animals slept. My feet carried me to the riverside, to our watering place. Knowing our home would soon be lost to us, I took pinches of witch hazel from my medicine pouch as farewell offerings. Mothers, as I reached to place the offering in the water, I saw that I was no longer alone. Brother Ka'wia had followed and was standing witness behind me. We continued together to another watering spot and repeated the offering. Then to the fields where Mother Esther's villagers had planted their crops."

Sisketung spoke softly but confidently. Cakoanos listened with special pleasure. Was this the timid fawn of Teaoga? Though her daughter still bore a child's flutelike voice, Cakoanos wondered if she was beginning to hear the sure delivery of a healer, even of a sakima. She shut her eyes and let Sisketung's story unfold.

"Mothers, we continued on to the Carrying Path, where we crossed the river by an enchanted canoe, Brother Ka'wia and I. We walked to the council grounds and left an offering. Under the moon, we proceeded on to the Painted Post, and to our fire circle, leaving offerings.

"Finally, Mothers, we approached the ridgeline from below. My purpose was clear. I went to the top of the ridge. Mother Esther's spirit was guiding me, leading me to that place. Truly it is a powerful place, because there on the ridge, Mothers, the world has cracked apart! Below it lies the ancient, precious Teaoga ground where our people congregated. Above has become yengwe town, yengwe land. In my spirit, I saw the long, glowing wound that marks where the two worlds divide.

"Mother Esther's hands were leading me. With Brother Ka'wia's help, I dug a hole beside the path, just below the crest of the ridge, where the pain of the land glows bright. Into it I placed my sacred possessions. There I placed a bundle of witch hazel as balm for the spirits of innocent yengwes our people had killed. Another I added for the spirits of our own innocents killed by yengwes.

"Next, Mothers, in the hole I placed a single string of sacred white peace wampum. It is a powerful offering, powerful medicine for any yengwes who might still wish for peace with our people. Finally, I reached into my pouch and took an ancient pearl. As I held it in my hand, Mothers, I saw the entire world reflecting off it! It was beautiful, the world as it should be! I placed it inside, too. Then I covered the hole.

"Brother Ka'wia and I remained for a time in prayer to the Preserver. We prayed that our offerings might help heal the spirits of all dead innocents. We prayed that our offerings might soften the hearts of the yengwes who foolishly claim Teaoga as theirs alone. We prayed that peacemakers might draw strength from our offerings as though from a pure wellspring.

"And we prayed that these offerings would remain for as long as the rivers flow. We prayed that their presence in that broken ground would uphold all people with good hearts—people who come near now and in all the seasons to come."

Chapter 20

Wouldn't my little bro just love this, Maddy thought. Here she was, pedaling along with two boys her brother's own tender age—voluntarily and loving it. She was leading the way into the hot afternoon wind, Curtis and Tommy trailing behind, pushing south out of town along the side of the road. Destination: the Queen Esther monument.

After leaving Round Top Park with the Tulowitskys, she'd borrowed Cowgirl from Katie with a vague story about how she had to make one last farewell swing through town. She promised to be back before Mrs. T's sloppy-joe supper was on the table. Thankfully, Katie and her mom didn't ask any questions. Maddy simply slung her new fringed handbag—now bulky with private gifts— over her shoulder, donned Katie's scuffed bike helmet, and off she went. Curtis and Tommy met up with her in the museum driveway as she'd arranged. Sensing Maddy was on a personal mission, the boys fell in behind her without a peep.

Just a week ago, Maddy mused, Mz Snarkley would have scoffed at the sight. But her inner cheap-shot artist had remained blessedly quiet the last few days. Same with Rockn Grl, actually. *I think I'm done ricocheting like a pinball between them. They both have their place, just so they tone it down and don't try to take over. Yeah, that works for me.*

Maddy glanced backwards. The boys were following at a safe distance, single file, content and alert. *Two short weeks ago I didn't even know these kids, and now we're, like, in a secret society together. Talk about going with the flow!*

They reached the old railroad tracks paralleling the highway, ditched their bikes, and continued on foot for the final leg. Maddy was still in the lead. She moved to the shoulder of the tracks and found a comfortable stride, glad to be wearing sneaks. Her brisk pace made her realize she'd grown fitter in the last two weeks.

A pair of crows broke into flight up ahead. They dipped and then rose, cawing into the headwind. What sheer pleasure that must be, Maddy thought. To be airborne meant she could glide to the monument in a flash. More than that, the vantage point from overhead would be magical.

From the crows, her eyes moved to the treetops and then to the mountainsides that flanked the long valley. She imagined the straight green slopes to be pointing her forward on her mission. *These hills have seen everything. They've seen the encampments, the fights, the gantlets, the harvests, the councils, all of it. They're silent witnesses, solid, 'stolid' I think is the word, through time immemorial.*

That brought to mind her classmates back home and how utterly un-solid they were. Most were still in flux—and reveled in it, in their personal changeability. Maddy had to admit that most of the time she appreciated the way the kids tried on different guises. She could picture all the types on display in the hallways: the fashion plate, the clown, the philosopher, the nerd, the jock, the tease, the Goth, the loudmouth, the artiste, the cynic. It was like an endless costume party. She also was struck by how they would change looks, seemingly on a whim, as they sampled what felt most "authentic." That was a word she heard a lot. Though Maddy hadn't been an identity-shifter, having a parade of metamorphosers to observe helped her sort out her whims from her true nature. The process had felt normal, somehow even necessary.

But now, at her detached distance, she was not so sure. Esther and the spirit girl jumped to mind. They knew who they were, and they tried to be as steady and firm as the hills. To them, change entailed peril. It was something forced on them from outside. Their challenge was to keep solid ground under their feet. *Our playing around with pseudo change is such a luxury. Frivolous, I guess, and pretentious. It's the sort of indulgence our ancestors would have dismissed as vain and the Indians couldn't have grasped.*

But that, too, brought a frown. Pacing swiftly along the tracks, Maddy wondered if maybe she was being a bit too harsh. *Isn't it normal to experiment? Does that automatically make you a poseur? Did Indian girls never push against their traditions?*

"MA-DEEE!!"

Thirty yards back, Curtis and Tommy had stopped. Curtis was hailing her through cupped hands. She turned to see Tommy pointing inland to the bluff along the highway. Lost in introspection, she'd marched right past the cutoff to the Esther monument.

Moments later, the trio arrived across the field to the granite block. Maddy took charge while the boys stood a few steps back, observing silently. After focusing herself for a moment, she knelt and ran her fingers across the lettering on the bronze tablet. "South door ... Esther's Town ... Hartley ..." Passing motorists slowed to check them out.

A wave of self-consciousness came and went. Maddy persevered.

She took the floppy handbag off her shoulder and reached inside. The boys watched her movements intently.

The bag was filled with presents. The night before, Maddy had sat on her motel bed and made the gifts one by one, working until almost midnight, while her dad slumbered obliviously in the living room. Now she felt around for a nice one and lifted it out.

In her hand she held a limp, woven figure-eight shape. She had bunches more in her bag. They were her brainstorm—licorice lace wampum. She'd tightly entwined strands of the red candy, three strands per circle, then linked the woven circles together in pairs. For the final touch, she'd figured out how to pinch the rubbery ends together so the whole thing wouldn't come undone.

Satisfied that this particular figure eight was intact, Maddy lifted it to her nose to enjoy the familiar sweet scent, then pressed it to her lips. *For you, Queen Esther. I'm so sorry for your sufferings. Please accept this as, like, my parting tribute.* Maddy pushed her gift down into the little crevice between the ground and the base of the monument. Seeing that it was safely in place, she rose to her feet.

Tommy came to her side. Together they backed up like pastors at the altar and looked out across Esther's Flats. What memories this land holds, Maddy thought. *Just like the mountainsides, the monument stands vigil, forever mute.*

Tommy surveyed the scene as though he knew every inch of it. Maddy admired how he scanned with his keen eyes—*a natural Indian scout.*

Curtis, meanwhile, was crouched in front of the monument, peering down at her sunken gift. "What is that in there," he said, "a bunch of licorice or something?" The way he leaned close, she could tell his mouth was watering.

Tommy understood better. "Perfect, Maddy," he said. "It's a perfect offering."

AWARE THAT TIME WAS limited, the three proceeded rapidly to the boys' base camp. There, seated in the shady grove, Maddy took out two more of the figure eights and presented one to each boy. "Please," she said. "Things happened here that never would have happened without you. Thanks for accepting me."

Tommy dangled his gift from his fingertips, studying the handiwork. "I'll have to try this, too," he said. "Red and black strings would look right together, strong together. Those were the warriors' favorite colors, you know. Red was for victory. I'll show this to my mom tonight. Thank you, Maddy."

Curtis pressed his gift to his nose and inhaled. He began nibbling at the ends like a chipmunk. "Don't worry, I'll save some," he said. "And hey, Maddy, here, for you."

Curtis reached into his pouch and withdrew a flint arrowhead. "I made it myself. Don't worry, I can make another. It's Iroquois-style. Don't have these down in Texas, I bet!"

Next they headed to the Chemung shoreline, to the spot where the visions had first appeared. Maddy shut her eyes. Nothing unusual, but she wasn't surprised. She was pretty sure she'd figured out when the spirits would show and when they wouldn't. She waited until the boys reopened their eyes. Shrugging an "oh, well" shrug at them, she proceeded with her silent offering. *For you, spirits of the watering hole. I grieve for your suffering and your losses. I'm honored you appeared to me.*

This time she pushed her tribute gift into the mud at the very point where she'd stood in amazement a week earlier. Curtis looked anguished as the candy disappeared into the ooze.

"Perfect," Tommy said again.

They returned to their bikes and continued onward. Maddy felt focused and sure. She led them to the road marker identifying the Carrying Path, where she dug a little hole and inserted another licorice offering. *For the rivers, which bore such changes.* Then onto the turnaround spot at the Point. Maddy walked onto the knoll and knelt. *For the watch town, and the fish racks, and the dancers, and the warriors ... and even the soldiers.*

As they wheeled past the hissing stone, Maddy asked the boys to hold their silence while she approached. Staying at arm's length, she dropped an offering toward the monument's base. A blessing was slow to emerge. Finally, one came: *For understanding. Complete understanding.*

Academy Park was next, their final stop. Dismounting her bike, Maddy noticed the pouch was getting low on presents. The boys trailed behind while she crossed the grass to her magic outpost along the far border. This time she was in no rush.

Maddy sat and took in the surroundings: the verdant treetops, the damp air, the buzz of insects. She closed her eyes lightly and waited for a fresh communication, perhaps even guidance.

Instantly, she apprehended a familiar figure in the distance. It was the spirit girl. She stood in the lowland. Beside her now was another shimmering spirit figure—an old woman whose hair was streaked with white. Both spirits glowed faintly. Maddy felt benevolence in their eyes. She experienced a rush of deep pleasure. *They're sending me a love beam, a personal love beam.*

But the figures would come no closer. Maddy knew why. Not all children were ready to process such powerful sightings, according to the ancient belief. Curtis and Tommy were simply not of age yet. So long as the boys were nearby, the spirits would keep a proper distance.

Still, they conveyed a message for Maddy. The spirit girl gestured to a spot in the land between them and where Maddy sat. It was at the very crest of the ridgeline. In her mind's eye, Maddy stood and approached it. The land had cracked open there. From the crack came a pulse of blood-red light. Maddy also sensed vibrations of pain. The girl was silently communicating instructions to her: *Place your offering there. There two worlds collided and split apart.* With that, the two spirits drifted back toward the Susquehanna and vanished. Maddy waited, but to no avail. They were gone.

She stayed in place, mulling what they'd told her, before opening her eyes again. Seeing her stir, the boys approached. "Was there anything?" Curtis said.

Maddy didn't answer right away. Instead, she rose and surveyed the overgrown ridgeline. "Help me out here," she said, tiptoeing forward to avoid the prickers and poison ivy. They worked their way to the designated spot. The magic crack was gone, but she saw signs of an old trail that led down to the lowland. "Let's dig a hole here."

A moment later, she took one of her final presents—a particularly well-knotted figure eight—and placed it in the shallow hole. *For you, spirit girl. You've shown me the bright path.* Remembering the old woman, she lay a second gift beside it. *For your endurance. If you were Queen Esther, to honor your strength.*

On the way back to their bikes, Tommy stopped her.

"Wait," he said. "To be really perfect, we ought to make an offering to the four directions, too. To the four winds." She and Curtis watched while Tommy took a pocket compass and placed it on the grass. Then, pacing two steps in each of the cardinal directions, he scraped out small holes in the ground to mark north, south, east, and west.

Though attuned to his gesture, Maddy knew she was short on presents. A solution came quickly. "Watch, guys." She plucked stalks of grass from the lawn. Recalling Katie's technique, she began to weave the grass into bracelets. "Easy. Weave, pull tight, weave, pull tight. Then I'll show you how to knot them."

Barely ten minutes later, she was holding their four floppy green figure eights in her palm. "How about I do north? Curtis, you do east, and Tommy, you do west, okay? We can do south together since this was the southern door. And say your own private blessing." She handed them the offerings, and they knelt at the holes. Her prayer flowed. *For this wounded land. Here two civilizations met and clashed. Here peace was tried. For this hallowed land. For the peacemakers. For the healers.*

Tommy started chanting, the guttural drone rising in the back of his throat. "This is what my mom does sometimes," he murmured. "She said the spirits hear it." Maddy and Curtis joined in, until their humming trailed off and Maddy grew aware of time again.

"This really was perfect. But hey, we'd better get back. People will be wondering where we are."

MADDY FLOATED PLEASANTLY THROUGH dinnertime at the Tulowitskys. Even the news that her father had suddenly been called away to check on a pressure reading didn't faze her. If he was still tied up later, Mrs. T would drive her back to the motel. *Fine, all fine.*

Over dessert, Mrs. T broke into her haze. "Maddy dear, you may not know it, but we were actually glad you rode off on Cowgirl this afternoon. It gave Katie and me extra time to work on *this.*"

Mrs. T went to the sideboard to retrieve a folded piece of construction paper that had been sitting on top, rolled up discreetly. She untied the string and unfurled the paper. She and Katie each held an end and displayed it in the light for Maddy. The sheet was rectangular, perhaps a foot high and three feet wide. Its surface was lined like graph paper, drawn freehand. The little squares of the grid pattern had been methodically filled in with colored pencil. Some squares were grayish, some whitish, some purple. Many were shaded for a three-dimensional effect.

Maddy knew immediately that she was looking at a personalized wampum belt. Katie and her mom had taken a lesson from their brainstorming sessions and brought it to life. They'd even superimposed a few large symbols on the belt, just as had been suggested—symbols representing an individual. In this case, representing Maddy.

She took the paper in hand and slowly examined the elements, left to right, right to left. There was a lavender bicycle. A pine tree. A pair of paintbrushes with an easel. An arrowhead. A framed caricature of Uncle Roscoe. And a thought bubble filled with #&$*!! curse symbols.

Seeing her momentary confusion, Katie pointed to the bubble and said, "That's a direct quote from the bullies. Curty told me what you did the other night outside the Handi. So awesome!"

All of it was awesome. Maddy started to giggle uncontrollably. Katie leaned in for a long head hug. "We had a blast together, girlfriend!" she said. "I can't believe you're leaving already. I'll miss-miss-*miss* you!" Maddy's laughter turned into blubbers. It was all she could do to shake her head in sobbing agreement. Mrs. T drew her into a long embrace.

"Oh my, my, my," Mrs. T said. "We will miss you. I know the campers will, too. Maddy, most of this picture is Katie's work. The pine tree is mine. If you're wondering, it's the Seneca symbol for a statesman-sachem. To me, it means a teacher, too. And that's you, dear, a teacher. You have it in you. As you go forward, I'd like you to think of yourself as a Pine Tree Teacher."

Maddy didn't believe it was possible to feel more love in a single day. She couldn't take her eyes off the paper belt. Through her tears, she noticed that

Katie had attached strings of fringe at both ends, and had decorated the top and bottom edges with a lacy green pattern to represent their grass weavings.

"Girlfriend," she sniffled, "I love how you shaded the squares to look like quahog shells. You're good! I wish we had time to draw together."

Katie had grabbed a hankie for herself. "Yeah, I imagine Budgie upstairs would be a good model," she snorted. That brought a fresh eruption of giggles.

"Speaking of drawing," Maddy said with a long sigh, "here." She reached into her pouch for her three remaining items. One was her last licorice figure eight. She gave it to Katie, who whooped and bounced with delight.

"Omigod, it's made like our grass bracelets! But you wove what, licorice lace! You totally rock, girlfriend!" She collapsed onto her chair and lolled her tongue. "Me want eat! No-no, KT! Me save! Be birthday treat!"

"And here." Maddy unfolded two pieces of sketch paper she'd slipped into the bag. One she handed to Mrs. T, the other to Katie.

Katie let out another shriek. Hers showed a girl with an enormous cartoon head. It was one of Maddy's caricatures. She'd dressed her friend in a yellow baseball uniform, a catcher's mask propped atop her ponytail, and a parakeet on her shoulder. This Katie was smiling zanily out of one side of her mouth while the other side bit down on a softball. Suspended around her were her BMX bike, a checkerboard, a first-aid kit, an ice-cream cone, an eagle in flight, and loops and loops of grass bracelets. Katie, the real Katie, swooned to the floor in a mock faint. "So awesome, friend-friend! Totally off the hook awesome-alicious!"

"And here." Maddy presented the other sheet of paper to Mrs. T. She'd sketched Katie's mom wearing a frayed apron, a yellow baseball cap sideways on her enormous cartoon head, a lanyard and whistle around her neck, a word bubble at her open mouth. She was saying "and in 1761, Esther is believed to have ..." Behind her was the museum with exaggerated Greek columns, plus a longhouse, a painted post, another eagle in flight, and a fat manila folder with papers spilling out. At her feet was a parade of tiny campers with kids' heads and baby-chick bodies.

Mrs. T held it up to her eyes and let herself spin in a delighted circle. "Perfect! You really got me, dear. Maybe you should go for a triple major. History, education, and art."

Funny, Maddy thought. She'd already imagined the same thing.

SOON AFTERWARDS, MR. WINTER called to say he was still in the thick of it at a compressor station west of town. He hoped to be back by nine o'clock. Mrs. T decided to drive Maddy back to the motel and stay to help her pack until Maddy's dad returned.

Lavish farewell hugs followed, along with pledges to stay in touch. Curtis even submitted to a squeeze, then gave Maddy one more gift. It was a stack of coupons to the ice-cream stand. ("They're good for a whole year. See, it says right there. Maybe you'll come back and use them. Only if you want.")

All the attention and emotion was starting to give Maddy a headache. She recognized the overwrought feeling from previous crying jags. So by the time they finally pulled out of the driveway, she was happy to be alone with Mrs. T.

Also, even though she was getting pooped, and even though the light would soon fade, a powerful urge was rising in her. It was an important one. She knew Mrs. T would understand.

"Can we stop at Academy Park first?"

Five minutes later, they were seated side by side on the grass. Without pause, Maddy shut her eyes. The two spirits were waiting.

She immediately felt the love beam touch her chest. The figures approached across the lowland and rose up to hover nearby. They seemed to radiate a warm female power, sending it outward in waves that washed over her. Yearning to touch the spirit girl's hands again, Maddy felt herself leaning forward. She was aware of Mrs. T shifting in the grass beside her, muttering to herself.

In a flash, the spirits formed a totem pole. The girl was perched on the grandmother's shoulders—and atop the girl now, a magical small mammal. Beaver? Opossum? From its glowing quills Maddy understood: a porcupine. Together the spirits transmitted a silent but distinct message: *Bring peace. Be peace. In your world, be peace women.*

They used the plural, Maddy realized. *Are they speaking to both of us?* She opened her eyes to glance over at Mrs. T. Her companion, eyes also open now, returned a look of astonishment. "Peace women," Mrs. T gasped. "You heard it, too? They meant us."

Maddy shut her eyes for more. Now the spirit girl was stretching directly toward her from the sacred totem pole. She held out a string of glowing white shells. Wampum, Maddy knew. She placed the string in Maddy's hand and clasped their fingers together.

Is for you, she communicated. *Means peace. For you, me, all.* Like Sisketung with Sarah, the young spirit raised her face to the treetops and swept an outstretched arm in a wide arc to encompass Teaoga and beyond. *Peace. You. Me. All.*

The spirit pulled away—then circled back closer than before. Maddy was aware of her penetrating gaze. The dark eyes looked deep inside her. It was as though the spirit recognized something. At this point, Mrs. T was no longer in her inner vision.

Suddenly the spirit girl spun wildly overhead. She returned, reached out to Maddy's face with a smile, and seemed to shudder. *Me! You! Blood! You! Me! Same blood!*

The spirit girl soared high again, taking the grandmother figure with her. They swooped away, then flew close. Suddenly Maddy was lifted aloft—perched now on one of the girl's shoulders. On the other shoulder sat the porcupine-spirit, love reflected in its eyes. An instant later, Maddy herself was flying like an eagle, Mz Snarkley on one shoulder and Rockn Grl on the other. Both of her unruly emoticons had grown composed and alert, and were communicating something like love back to her. The Indian girl flew alongside Maddy now, carrying the porcupine and the grandmother on her shoulders.

They flew high into the wind, rising above Athens, which now was old Teaoga. With supernatural speed, they swooped low over the crops and herds on Esther's Flats, then down the river to the huts at Sheshequin and Wyalusing. They returned upriver to Esther's Glen, Chemung, and the Tutelos' wigwam settlement.

The scenes below were as Maddy imagined them in Mrs. T's telling. The wigwams, the farmsteads, the shoreline, and the fields, all seemed to undulate as though alive on an ocean's surface. Groups of people came and went, villages grew, burned, were swept away. Crops spread and trees greened in vast radiant landscapes like ones Maddy had often painted in her imagination. Then the land heaved as armies clashed, with smoke and screams rising in the air.

Our story, the spirit girl was telling her silently. *Is my story. Is our story. Know it well.*

She guided Maddy back to her place on the grass. Even after returning Maddy fully to her body, the spirit lingered, alone now, floating like smoke from a campfire. Maddy sensed the spirit knew she must depart but was unwilling to go.

Then the spirit moved close and reached a hand toward Maddy's heart. In her palm, suddenly, was a pearl. It glowed white, pure white. She touched it tenderly to Maddy's sternum. A wave of blissful warmth almost knocked Maddy over. Then the spirit girl pulled her hand away. The pearl was gone. Whatever it was—love, strength, patience—had been passed into her.

She felt a brush on her cheek. The girl had stretched across so they could touch cheeks. Maddy experienced pure contentment. The spirit began to fade and withdraw.

Wait, don't go! Who are you? I'm Maddy.

But the girl was gone. Maddy knew she wouldn't return. It had to be so.

Chapter 21

"How about The Burgundy Bomb, Me-Madd? No, I've got it! Let's call her Ruby Red! Yeah, that's the ticket!"

Morning had come and a caffeinated Mr. Winter was popping with corny ideas. That's his way, to make the best of a disappointment. In this case, the car rental people had come through with a four-door sedan big enough to hold the full family—but it was a maroon color, like red wine, not the electric red he'd requested. Zipping down the highway now toward the Wilkes-Barre/Scranton airport and their inbound family, he lit up as he concocted wine names to christen the new wheels.

"No-no, here we go: Car-bernet! Well, maybe. The Chianti Cruiser? You know, actually, I like Ruby Red best. Whaddya say back there, girl? Should we stick with Ruby Red?"

"Sure. Ruby Red it is," Maddy replied absently from the back seat. She'd been trying to play along with his morning cheer but kept tuning in and out. Her brain was elsewhere. She needed to do some serious mental processing of things, and even though her dad was a good listener, Maddy wanted to keep these particular thoughts to herself. Stretching out on the back seat, alone and out of his view, seemed perfect for that.

"Well, okay then!" Mr. Winter stroked his goatee excitedly. "Ruby Red. It's a fine handle, if I do say so myself! Think I'll celebrate with some twist-and-shout time. Just lie back and relax, kiddo. I'll let you know if we come to any good landmarks."

He proceeded to explore the radio offerings, but Maddy barely heard it. Flat on her back, with two seatbelts cinching her in place, she grew transfixed by the treetops whizzing past. They reminded her of soaring aloft with the spirit girl. In her dreamy state, she felt unmoored again. *Did that really happen last night? If you'd put a videocam on me, would it show anything unreal going on?*

According to Mrs. T, something certainly had transpired at the park. She told Maddy afterwards that she too had perceived the two spirits floating above the ridgeline. She'd seen the porcupine totem join the spirits and speak. She said they'd communicated to her to be a peace woman in her own life, just as they had instructed Maddy. After that happened, Mrs. T said, the spirits disappeared, and she'd sat suffused with mellow vibrations inside herself and in the atmosphere around them.

She told Maddy all this the prior evening while they drove to the Cayuga Suites, and then when they sat together on the edge of Maddy's bed. Holding the girl's fingertips lightly again, Mrs. T searched for words to describe the experience. It was "otherworldly." It was "hallucinogenic." At the same time, she said, it confirmed positive intuitions she had about herself and about the purpose of the spirits. But that's where her own encounter had ended, Mrs. T said.

Maddy, leaning against the woman's shoulder, recounted the extra parts that she experienced. She told how the spirit girl had seemed to look into her soul and recognize something. "I think she said we share the same blood! She flew me—you won't believe this, Mrs. T—she flew me down the river and back up, like we were eagles! I went back in time to the Indian days! The land was alive! There were settlers and battles! She said this was *my* story, too!"

"You must be part-Indian, dear," Mrs. T said. "To look at you I wouldn't guess it, but there's *something* in there."

"Mrs. T, the girl spirit didn't want to leave me, even though she had to. I could tell. But before she vanished, she gave me something. She took a little white stone from out of nowhere, like a marble or pearl, and pressed it to my chest! And then it was gone, like my body just took it inside!"

Mrs. T stared hard at the motel carpeting, eyebrows working. Finally, she nodded, "A Tutelo pearl, a legendary Tutelo pearl. That girl must have been a Tutelo Indian. Some of them lived up here back then. I'll have to check. Lordy, lordy."

Maddy was near tears. "And I still feel it! When I put my hand on the bottom of my ribs, I feel a warmth, like a pump pumping goodness. It's something like that, anyway."

She pushed her unzipped purple suitcase out of the way and lay back on the bedspread. A massive sigh left her.

Mrs. T headed for the kitchenette. "Warm milk is always good for a sound sleep," she said. It was the last thing Maddy remembered until morning.

SPRAWLED ACROSS THE BACK seat of Ruby Red, Maddy now considered the preposterous possibility that her belly contained a pump pumping goodness. And if it did, why didn't it have an instruction manual? The thought made her smile. Could Mrs. T really find out anything about a girl from more than two hundred years ago, and about the power of the pearls? That morning, Mrs. T had dropped by again to quickly return some maps. She wrapped Maddy in a long final embrace, and said she planned to learn a lot more about Indian healers.

Now, warming her hand on her prone abdomen, Maddy continued to feel the strange but definite goodness. *I tink I must go mad.* The old phrase came to her, but it didn't really stick. She wasn't flipping out. No snarklies ambushed. In fact, she felt content and centered. Truth be told, that sense of ancient wisdom was settling over her again, as though she was wise beyond her years, and beyond her time.

In a good way, underneath it all Maddy also felt normal. She knew the spirits wanted her to be normal—better, kinder, stronger, but still in her regular, normal world. That was why they'd receded from her. It was like they had adopted her and were watching over her, uplifting her, but from a distance now, like parents are supposed to do.

In a funny way, every time she inhaled, Maddy felt like she was taking in the spirit girl's affirming love. *This is so amazing. It's like her pure love goes right into my heart, like through gills in my side. Love and confidence. I've got to put that goodness to use for others. I'm sure that's what they want.*

She flashed on a Jewish concept her friend Leah had talked about two months earlier in her bat mitzvah speech: *shalom*. It means peace in Hebrew, but Leah spoke proudly about how shalom goes deeper than that. It really means wholeness, the absence of conflict and oppression, the world in balance. Aspiring to shalom is hard work, but it's holy work, Leah told everyone. Maddy wondered if that's exactly what the Teaoga spirits longed for, to have their world be restored to balance again. Maybe that's what Esther tried to talk to the whites about—about how things could be, how the natives' Great Spirit wanted things to be. Maybe that's why the spirits reached out to people like herself—to enlist them in the difficult but undying cause of peace, and to send them off on that mission with confidence.

Lost in her reverie, Maddy was startled to see her father's face smiling in from the car's side window. She sat up and opened the door. "Like I was saying, it's an amazing view. Come check it out."

He'd pulled Ruby Red into the parking area of a scenic overlook. Maddy emerged to join him on the windy cliffside. They stood high above the eastern shore of the Susquehanna. Far below, a patchwork of farm fields spread west across the sunny river plain.

"These cliffs here are called the Wyalusing Rocks," Mr. Winter said. "You were so quiet I didn't want to bother you before, but we already passed the road to Camptown. Plus, I saw a marker back there about the French refugee colony that was built for Marie Antoinette herself. That was in 1793 during the French Revolution. She and her son were supposed to escape to safety here, but as we know, they didn't make it"—he smacked his neck to simulate a guillotine. "I'd heard of the place. It's called the French Azilum. It's up that-away."

To the north, where he pointed, the river curved gracefully back toward Athens. Maddy squinted silently. *Marie Antoinette! Here in the American wilderness? In Indian country? This place is too much.*

Maddy's eye was caught by a pair of kayakers in the distant river. She enjoyed how they moved in tandem, paddling smoothly to avoid a set of long sand bars near the shoreline. Were warriors that skilled in their birch-bark canoes, she wondered. A large answer came to her. *That's exactly what they were: adept, observant, savvy. And not only on the river. The Indians always had to be on the lookout for danger and deceit. Some were obvious, some were hidden. They had to steer the safest channel. That's what Esther did. She tried to find a safe course for her people, avoiding shoals and undertows, adjusting, finding the least resistance. Trusting that there was a bright path. That was her peace instinct. Until the danger and the treachery overwhelmed her, and she took her paddle and used it as weapon.*

Ruby Red continued southward toward the airport as Maddy toggled mentally between back in time and right now. Mr. Winter stopped periodically to recite the information on wayside markers. Most were about Sullivan's March along the river. Maddy did her best to listen. She found herself staring up at the ceiling light, hand relaxed on her sternum. Random mental images flickered in and out. The porcupine's eyes appeared. Uncle Roscoe. Moravian cabins. Popsicle-stick wigwams. The steamy poop bag. Katie's exhilarated collapses.

Descending steadily along the river toward the Wyoming Valley, the travelers eventually passed near the ravine where the warriors had ambushed the isolated farmers in 1778, and where young Elesoon was shot dead and buried.

Mr. Winter zipped past, failing to notice the small stone marker memorializing the slain white farmers.

At about that point, Maddy's whirling mind seized on another thought, a thought that turned into a wish and then a yearning. She realized that the spirit girl seemed in age like a younger sister, like the kid sis Maddy never had. Had the spirit revealed her own name? Sisk or something? Maddy wasn't sure she'd heard anything plainly—but she had a strong desire to call her Sis.

The prospect of a secret sister-companion was exquisite. Maddy shut her eyes and tried to summon Sis into the back seat with her. Nothing came. She imagined herself speaking to the girl. Nothing again. No, Sis was keeping Maddy in the present. The pearly glow within herself was always available—the term *Sis-strength* came to her mind—but the apparitions would be no more. There was to be no companion. Sis belonged to Teaoga. She knew that. Rubbing her ribs, she tried to accept it gratefully.

The car made a series of sudden quick turns, rolling her back and forth on the seat. A moment later, Mr. Winter shut off the engine and announced, "So here we are, darlin'. The Rock."

When Maddy didn't stir, he got out to look around. They were in the heart of an ordinary, working-class neighborhood full of frame houses, stores, barking dogs, and assorted parked cars and trucks. Kids rode past on bikes, indifferent to the visitors. When Maddy finally opened her door, she almost bumped into one of them.

Perhaps a hundred yards to the east lay the Susquehanna shoreline. Mr. Winter had his bearings. He pointed toward the riverbank, then gestured to a landmark across the street. It was a blue Pennsylvania historical marker that rose above the parked cars.

Though she'd asked her dad to stop here, Maddy wasn't sure she was really ready for it. Her stomach tightened as she approached the sign and read its words.

THE BLOODY ROCK
On the night of July 3, 1778, after the Battle
of Wyoming, fourteen or more captive American
soldiers were murdered here by a maul
wielded by a revengeful Indian woman,
traditionally but not certainly identified
as 'Queen Esther.'

Her Queen Esther, a demon of history. Maddy looked around dizzily. *Do those kids know anything about her? What are they told? Do they care? If I'd flown down here last night with Sis, what would I have seen? 'Murdered here by a maul?' I know what a maul is—a big, brutal club. What really happened? She probably did something horrendous, but I think she was beside herself. Literally, she was outside her normal self at the time, pushed over the edge. Because her real self was a peace woman. What would I have done?*

Maddy felt her heart racing. The surreal setting added to her anxiety. It was difficult to block out the bikes, the cars, the lawn ornaments and mailboxes, and manicured hedges that crowded in on the hallowed little plot. An old iron fence surrounded the plot. She opened its rusty gate and approached the heavy metal grate that covered the rock to protect it from souvenir-seekers. The boulder itself was nearly flat and lay at ground level. Being about the size and shape of a coffin, it gave the impression of an eternally open grave.

Maddy reached an index finger down into the grate but could barely touch the rock. She pulled her hand back, instantly glad she hadn't actually touched it. She squatted in place, imagining the events of that infamous night. Then she tried to push away the very images that came. Her dad stood nearby, solemn as a mourner.

Still queasy, Maddy shut her eyes and waited. No Esther appeared. No captives. No auras whatsoever. If any spirits inhabited the spot, they weren't coming to her. She sensed there were none. Esther may have left remnants of herself behind to inhabit some places, but not here.

Nonetheless, Maddy had come to pay tribute. She didn't care if the cyclists thought it was weird, or her dad, or even the spirits. It felt like a necessary part of her circuit.

From the pocket of her tab shorts, she pulled out a handful of stray gum wrappers, two dimes, and a few broken strands of red candy. She separated out the candy, brushed it off, and pressed the strands together to make two short, interlocking rings. Once they were ready for presentation, she held them up to her nose and inhaled. *For Esther, who bore so much. For her sins. For the soldiers. For their sins. For the bright path of peace.* Leaning forward, she pushed her offering through the grate and watched it drop down onto the doleful gray rock.

Mr. Winter witnessed the impromptu ceremony quietly. Once Maddy rose to return to the car, he opened her door like a chauffeur.

THE AIRPORT PICKUP WAS EASY. Within an hour, the Winter clan was heading east on the interstate, bound for New York City. Maddy, seated upright now, looked over at her little brother slurping loudly on the straw in his jumbo drink. Seeing him bop unself-consciously to the music on his ear buds—*mini-Dad!*—brought a burst of fondness. Directly in front of her sat her mother, hair and voice and earnest personality so totally familiar that Maddy found herself giggling. It seemed she'd been gone from them for five minutes, and five long years. Though their sudden presence was startling, she didn't feel put upon. Instead, she actually felt waves of a sweet, uncomplicated family love.

To her relief, Maddy was finding it easy to stay in the present. It was as though an unseen hand—Sis's hand—had lifted her out of mournfulness. She'd fallen into a perfect state of mind, a relaxed but full focus, which she also credited to Sis-strength. With sheer pleasure, she heard all about her brother's soccer scores and her mother's office stories. She dug her father's humorous descriptions of the motel, the Houston-like humidity ("the highs of Texas were upon us," he sang) and his fishing and cooking misadventures, and she chimed in with her own details. It was fun telling them about the campers' antics. Her brother yelped with delight to hear how she'd given the town bullies their messy comeuppance. Even her mother couldn't stop laughing at that one. Maddy basked in pride, knowing the tale would probably become a family favorite.

Once things quieted down and the only sounds were mellow jazz ballads on the radio, she caught her father stealing a few looks at her in the rear-view mirror. Concern was in his eyes. *He didn't tell them anything about Esther and The Rock and all that. Maybe it was for my sake, to steer clear of an intense subject. But still, he knows something's up with me. I wonder if Mrs. T dropped any hints. Probably not. Should I tell him? I'm still not sure he could handle that his little princess is, yes, bewitched.*

Maddy rested her head against the side window. They'd risen out of the Wyoming Valley into the windswept Pocono Mountains. The trees were low and patchy, the terrain filled with bogs and lichen-covered boulders. She could feel gusts of highland wind buffet the car.

From her reading, Maddy knew most of the Wyoming Valley's settler families had fled into these very mountains after the battle long ago, some of them to die in the perilous stretch known as the Shades of Death. A year later, Sullivan's army and its wagon train would struggle in the opposite direction across the same mountains and bogs as they launched their fateful journey up into Iroquoia. Maddy knew that, too, and her heart opened to all the suffering.

She felt herself lapsing into silent introspection. There was one more thing on her list to sort out. And it was a big one. It was Ana Estevez.

Her Tex-Mex classmate had been in the back of her mind for days. Ever since Tommy's angry eyes reawakened the memory of her own terrible slighting of dark-eyed Ana, Maddy had felt pangs of guilt. The incident had made her feel so ashamed that her mind at the time tried to repress it as a way to cope. Now, the challenge of becoming a peace person and a healer in her own life took her directly back to Ana. She sensed Sis guiding her to the task. Maddy had the same crystalline focus as before, turned inward now as she remembered.

She and Ana were only in one course together, third-period art. Several times they happened to sit at the same drawing table and share a box of pastel sticks. The morning of the incident, the art class was working on a still life. Maddy had noticed how skillfully Ana captured the light reflecting off the wooden apples. Ana complimented Maddy on her own shading technique. Maddy was sure she'd blushed at that, but something held her back from returning the compliment. She just didn't feel like being friendly. Ana was new to the school, and Maddy was sure they had no friends in common. She'd seen the girl get off one of the buses from the far neighborhoods. It was fixed in her mind that their circles didn't overlap.

Later, at lunch that very day, Maddy took a seat at her regular all-girl table. She and Melody had gotten into the group through another friend just that year, so she was still getting used to the girls and their edgy behavior. Maddy didn't want to play up to them, exactly, but she did like their approval and was envious of their quick, cutting humor. Plus, a few of them had boyfriends already, so she figured she might pick up some pointers.

Everyone was there except Melody, who was out sick that day. The girls were just settling in and gabbing about something. Then Maddy felt a tap on her shoulder.

It was Ana. She had slipped into Melody's spot beside her with her cafeteria tray.

All talk stopped. Ana gave her a small, expectant smile. The other girls stiffened and cocked their eyebrows. Maddy's mind began to reel. *Why is this girl putting me on the spot? Can't she see my friends want her to go away? Who the el does she think she is?*

Maddy shot Ana a hard look and grumbled, "What?" She noticed everyone else was studiously looking downward.

Without a word, Ana left. She grabbed her tray and moved to an empty spot two tables over. The whole thing was probably over in twenty seconds. The others resumed their chatter, but Maddy's head was pounding. She imagined running out of the lunchroom. Still, she felt immobile, as though tied to the table and this girl pack.

Twice she glanced over at Ana. That's when she saw the black eyes searing her. Ana was looking back with bottomless hurt and confusion. The damage was done. Maddy remembered looking away quickly, batting back tears, her breath a pant. She also remembered being hurt, herself, that none of the others at her table offered sympathy, even privately, then or later. They didn't even seem to notice. When it came right down to it, did they not care about her, or about Ana?

But in the end, Maddy shrank. She took the easy way out. She never broke with the pack. She never spoke to Ana. As the school year wore on, the two girls kept away from each other, even in art class. Staying in the comfort zone was just easier, Maddy figured, than inviting Ana's wrath or, worse, risking rejection if she strayed too far from the pack. So she mostly managed to push the problem out of her mind. Actually, she did mention it to Melody one day, but Mel replied that since she hadn't been there to witness things, she couldn't really, quote, "render an opinion." Big help she was.

Now, barreling toward New York City, Maddy was rendering her own opinion. And it wasn't pretty. *How did I get so close-minded? Put me to the test and that's what I do? Ana was reaching out—sticking her neck out—wanting to be a friend. I'm new in town and Katie rolls out the red carpet for me. Ana's new and what do I do? I give her the cold shoulder! How many Bible lessons about hospitality do I need to hear? What is my problem? When it gets right down to it, is it that Ana's Mexican? Do I look down on her—on all of them? She's different, and she has a little accent, but I've always told myself that didn't matter. I guess I'm just a stupid hypocrite. I hate the slurry names some kids have for the Mexicanos, but what do I do about it? Nothing, really. Truth be told, I just want to walk past them in the halls.* Maddy grew aware that this clear inner voice of conscience was a chorus of voices. From her folks, Mrs. T, Ana, Katie, Sis, Jesus. Even from good-judgmental Snarkley. Mostly, it was her own best self crying out. *Look at who my friends are. How did it get to be all Anglos? Why didn't I take Spanish, anyways? Ana didn't just look wounded. She looked lonely. Oh, Ana, please let's try again.*

One of her dad's favorite expressions came to mind: You don't know someone until you walk a mile in his moccasins. That's what she wanted to do. She wanted to jump out of the car and try on Ana's moccasins. In one magic mile she wanted to learn about Ana's whole family, her town, her culture, her religion, her dreams, her whole story. *I'll look her up in the school directory when I get home. I hope she likes licorice. We can go to the art museum together. I'll really, really give her a chance and hope she really, really gives me a chance. I wonder if she has any Indian blood. I hope....*

"Whoa, cool! Look!" Her brother was craning his neck like a prairie dog to see above the front seat. Up ahead, through the windshield, were the hulking steel towers of the George Washington Bridge, and the breathtaking New York City skyline beyond. Maddy felt Sis dropping her back into the moment.

BIG BUTTS. THAT'S WHAT Maddy was seeing as Ruby Red carried the family through Manhattan's forest of immense skyscrapers. Her brother howled with glee when she told him about the old settler term for primeval trees. No one could stop him then: "Big butt, big butt, look at that big butt! Ooo, there's a real big butt!"

A billion butts later, they arrived at the base of Manhattan and got tickets for the ferry to the Statue of Liberty. Mr. Winter was about to book them for three o'clock when Maddy asked for four o'clock tickets instead. She saw another opportunity awaiting. A half-block away was the National Museum of the American Indian, advertising its free admission. Maddy figured she could do a quick in-and-out. It had a big Eastern Woodlands collection, and a Southwestern room. Time to learn about the Tutelos, she thought. And who were those Indians from Texas? The Caddos?

Once inside, Maddy slipped into the galleries. Her parents kept an eye on the clock in the lobby.

"Do we really have time for this?" her mother asked.

"No," Mr. Winter said. "But I think I understand. This has been an amazing trip for her. She's been blown away by the Indian history. She even asked me if she had any Indian blood in her. She asked twice. I hated to have to say no."

"Well, I do love to see her learning stuff.... Wait a minute, did you say you told her no?"

"Well, sure."

"But why? You know about my great-great-great-grandmother. The one who we're told was some kind of Indian. Maybe it was great-great-great-great. I know I've told you about her."

"Since when?"

"Well, apparently it didn't stick if you don't remember, Russ. And who knows, maybe Maddy actually never heard.

"The family story goes that this Indian ancestor of mine married a white man and settled down in frontier Indiana to raise a family. The fellow was on our German side. We were told he was from some pacifist religious group that mingled a lot with Indians.

"As I remember it, he died, and then when she got to be old, her adult children somehow took her back to her homeland to live out her days and be buried there. One of the children stayed there and tried to live as Indian, too, like in an underground way. The story goes that it was along a big river. It could have been in Pennsylvania. I think the tribe name starts with T. You know who'd know? Old Aunt Pearl."

"You've got to tell this to Madd!"

"Think she'll want to know?"

Afterwards

Pickering's 1790 peace council at Teaoga heralded a new beginning for the United States government, being its first formal negotiation with the Iroquois following the adoption of the U.S. Constitution. At the same time, the event marked a sad finale—it was the last council ever to be held at the ancient treaty ground. Once the council fire was extinguished there on November 23 of that year, an era concluded. Never again would Teaoga witness such an assemblage of Indian nations.

Pickering promptly reported to President Washington that the natives had departed the proceedings "with their minds eased." For that outcome, he won Washington's appreciation and continued favor as a trusted public servant. He went on to be Washington's representative to crucial 1794 treaty talks with the Iroquois. Later, over his long career, Pickering served as U.S. postmaster general, secretary of state, secretary of war, and senator. He also avoided the personal bankruptcy that earlier had been his dread.

Red Jacket, Pickering's jousting partner at Teaoga, went on to a long run of his own in the public eye. He tried diligently to safeguard Seneca land rights, including at the 1794 Iroquois treaty talks, where he crossed paths again with Pickering. Though his rhetorical gifts were widely admired, Red Jacket failed over the years to dissuade other Indian leaders from ceding territory to whites. He is perhaps most famous for his 1805 speech to the U.S. Senate, called "Religion for the White Man and the Red." He argued for mutual respect, saying, "Since He had made so great a difference between us in other things, why may we not conclude that He has given us a different religion according to our understanding? The Great Spirit does right." In his later years, Red Jacket fell into hard drinking. He is quoted as lamenting of himself that while once "a lofty pine tree ... he has degraded himself by drinking the firewater of the white man. The Great Spirit has looked upon him in anger, and His lightning has stripped the pine of its branches."

And what became of Queen Esther? She is generally believed to have died around 1800 after living out her years in western New York State. Some accounts have her remaining in Ganogeh and being buried in honor on the western shore of Cayuga Lake, while another version has her taking up with a white vagabond named Thomas Hill and dying in a poorhouse near present-day Binghamton. Whatever the truth, her reputation as the bloodthirsty "Fiend of Wyoming" became burned in the white imagination for more than a century.

While Esther was presumably alive in 1790 and would have been aware of Pickering's November peace council, it is not known if she actually returned to Teaoga as Red Jacket's advisor. Similarly, while the Tutelo remnant might still have lived in the vicinity at the time, Pennsylvania's "Final Purchase" of 1784 may have already driven them westward by late 1790—or sent them underground into the hidden way of life that some Pennsylvania Indians managed.

Today, but for the work of a handful of hardy local historians and the scant information on roadside markers, the memory of the area's original people is little acknowledged, let alone honored. A tributary that trickles into the Chemung River across from Sayre bears the name Tutelow Creek. The public square in Athens is indeed named Teaoga Square. A set of streets in Sayre is named for the Iroquois tribes. On the way to Wilawana, one can find a rural lane named Queen Esther Drive, which leads uphill to a modern development called Queen Esther Estates. Beyond those faint references, however, is a silence that serves to reinforce the hissing stone's dismissiveness.

MRS. T CONTINUES TO brood about the hissing stone's conceits and appalling omissions. Her heart's desire would be to roll the thing across the grass and let it drop over the ridgeline. She'd organize a fund drive to replace it with a monument decorated like wampum that would honor the Teaoga treaty grounds. But since the boulder is anchored there in all its triumphalist glory, she's decided to work it into her curriculum as a glaring relic of the ideology known as Manifest Destiny. That belief in white Americans' divine right to the land had taken full force by the time the monument was erected in 1902. Figuring it's a concept middle schoolers are ready to learn, Mrs. T will propose that they visit the boulder—but only as a last outing, once they've gotten a better appreciation of Indian ways and tragic relations with settlers. Recalling Trevor's idea, she'll suggest that the students compose their own inscriptions for the monument. She hopes that will show how far most people, at least most youngsters, have come in their thinking.

Her vision in Academy Park that final evening with Maddy, happening just steps away from the stone, deepened her determination to present the Indian part of the story fairly. So even after Maddy left, Mrs. T pressed on with the group study sessions for another month. She let Curtis sit in on the brainstorming, too. Afterwards, she went off and wrote a set of multimedia lesson plans that she's very excited about. She thinks middle-schoolers will really be able to sink their teeth into the material. Trevor has promised to draw up some computer exercises, and Curtis said he'll flesh out an idea for phys ed classes using Indian lacrosse rules. All this will be in time for her presentation to the middle school principal later in the summer.

Mrs. T has returned twice to the enchanted spot in the park. She sensed something—a smoke smell, like from a wood fire—but no spirits, no message. She plans to go back with her completed curriculum. The day of her big presentation, she'll stop off at the park and lay her folder on the ground, maybe light some incense, before heading to the school. She's already been praying about the project in church, but she's gotten a tug on her heart telling her to seek a native blessing, too.

Meanwhile, Mrs. T has scheduled a public talk by her college intern Beth in the museum just before Labor Day. She knows the turnout might not be so great, but she's looking at it as a nice sendoff. Beth has been working hard researching the crazy but true episode in 1788 when Connecticut settlers kidnapped the one and only Timothy Pickering. Her lecture will be about how Pickering, a Pennsylvania official at the time, tried to evict the renegade Yankees and was abducted and held hostage in the woods for almost three weeks. She'll also talk about how the Upper Susquehanna became a last stand for the "Wild Yankees," also known as the Tioga Boys, whose dream of founding a breakaway state with Athens as its capital died a hard death. Public speaking isn't Beth's thing, but Mrs. T is assuring her she'll do fine, because the material is so eye-opening. It's history Mrs. T hopes to work into later lesson plans.

Curtis and Tommy, meanwhile, have returned a few times to the dip in the riverbank where Maddy said she saw the spirits. The boys have also frequented Academy Park. That's been Curtis's doing, mostly. They have yet to see anything special, just as Maddy would have predicted. Tommy isn't expecting any apparitions either, but he's gone along for Curtis' sake. Curtis also has been wheedling his folks to let him go with Tommy on a weekend campout alone up at Wilawana. Mrs. T told him to forget it, that his getaway fort along the Chemung is the most she's comfortable with. That set Curty to pouting, but no one's listening, not even Tommy.

Katie's summer has been hurtling along. Her Broncos got knocked out in the second round of the playoffs. She wondered if not having Maddy there for good luck doomed them. Afterwards, she was named a league all-star, and she put the plastic trophy in Budgie's cage just to be silly. Fortunately, the spell of stinky-hot weather broke, so Katie's final two weeks as a junior counselor were easy-peasy (her term). She tried to use some of Maddy's art projects. The cornhusk dolls were the best. Katie took some pictures of the campers with their dolls and posted them on her Facebook page. Maddy sent an immediate "OMG grlfnd!!!! Your kids rock!!" At first, Katie felt breathlessly sad that Maddy was gone—really, like she couldn't breathe for a minute—but then she'd go ride her bike and think about something else. More recently, she spent a week at church youth camp near Binghamton. She hit it off there with another girl from school who's a grade below her, and they've been spending lots of time together back home. Mostly, they're working on their strokes in the town pool so they can try out for the school swim team. Maddy's been rooting her on in her postings.

AND THEN THERE'S MADDY. When her mother finally told her the legend of her Indian ancestor, Maddy just about lost it. Her parents had decided not to say anything about it until their flight back home so she wouldn't mess up the vacation plans by, like, insisting that she return with her father to Athens *right then or else*. That decision might have made adult sense, but it meant Maddy ended up bursting with emotion in an airplane seat forty thousand feet in the air. She almost hyperventilated at the news, until she remembered to rub her belly. Once she calmed down, she turned to her mother and started in with the questions. Her mom had to repeat the family story three or four times. Maddy was a mix of overwhelmed and gleeful. Sis's lingering, loving gaze, the warmth of the pearl, it all made sense. Wisdom settled over her like a shawl. Beneath it, Maddy's belly was tingling.

Back in Houston, she bugged her mother to contact old Aunt Pearl for any extra information. One night, Maddy called the auntie herself, even though they hadn't really spoken since Maddy was little. She told Aunt Pearl she was researching their family tree. Aunt Pearl didn't have much to add, not even a name for their mysterious forebear, but she promised to "scour the attic."

Maddy is still waiting to hear back. It's made her a little frustrated—but not in the old moody-Maddy way. Mz Snarkley, in fact, was feeling like a thing of the past. Maddy wondered if the little demon had missed the flight home, or if Tiara-Cat had maybe trapped her somewhere in the basement.

Melody, meanwhile, was pumped to have Maddy back, and they've fallen back into their groove. No sooner did Maddy tell her about her ancestor than Mel posed the question, "So how much discrimination did your forebear have to forbear?" They'll never know, obviously, but their word-wonking was fun. Maddy gave Melody a quasi-lecture on the momentous history of Teaoga during Queen Esther's era, drawing as faithfully as she could from Mrs. T's info and anecdotes. She felt like a student teacher as she explained about the watch town and the Moravians and The Bloody Rock, as well as big themes like the vortex and commodification. She told her about the hissing stone, too, and showed her Katie's wampum picture. But Maddy still hasn't told her gal-pal about the spirit-sightings. It's been hard biting her tongue, but she doesn't want to scare Mel away. Plus, she feels Sis wants it that way. Sis seems to want her stay in the present and work on being her best self in the here and now.

That brings her to Ana. Maddy returned with a determination to repair things on that front, and she's proud of how it's worked out. She quickly tracked down Ana's home phone and called her. Ana was suspicious at first, thinking Maddy might be playing a prank. But the more Maddy apologized and explained her new awareness, the more Ana opened up. Next thing, Maddy invited Ana to the art museum. After a tentative start, they ended up whispering themselves hoarse in the galleries. Each came back with a poster of a favorite painting.

At dinner one night when Ana was over, Maddy's mom started pumping Ana for information. Maddy was worried until she saw how comfortable the girl was talking about her family. She learned that Ana's great-grandfather had been a governor of one of the Mexican states, and that Ana was distantly related to Geronimo's clan on her mother's side. Maddy's jaw dropped at that one! Ana told them she planned to become a lawyer handling immigration cases, and then become a judge. Maddy loved how Ana held her head high when she said that.

Ana had Maddy over to her house and then to meet her circle of friends from church. They even went to Mass together, which was Maddy's first experience with a Catholic service and the beautiful sounds of Spanish prayer.

But then, back at the Estevez house that day, Ana's tenth grade brother Hector abruptly pulled Maddy aside into the pantry. "Don't ever try any of your *mierda* on my sis again," Hector seethed. "Some reason she thought you were one of the special ones. Something about the way you drew pictures. You really messed up her year, you know. Be glad she's so *cortés*, so polite, 'cause I woulda popped you if you dissed me like that! No more, are we straight?" Maddy nodded hard. "No more," she whispered. "Never." Still muttering, Hector pulled his finger from her face and headed back to the kitchen. It was the chewing-out Maddy had been waiting for and felt she fully deserved.

Later, up in Ana's bedroom, Maddy apologized again. Ana gave her a long look before a smile crept onto her face. "*Paz, mi hermana*," she said. "Peace."

Fortunately, Mel isn't the jealous type. She's enjoying getting to know Ana, and has suggested the three of them go on a Hispanic history tour of Houston.

She found a special tour that visits Our Lady of Guadalupe Church, Talento Bilingua de Houston, the Tejano Center for Community Concern, the Pan American Ballroom, Hidalgo Park, and the New World Museum. Ana jumped at the idea, because even she didn't know about some of those places.

Maybe best of all was the time Maddy visited Ana's grandmother. The girls took the bus together to the lacy little apartment, Ana toting her pastels and sketch pad to continue working on her *abuela*'s portrait. Maddy was able to help with Ana's other summer project: a family oral history. While Ana sketched, Maddy ran the video camera and added a few questions that Ana then asked her granny in Spanish. The legends about Geronimo's exploits were amazing, as were the stories about the family's menfolk who fought in World War I, World War II, the Korean War, and the Vietnam War. The memory of a beloved great-Uncle Felipe, who was killed in battle in Vietnam, brought tears to all their eyes. When it was time to leave, there were lots of long hugs all around, and a bulging bag of homemade *galleta de coco* cookies to take home.

On the bus ride back, Ana told her that the war hero Felipe lives on in her heart, for real, giving her pride and purpose, and that sometimes Geronimo does that for her, too. They both stared out the window for a long time. Maddy found herself blinking back tears again.

Back at Ana's house, the girls feasted on the coconut cookies and practiced some dance steps. Ana has a favorite hip-swivel move that includes tapping her belly quickly. Maddy copied it but then turned it into giant, circular belly rubs, hamming it up until they both fell over laughing.

That moment, too, made Maddy's eyes moisten. *All this is too good to be true. It's as if Ana's been waiting for me to come into her life. She kinda picked me out, like she sensed something.* Maddy decided on the spot, lying there on the rug in Ana's bedroom, to learn Spanish. And to learn the words to those Tex-Mex songs about fiestas and siestas and dark-eyed girls, songs she'd barely paid attention to before.

But most of all, she decided to tell Ana her secret. She'd confide in her one day soon. She knows Sis would understand. Ana will, too.

Questions for Classroom
or Group Discussion

1. What are two or three new things the book taught you about Indians? About settlers?

2. In Chapter 3, Sisketung feels caught between world views "clashing like flintstones." Do you think the natives and the Europeans were fated to clash? Why or why not?

3. In Chapter 4, Mrs. T tells Maddy how many Indians regarded the woods with anxiety, as a place of wood sprites and troubling spirits. Did that surprise you? Can you relate to it?

4. In Chapter 7, Maddy feels she's observing things from afar as though she's on a helicopter. Have you ever had that feeling?

5. The Indians cherished oral history and storytelling skills. Try that skill by having one person carefully read aloud several paragraphs from the book. Assign one listener to memorize the first half on the spot, another, the second half. Then, have them recite their parts back to the group as exactly they can. Discuss the experience.

6. In Chapter 14, Mrs. T's study group imagines students debating whether Indians "were wasting the land by not developing it." Hold that very debate yourselves, dividing your group into pro, con, and judges.

7. In Chapter 20, Maddy offers a gift "to the rivers, which bore such changes." What is the significance of waterways to this period of history?

8. What are some of the values and emotions that wampum carry? Do our modern cultures have anything similar?

9. The author presents Queen Esther as a tragic figure trapped by circumstance. Do you agree?

10. Who was your favorite character, and why?

11. As Maddy discovered, seemingly ordinary Athens has a remarkable past. Does your area have a hidden history? Consider visiting your local history society, or go online, to research place names, heroes, scoundrels and other colorful chapters of the past. Focus on the historiography, on who told the stories and how complete and balanced they were.

12. Maddy felt the spirit girl was directing her to be her best self. In your own life, who would that self be?

13. How can learning from the past shape our futures, both individually and as a society?

For Further Study

Just as Sisketung and Esther prayed ceaselessly to the Preserver, the author offers up his own deep wish. It is that *Visions of Teaoga*, his ode to a lost world, succeeds in bringing local history fully alive for the reader. His heart's desire is that people, particularly young people, appreciate how American history glows underfoot nearly everywhere we live—tumultuous, poignant, magical history, filled with grit and gristle, with rollicking stories and unlikely heroes and scoundrels. Whether in Teaoga or in your own backyard, this history is a powerful legacy to be explored and appreciated.

With that in mind, you are invited to visit www.jimremsen.com and experience its interactive resources about the book and the history it portrays. On the website's *Visions of Teaoga* page, you will find:

Original maps and documents

Bibliography and lists of references

Recommended reading for students

Supplemental discussion questions

Author's research notes and acknowledgments

Links to related history sites

Made in the USA
San Bernardino, CA
27 September 2014